A Spiral of Moments

Robert Beech

First Edition

This is a work of fiction. Names, characters, places, organizations, and incidents are either the product of the author's imagination or used fictitiously, and any resemblance to actual persons, living or dead, business establishments, events, organizations, or locales is entirely coincidental.

ISBN: 979-8-9916357-1-4

To Chris, my love

Prologue

February 4, 1997
Los Angeles, California

The studio publicist stood by the side wall of the hotel ballroom, a mobile phone to his ear. Moments later, he hurried over, leaning across a table at the front. "I've tried multiple times. His driver's not answering."

"Adrien's never late. Something must have happened." Anna Nyholm tilted her head, looking past the publicist toward the restive gathering of Hollywood press. Two reporters left the cordon of velvet roping, navigating toward the rear entrance doors. "Should I get started without him?"

The publicist turned. "I guess you'll …" Flashing strobes interrupted his response, cameras clicking rapidly. He stooped low, hurrying aside.

The departing reporters tried to regain their former position but failed, relegated to the back.

"Hello, everyone," said Adrien Satorri in a loud voice. He proceeded across the ballroom from a side door, a commanding presence despite his diminutive size and advanced years. "Thank you for your patience. I know it's late in the day." He eased along the back of the table, stopping behind Nyholm's chair. His wrinkled face barely showed above her youthful visage, a defining image that would underscore the transition that followed. He placed one hand on her shoulder, raising the other.

A hush fell over the room. Handheld recorders extended outward.

"I'd like to start with a special announcement. Anna will be the director of our new movie. I will only be a part-time adviser."

The press was momentarily flatfooted. More flashing ensued, photographers capturing the generational moment—the proverbial passing of the baton. Questions erupted, escalating into strident competition.

Nyholm raised her chin, maintaining a calm smile. *That's it. Look slowly to the left and now back to the right. Good. Focus on the television camera. Broaden the smile. Live up to the moment.*

Satorri patted her shoulder, taking a seat alongside.

Reporters shouted, many asking the same question, "Are you retiring?"

He held up both hands. "Let's leave my plans for another time. Today is about the remarkable story Anna will bring to life. It's the reason we are here today." Satorri leaned over, his voice lowered. "The rest is yours, Anna. Good luck."

Nyholm scanned the crowd for a familiar face. She pointed to the right, midway back, speaking into the table microphone. "Steven?"

The room quieted.

The lucky reporter flashed a quick grin. "Thanks, Anna, and congrats on the big moment. The teaser sounds interesting. How'd you learn about the fighter pilot?"

Nyholm exhaled a sigh of relief. *A great way to start. Remember to give him an exclusive interview.* She glanced at Satorri. "Adrien introduced us to the gritty realities of twentieth-century combat, along with a dramatic focus on the lasting physical and emotional turmoil it inflicts on military veterans. Our new project will add to those stories. We learned about Lieutenant Simon Bronson from a brilliant series of articles by Fletcher Hastings, an investigative reporter with the *Tampa Sentinel.*" Nyholm pointed to her assistant standing at the end of the table. "Krista will be handing out detailed briefing packets. Reprints of the Hastings articles are included for your review."

Krista moved quickly across the front row, providing packets for distribution from front to rear.

Nyholm continued, "The screenplay will be based on actual events but subject to creative interpretation. Which is a formal way of saying that the truth will be stretched to ensure we make a damn great movie."

Laughter followed. Nyholm flashed her trademark smile, pointing to an older woman at center left, another familiar face. "Deidra?'

"Are you ready to run the gauntlet of critics? Expectations will be high."

Nyholm responded without hesitation, "It would be presumptuous to say I could achieve what Adrien has accomplished. But yes, I'm ready to blaze my path."

Nyholm pointed at a woman standing beside the television camera. "The *Entertainment Today* reporter. I'm sorry, I don't recall your name."

"Casey Remington. Do you have a lead actor in mind?"

"Most definitely, a wonderfully talented young man, but he's not yet a household name." *That should keep them busy.*

Energetic waving caught her attention, a man she didn't recognize. "Wearing the red vest in the back."

"So, not John Clanders?" The man grinned smugly.

Gasps rippled across the room, intermingled with nervous laughs. The sudden termination of Nyholm's engagement to Clanders had dominated the pages of entertainment tabloids for the past two months, the articles filled with indelicate rumors of Clanders's trysts with his latest co-star, a starlet barely of age.

Nyholm struggled to maintain a calm expression, inwardly seething at the insensitivity of the question.

Satorri grabbed the table microphone, glaring at the man. "I don't believe we have met, sir. Could you state your name? I want to remember it."

Strobes flashed toward the man, cameras clicking like a firing squad. He exited hurriedly, his face the color of the vest.

"That's why I don't make movies about cowards." Satorri replaced the microphone and sat back, arms folded against his chest, scanning the room.

Nyholm exhaled slowly and looked to the right. "The older gentleman on the perimeter. Tweed sport coat."

"Glenn Rooney, *LA Times*. What's so special about this fighter pilot? Many have been the subject of Hollywood movies."

Time to lay it out. Nyholm sat straighter, her exceptional height dwarfing Satorri. "For starters, Lieutenant Bronson flew in Burma, now called Myanmar, a mostly forgotten area of World War II. Allied and Japanese forces waged a brutal air campaign over mountain ranges and terrifying jungles amidst rapidly changing weather.

"Lieutenant Bronson accomplished over one hundred combat missions in those difficult conditions, well beyond the average of other World War II theaters. Pilots in Burma were in short supply due to attrition and the remoteness of the region.

"Most notably, and central to the story, Lieutenant Bronson was awarded the Distinguished Flying Cross for accomplishing a mission so dangerous the Allied command would only risk one pilot. He volunteered, diving steeply into a ravine and bombing a critical bridge, returning to strafe the enemy positions multiple times. The courageous action saved the lives of several hundred British soldiers who were at imminent risk of being overrun.

Lieutenant Bronson narrowly survived the torrent of antiaircraft fire he encountered. Against the odds, he returned to his jungle air base, wounded and bleeding profusely. His plane was damaged beyond repair.

"Soon afterward, Lieutenant Bronson returned stateside and was honorably discharged. He disappeared from mainstream society, working for decades as a reclusive bridgetender on a remote wooden bridge in southwest Florida, never divulging his World War II heroics. The rescued British soldiers tried in vain to locate him, wanting to express their enduring gratitude. All they could do was honor his courage at their annual reunions."

A reporter shouted, "Is he still a bridgetender?"

Nyholm shook her head. "No. Lieutenant Bronson was killed in July of 1994. What occurred adds an unfortunate outcome to the story. A suspicious fire engulfed the Florida bridge, killing him instantly when a pair of propane tanks exploded next to the bridgetender's shack—almost fifty years to the day after his special mission in Burma."

She paused for a few moments, allowing the overview to take hold. "Hopefully, my discussion gives a good sense of what we will bring to life." Nyholm noted the nodding heads. *It's resonating—time to wrap.* She gave the preplanned signal, glancing at the publicist and leaning back.

He stepped from the side wall. "There's time for two more questions." He pointed to a young woman on the front right. "Molly?"

"What do you mean by *suspicious fire*?"

Nyholm leaned to the mic. "The wooden bridge protected the natural beauty of a barrier island and the old Florida heritage of its tight-knit community. It was too narrow and rickety to support all the heavy construction vehicles and supplies required to build condos, resort hotels, large mansions, golf courses, and other modern structures. The bridge literally stood in the way of billions of dollars of prime real estate."

She held up a copy of the distributed packet. “I suggest reviewing the sequence of events that occurred on the evening of the fateful bridge fire. As you will learn, an arsonist started flanking fires, trapping Lieutenant Bronson. The bridge was all but destroyed—only a short section remains, now a memorial fishing pier.” Nyholm replaced the packet.

“Last question,” announced the publicist, gesturing toward a heavyset man in the middle. “Norman?”

“Where exactly is the island located?”

“Marcosta Island sits below Naples and immediately north of the Ten Thousand Islands National Wildlife Refuge. Access is limited to waterborne transportation. Shortly after the fire, the islanders held a special referendum. They voted against allowing the State of Florida to build a new bridge, returning to the earlier use of ferries and barges—a rather pointed statement about protecting the island and their way of life.”

The publicist moved between the table and roped cordon, raising both hands in the air, ending the event.

Adrien Satorri stood, turning to Nyholm. “Well done, champ.” He headed for the side exit, ignoring the barrage of questions.

Nyholm exhaled slowly, allowing the tension to drain away. She surveyed the milling press and caught the attention of the first reporter she called upon, gesturing for him to come over.

PART I

Chapter 1

Ripples raced across the surface of the marine lab harbor, driven outward by the spinning thrust of overhead blades. The corporate helicopter finished its sliding rotation and lifted away to the north, heading up the bayside of Marcosta Island, bound for Tampa. The sole passenger aboard was Geraldo Diaz, general counsel for Nielsen Enterprises, the Florida real estate empire of billionaire Derek Nielsen.

Mayor Jake Crawford stood near the harbor fuel dock, watching the helicopter disappear in the morning sky. A screen door slammed shut. His wife, Caitlin, walked toward him from the lab's front office, her auburn hair flowing in the onshore breeze. He waited until her questioning eyes stared up at his, lovely ovals of emerald green and reflected blue sky.

"Nielsen just terminated the negotiation," he said tersely.

She reacted with surprise. "But you agreed to make the public statement … about your belief in his innocence."

"He no longer cares about the suspicions, or so claims his attorney." Jake looked skyward. Frigate birds soared in widening circles above Munson Bay, spiraling upward in the warming air.

"Something's afoot. It would explain why the negotiations were delayed for two months." He refocused on Caitlin. "There's something else. Nielsen turned the table and made an offer to buy this property."

"What's he thinking? Ida would never sell."

"It's a big offer."

"How big?"

"A hundred and seventy-five million in cash, plus a fifty-five-acre marina and boatyard on the east side of Charlotte Harbor, south of Punta Gorda. Nielsen bought it out of bankruptcy recently."

"You mean, move the lab there?"

"His attorney said it could be accomplished for under $125 million, including new building construction, leaving at least $50 million for ongoing research and operations, five times the lab's annual budget."

Caitlin glanced down, shaking her head. "Ida must be devastated. She so wanted Nielsen's land for a nature preserve."

Jake looked in the direction of Ida Hoefler's office. "I need to get back with her. I'll stop by the front office before leaving for City Hall."

"You forgot. I won't be there."

Jake tapped his forehead once, reminded of their breakfast discussion. "I'm glad you're finally going for a checkup."

"You know how much I dislike the clinic."

"Yes, but it's not a smart choice at your age.

"And when was the last time you went? People in glass houses …"

"Okay, fair point. Give Doc Harris my best." Jake started for Hoefler's office.

"Do you want anything special from Hawker's?" asked Caitlin. "I'm picking up fresh grouper and shrimp after work."

Jake paused, turning. "No, that sounds good. I should be home by seven, hopefully sooner."

****

A cardboard tube occupied the corner of Ida Hoefler's office. Its contents displayed aerial overlays of the planned nature preserve, replete with wooden walkways and elevated viewing stations. She eyed the tube with dismay.

A courtesy knock preceded Jake's entrance, his head almost touching the top of the doorway. He traversed the distance to a corner conference table in three long strides, snatching Nielsen's offer and extending it her direction. "Are you considering this?"

"Good grief, not for a second."

"It's a huge sum. What about your board of directors? Will they think otherwise?"

"They detest Nielsen as much as you and I do."

Jake sat, placing his elbows on the table, head down, fingers massaging his temples. "A marina and yacht club were missing from Nielsen's original plans. This property is the obvious solution."

Hoefler grimaced at the thought of Nielsen's plans, envisioning the island overrun with thousands of wealthy snowbirds. The southern boundary of the mega-resort would abut the marine lab property.

Someone knocked briefly, partially opening the door.

"Yes?" Hoefler asked curtly. Her gray-blonde eyebrows started twitching, evidence of annoyance.

Judith Kerner's tanned face peered around the door. "Sorry for the interruption." She looked toward the conference table. "Hi, Mayor Crawford."

"Dr. Kerner."

"What is it, Judith?" Hoefler asked impatiently.

"Billy Watson is stumbling around in his mullet skiff by the shark pond, hollering and cussing a blue streak. I think he's drunk."

Jake jumped up, going to the bayside window. "Dammit,

Billy."

Kerner pushed the door open, stepping aside as he hurried out. She looked at Hoefler. "Should I go with him?"

"No. They're best of friends."

"A former cancer scientist and redneck commercial fisherman? Not your typical match-up."

"They grew up together on the island."

"How'd the meeting go?" asked Kerner, glancing at the conference table.

"Surprising," Hoefler replied.

Shouting erupted, the two men arguing. The roar of an outboard motor echoed through the open bayside window, racing away at full throttle.

"Surprising in what way?"

"Mayor Crawford and I are still discussing what happened. I'll update the leadership team after we're done."

Jake came through the doorway. "Billy's upset at someone named Dirty Dick. Claims the guy called his mother a whore at the tavern last night."

"I'll speak with Richard," said Hoefler.

"One of your dockhands?" asked Jake.

"No, our longtime cook."

"Our longtime, *disgusting* cook," clarified Kerner.

"Richard is eccentric, but a good person at heart," countered Hoefler.

Kerner rolled her eyes. "Not toward scientists."

"Sounds like a character," said Jake. He looked at his watch and then at Hoefler. "I have fifteen minutes to finish our discussion. You can update me later about Dirty … Richard. Try to find out his version of what happened."

Kerner headed for the doorway. "I need to check an experiment."

****

Jake exited the marine lab entrance. The drive north to City Hall would traverse the entire length of the island, just over five miles. Wispy horsetail clouds streaked across the sky. Cool, less humid air swirled through the open car windows, typical for late January in southwest Florida.

Native flora flanked the road, covering a continuous three-mile stretch of undeveloped land, eleven hundred acres in total. The elderly Garrett siblings had sold the acreage to Nielsen two-and-a-half years ago, in the summer of 1994, shortly before the old wooden bridge had burned down. Their great-grandfather had settled the island in the mid-1800s.

Jake shook his head. *Ole Cyrus must have rolled in his grave.*

Egret Avenue eventually appeared on the right, demarcating the northern boundary of Nielsen's holding. Jake slowed, thinking about the progress on the sustainability complex at the east end of the avenue, close to Munson Bay. Several hydroponic greenhouses were already producing lettuce and cherry tomatoes, fed by captured rainwater from advanced cisterns. Three prototype windmills could be seen spinning above the palms and Ficus trees, generating enough power to run the greenhouse fans and pumps that circulated the water.

The City and its university research partners had formally broken ground on the complex a little over a year ago. It was easy to remember the date: *January 23, Caitlin's forty-second birthday*. The two of them had celebrated afterward with a leftover bottle of champagne, laughing and fooling around behind a dune on Sand Point, pretending to be teenagers again.

Jake checked his watch. *Late for the lunch meeting.* Nielsen's land receded in the rearview mirror as he accelerated. Ahead, a grove of magnificent banyan trees appeared on the right, bordering the St. Andrew's Catholic Church. The trunks and aerial roots spread for an entire block, providing decades of enjoyment for island kids, playing tag or hide-and-seek, climbing and balancing on the branches, daring to jump from unnerving heights. Jake navigated the curve around the church property, entering the modest stretch of downtown buildings that paralleled Passage Channel. He turned left into his reserved parking space in front of City Hall.

****

Two blocks away, Caitlin reclined on an exam table at the island clinic, startled by the troubling discovery. Doc Harris pressed harder, probing the mass deep within her left breast. The expert fingers moved to the side, on an arc toward her underarm. His neutral expression masked what she sought. The room suddenly felt cold. She shivered.

The probing stopped. His hand appeared from under the paper apron, touching her shoulder. He met her look, a furrow forming across his brow. "It's probably a benign cyst, but we'll need to get it biopsied, just to make sure."

The attempt at reassurance didn't match the furrowed brow, failing to calm the rising fear. She bit her lower lip.

He went to her medical chart, flipping to a page. "Your last mammogram was five years ago. You should be getting one every year at your age."

Obviously. She shifted her eyes to a watercolor painting on the wall. It depicted Sand Point, the small peninsula at the northwest corner of the island, captured from the perspective of the gulf. Sugar-white dunes and yellow sea oats stood out vividly against the backdrop of dark-green Australian pines. A squadron of pelicans flew overhead in a loose formation.

Doc Harris discussed the referral to a Naples surgeon, describing the likely biopsy procedure.

Caitlin stayed focused on the painting, attempting to blunt

his words. Sand Point held such special memories. Many beautiful sunsets had fostered her youthful romance with Jake, their most intimate moments hidden behind those sugar-white dunes.

When do I tell Jake about the breast mass? She thought of what happened to his mother, all the suffering Jake had witnessed at a young age. It had been the reason for his research career, driven by the desire to conquer the enemy that had caused his mother such pain and, ultimately, an early death. *I'll wait for the biopsy results*. She shivered again.

****

Two hundred miles to the north, Derek Nielsen watched a cargo ship heading toward the Port of Tampa. A corporate helicopter flew past the ship's stern, approaching rapidly from the south. It climbed before flaring, descending toward his penthouse office suite above the northern edge of Tampa Bay, disappearing overhead.

The intercom came alive. A woman spoke in a calm, professional tone. "Mr. Diaz has arrived on the helipad. He will be down momentarily."

"Just send him in."

"Yes, Mr. Nielsen."

A pilot boat moved in front of the cargo ship, guiding it toward the port channel. Men could be seen lining the ship's railing. Nielsen wondered how long they had been at sea.

A nearby floor vent vibrated from a pressure change. A stocky, middle-aged man hurried through the inner office door, his black hair slicked back, briefcase in hand. Nielsen turned, gesturing toward a set of chairs in front of an elegant glass desk.

Geraldo Diaz settled in, retrieving a yellow legal pad.

"And?" Nielsen asked as he seated himself.

"Only Hoefler and Crawford were present at the meeting.

She went quiet after I terminated the negotiation and made the offer for the lab property."

"What about Crawford?"

"Visibly irritated. He asked if we'd take $14 million for the island land."

"He added $2 million to their previous amount?"

"That's right."

Nielsen laughed, swiveling to face the bay. The cargo ship had disappeared behind the other high-rise buildings at left. *Nice try, Crawford. Millions are a pittance against billions*. "How'd you respond?" Nielsen asked over his shoulder.

"I didn't."

"Good. I'd never accept the pathetic offer."

"I'll send a letter declining it."

Nielsen spun back. "No, do nothing. Let them stew. Hoefler will sell the lab property when the bulldozers get going."

****

The rear windows of the mayor's office offered an expansive view, encompassing Passage Channel and the Florida mainland, a half mile away. Jake stared toward the northern horizon, deeply troubled by what had transpired that morning, wondering what had encouraged Nielsen to reverse course.

The passenger ferry came into sight, heading from the island transport dock toward the Gulf of Mexico, destined for Naples. A departing group of tourists lined the railing, aiming their cameras toward the island.

Jake identified the reason for their interest, a scene he had witnessed many times. A rampaging pod of porpoises worked the edge of Passage Channel, bulging torpedoes chasing a large school of mullet, repeated tail slaps scattering the panicked prey. Panting exhalations glistened above exposed blowholes—sunlit puffs of mist shot upward in an energetic display of predatory coordination.

The intercom beeped, followed by a young woman's voice. "Fletcher Hastings from the *Tampa Sentinel*. Line 1."

"Thanks, Sandra." Jake turned to the desk phone, punching a button. "Fletcher, my man. It's been a while."

The familiar New England accent came through the speaker. "I just received a call from our branch office in Tallahassee. There's something you oughta know."

No pleasantries? Jake masked the sinking feeling, responding lightly, "What's cooking in Tallyho?"

"A new bill is circulating in the legislature. If it passes, the State can overrule your no-bridge referendum."

The sinking feeling went deeper. "On what grounds?"

"That the lack of a bridge is severely limiting the development of Marcosta Island, which in turn is harming Naples … all the missing snowbirds that would otherwise be driving up there to shop, dine, visit spas, engage wealth managers … all the fancy stuff they do."

Jake shook his head. "Who sponsored the bill? Grimm?"

"No, some two-bit representative from Zolfo Springs. A guy named Wilbur Blake."

"Why would he care? Zolfo's far from here."

Hastings explained, "The legislation is broadly worded. Any local action can be overruled if it causes economic harm to another city or region of the state."

Jake connected the dots. "I'll bet Nielsen's driving this. The Zolfo guy is just a decoy, making it appear like statewide interest."

"Interesting thought."

Jake reacted swiftly to the troubling realization. "Marcosta will mount a legal challenge if the State tries to overrule our referendum. We've controlled access rights to our island since the 1800s."

"I highly doubt a state court would rule in your favor …

particularly if Nielsen is in the mix. Many judicial campaigns have likely benefited from his influence peddling."

Jake emitted a sigh. "You're full of optimism."

"Well, I do have some *good* news … something I learned from my father last night. You've heard of Adrien Satorri?"

"The movie director?"

"Uh-huh."

"Why's he good news?"

"Dad's been a major investor in Satorri's movies, including the two blockbusters about Vietnam veterans."

"He's done well."

"Dad sent him my investigative series about the 1994 bridge fire, including the posthumous discovery of Simon's heroic mission in World War II. I guess the articles galvanized Satorri's creative imagination. His production company has already started on the movie project."

Jake glanced at the large watercolor painting. It had been on the wall of the mayor's office for decades. The old wooden bridge had been captured with exquisite detail, spanning Passage Channel in the warm light of an early sunrise. Simon stood in the control shelter next to his bridgetender's shack. The local shrimper fleet paraded through the drawbridge opening, seagulls swooping around the laden vessels.

Hastings continued, "Something else of relevance … Satorri is big on protecting the environment. He's used much of his wealth to preserve a large tract of land north of Santa Barbara, saving it from development. Apparently, he detests what Nielsen has done to the Florida Gulf Coast, including the suspicious events surrounding the '94 bridge fire."

Jake felt a familiar twinge. "Are you saying Satorri plans to implicate Nielsen?"

"I doubt he would point the finger directly—it would be a clear case of libel. He'll likely dramatize the suspicious events and let the audience draw their own conclusion."

Jake remained quiet, troubled yet again by the conflict of conscience: *violate solemn promises or continue allowing the unwarranted vilification of Nielsen?* Both choices lacked integrity.

"Pretty exciting, don't you think?" asked Hastings.

"Yeah. Where does Satorri stand in the movie process?"

"He has the financial backing lined up, including a chunk of Dad's money. The creative team is underway with pre-filming activities. Speaking of which, expect a call from Satorri's protégé, Anna Nyholm." Hastings spelled her surname.

"Why's Nyholm calling *me*?"

"They want to survey the island and surrounding waters."

Jake reacted skeptically, "To film here? There's no bridge. What little could be saved is now a fishing pier."

"I said the same to Dad. Apparently, they've struggled to find a wooden bridge with a drawbridge and co-located bridgetender's residence—modern concrete and metal bridgeworks are not an arson opportunity. They're considering filming background scenes at Marcosta and then integrating them into studio replicas of the bridgeworks … using blue screens and CGI.

"It's amazing what they can do these days. Okay, thanks for the heads-up. It should be an interesting discussion."

****

Jake's new assistant entered his office on the heels of the call with Hastings. Sandra's compact physique reminded him of an Olympic gymnast, taut muscles ready to spring. Dark-brown eyes complemented the jet-black, pixie-cut hair. He thought of her recent arrival on the island, wondering if she was adapting to its slower pace.

"Ms. Hoefler called while you were on the phone with Mr. Hastings. She wants you to call back. Something about the lab's cook."

Jake glanced at his watch.

Sandra placed a document on his desk. "Ms. Wilson said to sign at the red sticker. It's the annual emergency services contract with the County."

Jake signed, handing it back. "How's the garage apartment working out behind Ms. Vickers's house? It's a big change from your swinging condo life in Tampa."

"It's okay. Kinda old and creaky. Ms. Vickers is super cool. She invites me over for after-dinner drinks most evenings. We chat on her back porch until the no-see-ums show up. They were awful last night—look at all the bites." Sandra thrust a muscular leg horizontally in the air, easily balancing on one foot.

"Trying smearing bath oil on exposed skin. It clogs their tiny mouths, preventing the bites. Commercial fishermen swear by it. Horseshoe Basin smells like a fragrance shop most evenings."

"Seriously?"

"Yep. Hey, before I forget, I'm expecting a call from Anna …" Jake glanced at his note. "… Nyholm. I need to take it, regardless of what I'm doing."

Sandra's eyes went wide. "*The* Anna Nyholm? From Hollywood?"

"You know about her?"

"Are you kidding? She was engaged to John Clanders … but he backed out right before their wedding date, dumping her for his latest co-star. Katrina … Katrina … shoot, I can't recall her last name. It's Eastern European … maybe Russian. She's younger than me, only nineteen, I think."

"Who is John Clanders?"

"*What?* He won the Academy Award for Best Actor last year. Didn't you see Anna with him? You can't miss her, super tall, slender, gorgeous blonde hair in a long shag cut, stunningly beautiful. John looked so short next to her." Sandra struck a movie star pose, hands on hips, twisting to the side, chin raised.

"I'm more his size."

"We don't have a TV."

"Oh, that's right … I forgot. So, why's Anna calling *you*?" Sandra put a hand to her mouth. "Goodness, that came out super wrong."

Jake chuckled. "Relax, I'm definitely not a movie star. Listen, I can't discuss why she's calling." He gave Sandra a stern look. "You need to keep quiet about Ms. Nyholm, understood? I'll let you know when you can tell others."

"Sure thing, but can I guess?" Sandra lowered her voice, sounding conspiratorial. "I bet she's coming for a romantic getaway with a hot new movie star boyfriend. You know, the Hollywood rebound thing. No one would suspect them staying here."

"I doubt she'd call the mayor to make romantic arrangements." He pointed toward the office doorway.

"Unless she wants special treatment." Sandra headed to the outer admin office, an extra spring in her step.

Jake shook his head. *She must devour the* National Enquirer.

****

A call with the county manager ended the long workday. Jake's thoughts returned to the troubling Blake legislation, pondering the seriousness of Nielsen's maneuver. The ruminations led back to the Satorri movie.

Jake studied the fishing pier from the office window, thinking of the expected call from Anna Nyholm. He wondered if a replica of the drawbridge and bridgetender's shack could be erected on the far end. Depending on the filming angle, the downtown waterfront would be seen in the background, along with parts of the gulf and Munson Bay. A scaled-down version of the full bridge could be filmed in a studio using distant perspectives and special effects.

He returned to the desk and opened a side drawer, retrieving the projected city budget for the year. The income barely covered expenses, leaving little cash for capital improvements. He had considered debt financing, but the municipal bond brokers had only laughed, citing the island's lack of a bridge and tenuous economic status.

The movie might provide the needed cash. He wondered how much the filming fees and extra tax revenues would add to the city's income. The hit movie *True Lies* came to mind. Many of its scenes had been filmed in the Florida Keys, recalling that Hanna Sawyer had run the Monroe County Film Commission before becoming mayor of Key West. She would know the financial contribution, along with other insights. *I'll contact her first thing tomorrow.*

He returned to the window. The car ferry was on the other side of the channel, loading vehicles at the mainland transport dock. The activity triggered another realization: if the Blake law succeeded, the new bridge construction would likely interfere with the pier location, removing the filming option. *I need to contact Fletcher and alert his father. Maybe Satorri can help delay the State, buying more time to fight Nielsen.*

Sandra came into the office, sounding breathless. "Anna Nyholm's assistant is on the phone from Los Angeles. Can I schedule the call for 11:00 a.m. tomorrow, Eastern time? You're available."

****

Caitlin prepared dinner, sniffling. The paring knife cut cleanly, slicing a large onion into small chunks. A bubbling sauce simmered on the stove to her right, filling most of a cast iron skillet. A bowl of shelled shrimp and grouper chunks sat nearby, to be added last.

A car door slammed. Jake came into the kitchen through the

cabin side door. He recoiled immediately. "*Whoa* … that's one strong onion."

Caitlin wiped her eyes with the back of a hand. "I know. Could you grab me a tissue?"

Jake pulled her close, using the tissue to dab the tears. "You need to wear a dive mask next time." He kissed her briefly, letting go and extracting a beer from the refrigerator, taking a long swig.

Caitlin returned to the task. "How'd it go with Ida this morning?"

Jake placed the beer on the kitchen table and took a seat, wiping drips from his beard with the back of a hand. "You were right. She's devastated."

Caitlin cleared her throat. "Ida had plans drawn for the nature preserve … about a month ago."

"Interesting. She's never showed those to me."

"She wanted to surprise you—once the purchase of Nielsen's land was finalized."

Jake watched as Caitlin chopped the onion, appreciating his spousal good fortune. Entry into middle age had done little to diminish her natural attractiveness, a wholesome blend of Scottish ancestry and unassuming self-confidence. The appreciation brought a reminder. "How'd your appointment go with Doc Harris?"

"You'll have to put up with me a while longer. Before I forget, you've postponed *your* checkup three times. I told him you've been consumed with the challenges of being mayor."

"To say the least."

"I hope you're hungry," she said.

"Can you hear my stomach growling? Is it what I think?"

Caitlin pointed the knife at the skillet. "Spicy jambalaya sauce, fresh garden okra, and in a moment, the rest of this onion … followed by the shrimp and grouper."

"Smells delicious."

“Speaking of being mayor, how was the rest of your day? It certainly didn’t start well.”

“Fletcher Hastings called this afternoon. There’s troubling news out of Tallahassee … proposed legislation that would enable the State to overrule our no-bridge referendum. It explains what happened this morning.”

Caitlin spun in surprise, the knife pointing at him. “Overrule us? How?”

He glanced at the knife, eyebrows raised in mock concern, teasing her. “Careful now.”

“Oh, sorry.” She dropped her arm, pointing the knife at the floor.

Jake described the proposed legislation and the seriousness of the threat.

“Can the State get away with it?” She placed a steaming bowl of white rice on the table, returning to the dinner preparations.

“We’ll need to file a lawsuit challenging the action in state court, although Fletcher doesn’t give it much hope. I asked Miriam to research relevant court cases to verify he’s right.”

Caitlin shook her head in dismay, stirring the skillet. “You’ve had a crazy day.”

“More than you realize. Ever hear of Adrien Satorri and Anna Nyholm?”

Chapter 2

Anna Nyholm waited patiently, reflecting on the morning call with the mayor of Marcosta Island. An open notepad rested on her lap.

Adrien Satorri stood at the far edge of the broad wooden deck. His Japanese-style villa rambled through copses of trees and bushes, all native to the central California coast. Stone walkways interconnected simple, one-story structures of lacquered cypress, teak, and bamboo. The architectural artistry had no apparent symmetry, enabling an interwoven flow that conformed to the slopes and undulations of the terrain.

Nyholm loved the elegant minimalism—*Adrien's pride and joy*.

The Pacific Ocean was visible in the distance, a dark-blue line at the bottom of gently sloping foothills. The hillsides and valleys were covered in sage and chaparral. A late afternoon sun cast a shadow across the deck, compliments of a nearby Monterey pine. Creeping coolness filled the air.

Nyholm tugged at a new shawl, a recent birthday gift from

her mother in Stockholm. The smell and texture of the lambswool brought memories of childhood.

Thirty-four? How can that be? Her fingers traced the renewed tightness around her eyes and cheeks. The recent plastic surgery helped defeat the outward progression of time, yielding the appearance of being in her mid-twenties. *But I should have done it sooner.* She remained deeply offended, resentful of Clanders and his latest co-star, the feeling amplified by their lack of public discretion, the flaunting of the starlet's more youthful sexuality.

"What's with Stevansky and Jones?" Satorri inquired, walking toward her. "They should be here by now."

Nyholm glanced at her watch. Ten minutes remained before the scheduled start. "There was a backup on 101. I expect them any minute." She had arrived a half hour early, well aware of Satorri's obsession with punctuality.

"Let's get started. Have you reviewed my outline?"

"I did."

"There are numerous gaps. Those are your job now."

"Understood."

Satorri pointed at a voluminous binder on the adjacent side table. "The investigative articles by Fletcher Hastings, plus the initial research from Kurt … you've been through it all?"

"Multiple times. It oozes with dramatic potential."

Two men appeared, entering the deck from the side steps. Merv Stevansky led the duo, a burly older man with straight, graying hair pulled tight in a long ponytail, the director of photography. The screenwriter, Kurt Jones, trailed behind, a much younger man, thin and mousy looking. His unkempt, curly hair reminded Nyholm of another Kurt, the famous novelist. A congenital hip malformation caused Jones to gyrate between downward sags and upward thrusts. *Difficult to watch.*

Satorri gestured at the empty chairs, flicking his fingers impatiently. He began pacing, fiddling with a shirt button, clearly lost in thought. He stopped in front of Stevansky. "Merv?"

"Yes, Adrien?"

"Your latest thoughts on filming the Florida bridge scenes?"

Nyholm preempted Stevansky's response. "I spoke with the mayor of Marcosta Island early this morning. Two hundred feet of the old wooden bridge remains connected to the island's north end, what the fire department could save. It's now a memorial fishing pier."

She focused on Stevansky. "The mayor suggested the pier could be used for filming most of the bridge scenes, adding a full-scale replica of the drawbridge and bridgetender's shack to the far end. The downtown waterfront would be the primary background, augmented by angles toward the Gulf of Mexico and that large bay to the east." Nyholm smiled before continuing. "I had to chuckle. He referenced the Seven Mile Bridge scenes in *True Lies*, mentioning how they used a scaled-down model for the famous missile strike and teetering truck scene, suggesting we could do a similar model for distance shots and integration of special effects, like the nighttime fire and explosion."

Jones piped up, "The pier could also be used for the bridge fishing segments. The back of the binder contains photos of Lieutenant Bronson holding up some damn big fish."

Nyholm watched as Stevansky stared toward the distant Pacific. *He's considering it.*

She took the opportunity to convey another suggestion from the mayor. "There's a seventy-acre marine lab on the island's south tip with a large boat harbor. The mayor claims it can house around two hundred adults. There's plenty of storage for props and equipment, plus space for makeup, wardrobe, and our other requirements. A good number of the lab's research vessels have wide, flat decks that could be used as floating camera platforms."

Satorri turned, coming toward her, clearly intrigued. "What about housing for the lead actors?"

"The mayor had a fun idea. Position luxury yachts in the

marine lab's harbor. I like having the actors trapped on location … minimal distractions."

"Is the marine lab a significant operation?" asked Satorri. "We would need to take over the place."

"The mayor acknowledged the disruption. He believes the lab could continue its research projects, being mindful of our filming activities, but their ecotourism programs would need to be suspended."

"And would the lab expect us to cover that lost income?"

"I'll need to check. The mayor is discussing his ideas with the head of the marine lab. He promised to get back to me in a day or so."

Stevansky reengaged. "We'd still need to shoot the shack interior scenes at the studio. It removes the weather challenges. Florida has frequent pop-up thunderstorms in the summer … with plenty of lightning. It would be a nightmare moving the equipment and everyone back and forth to the end of that pier, particularly in a rush."

Nyholm proposed another option. "It might be possible to recreate the shack interior at the marine lab, directly adjacent to the seawater and accessible shelter. You could use blue screens to integrate window scenery. I prefer having actors perform in the actual setting, including indoor scenes."

"Like we did in the Philippine jungles," noted Jones. "Although the actors hated the heat and humidity."

"And all the bugs," added Stevansky.

"But it gave an edginess to their performances," noted Satorri. "And got Clanders his Academy Award. Speaking of the Philippines, what about the Burmese bridge and jungle air base locations? Where do we stand with those?"

"I'm working through the requirements with Merv," Nyholm replied. We'll likely film in Thailand."

"Why not Burma?"

Jones explained, "Myanmar is a mess … all the government

crackdowns."

"Right. Myanmar. I must stop calling it Burma."

"They hate that name," said Jones. "It's linked with the British colonial era. George Orwell wrote about it in *Burmese Days*."

Satorri came close, looking down at Jones. "You are truly encyclopedic about everything, momentous and trivial."

The comment sounded sarcastic, but Anna knew how much Satorri respected the talents of the young screenwriter. *Adrien's assignment of the two men is a godsend.* Stevansky directed photography for the blockbuster Vietnam movies. Jones wrote the screenplay for the most recent one, winning a Golden Globe.

Satorri turned toward Stevansky. "Don't tell me we must transport a World War II fighter plane to Thailand and back. Can we please find one in the region?"

Jones interjected, "Finding an operational P51-A Mustang will be challenging. The first version of the P51 is much rarer than later versions."

"Does that matter?" Nyholm asked.

"Yes, to be historically accurate. Bronson would have been piloting the 'A' version during his deployment years, the 1943–44 timeframe."

Satorri went after Jones again. "Remember, we have creative license. The movie is not a damn documentary. Forget the specific version of the plane. Just use whatever is over there: A, B, C, D, or whichever letter is available."

Jones looked away in apparent frustration.

Nyholm made a mental note to check back with him. The version of the fighter plane might matter to World War II buffs, including historically minded critics. *One never knows what could trigger a negative review.*

Satorri left Jones, walking briskly to a tall table at the side of the deck. A coffee carafe sat perched on top alongside a rectangular plate of assorted pastries. He refreshed his cup, drank a few sips, and returned to the trio, querying as he approached. "Ideas about the lead actors? Or do you need more time?"

"I definitely need more time," said Jones. "There are numerous gaps in the storyline. I want to find some of the surviving British soldiers. They'll have firsthand knowledge of what Bronson encountered at the Burmese bridge. It sounds like a suicide mission, given the thicket of antiaircraft guns at the ravine. I'd also like to interview surviving pilots from his fighter squadron … and maybe get the Japanese perspective of what transpired." Jones made a tangential leap, later to prove insightful. "Plus, something is nagging me about the Florida bridge fire."

"Like what?" asked Satorri.

"Why didn't Bronson escape the fire by jumping in the channel? The drop was only fifteen feet or so."

"Maybe he couldn't swim," suggested Satorri. "Or perhaps the arsonist had already killed him or knocked him unconscious. Forensics couldn't determine if there was foul play or not. The explosion scattered small pieces of the man all over the water."

Nyholm stood and headed for the carafe. She spoke while refilling her cup, returning to Satorri's question about lead actors. "We'll need to cast a younger man for Bronson's character. Make-up will age him as we shift to later timeframes, ending in his early seventies." She took a sip. "I have a particular candidate in mind. Draven Barlowe gave an impressive supporting performance in *Taming of the Many*, exhibiting broad dramatic range, which we'll need. Bronson's character will start as a dashing young fighter pilot, gregarious and eager for combat. The horror of warfare transforms him into a reclusive bridgetender. We need to learn more about the specifics, but I think Barlowe could be a great fit—and stardom hasn't affected him."

"*Yet.* Only a matter of time," Stevansky predicted.

Satorri stared skyward, in the direction of a contrail cutting across the late afternoon sky, high above the Pacific horizon. Minutes passed before he spoke. “I can picture Barlowe in the role. Will he be available in four months?”

“Krista’s checking schedules with agents. Are you moving up the timetable?” asked Nyholm.

“That’s something we need to discuss. Charles Hastings called me last evening. Sounds like that Nielsen bastard is at it again, working against the wishes of the island residents. Charles said it would help if we gave an early presser announcing the movie project and why the Bronson story needs telling, including mention of the suspicious events surrounding his death and our interest in filming on the island. It would resurrect awareness of what transpired in ’94 and shine attention on Nielsen’s latest maneuvers.”

Jones jumped on the comments. “The *Sentinel* articles all but pointed the finger at Nielsen. He had a clear motive for torching the bridge that night. It had to be arson-for-hire.”

“You need to avoid crossing the line when depicting Nielsen’s character,” Satorri reminded. “Make sure our law firm reviews your drafts. We must avoid libeling him. Otherwise, he’ll have us by the balls.”

Stevansky added another concern. “Paparazzi might head to Marcosta Island after the presser, anticipating our surveying, particularly with Anna in the mix. The island mayor needs to be alerted.”

“He can’t underestimate them,” said Jones. “Remember what happened in the Philippines?”

“Remarkable that no one got killed,” said Stevansky.

“Which is another reason to like the marine lab location,” Nyholm noted. “The mayor said it’s isolated on the island’s south tip, separated from the small town on the north end by several miles of undeveloped land—the same land where Nielsen wanted to build that massive resort complex. A single, two-lane road connects the lab to the north end. It should be a straightforward security setup."

"This island mayor, he sounds fairly savvy," said Satorri. "Does he have a name?"

Nyholm checked her notes. "Jake Crawford. He grew up on the island and knew Lieutenant Bronson well. I expected a backwater hick. The guy reminds me of a big-city mayor … smart, articulate, thinking steps ahead. He knew far more about our filming requirements than I expected. Kurt's team is preparing some information about him."

"I've received an initial summary," said Jones, referring in turn to his notes. "Forty-three years old. Holds a doctorate in human genetics—the former chief science officer of a highly successful biotech company in Boston. He made a huge fortune when the company went public but donated his unsold company stock to the American Cancer Society, something like four hundred million dollars' worth, most of his net worth at the time. He quit the biotech industry in July 1994 and moved back to Marcosta Island, his hometown, arriving in the early morning hours on the day of the fateful bridge fire and …"

Satorri interrupted. "I've encountered exceptional people in the most unlikely places." He spun an index finger. "Let's keep moving."

Nyholm looked up from her notes. "One more thing. Mayor Crawford invited us to visit the island at our earliest opportunity. Said he'll roll out the 'redneck' carpet, old Florida style."

Satorri finally smiled. "So, this scientist-turned-mayor also has a sense of humor." He scanned the trio. "Go verify what he's saying and …" Satorri stopped himself. "… but don't head there yet." He focused on Anna. "I'll be announcing your directing debut at the presser. You need to be there to field questions. Get with our publicist to arrange the event for early next week."

Anna grinned broadly, striking a dramatic pose. She threw her left arm outward with a flourish, the other hand raised skyward, holding the notepad. "Ta-dah … I can't wait."

Chapter 3

Jake waited patiently at his corner conference table, allowing Ida Hoefler time to visit the wall painting. A sheet of notes lay before him, highlights from the previous day's call with Anna Nyholm.

"Delores is *such* a talented artist. I never tire of seeing this." Hoefler turned and ambled over, seating herself on the opposite side of the table. "Before we start, how's Caitlin? Is she doing okay?"

"Why do you ask? She's been fine around me."

"I … well … she went to Naples today."

"I know, running errands for the lab."

Hoefler avoided his stare, glancing downward.

Jake felt immediate concern. "So, she's *not* running errands for the lab?"

Hoefler looked up. "I may have caused a problem here."

"What did she tell you?"

"Only that she needed to go to Naples for an appointment … but she looked worried. That's why I asked."

Jake pushed away from the table, standing. *Why did Caitlin mislead me?* He glanced at the wall clock before turning to face the back windows. The car ferry was heading away from the island, across the channel toward the mainland transport dock.

"I'm sorry. I just assumed that …"

Jake ignored the rest of Hoefler's explanation, wondering if Caitlin would be aboard the return crossing.

He resumed sitting, leaning forward and placing his elbows on the table, palms together as in prayer, tapping thumbs to his forehead. *Maybe it's something she doesn't want to discuss. A gynecological issue?* He had become more aware of the abuse that Caitlin endured in her first marriage, piecing most of it together despite her unwillingness to discuss what had transpired. The limits of their lovemaking spoke the loudest, the boundaries evident. Island rumors provided additional insight, at least to the extent they could be believed.

He refocused, hearing the last of Hoefler's words: "… I can return tomorrow."

Jake forced aside the concern. He leaned back. "No. It's important we talk." He gathered his thoughts. "I mentioned the Blake legislation when I called. A source has confirmed that Nielsen is using widespread campaign donations to expedite the bill through the legislature and across the governor's desk."

It was Hoefler's turn to lean forward, planting her stout forearms on the table. The blue eyes were focused intently, eyebrows twitching.

Jake continued, "Nielsen lulled us during the delayed negotiation—the whole bit about needing time to consider a donation of the land to the lab, the potential tax advantages. It was utter bullshit, a deceptive smokescreen, purposely designed to entice us. Meanwhile, he used the delay to put the Blake legislation in play. He's caught us off balance. We should never have believed the bastard."

"Are you saying there's no time left to fight him?"

"Not in the legislature, and the governor's deep in Nielsen's pocket. We'll need to file a lawsuit, seeking a preliminary injunction against the application of the new law."

"Can the City afford a lawsuit?"

"We won't incur a significant budget hit," Jake replied flatly. "I contacted Fred Thompson in Miami. As you may be aware, he harbors a longstanding grudge against Nielsen. He's agreed to do the litigation work pro bono. I'd cover the remaining expenses personally, but it causes a conflict now that I am mayor."

Jake shifted to the primary reason for the meeting. "I need to bring you into the loop on something else. If I'm right, it should delay the State, buying time for our legal strategy to take hold. The marine lab has an important role to play."

"Go on."

"Adrien Satorri is planning a movie about Simon."

Hoefler looked perplexed.

"You've heard of Satorri, the movie director?"

"Of course, he made those grim movies about Vietnam War veterans."

"Challenging to watch but highly acclaimed. As it turns out, Fletcher Hastings's father provided Satorri with copies of the *Sentinel* articles about the 1994 bridge fire and Simon's combat heroics. Satorri Productions has already started on the project."

"And how does this involve the lab?" Her eyebrows started twitching again.

"They're considering filming here, which, aside from potentially delaying Nielsen, would provide a significant financial boost to the local economy and city budget. But they will need a place to house the production staff and actors, store equipment, construct props, and do a range of other stuff."

The eyebrows twitched faster. "And did you suggest the lab?"

"Yes, but I explained it would need your approval."

"How many movie personnel would be involved?"

"Over a hundred. Well … actually … closer to two

hundred."

Her voice rose, confirming what the eyebrows already stated. "You should have asked me first. Your suggestion is entirely unacceptable. It would completely disrupt our operation."

"Only the ecotourism programs. The scientific research could continue … being mindful of the filming activities."

"The eco-programs are just hitting stride. It would take at least a year to get those back on track, more like two years. Think of the lost momentum and revenues, all the affected staff." She leaned back, forearms firmly crossed in defiance.

Jake raised both hands, palms facing outward. "You need to hear me out."

Hoefler maintained the defiant posture.

"Here's the deal. Satorri Productions would pay for the use of the lab facilities. And I'm willing to offset the remaining lost income through an additional donation to the lab—it's not a conflict with me being mayor. Affected staff can be redeployed to research assistance or other purposes, maybe helping with the movie. I bet they'd enjoy it."

Hoefler looked toward the wall painting, eyebrows slowing.

"I need your full support, Ida. Nielsen has the upper hand with the Blake legislation. We must win Satorri's affection for filming here. The politicians will catch hell if the State interferes with his making a movie about Simon, a decorated World War II hero—especially if they've taken campaign money from Nielsen, which is likely. It will buy time to fight back before it's too late."

Hoefler turned to face him. The twitching had stopped.

Jake pressed the moment, targeting what mattered most to her. "If Nielsen succeeds, you'll be dealing with the full extent of his plans, starting at the edge of the lab property. Any shot at the nature preserve will be lost forever. And forget the eco-programs. Very few ecotourists would want to visit an island that's become a manicured playground for thousands of self-indulgent snowbirds."

Hoefler unwound from the chair. "I'll speak with my leadership team and our board of directors. I can't move forward on this without their full support." She headed for the office door.

"I'd appreciate a timely decision," said Jake. "Satorri's creative team is eager to survey the island. I'd like them to know in advance that the lab is available. They could stay in the visiting scientist quarters while here, experiencing the location firsthand."

Hoefler paused at the doorway. "I'll get back to you by late tomorrow, possibly sooner."

Jake threw out a final request, more of a demand. "Make sure your leadership and board keep this quiet. The planned movie will be big news. We can't get ahead of Satorri's press event."

Hoefler exited without acknowledgment.

Jake's thoughts shifted immediately to Caitlin, wondering if she had returned on the latest ferry crossing. He quickly gathered paperwork into his brief bag, instructing Sandra to reschedule the remaining calls and meetings as he hurried out.

****

A twisting road connected the Tamiami Trail to the transport dock on the mainland side of Passage Channel. Caitlin winced as she turned the steering wheel, navigating another curve. The side trip to an Asian grocer in Naples had delayed her return, enabling the local anesthesia to wear off. She glanced at the two bags of lychees on the passenger seat. The exotic fruit had been Simon's favorite, a taste he acquired during deployment to Burma. The affection had rubbed off on Jake. Caitlin found the taste and texture unappealing.

Rounding the last curve presented a welcome sight. The car

ferry was still at the mainland dock, loading vehicles for transport to the island. Hers was the last to board.

She remained in the car during the crossing, privately supporting the sore breast to minimize jostling from the channel waves. The ferry soon came tight to its island dock, the ramp lowering into position. She followed the other cars onto Gulf Drive, turning left at the first side street. *Ouch!* The needle had pierced close to the underlying pectoral muscles. She dropped her left hand, continuing to drive with the right, hoping she could suppress the wincing when Jake arrived home from work.

Their cabin lay nestled in an array of tropical foliage, situated on an acre of land on the island's northeast tip, at the end of Eletz Point Lane. Her tires crunched on the oyster shell driveway, weaving between a grove of banana trees and a long stand of bamboo. Large hibiscus bushes framed the gated entrance to the parking area—each displayed white flowers with purple and gold centers, her favorite color combination.

The gate was open. She skidded to a stop, leaving trails in the oyster shells, startled to see Jake's car alongside the cabin. *Why's he home so early?*

She pulled forward and parked. Jake sat on the bench at the end of their T-shaped dock, facing the bay. *Something must have happened—probably related to Nielsen.* She wished the billionaire would stop the deceitful maneuvering, hating the burden it placed on Jake.

The combination of purse and grocery bags required a solid push of a hip to close the car door. It slammed loudly. Jake stood and turned, cutting a tall figure amid the backlight from the bay. She couldn't raise an arm to wave, but neither did he.

No greeting? She paused momentarily, staring at him before proceeding through the side door. She placed the purse and bags on the kitchen table. The lychees went in the freezer. She stepped back, looking toward the dock through the bayside windows of the cabin. Jake remained standing alongside the bench.

She carefully removed the windbreaker and entered the bathroom, closing the door and unbuttoning her blouse, pulling the left side over the shoulder, exposing the biopsied breast. Her bra was in the purse. The surgical nurse had said it would be too uncomfortable to wear once the anesthesia wore off. *Right about that one.*

The large Band-Aid came off easily. She leaned toward the mirror above the sink. A raised bump was visible on the upper part of the breast, reddish in color. Black marker lines formed an X across it, the intersection designating the entry point for the biopsy needle. She used her right hand to retrieve cotton balls and a bottle of rubbing alcohol from the shelving above the toilet, pulling her left arm in close to ease the pain. She rubbed at the marks. The porch screen door slammed shut, almost causing her to knock over the bottle.

The floorboards creaked, growing louder. "You okay in there?" Jake's voice sounded flat, almost terse.

"I'm fine … just need to pee. You're home early." She soaked another cotton ball and rubbed it in circular motions to finish the job.

The floorboards creaked as he moved away.

She raised her voice. "I grabbed some lychees while running the errands. They're in the freezer."

She flushed the unused toilet and turned on the sink faucet, washing her hands. A quick check in the mirror confirmed the marker lines were gone. Haunting eyes stared back, appearing deep set, the cumulative effect of sleepless nights. Windblown hair amplified the distressed appearance. She buttoned her blouse and brushed out the tangles. *Stand straight, shoulders back. Ow!* She hunched forward, pulling her shoulders inward to reduce the pain, pausing to calm herself before opening the door.

Long fingers drummed the armrest of Jake's reading chair. He faced the bayside windows, right leg crossed over left. A palpable tension filled the room. She decided to leave him alone, turning toward the kitchen.

"You weren't running errands for the lab."

His words stopped her cold. *Oh, no.* She braced for the unwanted discussion.

"Whatever is going on may be something you don't want to discuss. If that's the case, just say so. I'm concerned but will respect your need for privacy."

Take the offer. But wait, what if the biopsy result is bad news? Jake would know in a few days. Feelings of apprehension and loneliness enveloped her, tears forming. The onset of sobbing defeated an attempt to explain.

Strong arms pulled her close. A large hand brought her head against his chest. The steady thump of his heart became a calming influence. He caressed the side of her face, helping the sobbing to dissipate. She looked up. His eyes stared deeply into hers, a mix of kindness and concern.

He slowly released the embrace, leading her to the couch, reclining against a corner cushion. She nestled alongside, under the protection of his outstretched arm. His fingers gently pushed the dangling hair from her face.

"Do you want to discuss it?" he asked softly, grabbing a tissue from a box on the coffee table.

She bit her lower lip, working to gather herself. The tissue became the center of focus.

He wiped away the leftover tears. "It's okay if you'd rather not. Just know I care, whatever is going on."

She inhaled deeply and exhaled, committing to the moment, dreading the impact of her words. "They biopsied a large mass in my left breast."

His muscles tensed, coinciding with a sharply inhaled breath.

"I didn't want you to worry," she added quickly, trying to offset the reaction. She imagined the thoughts racing through his mind.

It was her turn to wait, allowing him to process the sudden

news. She reached for his hand, holding it.

The tension in his muscles subsided. “When do you learn the results?”

“Doc Harris won’t receive the report until midday Monday, given the weekend.”

He went quiet again.

“The surgeon told me it’s probably a large cyst.”

“Is the mass irregular? Can it be moved around or is it …” Jake stopped, looking away.

“Please don’t worry. I should be fine.”

More moments passed. Jake finally looked back, his eyes once again a mix of kindness and concern. “You’re right. The probabilities are in your favor. Let’s keep a positive outlook.”

Chapter 4

A copy of the pathology report occupied the passenger seat of Jake's car, contained within a red folder. Doc Harris had shared it with Caitlin the previous afternoon. Jake looked ahead as Caitlin's car curved around the grove of banyan trees on Gulf Drive, heading to work. *She's being brave.*

He swung into his parking spot at City Hall and turned off the ignition, considering the findings. The mass was not a cyst. No cancer cells had been identified; however, there were disconcerting concentrations of atypical, precancerous ones. *Suggestive.*

He grabbed the folder and stepped from the car, worried that the biopsy needle may have missed cancerous cells. The most conservative protocol called for the mass to be excised and subjected to comprehensive microscopic and genetic analyses. He knew the best place to get the surgery and diagnostics performed. *Hopefully, Caitlin will agree to visit Boston.*

Officer Pearson rode up on a patrol bike. "Morning, Mayor."

"Hey, Michael. Getting some exercise?"

Pearson straddled the bike, both feet planted on the tarmac, grabbing his midsection for emphasis. "Down fifteen pound-a-roozies."

"Good for you—that's serious progress. All secure on the home front?"

"Yeah, other than Billy. He started howling at midnight … like some kinda red-headed werewolf. Neighbors are royally pissed."

House arrest must be driving Billy crazy. Jake stepped to the brick sidewalk. "Have the charges been finalized?"

"Yeah. Shooting a firearm in a public facility. Reckless endangerment."

"Misdemeanors?"

"Reckless thing might be a felony, the gun being so close to the cook's head and all."

Jake recalled Pearson's earlier remark. "What'd you call Billy? A red-headed werewolf? Did you come up with that?"

"Naw. The commercial fishing dudes started it. Some are calling him 'ginger wolf.' It's the full moon shit."

"Full moon?"

"They stay clear of him them nights. Billy gets dark in the head—meaner'n hell. Least now, he's stuck at home."

Jake considered the incident on the back deck of Harry's Tavern three nights ago. Billy had shot the button off the top of Dirty Dick's baseball cap. *Huh, it was a full moon. Tide was way up.* The feud with the cook needed to stop before somebody got killed. "I'll talk to Billy about the howling. He's probably doing it to annoy the fishermen that live at the basin, seeing they called him a werewolf. Let me know if you hear anything more about the charges."

"Roger that." Pearson gave a playful salute and pedaled away, crossing Gulf Drive and dismounting in front of Spud Nut, the local donut shop.

Good thing he's exercising. Just breathing the air in Spud

Nut will add pounds. The thought of fresh donuts grabbed Jake's interest, quickly dismissed. *Stay focused.* He hurried up the sidewalk and entered the main door of City Hall. A twelve-foot stuffed alligator sat in the middle of the circular foyer, mouth open wide. The beast straddled an inlaid city logo. Someone had stuck a toy pink flamingo on the gator's snout, looping a wire around the bird's feet and through the gator's nostrils.

Jake followed his customary route, stepping over the long tail and heading straight for the mayor's suite. Sandra wasn't at her desk. He entered his inner office, pausing to look at the bridge painting, a ritual he adopted after becoming mayor. It helped with regaining perspective. *Nothing I'm dealing with comes close to what Simon endured.*

Keeping the right perspective yielded the best attitude, an early truth he had learned in cancer research, where failures abounded. He thought of it mathematically: *attitude is a function of perspective.* Jake recalled stopping by the Vietnam War Memorial whenever he had reason to visit DC, staring at the names on the hallowed wall, quickly regaining perspective.

He came around the old desk and took a seat. Sandra had left the day's schedule in the middle. *Good, a full plate.* The meetings and calls would leave little time to dwell on Caitlin and the pathology findings.

Jake noticed that one of the day's meetings involved a discussion with Police Chief Wilkinson. It reminded him of the update from Pearson. *What's with Billy these days?* Jake knew his relationship with Billy had become strained over the past year. The mayoral duties had proven omnipresent, leaving no room for the outdoor pastimes that had forged their relationship in younger years, mostly netting skiff-loads of mullet in Munson Bay. Billy had become increasingly resentful, leading to outright petulance. And now this escalating feud with the lab cook. Billy's increasingly dark behavior made Jake wonder if his longtime friend had become depressed.

Jake pushed the red folder to the side of the desk, reaching for a stack of documents to review. His eyes drifted back to the red folder. The earlier thought about the omnipresent mayoral duties intersected with Caitlin's medical situation. Becoming mayor had coincided with being newly married, causing the postponement of their planned honeymoon, a monthlong private cruise of the Bahamas. *My priorities need changing—sooner than later.*

He thought of the used power yacht he had recently located up in Manatee County. It would take several months to restore to cruising condition. *I should purchase it and get the repairs started.* The much bigger decision was how and when to exit the mayor's job. Especially with Nielsen back on the attack.

****

Caitlin slowed on Gulf Drive, pulling onto a sandy shoulder about a mile short of the marine lab. No cars were visible ahead or behind. A narrow path could be seen through the passenger window, cutting between a mixed collection of sea grapes and scrub pines. She opened the driver's door with her right hand, avoiding the lingering pain.

The path was overgrown from lack of use, the gulf hidden by the aggregation of native flora and dunes. Sand spurs pricked her ankles as she worked her way toward the beachfront. The path curved around a high dune. She looked up. A single scrub pine resided on the top, its gnarled trunk and limbs bent toward the island and away from the gulf, the onshore winds having directed the tree's growth.

She reached the upper beach and kicked off her sandals, leaving them as they fell. A circuitous route to the water's edge avoided the accumulations of broken shells in depressions of sand. No one could be seen on the beach to the left or right. The expanse of gulf lay before her. Small waves came ashore, gentle curls caressing the sand.

Trips to the remote beachfront had become a necessity during her first marriage, four years of hell in her early twenties. Coming here and floating naked in the gulf water had helped to ease the physical and emotional pain, countering the latest toxicity she had endured.

Her bare feet entered the cool water, causing her to shiver. The waves slid up and down her calves. She wiggled her toes in the sand, observing the line of white clouds on the horizon. Other senses joined the moment, melodic liquid tones and salty smells, the warmth of the rising sun on her back.

A mockingbird sang a rotation of mimicked songs. She turned and looked toward the high dune, locating the avian soloist on the topmost branch of the resilient pine, silhouetted in the morning sunlight. The tree's disfigurement brought recognition of a future possibility.

The pine beckoned. She exited the water and retraced her steps to the dune, navigating its slope at an upward angle, placing her right hand on the sand to maintain balance. The mockingbird broadcast a blue jay's warning and flew away.

She arrived at the top, grasping the largest branch for support, amazed she had never viewed the island from this vantage point. Sand Point was visible to the northwest, extending into the gulf, the mouth of Passage Channel just beyond. Her vision shifted eastward, scanning across the tall row of Australian pines to the downtown buildings. The sight of City Hall brought loving thoughts of Jake. His respect and kindness stood in sharp contrast to her first husband.

The island warmed in the advancing sunlight, initiating an onshore breeze. Wisps of hair drifted across her eyes. A soft whistling could be heard as the breeze came through the pine needles, gaining in volume as the minutes passed.

She raised her left arm slowly, grasping the gnarled branch with both hands and closing her eyes, forming a bond with the enduring tree, absorbing its resilience.

****

Jake returned to his desk from the third meeting of the day, the last hour spent with Chief Wilkinson at the adjoining police station. They had discussed several pressing issues, most notably Billy's erratic behavior and escalating hostility toward the lab's cook.

The voicemail light blinked on the desk speakerphone. He punched the play button.

"Fletcher here. Satorri is announcing the movie project today at 4:00 p.m., Pacific time. They've provided a call-in number. I'll be listening remotely along with our entertainment reporter. She'll write the presser article and reference it to the one I've been readying about the Blake legislation. Both will hit the front page tomorrow morning and …" A muffled voice could be heard in the background. "Gotta run, but one more thing. According to Dad, Anna Nyholm will be directing the movie—it's her debut. I guess Satorri's retiring soon." The voicemail stopped.

Jake crossed his fingers, hoping the press event and *Sentinel* articles would trigger a disruption of Nielsen's plans. He glanced at the day's schedule, orienting to the next meeting. Sandra poked her head through the doorway. "Ms. Wilson needs a quick moment."

"Okay."

The no-nonsense city attorney walked into his office shortly afterward, a thick folder in hand.

"Afternoon, Miriam."

As usual, she wasted no time on pleasantries. "Do you have five minutes to discuss the Blake legislation?"

Jake glanced at the wall clock. "Ten."

Wilson opened the folder and retrieved the top sheet, passing it across the desk. "I reviewed past state court rulings, as requested. Several exemplary cases are summarized on the page. As you'll see, each court decision favored the plaintiff claiming economic harm, regardless of the defense arguments about loss of local heritage or damage to the natural environment. All the other cases have resulted in similar decisions. The Blake legislation essentially codifies the judicial precedence into law."

"Unsurprising for Florida," said Jake, scanning the summary sheet. "Economic progress is the sole arbiter of the state's future, the environment be damned." He paused for a moment. "Given what you found, why didn't Nielsen file a state lawsuit contesting our '94 referendum?"

"The plaintiff must be a governed location, like a city or county, not a real estate developer. And courts move slowly. The Blake legislation offers a faster route."

"Got it." Jake reached for a used Post-it Note, sticking it on the sheet and handing it back to her. "We'll need to bypass the state judiciary and file a federal lawsuit. I've attached the mobile number for Fred Thompson in Miami. We should consider hiring him to seek a preliminary injunction against the State."

"Federal courts don't have jurisdiction," said Wilson.

"You've forgotten that the Ten Thousand Islands National Wildlife Refuge is immediately to our south. We'd point to the predicted harm to the refuge if Marcosta is developed as Nielsen plans, and why the new bridge enables that to happen. The rest goes to showing his connection with the Blake legislation and related influence peddling. The legal strategy should overcome the jurisdiction issue."

"We can't afford Fred Thompson."

"He'll work pro bono."

Wilson reacted with surprise. "How do you know?"

"I know."

"Huh … okay. But the city council must still approve his hire and the lawsuit filing."

"I'm waiting for some news to break before scheduling the

public council meeting."

"What news?"

"You'll have to wait until tomorrow morning."

"But I'm the city attorney."

Jake smiled. "Even more reason to wait. You can deny foreknowledge of it."

Chapter 5

Derek Nielsen headed down the stairwell, bypassing the helipad elevator atop his headquarters. The short morning commute across Tampa Bay had barely provided time to read the *Sentinel*'s front-page articles. He exited the top-floor stairwell at a brisk pace, pushing through the double wooden doors and into his outer office.

"Oh, Mr. Nielsen … good morning." His executive assistant jumped from behind her desk, looking startled. She hurried to prepare his customary cup of Ospina Grand Cru coffee. Nielsen stopped, turning back in her direction. She froze.

"Get Diaz up here … *now*."

Nielsen entered his palatial office. The newspaper flew onto a lacquered coffee table to the right. His sport coat followed, landing on the companion couch. The angry traversal halted at the floor-to-ceiling windows behind the glass desk. He stared at the bay, fists clenching repeatedly, a defining contrast to the tranquil waters beyond.

The floor vent vibrated. Nielsen swung around. Diaz hurried

through the inner doors, exhibiting a worried expression.

Nielsen pointed at the newspaper. "Did you read the front-page articles? About the Satorri movie? And the Hastings one about the Blake legislation?" A hateful intonation enveloped the reporter's name.

Diaz sounded nervous in response, "I … I read them."

"It's no coincidence how they're written—the joint timing. It's a coordinated attempt to discredit me."

"Neither article mentions you by name."

"For Christ's sake, Geraldo, they don't have to. Most of Florida believed I caused the bridge fire and the death of that old bridgetender. I've spent more than two years letting the suspicions subside, setting the stage for my next move. Now the goddamn *Sentinel* has pushed it all back to the surface and connected it with a fucking Satorri movie, of all things. You've got to stop this shit in its tracks. Kill the goddamn movie before it gets going. Nip this shit in the bud."

Diaz stayed quiet, looking down and grimacing, slowly shaking his head.

Nielsen studied him, eyes narrowing. "And how the hell did Hastings learn so much about my involvement in the Blake legislation? Is there a mole inside this building? I want all outgoing and incoming phone numbers for the past three months thoroughly analyzed. And what about Hastings? I thought we had him under surveillance."

Diaz looked up, sweat forming on his brow. "I've had him trailed everywhere possible. No sources have been exposed that are connected to us. We thought about bugging his desk phone, but it doesn't matter. He's using a mobile one now."

"Where was your Marcosta source about this? Why didn't she know something? Instead, I learn about the goddamn movie from *Sentinel* headlines? Fucking wonderful."

Diaz glanced at his notepad. Sweat formed on his brow. "She notified me about Anna Nyholm, but it was wrapped in a story about a romantic getaway with a new movie star boyfriend."

Nielsen shook his head in frustration, pointing toward the coffee table. "Nyholm's the director. Am I right?"

Diaz grabbed the newspaper from the table, studying the front page. "Her directing debut was just announced. Regardless, it would have been a gigantic leap to think she'd be making a movie about the bridgetender."

Nielsen's frustration boiled over, the angry tone rising in volume. "Why the hell would someone of Nyholm's sophistication go to that island for a romantic getaway? It's mostly a rundown commercial fishing village with a minor, shark-hugging marine lab stuck at the bottom. There are thousands of better islands. Did you ever stop to think about the subject of Satorri's movies? They're about troubled war veterans, for Christ's sake. Like guess who? The damn bridgetender! You need to get your head out of your ass. You're paid to think ten steps ahead, not twenty behind."

Diaz hunkered down, adopting the pose of a dog about to be cuffed.

Nielsen turned back to the window. *One more strike and Diaz is history.* He spoke while facing the bay, his voice coldly monotonic. "What else have you learned that I don't know?" His inquiry initiated the sound of flipping pages.

"Mayors Crawford and Sawyer had a phone discussion. I assume about the Blake legislation. Maybe she's learned about the State's intentions to also overrule the Key West referendum … regarding the size and number of cruise ships in their harbor."

Nielsen's assistant hurried in with the coffee, quickly placing the cup on the desk and retreating.

Nielsen returned to the desk, sitting with forearms on the desktop, hands clasped together, staring into the dark liquid. *Crawford's behind this shit, working in concert with Hastings.* Nielsen kept staring at the coffee as he queried Diaz. "Anything else about Marcosta … or Crawford?"

"Nothing of much merit. More drama involving Crawford's close friend Billy Watson, the red-haired commercial fisherman —he got into another altercation with the lab's cook. Snuck up and leveled a pistol barrel behind the button on the cook's baseball cap, then pulled the trigger. I guess the bullet and button flew into Passage Channel. The cook pissed himself in front of the tavern regulars."

"I'd have pissed myself too. Unbelievable. Yet another outrageous story involving a Florida redneck."

"Watson's under house arrest pending appearance before a county judge."

Nielsen recalled the interactions between the red-haired fisherman and Crawford on the evening of the '94 bridge fire. Watson had been Crawford's loudest supporter at the public meeting. "Keep 'Billy-the-Kid' on the side burner. Maybe we can learn something useful."

"That's all I have," said Diaz.

Nielsen narrowed his eyes, circling back to an earlier topic. "I want you to file a libel suit against the *Sentinel*. They attacked me in that Blake article. You also need to send a letter to Adrien Satorri, warning him not to implicate me in the bridge fire."

"I think both actions would backfire," Diaz counseled, acting braver than usual.

Nielsen stared long and hard, finally sighing and slumping back in the chair. "Out with it. Why?"

Diaz sat straighter. "For starters, we'd be handing the *Sentinel* legal team the keys to hidden doors. They would depose every politician in sight about the Blake legislation. Most are already petrified of getting in Hastings's crosshairs."

Nielsen stroked his chin. *Diaz is right. It would open a can of worms*. "I'll think about it. What's wrong with a letter to Satorri?"

"The movie won't be a documentary. Satorri is adept at basing movies on true events, while altering the storyline enough to claim a fictive product. He'll simply claim that any resemblance to you is coincidental. Legal precedent is strongly in his favor."

Nielsen shook his head. "A forceful letter can't hurt, regardless of the damn precedent. At least we would have him on notice. And who knows, it might rattle him." Nielsen paused, realizing an opportunity. "After you send the letter, figure out how to get a copy of the movie script. It'll get shared with agents and contractors as part of the production process. If it turns out Satorri is implicating me, I want you to make a preemptive legal strike. Understood?"

"Understood," acknowledged Diaz, writing on his pad.

Nielsen stood and returned to the window, watching sailboats race each other across the bay. Whitecaps were visible on the waves, the onshore wind gaining speed. "Dammit, I hate going through another round of suspicion."

"They'll make a misstep," said Diaz. "When they do, I'll hit them hard and fast."

The competing sailboats reminded Nielsen of the advice of his father, the patriarchal founder of Nielsen Enterprises and an accomplished sailor, long deceased. They would sit together in the cockpit of his father's racing sloop, sailing together in Tampa Bay, beyond the earshot of others. "Always find the soft spot, Derek. Every adversary has one. Focus the pressure there and keep at it … never let up until you've soundly defeated them."

Nielsen considered what he knew about Crawford. He turned to Diaz. "I want a daily summary from every source you have. Anything related to the Blake legislation and the Satorri movie … and also Crawford, like his red-haired buddy. All information comes to you first. Bring the relevant updates to me in person—nothing in writing or voicemail. Whatever you share remains under attorney-client privilege. Am I clear?

"Very clear."

"That's all for now." Nielsen turned back, watching the

sailboats slice the waves.

****

The Marcosta City Council assembled in Jake's office. Four of the five members sat at the corner conference table. As the current mayor, Jake served as the fifth member and council chairperson. He remained apart from the others, partially seated on the front of his desk, one foot on the floor, the other dangling. Two of the council members stared at him with obvious displeasure. He glanced at the wall clock—9:25 a.m. Barely two hours had passed since copies of the *Sentinel* had arrived on the island. *Didn't take long.*

Miriam Wilson stood nearby, vocalizing a concern about the impromptu meeting, a potential violation of Florida's Government-in-the-Sunshine Law, the requirement of public transparency. "Please stay focused on matters involving the confidentiality of third parties and related proceedings. Otherwise, you need to disband and reengage this discussion in a public session."

Ed Dickerson didn't hesitate, quickly addressing the cause of his irritation. "Dammit, Jake. Miriam briefed each of us about the Blake legislation, but we didn't hear a damn thing about the Satorri movie until the news broke this morning. Did you know about it?"

Wilson defended herself before Jake could respond. "I didn't know anything about the movie."

"I watched the entertainment channel last night," said Vickers excitedly. "Is Satorri planning on filming here?"

"Hopefully not!" exclaimed Delores Perkins. "It will attract all kinds of unwanted visitors."

Jake observed Vern Tompkins staying quiet, unusual for the outlandish former mayor. *Probably hoping to appear in the movie.*

Dickerson picked up where he left off. “I got asked a thousand questions at Spud Nut this morning. Looked like a damn fool not knowing anything.” He reiterated his question to Jake, “Did you know?”

“I did. But it was a highly confidential matter. I couldn’t risk the news leaking before the Satorri press event.”

Dickerson’s face reddened. “So, that’s your excuse? You don’t trust us with confidential information?”

Jake looked at him skeptically. “It’s difficult to keep anything confidential on this island, especially among the Spud Nut regulars.”

Perkins demanded to know, “Do they plan to film here?”

“I hope so,” answered Jake. “Keep in mind that hosting a movie production would mean substantial fees, plus revenue gains to the local economy, yielding more taxable income.”

“And a transformational change to the island’s character,” countered Perkins. “Look at what’s happening in Dyersville, Iowa.”

“Which is what?” Vickers asked.

“*Field of Dreams* was filmed there,” noted Dickerson.

“And the town is fast becoming a tourist destination for baseball fans,” said Perkins.

Tompkins broke his silence, teasing Perkins. “Hell almighty, Delores, you saying all them bridge-tending fans would come here? Lord, help us. We’d be overrun.”

She rolled her eyes, shaking her head in apparent disgust.

Vickers shrugged. “Filming the movie on the island sounds like a big positive to me.”

Wilson interrupted the discussion. “The Satorri movie is no longer a confidential matter. The remainder of this discussion needs to be aired in a public session.”

Jake stood, straightening to full height, towering above the others. “Miriam’s right. Let’s shift this discussion to a town hall meeting.” He turned toward her. “I need a moment longer. It’s about the Blake legislation."

"Okay but stick to something confidential."

Jake refocused on the council members. "You read about the Blake legislation. Nielsen thinks it's the ticket to getting a new bridge built. If that happens, his mega-resort will finally get constructed. I'll also use the public session to explain what's at stake and then seek council approval to file a federal lawsuit. We'll seek a preliminary injunction, preempting the State action, blocking application of the new law before they can get started."

"A federal lawsuit based on what?" asked Vickers, the skepticism apparent.

Jake stared at her. "You know the predicted environmental harm if Nielsen's plans move forward. Or have you forgotten?"

"What will it cost to file the lawsuit?" Dickerson asked. "Sounds expensive."

"The foremost environmental attorney in Miami is willing to take our case pro bono. The other costs are manageable."

Wilson stepped forward. "Okay. That's it. I'll provide a written briefing about the proposed lawsuit and estimated costs before the public session."

"When are you calling the meeting?" Perkins asked.

Wilson reminded Jake, "A minimum of forty-eight hours' notice."

"Let's go with this Friday evening," suggested Jake. "Seven p.m. start. Any objections?"

No one objected.

"Miriam will get the public notice issued. Encourage everyone to attend."

****

Sandra came through the doorway on the heels of the departing council members. "My phone has been ringing off the hook about the movie. Some are residents, but most are calling from elsewhere. Seems like the entire world wants to know how to get here and where to stay. What do I tell them?"

Wilson had remained behind. Jake tipped his head in her direction. "Work with Miriam on how to respond to our residents. We'll be holding a public meeting Friday evening to discuss the movie. As for the outsiders, politely inform them that most travel agencies know about Marcosta Island. The mayor's office can't serve that purpose."

Wilson looked at her watch, directing the comment to Sandra. "I need to make a quick call to the *Gazette*. I'll be back to discuss the public meeting preparations."

Sandra remained in Jake's office, looking at her notepad. "A Dr. Zhou called from the Albright Medical Center in Boston. She said you tried to reach her early this morning. I didn't want to interrupt the council meeting."

"Did she say when I should call back?"

"No. She said to have her paged."

Jake scanned the daily schedule. "Reschedule the next two calls. Apologize for the late notice … and close my door on the way out." He glanced at a sticky note while picking up the handset, dialing the Boston number.

"Dr. Zhou's office."

"Is Vivian available?"

"May I ask who's calling, please?"

"Tell her it's Jake Crawford."

"Oh, Dr. Crawford. Yes, yes, just a moment."

Muzak played through the handset. Jake considered his discussion with Caitlin and the reasons for going to Boston.

The music stopped. "Ah, Jake. So good to reconnect. What has it been? Almost three years since we last spoke?"

"Hi, Viv. Yes, far too long. How are you these days? Still terrorizing pathology residents?"

A familiar cackling echoed in the receiver. "Ha, ha, yes, the idiots. They're all so smart, yet so little do they know."

He laughed in return. “And you know so much, about so very much.”

“You are too kind.” She paused for a moment. “Jake, before we go further, there is something you should know. All of us greatly appreciate your unprecedented donation on behalf of cancer research; much has been accomplished because of it. You should visit Albright soon. We would love to showcase our latest data; exciting breakthroughs are happening with the targeting of oncogenes. Wait until you see the solid tumor results; the shrinkage rate is highly encouraging. Progression-free survival has been extended significantly.”

“I can’t wait to see the results. Actually, I’m calling about a need to visit Albright.” He could imagine her immediate concern, promptly confirmed.

“May I ask about your health? Are you doing okay?”

“It’s my spouse, Caitlin.”

“Ah, you have finally married, such wonderful news. Now, about your Caitlin.”

“Unfortunately, she has a longitudinal 2.8-centimeter mass in the base layer of her left breast. It may have infiltrated the pectoral muscle.”

“So sorry to hear of this. Has malignancy been confirmed? Are lymph nodes involved? Staged? The tumor genetically profiled?”

“A local clinic performed a needle biopsy. There are numerous groupings of atypical, precancerous cells.”

“I see. And you would like to bring her here for excision of the mass and its subsequent analysis?”

“Yes, along with several of the ancillary lymph nodes, unless recommended otherwise. Caitlin and I discussed the importance of a thorough diagnostic work-up using your latest developments in the genetic profiling of suspicious tumors. She’s agreed to the visit. I’ll cover the costs, whatever it takes.”

“Please, please, do not think of paying. All of us will work night and day to help Caitlin. Our foundation will cover whatever costs are involved. It's the least we can do in deference to your outsized generosity."

"That's very kind. Thank you."

"Now, back to Caitlin. Has she received the proper emotional counseling about the potential for a single or double mastectomy, depending on what we determine?"

"She understands why I want the excisions and a comprehensive work-up. We haven't discussed the treatment possibilities. I'm still getting her comfortable about flying for the first time and visiting New England in the jaws of winter. She's native to southwest Florida and absolutely hates cold weather."

"I share her sentiment. Okay, please keep in mind we have excellent counselors; kindly let me know if you need their help. Perhaps a pre-visit videoconference could be arranged."

"Thanks. Is Dr. Adams still doing reconstructive surgery, if it's needed? I recall he was close to retirement."

"Cornelius retired last summer, but he still consults on special cases. I'm certain he would perform the procedures for Caitlin. He's always been a fan of your biopharmaceutical research and inventions."

"That's good to know. Well, let's hope he won't be needed. Hey Viv, I've caught you at a busy time. Who should we contact to schedule the appointments?"

****

Caitlin smiled at the photograph of Tommy in his army fatigues. She returned the picture frame to its central position on her office desk, recalling rocking him to sleep while breastfeeding, humming her mother's favorite Scottish lullaby, cradling him close. *Such a sweet baby.*

Unfortunately, the tender moments with Tommy resurrected the other memories from her first marriage, the horrible ones.

She had sworn never to remarry, not wanting to take the risk. But Jake finally came home, long from sight but never from her heart. *The only man I could trust again.*

The other night stood in confirmation. Jake immediately shifted to caring attention, providing the loving embrace and holding her until after the sobbing subsided. She knew he wanted to ask more questions about the breast mass and biopsy procedure but focused instead on being kind and caring, waiting patiently until the results came back.

Even then, he was mindful of her feelings, carefully explaining what he believed should happen next and why it mattered. The irony had not escaped her. If Jake had never left the island for Boston, the world-class team at the Albright Medical Center would not be available to her at this point in the process, if ever.

The thought of flying for the first time caused her much apprehension, but Jake had flown extensively, traveling the world to medical conferences, often as an invited speaker. He also knew Boston inside and out. His presence would be the reassuring part, supporting her throughout the process.

Tommy's picture came back in focus. *Should I write and tell him what's happening?* Jake had suggested waiting for the Albright results. She wondered what Tommy was doing right now. Bosnia was six hours ahead. It would be late afternoon over there. Hopefully, he's staying out of harm's way. It may be a peacekeeping mission, but it still sounded dangerous.

A stout silhouette came through the front office doorway, backlit by the bright sunlight. "I'm checking to see how you're doing," said Hoefler. "All okay?"

Caitlin hesitated as Hoefler came alongside the desk. Jake had said the Boston trip might require more than a week of absence, depending on what was discovered. "I hope so. I need more testing. Jake wants it done at a medical center in Boston."

Concern dominated Hoefler's expression. The words that

followed attempted to sound otherwise. "I see. Well then, let's hope for the best. You take whatever time is needed. Melissa and others can cover the front office until you get back."

"Thanks for understanding." Caitlin reached to the left of the desk, no longer wincing. "I was about to bring this to you." She handed Hoefler the copy of the morning *Sentinel*. "Jake called earlier. He said you should read the front-page articles." She watched, wondering which passages caused the eyebrow twitching.

Hoefler refolded the paper and handed it back. "Did you read the articles?"

"Yes."

"What do you think?"

"I wish Nielsen would leave us alone."

"You, me, and most of the island. What about the movie announcement?"

"Goodness. It's beyond exciting."

"Did Jake mention that the production team and actors will need to stay at the lab if they decide to film here? We're the only facility that could handle all the personnel and equipment."

Caitlin hesitated, not wanting to divulge something Jake might have shared in confidence, choosing to respond with a question. "Is that okay with you?"

"I spoke with our leadership team and board of directors," Hoefler replied. "Everyone agreed with using the lab as a base for the moviemaking. It would be a big disruption, but it should be worth it in the long run, particularly given Jake's support."

Caitlin noted the last phrase and Hoefler's close observation. "That's wonderful to hear. I'm certain he will be pleased."

Hoefler smiled, glancing at her watch. "I must scoot. Oh, I almost forgot. Jake said Anna Nyholm and a few members of the movie's creative team would be visiting soon. They might stay in our visiting scientist quarters."

"That's exciting. Should I start preparing?"

"Not yet. I'll let you know. Now, you take care of yourself." Hoefler departed. The screen door banged shut.

Anna Nyholm. Caitlin recalled the photos in *People* magazine showing John Clanders standing alongside her at the Academy Awards. She wondered what a glamorous Hollywood life would be like, dating famous movie stars and attending red-carpet events. *Thrilling, perhaps, but I'd never trade my life for hers.*

****

On the opposite side of the country, Nyholm reclined by the backyard pool at her home in Brentwood Park, northwest of downtown Los Angeles. Less than a day had passed since the press event announcing her directing debut, the subsequent hours filled with a constant stream of well-wishers and interview requests.

The current call was different. She switched the portable phone to the opposite ear. "So, should I call you Mayor, or *Doctor*, Crawford?"

There was a short pause at the other end. "How about … Jake?"

"Lovely, but only if you stop calling me Ms. Nyholm. It makes me feel old."

"All right then … Anna."

"Much better. Is it already dark in Florida?"

"Nightfall is about an hour away."

"And warm?"

"Not by our standards. Low sixties. A warming trend starts this weekend. It should be in the high seventies by the time you arrive."

"Sounds delightful. We so look forward to visiting the island. I can't wait to meet in person."

"May I ask why you offered to call me Doctor Crawford?"

"I was mostly teasing, but you have quite the resumé for a small-town mayor."

Another pause ensued. "It sounds like your researchers are hard at work."

"It goes with the territory. Kurt is incredibly thorough … almost to a fault. He's the best screenwriter in Hollywood, but I'm biased."

She waited for Jake to say something. *Strange, he wasn't this reticent last time*. She continued, "Speaking of Kurt, he had a fabulous discussion with Fletcher Hastings from the *Tampa Sentinel*. Fletcher's father has been a major investor in Adrien's movies. He's making a big investment in this one."

"So I've heard."

Nyholm leaned forward to adjust the towel covering her legs. "But I digress. Shall we get back on topic? Fletcher informed Kurt about your close relationship with Lieutenant Bronson, starting as a little boy … and how you returned to the island after such a protracted absence, spending hours in Simon's bridgetender shack, on the very day of the fateful fire. You were gone for what, twenty-something years?" She waited for a response. More silence ensued.

"Are you still there?"

"I was gone twenty-three years."

"I thought our phone connection had dropped. Well, that's quite a long time. Kurt will have numerous questions about your memories of Lieutenant Bronson and the inside of the shack. Your insights and descriptions will be essential to him and our set designers, providing valuable context and content. Perhaps you can guide Kurt to others he should interview. I know he's banking on it."

"Okay."

Why the lack of enthusiasm? She felt a need to reassure him. "I'm certain Kurt will be sensitive. We are intrigued by your reason for coming home and choosing to spend your initial hours with Lieutenant Bronson. The interactions will likely offer special moments that we can portray, leading up to the fateful events that evening." She paused, recalling something. "Oh yes, and your passionate speech that night? During the town hall meeting? We read the public transcript. It's made for the movies … very much a Jimmy Stewart moment."

"It sounds like my character will be a central part of the movie," said Jake, his voice flat. "Is that what you're saying?"

"Well, yes, of course, that's indeed what I'm saying. Bronson's exploits as a fighter pilot in Burma offer great action scenes. However, the intervening time between then and the deadly bridge fire lasted almost fifty years. We'll use creative ways to span the decades: flashbacks to the war, him catching huge fish off the bridge, including you fishing with him as a young boy, plus other scenes and interactions we have yet to determine. But your visit to his shack, after such a long absence, on the very day of the fire and his horrible death? My goodness, it offers dramatic, character-driven intimacy. So, yes, absolutely, we will portray your character as a central part of the movie. You're the quintessential protagonist's helper."

Jake remained silent.

"I assume that meets with your approval?" she asked, pushing him to respond.

"I'd rather not be portrayed as a central character, but I understand why you're considering it."

Nyholm shook her head in disbelief. Millions would beg to be portrayed in a good-guy role in a Hollywood movie. She thought back on what Jones had shared, the details about Crawford's enormous donation to cancer research, the bulk of his net worth at the time. He had tried and failed to hide it from public view. No one she knew in Hollywood would donate nearly their entire net worth, and certainly not while trying to keep it anonymous. *Crawford's an intriguing man, almost too good to be true.*

"Trust me, we'll do an outstanding portrayal of your character," Nyholm said. "Let's switch to the upcoming visit. Four of us will arrive by private jet on Sunday evening, staying at the Naples Ritz; Kurt, Merv Stevansky, and Krista Sundstrom will accompany me. I've spoken of Kurt. Merv is our director of photography, and Krista is my personal assistant. Merv's arranged for a helicopter to fly us to the island the following morning. He wants to assess different filming perspectives from various heights and angles. We'll land at the marine lab, get a tour, and then start performing local interviews, first and foremost with you."

"Everyone looks forward to your visit," said Jake, sounding more upbeat. "Arrangements have been made for you to stay in the visiting scientist quarters at the marine lab, unless you prefer going back and forth to the Ritz. The lab accommodations are spartan."

"I've never been to a marine lab before. We'd love to stay there, pretending to be adventurous explorers of the aquatic world."

"Very well then, my assistant, Sandra, will work with Krista to finalize the arrangements. And regarding my interview, I can meet with you in one of the lab offices, or better yet, inside their chickee by Munson Bay; it's a lovely spot."

"What in the world is a *chickee*?"

"It's an open, thatched-roof structure the Seminole Indians have built and used for centuries. The lab had one constructed by an older Seminole that lives in the area."

"How delightful. We need to see as much of the island character as possible."

Jake chuckled. "Watch what you wish for."

"Why's that?"

"Let's just say the island has lots of character … and characters."

Nyholm smiled. *Good. He sounds less uptight*. "Well, I can't wait to see the island and meet the characters firsthand. So, as it stands, we'll be buzzing around early Monday while Merv performs the aerial assessment. The copter pilot will contact the lab about the best landing spot. Let's plan to start the tour at, say, 9 a.m. and go from there. Work for you?"

"Sounds great."

"Excellent. We're scheduled to finish the island trip by late afternoon on Wednesday. There's an outside chance we might need to stay an extra day, depending on what we learn."

"I'll be flying to Boston on Thursday. Sandra can set up additional interviews if you need to stay longer."

"Delightful. We shall see you bright and early on Monday. Ciao."

****

Jake hung up from the call with Nyholm, spinning his chair to view Passage Channel. The daily parade of shrimp boats was heading into the gulf for another night of trawling the offshore grass beds.

The tranquil scene did little to assuage his concern. He had anticipated being portrayed in the movie, but not as a main character, disliking the self-serving appearance of it, being mayor and pushing for the filming on the island.

A large crab boat entered the channel from the gulf, returning from a long day of pulling trap lines to the north. *Tequila Annie* would follow the channel eastward, around Eletz Point and into Horseshoe Basin, headed for her spot at the commercial fishing docks.

Soon to pass our cabin. The thought shifted his focus to the counseling offer by Dr. Zhou. Caitlin hadn't mentioned any concern about a potential mastectomy. Her lack of apparent worry caused his reluctance to bring up the topic; plus, the odds were still in her favor. *But what if it were me? Wouldn't I want to know it could happen while in Boston?* He imagined the equivalent for a man with testicular cancer. *Of course, I would.*

Sandra disrupted his contemplations, coming through the open doorway. “Mayor Crawford?”

Jake spun around. “I thought you had left for the day. Have you been at your desk all this time?” He wondered if she had overheard his comments during the call with Nyholm.

Her reply sounded defensive. “I’m preparing what you requested for the public meeting.”

“Ah, I forgot. Thanks for working late.”

“I have questions about the agenda. I tried Ms. Wilson, but she said you need to answer them.”

“Fire away.”

“Should the meeting start with the movie? Or the other issue about filing the lawsuit?”

First, get everyone riled about the State and Nielsen. “Lawsuit first.”

“That’s what she thought you’d say. Second question: Do I give each issue the same amount of time?”

He decided on equal weighting. “Forty-five minutes each. If everything stays on track, we’ll be done in under two hours, including the opening prayer and pledge to the flag.”

Sandra jotted a quick note and then handed over a printed page. “Here’s the final draft of the public meeting announcement from Ms. Wilson. I need to take it to the *Gazette* office before 7 p.m.”

Jake scanned it. “Looks fine.”

“Okay. That’s it. I’m heading out.” She stopped at the office doorway and turned, one hand against the door jamb. “Sounds like I have some things to do before the movie people arrive.”

She was listening, after all. Jake adopted a stern tone. “I’ll let you know when you need to do something. And I want to remind you, many aspects of the movie must remain confidential. You should only share the information on a need-to-know basis. Understood?"

"Yes, sir. Understood."

"I'll follow you out and lock up."

Sandra led by a few steps. Jake locked the front door of City Hall and headed toward the parking spaces. *What the hell?* A bright-blue Toyota Corolla was parked alongside his old Honda Accord. He caught up to Sandra. "Is that brand new?"

"Yes. Isn't it cute? I bought it over the weekend."

"I don't recall confirming your employment for a bank loan."

"My sweet uncle loaned me the money. He never married and treats me like his daughter—lives in Ohio."

"Sweet indeed," said Jake. "Well, keep it away from the salt water. Otherwise, it'll end up looking like Billy's rusted pickup."

She grimaced and jumped in the driver's seat, heading across Gulf Drive and down Heron Avenue.

Jake opened his car door. "Hail to Claude" rang out from Harry's Tavern next door. A loud "Yeah!" was followed by the clinking of bottles and glass tumblers. He wrangled into the front seat and departed for the cabin, refocusing on Caitlin. When he arrived, his decision was made, along with a critical self-reminder: *first and foremost, be a loving husband, not a cancer scientist.*

****

Caitlin pulled the blanket tighter, snuggling closer to Jake. They sat on the bench at the end of the cabin dock. Waves lapped against the dock pilings. The evening stars were vivid and distinct, a benefit of the cooler temperature and lower humidity.

More than an hour had passed since Jake discussed his call with Dr. Zhou. Caitlin had listened intently, ultimately declining the offer of emotional counseling, allowing Jake to explain why a single or double mastectomy was possible. It was something she had already surmised from reading women's magazines but wanted to hear from Jake's clinical perspective.

She could sense that Jake was apprehensive about what Dr. Zhou's team would discover, despite his attempt to appear otherwise. The complexities and failures of cancer research had to be part of it, but the memory of his mother must loom the largest.

Caitlin recalled attending his mother's funeral. Jake had stood quietly, acting stoic throughout the ceremony. He had just turned nineteen. His father had drowned years ago in Passage Channel, back when Jake was seven. No family remained after his mother's passing, never having siblings. Caitlin had watched him and wept, feeling his familial loneliness.

And now this scary mass in my breast. Will it be the same cancer that took his mother? Her fear wasn't about the potential of physical pain. She had endured plenty during her first marriage, learning to be resilient despite the hidden insults. Nor was she fearful about losing a breast and the corresponding stigma, living in a small town where everyone would know. No, the fear was of cancer itself, the insidious way in which it could violate and ravage the human body.

Unfortunately, Jake's expert knowledge had made cancer much scarier, replacing her ignorance of what it meant. She had overheard his discussions with scientists at the marine lab, about why anti-cancer treatments were often a Faustian contract, buying time and the illusion of success, only to be followed by a resurgence of the most resistant cancer cells. She shivered at the thought of harboring those awful cells in her body.

"Are you warm enough?" Jake asked, pulling her closer.

"It's chilly out here."

He pointed, his long arm backlit by the hazy band of the Milky Way. "There's the Perseus constellation. We normally don't see it this distinctly."

She followed his finger as it traced the telltale geometry. "Ah yes, I see it now. What's that moving away to the right?"

Jake's finger found the object. "Probably the Mir Space Station."

"We can see it without a telescope?"

"Its solar panels are large enough to reflect sunlight to the naked eye at night. It helps that Naples is miles away. Minimal light pollution."

She rested her head against the side of his chest. "I appreciate what you said earlier."

"I meant it. You're stuck with me no matter what. If a mastectomy were to happen, I would only love you more, if that's even possible."

His words made her smile. "Hopefully, all this won't be too hard on you. But let's think positively. As you said, the most likely outcome is a good one."

"Yes, we need to stay focused on probabilities, not possibilities."

He switched to a tangential topic, given the upcoming Boston trip. "What do you think of Sandra? You've dealt with her on matters involving the lab."

"Why do you ask? Is she becoming a problem?"

"She's starstruck, trying to overhear everything about Anna Nyholm and the movie."

Caitlin chuckled. "I'm a little starstruck too. Remember, you were out in the big world."

He remained quiet for a while. "I guess I need to cut her some slack. But she can't get ahead of me, not with Nielsen maneuvering. Word travels fast when movie stars are involved."

"I tell you what, I'll reach out to her. We can do the starstruck thing together. Maybe I can be an outlet for her excitement."

"There's a reason I brought her up. It would be easier if she could make our travel arrangements, including your appointments at Albright. She needs to keep those appointments confidential."

"That's fine."

"Okay then, I'll have her coordinate with you about the trip. She'll also be in touch regarding the arrival of Anna Nyholm and three of her team members on Monday morning."

"Ida mentioned they might be staying in the visiting scientist quarters. I'll need to get going on preparations. I hope they're ready for basic living conditions."

"We might be surprised by what they've endured at remote locations."

"True, but they've never encountered Dirty Dick's cooking."

"What's with that guy? He's certainly gotten under Billy's skin … deeply."

"Dick's been nice to me, but we only discuss kitchen supplies. I've heard he's awful toward the scientists. They often question the source of the meats he serves them. I try to avoid those dishes."

"I've witnessed Ida defend him," said Jake. "There must be something in his past that's important to her."

"I've heard rumors. Supposedly, he was a brilliant, Yale-trained psychologist, specializing in helping abused children. He had some kind of emotional breakdown and walked away from it, coming here."

"Burnout is a frequent occurrence in that profession. It would be a very tough job, day after day, especially for a highly intelligent person. For some, the mental turmoil becomes unbearable, leading to bizarre behavior. It's the opposite of saying ignorance is bliss."

Caitlin shifted, looking up at him. "That sounded a little too familiar."

Jake chuckled. "Hopefully, I wasn't acting bizarre."

"No, but I was worried when you returned. You were certainly in some kind of turmoil."

"Coming home took care of it. Thanks in great part to you."

Caitlin rose upward, moving a hand around his neck, pulling him down for a prolonged kiss. She snuggled close again.

"Billy is likely headed to jail for a couple of months," Jake informed her.

"Speaking of bizarre behavior. Shooting the cap button? I heard that Dirty Dick started the feud, calling Billy's mother a whore at the tavern."

"I doubt Dirty Dick used that expression. More likely, he called Billy a bastard, but colloquially not literally, like calling him a son of a bitch. Billy's hypersensitive about his mother's rumored infidelity. He and Harry look and act very different."

Caitlin reminded him, "I was at the school playground too. I witnessed the teasing Billy encountered."

"Do you recall me trying to stop him from fighting?"

"And he would turn on you instead. I'm amazed you stayed close friends."

"He would always apologize afterward. We spent all those years on the water together, netting mullet and fishing—the hundreds and thousands of hours it takes to form a lifelong bond, regardless of individual differences. In many ways, Billy is the brother I didn't have. I could always rely on him when something truly mattered."

"Does he have to do to jail time?"

"Dirty Dick pressed charges, plus the prosecutor wants a cooling-off period. Sticking Billy in jail keeps them apart for a while."

"Won't that backfire? Billy might get angrier."

"It's the counter risk. I've never seen him remain this sullen and vengeful. Normally, he snaps back quickly, a bundle of positive, playful energy. Hopefully, he'll break out of the funk. I expect the judge to order anger-management counseling as part of the sentence."

"Have you spoken with Billy since his arrest?"

"I've tried. He's unwilling to talk with me. From what I can tell, he's become deeply resentful of me being mayor." Jake paused before continuing. "I'll stop by his cottage first thing tomorrow and try again."

Chapter 6

The commercial fishermen were busy preparing for another day. The smell of Cuban coffee rode the morning air, combining with the odor of diesel fumes and recently harvested seafood. Billy's mullet skiff sat alongside a dock at Horseshoe Basin across the road from his ramshackle cottage. Jake noticed the cast nets were missing from the blood-specked stern.

Cursing ricocheted off the cinderblock wall of Hawkers Fish Company. Jake traced the flowing profanity, crossing the oyster shell road. *Billy's behind his cottage.*

Scavenged boat motors sat in a fatal state of dismemberment, randomly perched on wooden stands in Billy's overgrown yard. Many islanders considered the display an eyesore. Jake saw it differently, imagining all the special moments those engines had enabled.

Navigating the yard became tedious. Rusted parts lay hidden in the weedy grass, long impossible to mow. A mature Ficus tree stood amid the mechanical carnage. Its trunk wore the scars of repeated impacts, likely the target of broken parts thrown in moments of frustration. The largest limb held the dangling frame of a fully disassembled Harley-Davidson motorcycle. The recently sandblasted metal showed early signs of rust, in need of primer paint.

Jake homed in on the profanity. “Gonna kill his ass,” echoed repeatedly, a recurring refrain within the fuming tirade. He peered cautiously around the back corner of the cottage. All but one of the cast nets sat in a tangled heap. The exception was spread wide, at least ten feet in diameter, dangling from a taut rope between two palm trees like an enormous spider web. Gaping holes were evident.

Billy stood barefoot with his back to Jake, patching the widest hole, a black GPS bracelet on his left ankle. A pile of crushed beer cans surrounded a dilapidated Igloo cooler.

Jake pulled behind the corner, raising his voice loudly. “Billy, it’s Jake.”

The stream of cursing stopped. “Git lost, Guts.”

My boyhood nickname—he’ll always use it. Jake peered around the corner and stepped into the open. “The basin sounds like a one-man cussing match. What happened to the net?”

“I done told you to git … now git, dammit.” Blue eyes glared within the tangled mess of curly red hair, the look of an Irish kern preparing for attack. One cheek bulged with chewing tobacco.

“I heard you the first time,” Jake replied calmly.

“So, why’s you standin’ there?” Billy returned to mending the net.

Jake came closer. “Are all the nets like that?”

Billy pointed at the pile, spitting a large stream of tobacco juice to the side. “Shithead cook done it. Fucker’s a dead man.”

“Dirty Dick did this?”

“Damn right he done it. I ain’t shootin’ no button next time.”

Jake went to the remaining nets, pulling them apart. Each had been slashed multiple times. “When’d this happen?”

“Found ’em this morning.”

"So, overnight?"

"Yeah."

"Any other damage? To your skiff or anything else?"

"Ain't seen nothin'."

"How do you know it's Dirty Dick?"

"Nobody else stupid 'nuff."

Jake grimaced. *Billy's probably right. None of the commercial guys would do it to a fellow fisherman. It would be a cheap shot ... cowardly.* They fought face-to-face using fists, not sneaking around at night and vandalizing the other guy's livelihood. "This must be payback for the button shooting."

"Didn't hurt him much."

"You literally scared the piss out of him, in front of everyone at the tavern."

Billy screwed up his face, spitting more tobacco to the side. "Ain't no man gonna call Momma a whore."

"Did he use the word *whore*? Or did he call you a bastard?"

"Same thing, dammit."

Jake sighed. "I don't think he meant it that way. Look, you're already in serious trouble about the shooting incident. You could have accidentally killed him. I've spoken with the prosecutor. He's working a plea deal with the public defender—two months in jail and a probationary period. Enough time for you to calm down."

"Ain't gonna matter. Asshole done cut my nets."

Jake sighed again, louder for effect. *Best to get tough. Otherwise, he'll end up on death row.* "Listen to me. I came here as your friend, but I'm also the island mayor. Watch what you're saying."

"Yeah. You's the fancy-ass mayor now. Sure gettin' a big head 'bout it." More tobacco squirted, almost hitting Jake's shoe.

"Dammit, watch where you're spitting. And cut the shit about me being a fancy-ass. You know that's not true." Jake glared back at Billy, straightening to full height, becoming more imposing.

Billy shifted to a defensive stance, leaning back.

Jake bore in, anger rising. "I'm sick and tired of this tit-for-tat shit you and Dirty Dick are doing. Rest assured; I'll have the police investigate his whereabouts last night. You will not, I repeat *not*, retaliate, particularly after the stunt you pulled the other night. If you do something that stupid again, you'll be put away for years, not months. Let the police handle it here forward."

Billy turned away, heading toward the back door of his cottage.

Jake followed him. "Hey, dammit, I'm not done. What's with the howling at night?"

Billy stopped and pointed in the direction of the commercial fishing fleet. "Howling stops when they do. I ain't no damn werewolf." He spat and stomped into the house, slamming the door.

Jake waited to see if Billy would return, finally deciding to leave. The heap of nets blocked the immediate route. Jake scanned the damage. *I'll get the police to interrogate Dirty Dick.*

****

Judith Kerner rubbed her temples, closing her eyes. *Damn, hangover.* She stood next to the lab dining hall, listening to two of her colleagues.

Ned Callahan specialized in shallow-water sharks. Harold Decker studied marine invertebrates, mostly sea urchins. The men were engaged in a spirited debate about the contents of the morning omelet. Callahan was convinced that Dirty Dick had just served another unsavory meat to the scientific staff, or "the intelligentsia," as the cook derisively called them.

Callahan glanced at Kerner and winked, obviously enjoying the argument with Decker. He returned to the task. "I doubt you've eaten their gonads, Harold—you treat your urchins like spiny pets. I attempted it once, over in Japan. It's one of the stranger sushi delicacies—smells like the bottom of a drained fish aquarium."

Kerner covered her mouth and gagged, the nausea reaching upward.

Decker responded to Callahan with indignation. "The sea urchins are not my pets. Stop being paranoid about the meat. It was extra-salty sausage. Keep poking tags in sharks and leave invertebrate anatomy to an expert."

Callahan emitted an elaborate sigh. "I must say, your faith in that culinary reprobate is rather excessive. You might want to count the urchins in your holding tanks—I'd bet you're missing a dozen or so."

Decker glanced toward the wet lab building, sounding less confident. "You better be wrong. If he killed any of them, I'll …"

The kitchen door slammed shut, causing the threesome to turn in unison. A mangy Australian terrier ran toward them, his short legs pumping furiously.

The door reopened. Dirty Dick stepped outside, a lit cigarette in one hand, the other holding a can of Budweiser. A sweaty bandanna surrounded a thinning mop of gray hair. A stained T-shirt showcased a fist with raised middle finger on the front; the flap of a beer belly drooped below; thin legs protruded from a loose pair of fraying gym shorts. Cheap flip-flops completed the "I-could-give-a-shit-what-you-think" appearance.

The terrier circled erratically between the scientists' legs, yapping incessantly, then suddenly targeted Kerner's left ankle with his forepaws. She fended him off, well aware of the dog's salacious affection for available extremities.

"Attaboy, Dingo!" Dirty Dick hollered, followed immediately by cackling laughter.

Decker chased Dingo back toward the kitchen, approaching

Dirty Dick, "That had better be sausage in the omelet this morning."

Dirty Dick pointed at the T-shirt graphic and retreated inside the kitchen with Dingo, slamming the door shut. The clatter of a latch followed.

Decker yanked at the doorknob. "Come out here, you incorrigible scoundrel."

Kerner shook her head, trying to imagine a tough guy using that description in a movie.

Decker walked back. "There better be no missing urchins. I swear to God, I'll have him arrested."

"Well, here comes your opportunity," said Callahan, gesturing toward an approaching police cruiser.

The cruiser stopped short of the dining hall. Michael Pearson got out, walking over. "I'm looking for the lab cook. The fellow called Dirty Dick."

Decker pointed at the kitchen door. "He's in there. Do all of us a favor and arrest him for incorrigible behavior. His dog too."

Pearson raised an eyebrow. "Arrest him for *what*?"

Decker started to explain.

Callahan put a hand up, interrupting. "Thank you, officer. We'll let you do your job." He briefly placed a hand on Decker's back. "Come along, Harold, let's check your tanks before the officer leaves, just in case."

They headed away, Decker muttering.

"You doing okay?" Pearson asked Kerner. "You look kinda green around the gills."

"Just not feeling well."

Pearson looked toward the kitchen. "How big's that dog? Do I need to get my pepper spray?"

"It's a small terrier. He doesn't bite, but watch your ankles." She made a descriptive gesture, pumping the butt of her hand against the opposite wrist.

Pearson's eyes went wide. "I'll get the pepper spray."

****

Nielsen finished a late breakfast on the veranda of his villa on the northeast corner of Anna Maria Island, at the bottom of Tampa Bay. He downed a third cup of espresso and yawned, marveling at the libido of his overnight companion. She had been more than he could handle, leaving her unsatisfied. Waning stamina had not been a problem until recently, an unwelcome reminder that his sixtieth birthday was only a year away.

The villa property manager approached the veranda from the bay's edge, stopping short of the entrance steps.

Nielsen gestured for him to come forward, reaching for the mobile phone on the table.

"The signal amplifier should work much better," said the manager. "We installed a higher-wattage antenna."

The mobile phone indicator displayed a full five bars. Nielsen showed him the screen. "Looks good. I'll let you know if I encounter more problems."

The property manager exited the veranda through an arched doorway, passing a uniformed servant on her way out.

She delivered a message while clearing the breakfast dishes. "The helicopter will arrive in fifteen minutes, Mr. Nielsen."

He stood, brushing some crumbs from the front of his golf pants. The mobile phone rang. He noted the caller ID and answered. "Do you have the movie script yet?"

"From what we can tell, no copies have been distributed," answered Diaz. "It's most likely a work in progress."

"So, it will be a while before they start filming."

"I would guess a few months, maybe more."

"What else do you have?"

"An update about Crawford."

Nielsen looked toward the Skyway Bridge. The helicopter wasn't visible. He retook a seat. "Go on."

"His wife must have a serious medical problem. They're

heading to Boston next Thursday. She has several appointments at the Albright University Medical Center. I did some quick research. It's a top cancer-research facility and one of the primary recipients of Crawford's big donation."

Nielsen glanced down, slowly drumming his fingers.

Diaz continued, "Albright was also a clinical trial site for Crawford's blockbuster drug."

"Isn't the drug for breast cancer?"

"Originally. It's since been approved for treating other types of cancer."

"Any other updates?"

"No."

Nielsen studied the sky, spotting the helicopter exhaust plume a few miles away. He left the veranda, heading toward the helipad, continuing the discussion. "The *Sentinel* articles have caused tension in Tallahassee. I've received nervous calls."

"Some of the legislators called me as well. The governor's chief of staff says the majority remains intact. The bill will pass."

"The vote is tomorrow?"

"Yes."

"Have you learned anything further about the Marcosta lawsuit?"

"Their public council meeting is tomorrow evening. I expect them to vote in favor of filing. Crawford will also provide a public update about the Satorri movie. Rumor has it that filming will be done on the island and surrounding waters. Anna Nyholm and part of her team fly into Naples on Sunday to do some surveying, arriving on the island by helicopter on Monday morning. They'll stay at the marine lab through Wednesday, possibly longer."

Nielsen's eyes narrowed. "I want timely updates about both matters. Make sure your source calls you right after the council meeting." He paused for a moment. "In fact, plan to take her call at my villa. Bring your mobile phone. I want to listen on speaker without my presence made evident."

"I've hesitated to give her my mobile number."

"Give it to her. It bypasses your assistant. The fewer intermediaries, the better."

"Should I drive to Anna Maria?"

"No, hitch a ride with me in the helo after work. The pilots will wait until we're done and fly you back."

"Thanks. I forgot one item. I heard back from Satorri's legal counsel regarding my letter."

"And?"

"She thanked me for sharing legal concepts she learned during her first week of law school."

"Whatever. They're on notice." The helicopter flared toward the helipad. Nielsen raised his voice above the noise. "I'm headed to the golf club for a round with Senator Hoxman. Only call if it's urgent."

Chapter 7

Last-minute stragglers entered the town hall. A light breeze came through the open side windows, cooling the room. Jake noticed that most of the seats were taken. A strong showing for a Friday evening.

The five council members sat behind a draped table on a stage at the hall's east end, Jake in the middle. Miriam Wilson sat apart at the far left. Old Glory and the flag of the State of Florida flanked the stage.

Jake glanced at the clock above the doors at the back of the hall—7:07 p.m. *Almost on schedule.* He banged the gavel to quiet the room.

Pastor Burnside rose from the front row, turning to the audience, leading the assembly through the customary prayer and Pledge of Allegiance.

Jake called the meeting to order, reaching for a sheet of paper and holding it high. "Good evening. Please refer to the agenda found on your seat." He scanned the room, finding Caitlin midway on the left. She acknowledged his attention, giving a thumbs-up.

He replaced the agenda and continued, "There are two important matters. The first involves a proposed federal lawsuit against the new Blake legislation, which passed the Statehouse and was signed into law by the governor late this afternoon. I'll discuss the basis for the lawsuit in short order.

"The second matter involves the movie depicting the life and death of Simon Bronson, our beloved former bridgetender. As many of you know, Satorri Productions is considering filming here. If approved by council, the filming activities would impact our lives for two to three months, likely starting this summer.

A few shouts came from the audience, clearly supporting the island filming. Jake raised a hand. The room quieted. "Thank you. Kindly note there are two public comment sessions on the agenda, one for each matter."

Jake looked left and right. "Do other council members wish to add to my opening remarks?"

None responded.

"Okay, then. I'll start by explaining the need for a federal lawsuit."

Jake reached for a water bottle and took a sip, glancing at the clock—*almost back on schedule.* He replaced the bottle cap, leaning toward the table microphone. "How many voted in favor of the no-bridge referendum in August of '94?"

Almost everyone raised a hand.

"Excellent. You exercised our longstanding right to control access to the island. As many here know, our city founders adopted the ordinance in the late 1800s, patterned after Key West. The State has always respected our right … until now."

Someone hollered, "To hell with the State!" Others shouted similar expressions. Spontaneous discussions broke out.

Jake banged the gavel, quieting the hall. "I thought you would be outraged. So am I." He continued, describing the impending State action. "And to no one's surprise, Derek Nielsen has been funneling campaign donations to many legislators, effectively buying their votes."

The hall erupted. Much of the shouting involved harsh cussing from the back right, where the commercial fishermen congregated.

Jake stood to his full height and banged the gavel repeatedly, gesturing up and down with his free hand for quiet. The hall finally settled. "Everyone gets it," he said, retaking his seat. "The new law would pave the way for Nielsen to build the mega-resort."

Someone hollered midway back, "What happened to his land sale?"

Jake noticed a vigorous motion to his right, down at the end of the council table. It was Miriam Wilson, waving her hand back and forth while shaking her head, trying to stop where he was headed. *To hell with confidentiality. Let Nielsen sue. Hastings would skewer him in the press.* Jake looked back at the audience. "Nielsen recently terminated the negotiation for his island land and turned the table, offering to buy the marine lab property. He wants to create a fancy yacht club and marina for his resort visitors and residents. As you can see, he expected the Blake legislation to pass."

Jake explained how the tidal flow of South Munson Bay communicated directly with the waters of the Ten Thousand Islands National Wildlife Refuge, and how it would enable the city to file a federal lawsuit. "We hope to get a timely preliminary injunction based on the predicted harm to the refuge, preventing the State from acting on the new bridge and enabling development of the mega-resort. The evidence of Nielsen's vote-buying should help our cause."

He gave the audience a few moments to consider what he had presented. Numerous discussions broke out. He spoke above the noise. "Okay, it's time for the first round of public comments, to be followed by the council discussion and vote. Please limit your remarks to the lawsuit."

****

Officer Pearson pedaled his patrol bike along the perimeter of Horseshoe Basin. Most of the shrimp boats had remained at the docks for the night, their captains and crews in attendance at the town hall meeting. Hawker's Fish Company passed to the right. A refrigerated seafood truck sat parked at the loading dock, its cooling unit running loudly.

Pearson stopped alongside a rusted pickup, straddling the bike. Light flickered through a translucent curtain covering the front picture window of Billy's cottage. *Good, he's watching TV, but best to check, just in case.* Pearson recalled the interrogation at the marine lab dining hall early that morning. Dirty Dick had denied cutting Billy's nets. *Seemed uptight, though. Acting kinda guilty.*

He dismounted and navigated to the side of the cottage, tripping several times on discarded motor parts. *Yard's a damn minefield.* The kitchen window stood higher than the others. He crouched beneath the window, slowly raising his head to view the interior. A mess of curly hair rested above the back of an easy chair. Pearson watched for a while, observing no movement. *Must be asleep.*

Pearson noticed a small gap between the front curtains. He navigated the outside wall, going to the front, peering cautiously through the gap. *What the hell?* Light from the TV exposed a red-headed dummy composed of stuffed pants and shirt. A short wooden pole extended out of the shirt's neck. Impaled on the upper end was a crab float wearing a curly red wig. The GPS ankle bracelet lay on the floor nearby, next to a can of marine grease and an oily rag. *Why, that wily son of a bitch—the bracelet musta been too loose.*

Pearson navigated to the patrol bike, grabbing a large flashlight and turning it on. He headed hurriedly up the stone walk and banged on the front door, stepping aside and unsnapping his holster. “Billy! Officer Pearson. Open the damn door.”

He listened intently. Only the sound of the TV was evident. He repeated the command and waited. Nothing. He headed to the back of the house, navigating the yard debris with the benefit of the flashlight beam. The damaged cast nets were arrayed in a heap near a beat-up cooler. Pearson went to the back door, pounding and hollering again. Again, no answer.

He went to the front and crossed the road. Billy’s skiff was missing from the dock. *Shit! He musta gone to the lab.* Pearson keyed his radio. “Dispatch. Pearson.”

“Go ahead.”

“Billy Watson ain’t at his house. Skiff’s missing. Get Glenn down to the lab. Pronto. Billy might be after the cook. Have Glenn report what he finds.”

“Roger that. Sending Glenn.”

The noise from the refrigeration truck prevented hearing a boat motor running in the bay. Pearson hustled over and unplugged the 240-volt cord, returning to the dock and listening intently. *I’ll be damned.* An outboard engine could be heard in the distance, the noise getting louder. He looked skyward, somewhat relieved to see a three-quarter moon.

The motor quieted, slowing to idle speed. He could make out the shape of Billy’s skiff in the moonlight, slowly rounding the south corner of the basin. Pearson remained alongside the bike.

Billy secured the skiff and jumped to the dock, heading toward the cottage.

Go now. Pearson went toward him, placing a hand on the pistol butt, ready to draw if needed.

The two men came together in the middle of the road.

“Where you been?” Pearson demanded.

Billy stood speechless.

“Don’t make me ask again.”

“I ain’t done nothin’.”

"Oh yeah, you did—violated house arrest. You been down at the lab? Looking for Dirty Dick?"

"Naw."

"You sure?" Pearson could smell alcohol.

"Damn sure. I ain't been down there."

"You better be telling the truth."

Billy stayed quiet.

"You packing a pistol?" Pearson asked, retrieving handcuffs with his left hand.

"Y'all done took it."

"Turn around. Hands behind your back."

"What the hell?" Billy stood still, arms by his sides, fists clenched.

"You want to add resisting arrest?"

"Shit. Just out takin' a damn ride. Needing to get some salt air."

Pearson went around, pulling Billy's arms back and locking the cuffs. "Where's your truck keys? I'm driving … bike's going in the back."

"Where the hell you takin' me?"

"Where the hell do you think? You'll be in the slammer the rest of the night. Maybe more. We'll see what the chief says."

"Hell, it's a fuckin' zoo in there. Like a damn monkey on display. Noisy as hell. Food tastes like shit."

"You shoulda thought of that before heading out. Now, where's the truck keys?"

"In the damn ignition."

Pearson lifted his radio. "Dispatch. Pearson."

"Go ahead, Michael."

"Got Billy. Bringing him in. Glenn needs to find the cook and see if he's okay. Have him check around. See if anyone saw Billy down at the lab."

****

About twenty public meeting attendees had vented at the standup microphone, their anger aimed at Nielsen and the State. Most of the council paid heed. Only Glenda Vickers voted against filing the lawsuit.

Jake glanced at the clock. *Fifteen minutes behind schedule.* The sound of Billy's pickup reverberated through the open windows facing Gulf Drive. The unmuffled engine revved once, coming to a fitful stop. A truck door screeched open and slammed, followed by another. People on that side of the hall craned to look out the windows.

Why's Billy out of the house? And who the hell's with him? Jake shook the thoughts. "We're behind schedule, folks. But, hey, I'm sure this is more fun than saluting ole Claude at the tavern."

Laughter broke out, along with a few hoots from the commercial fishermen.

"Let's proceed to the second matter. The movie's director, Anna Nyholm, and several of her creative team will be visiting us early next week. They want to survey potential filming locations and perform some local interviews. Assuming they decide to film here, I will seek council approval of a negotiated contract with Satorri Productions. Among other benefits, we should realize sizable fees to the city, plus added income for local businesses."

Jake scanned the audience. There were lots of smiles and excited expressions, including Caitlin's. *Good to see her smiling.*

He continued, "But let's also keep in mind the trade-offs. The filming will disrupt our daily lives. We will be set upon by paparazzi and movie groupies. News crews will show up seeking coverage opportunities. The lack of a bridge should minimize the worst of it, but all of us will be impacted, often trying our patience and straining city resources."

Thoughtful looks and grimaces replaced the smiles.

"I hope that frames the big picture, so to speak. The goal for tonight is to hear your questions and concerns about the proposed filming." He paused, deciding to make a switch. "Delores? Anything to add before the public comments?"

Perkins pulled her microphone closer. "Are you changing the order?"

"I am."

She turned toward the audience. "Well then, I am deeply concerned that using our island as the movie setting will bring unwanted consequences. For example, Dyersville was a quiet farm town in rural Iowa. Then came the *Field of Dreams* movie. The town is fast becoming a shrine for baseball lovers from all around the world, changing the character of …"

Vern Tompkins interrupted her, not teasing this time. "I hear you, Delores. But dang, the potential movie fees could be a mighty big help."

Vickers piled on, "Vern's right. We'd no longer need to advertise to attract tourists. The movie will have done the job. It'll boost our economy and leave extra budget money for other purposes."

"Ed?" Jake asked, intervening before Perkins could respond.

Dickerson spoke in a slow drawl. "I do worry about that new Blake law. What happens if we allow the movie, and the State constructs a new bridge? Hell, we'll be overrun by snowbirds *and* movie tourists. A Satorri movie plus Nielsen's big resort? You can kiss old Florida goodbye … for good."

Perkins took another angle, catching Jake off guard. "How would Simon have felt about his life being dramatized in a movie? He valued his privacy above all else."

A rationalization came quickly to Jake. *Surely, Simon would favor the movie if it kept Nielsen at bay.* He believed that Simon had committed arson-suicide to help protect the island, stranding the island without a bridge and casting suspicion on Nielsen—it would explain the timing of the fires and explosion that fateful evening.

But the rationalization needed to stay private. Jake shifted his thinking, seeing a different counter to Perkins's challenge, something he could state publicly. He glanced at the wall clock. "Thanks for the council comments. Delores just raised the question about what Simon would want. Keep in mind that Satorri can simply make the movie elsewhere. Nothing stops him from portraying Simon's life and death using a different island setting.

"And Ed, I appreciate your concern about the combination of snowbirds and movie tourists, but it's unwarranted. The filming won't happen if the State gets started on the new bridge—the construction activity would be too unsightly and disruptive. In fact, they'll likely demolish the pier right from the start, clearing the way for building the connection to Gulf Drive."

Ray Garrett jumped up. He bellowed loudly, shaking a big fist, "Over my dead body!" Other pier fishermen came to their feet, yelling in support.

Jake stood and quieted the room, scanning the hall for effect. "Okay, let's hear the public comments."

About a dozen people jumped up, heading toward the microphone, eager to speak. Others quickly followed, about thirty in total.

Far too many; we'll be here all night. Jake realized how to cull the numbers while also making an impression. He raised a hand while speaking. "Hold up a second. Please refrain from using the public session to express your support for the movie. The council only needs to hear your questions and concerns."

All but four people returned to their seats. *Good, a time-saving way to demonstrate the overwhelming support.* Of the remaining four, the last in line was positioned at Jake's request. He acknowledged the first. "What's on your mind Ms. Douglas?"

She stepped to the microphone. “Where’s all them movie people gonna stay? And get their meals? We’ve only got lodging and dining for the current level of tourists, including them eco-folks from the lab.”

Jake nodded. “Great question. As currently envisioned, the movie personnel would be housed and fed at the marine lab. It would also function as their base of operations. The scientific research will continue while the movie is filmed, but the lab’s ecotourism programs would be suspended.”

Douglas remained at the microphone. “But plenty of them eco-folks shop and eat downtown. Are you saying we’d be losing that money?”

“Not to worry,” Jake replied. “The movie personnel would number about the same. They’ll also want relief from the lab. I expect them to frequent the downtown establishments, just like the ecotourists.”

Chatter broke out across the hall. *Probably excited about seeing movie stars.* Douglas seemed satisfied, stepping away.

Jake leveled a stern look at the second speaker. It was one of the younger commercial fishermen. Jake had noticed him looking back and grinning several times. His buddies were giving him a thumbs-up.

Jake flattened his voice. “Next.”

The young man stepped forward. He wore a backward baseball cap and a T-shirt that proclaimed: “I’ve Got Crabs.” He glanced at his buddies a final time before speaking. “Can us fishing dudes get a picture with that Nyholm chick? She’s hot as hell. Damn, *hot*!” The back right erupted in hoots and catcalls. He hurried away, mission accomplished. A collective groan trailed him to the back of the room. The buddies whacked him on the back.

The gavel came down hard. “Okay. Enough. You had your fun.”

Next in line was the certified public accountant on the island.

Jake waved him forward. “Evening, Connor. What’s up?”

“Good evening, Mayor. Some of us are concerned about the added expenses to the city budget—things like extra police security and liability insurance. Will the movie fees and increased tax revenues be enough to offset those added expenses and still enhance the bottom line … significantly?”

“Great question. Based on what I’ve learned from Mayor Sawyer of Key West, the realized income should be much more than the added expenses. She was the Monroe County film commissioner before entering local politics. How many remember the movie *True Lies*?”

Many raised their hands. Someone yelled, “*Owlll* be back,” mimicking the famous actor’s accent.

“Right actor, different movie. Sorry, Connor, please continue.”

“Thanks. How much more?”

“Close to a million dollars, but we won’t know the full impact until they’re done filming. It could be more.”

Connor nodded and stepped away.

Jake signaled for the final speaker to come forward. Everyone knew who she was, at least anyone who had spent time eating donuts at Spud Nut, which was nearly everyone. The longtime counter attendant was an older, straight-talking woman who didn’t take shit from anybody. She detested Nielsen.

“Hello, Ms. Appleton. What brings you to the microphone?”

“Is the movie gonna show who killed Simon?”

Miriam Wilson started waving again.

Jake ignored her. “Ms. Appleton, I don’t know how they will characterize the suspicious events of that evening. We’ll have to wait and see.”

“Far as I’m concerned, that fancy-pants Nielsen fella did it. He oughta be double fried in Old Sparky.” She spun around and headed toward the back rows.

Some in the audience clapped. A commercial fisherman

hollered, "Yeah, fry his rich ass."

Jake banged the gavel, intervening before the anti-Nielsen sentiment got out of hand, finally making the public statement about Nielsen's innocence, albeit in a backhanded manner. "Remember, Derek Nielsen was never charged with wrongdoing —he is innocent unless proven otherwise." He glanced again at the clock. "Thanks for your attention and comments. Many would like to get home or salute ole Claude at the tavern."

"Hell yeah," sounded from the back right.

"There's no need for a council vote until a contract is negotiated with Satorri Productions. Do any council members wish to add a final comment?" Jake checked left and right. No one spoke up. "Okay then, there being no further business, this meeting is adjourned." The gavel banged for the last time.

****

Jake stood, preparing to leave the stage and join Caitlin. Officer Pearson approached from the side stairs, Sandra directly behind him. Glenda Vickers hovered close by, apparently waiting to discuss something.

Jake focused on Pearson first, remembering the sound of the truck. "What's going on with Billy?"

Pearson cocked his head in the direction of the station. "Violated house arrest. He's in the slammer."

"Dammit. What happened?"

"He stuck a red wig on a dummy in front of the TV, then took his skiff into the bay. Denies going down to the lab. We checked and the cook's okay. Nobody at the lab seen Billy around."

"He put a red wig on a dummy?" Jake shook his head in disbelief.

"Yeah. Stuffed the pants and shirt with towels. Hell, he used a crab float for the head. It's a clown wig I'm guessing."

"What about the ankle bracelet? Can't you track where he went?"

"It was lying on the floor next to the dummy. Worked the damn thing off using engine grease—must not have been tight enough."

Good grief, Billy. Jake noticed Sandra writing in her spiral-bound notepad on the council table. "What are you doing?"

She seemed startled by the challenge. "Oh … just finishing the public meeting notes. I need to get the equipment back in storage." She closed the notebook and grabbed a microphone off the table.

Jake turned back to Pearson. "How's Billy? Quiet or hollering?"

"Not cussing like he was. Just sitting there, arms folded. Chief's keeping him in the slammer until the judge hears what he done."

"Probably best," Jake observed. He turned to speak with Vickers. She and Sandra were departing the stage together, microphones in hand, heading toward the exit door.

****

Nielsen paced slowly in the elegant study at his Anna Maria villa, casually smoking a contraband Cuban cigar, a bourbon in the other hand. A woman's voice came through the mobile phone speaker on the coffee table.

Diaz sat at the edge of a companion couch. He interrupted her depiction of the public meeting. "Sorry, but could you restate your last comment? What the elderly waitress said about Mr. Nielsen?"

"Certainly. That he should be double fried in Old Sparky."

Diaz glanced up, a look of disbelief on his face. He followed with another question. "And did Mayor Crawford agree with the waitress?"

"No. He reminded the town folk that Mr. Nielsen is innocent unless proven guilty."

Nice move, Crawford. Nielsen signaled to move on, spinning the cigar hand.

"Anything else of interest?" asked Diaz.

"Billy Watson violated house arrest. He stuck a red wig on a dummy, then snuck out."

"Where? To do what?" Diaz queried.

"The police thought he had taken his skiff to the marine lab … to get back at the lab cook for cutting his nets. No one saw him at the lab. The cook is fine."

Nielsen signaled to stop the discussion, swinging his cigar hand in a level plane.

"Okay, thanks for that. I know it's late. Use this phone number from now on. Remember, don't leave a voicemail. Call back later if I don't answer."

"Okay."

Diaz pressed the cancel button, wasting no time reacting. "Crawford orchestrated the interaction with the elderly waitress. It sounds contrived, almost scripted."

"I found it entertaining," Nielsen said, downing the rest of the bourbon. He raised the empty tumbler in a mock salute, facing south. *Well done, Crawford, a clever adaptation of the good cop/bad cop routine.*

"But he slandered you in a public forum, purposely resurrecting suspicions of your involvement. That's defamation with malicious intent, a serious misstep, more than enough grounds for a lawsuit."

"That's not how I heard it," Nielsen countered. "It was the old woman who slandered me. Crawford used the opportunity to emphasize my presumed innocence. We don't gain anything by going after her. Hastings would have a field day."

"Unless I depose her, and she acknowledges colluding with Crawford."

Nielsen shook his head. “He’ll just claim she misunderstood their conversation and that he publicly corrected her.”

“So, do nothing?”

“That’s right. Nada.” Nielsen took a puff of the cigar. “Stay focused on getting a copy of the movie script. Satorri has a global audience. No one is paying attention to a shitty little public meeting.”

“What about Crawford’s violation of the confidentiality agreement? Regarding the land negotiation?”

Nielsen walked over and punched a button on the wall intercom.

A deep voice responded, “Sir?”

“Tell the pilots to spool up.”

“Yes, sir.”

Nielsen returned to Diaz. “Hold the violation on the back burner. We’ll see what happens in the weeks ahead. Enjoy the view flying back.”

Diaz retrieved the mobile phone and his notepad, exiting the study.

Nielsen went to the edge of the master suite balcony, scanning the bright glow of lights around Tampa Bay. The helicopter soon lifted away, heading toward the Skyway Bridge. He reflected on what they had just heard about the federal lawsuit, reminding himself to meet with Senator Hoxman at the earliest opportunity.

Chapter 8

Dawn's light hinted behind the bedroom curtains. Caitlin lay curled under a warm blanket, unwilling to expose herself to the morning coolness.

The clang of a cast iron skillet sounded through the wall. The silverware drawer opened and closed, followed by the refrigerator door. The sound of sizzling bacon would be next. Jake's Sunday morning ritual was underway, the weekly respite from mayoral duties.

The thought of a leisurely morning together caused her to smile. A satisfying soreness provided another reason.

Jake had been overly cautious during their initial lovemaking. The second time was different but of her choosing. He had fallen asleep after the first. She had remained awake, eventually arousing him in a way that wasn't typical, removing his cautiousness. The primal passion she unleashed brought them both to an exhilarating climax.

She had wanted him to lose control, accepting the consequences of his exceptional height. The initial lovemaking had left her feeling incomplete, unsatisfied. After a while, she realized why. The insight drove what followed, the desire to make him forget the worrisome breast mass, employing tactics she had been taught to hate in her first marriage.

Plates rattled in the cupboard. Jake whistled an upbeat tune, bringing her another smile. *Okay, time to get up*. She braced herself. The covers flew aside, the coolness yielding immediate goosebumps. She snatched the blanket from the bed, wrapping it tightly.

Jake embraced her with one arm as she entered the kitchen; the other held the spatula wide. He stared into her eyes. “You’re awfully beautiful.”

“Awfully?” She made a slight pout, unwinding from his grasp and sitting at the kitchen table, pulling the blanket tighter.

“Well, then, would you prefer exceedingly, exceptionally, or exquisitely?”

“Hmmm … let me think. All the above?”

Sizzling and popping returned him to the task at hand. He spoke over a shoulder while flipping the bacon strips. “You were rather energetic last night.”

“Too much for you?” She assumed a teasing expression, chin raised, head tilted slightly.

“Not in the least. How about you?”

She hesitated, glancing downward, thinking of what had transpired the first time.

He turned. “Everything okay?”

She looked up, slightly startled. He was staring at her with an expression of concern.

“Oh, of course … it was wonderful.”

“Sorry if I caused any discomfort.”

“That’s okay. I asked for it.”

“I want to be sensitive.”

“Why? Because of the mass in my breast?”

“Partly that, but also what happened during your first marriage.”

"What exactly do you mean? That's not something we've discussed, at least not in detail."

Jake turned off the stove, shifting the skillet to a different burner. He sat at the table. "I've pieced most of it together. There aren't many secrets on the island."

She looked away, wondering if the sealed evidence had been shared. Keeping it confidential was the reason Mark Jenkins left the island, the trade-off for avoiding prosecution.

Jake reached across the table, taking her hand. His eyes were filled with kindness. "I never want to cross a line that resurrects that difficult past. You need to guide me on the limits."

"Jake, you're not Mark. You're kind and respectful. He belittled and dominated me, never stopping, even when I screamed. He would force me to …" She stopped, shaking her head. "I stayed with him much longer than I should have. I didn't want Tommy to lose his father."

Jake squeezed her hand. "No need to explain further. I understand."

She wished for the millionth time he had never left for Boston.

Jake returned to the stove, shifting to levity. "Should I cook the omelet now or wait until you are dressed in a snowsuit?"

"You know how much I hate cool weather."

"The understatement of the year. So, what's it to be?"

"Go ahead. I can eat with this blanket around me."

"Unless you want me to remove it and go for round three. The omelets can wait."

"I need more time to recover."

"As you wish, my love." Cracked eggs soon filled a bowl.

The discussion about Mark Jenkins reminded Caitlin about his younger brother. "Do you remember Eric Jenkins? He was in the grade above ours."

"I recall Billy and Eric fighting when we were kids, at least until Mark flattened Billy one day."

"Eric remained here after Mark moved to Apalachicola, calling me awful names at every opportunity. Billy became protective, defending my honor."

"So, they fought again?"

"Multiple times, until Billy broke Eric's jaw. Eric moved to Copeland and started hunting gators."

"Good riddance. Hey, I thought I'd stop by the police station after lunch … if that's okay. I visited Billy on Friday, but he refused to talk. Maybe he'll be more agreeable on a Sunday. The station should be much quieter."

****

Jake pulled into the tavern parking lot, turning off the engine. He sat in the car for a while, reflecting on the remainder of the morning with Caitlin.

She had lain on the dock bench, reading a novel, the cause of frequent laughter, a refreshing sound. He had fished nearby, casting up current in the outgoing tide, retrieving a pinkish-gold jig along the sandy bottom of the channel, flicking his wrist. The shrimp-like action did its job. A redfish lay on the dock, about four pounds in weight, perfect eating size. The two filets were grilled for lunch, served blackened atop dirty rice. The tasty fare prompted a thought about his impending visit to the police station: a tavern box lunch might ease the tension with Billy.

Jake stepped from the car. The entryway to the fishing pier stood to the right of the tavern parking lot, extending into Passage Channel. A handful of locals fished at the far end, near the memorial showcase. A group of kids ran up and down the wood planks, playing a game of tag. Seagulls and pelicans worked the waters on the bay side, attacking baitfish that schooled in the early afternoon shadows of the pier.

Patrons filled half the tavern dining area, primarily churchgoers who had attended the late services. He acknowledged several waves. A few hardcore drinkers camped at the bar. A colorful balsa wood stone crab dominated the back wall, overtop the cash register. *Ole Claude himself, the longstanding recipient of inebriated idolatry.*

The hostess spotted him, coming over. “Howdy there, Mayor. Where’d you like to chow down?”

“Hey, Cindy Lou. I need a take-out order. A fried shrimp box.”

“Six or twelve shrimp?” She pronounced it “shrump.”

“Eighteen. It’s for Billy.”

She acknowledged with a knowing look. Billy consumed prodigious quantities of fried seafood at the tavern, courtesy of his older brother.

“Harry was at the station earlier,” she noted.

“Did he already take lunch to Billy?”

“Not that I seen. He weren’t there but a bit. Been a big grump ever since.”

“How long will the order take?”

“Fifteen or twenty.”

“Okay. Back soon.” Jake headed out the tavern door, striding across the parking lot and onto the pier. Rippling wavelets ran toward the mainland, driven northward by a southerly breeze. He glanced at the sky. Small cumulus clouds had replaced the wispy cirrus ones, signs of the warming trend taking hold.

Children ran past him, laughing and teasing each other, enjoying the escape from church-minded discipline. One boy stopped and made a solemn face, saluting as Jake walked past, then burst out giggling. The others pushed at him, laughing and scampering toward the tavern.

Jake reached the far end, stopping in front of the memorial showcase. Copies of old photos were arrayed behind a four-by-eight-foot plexiglass panel, affixed to a cork board. Most of the images depicted the chronology of the wooden bridge. One showed it under construction back in the 1920s. Another captured its demise, the terrible fire and explosion that killed Simon. The nighttime photo showed fiery debris on the dark surface of the channel, along with the burning tops of wood pilings, lit like candles stuck in licorice icing. A caption marked the fateful day: July 20, 1994. *It still seems like yesterday*. The horrible event remained scorched in Jake's memory, the subject of lingering remorse and periodic nightmares.

Another section included photos of Simon, mostly hoisting large fish that he had caught from the bridge, historical advertising for fishing the pier. A favorite photo showed a young boy holding a small fishing rod and speckled trout. Simon stood alongside, his hand on Jake's shoulder. *All those times together, fishing the bridge. The many lessons imparted. Simon was more of a surrogate father than I realized.*

An official declaration was prominently displayed at the center of the board. Jake leaned closer, rereading the inscription:

> Her Majesty's Government hereby awards Britain's Distinguished Flying Cross to Lieutenant Simon J. Bronson, United States 10th Air Force, in posthumous recognition of his heroic actions in Burma on July 13, 1944. His unselfish courage saved three hundred and thirteen of Britain's finest. Her Majesty and all the subjects of her realm remain deeply indebted to Lieutenant Bronson for perpetuity.

Jake turned and looked at the emptiness beyond the pier, toward the middle of the channel where Simon had lived for decades. It was easier to feel his presence out here, on what remained of the bridge he loved.

"Well, if it ain't Mayor Jake." A burly man with a bushy gray beard leaned against the railing to the left, fishing pole in hand.

Jake walked over, extending a handshake, preparing to wince. "How's it going, Mr. Garrett? Catching anything of interest?"

The bear paw engulfed Jake's outstretched hand, inflicting the customary pain. Garrett stuck the butt of the fishing rod in a worn knothole. An ice cooler was strapped to a rusty roll cart nearby. He removed the top.

Jake peered inside. Pompano were stacked halfway up, each fish about fifteen inches long. "Now that's a tasty catch."

"Running strong as hell. Cooler water has 'em biting."

A slapping commotion followed the landing of a fish nearby. The two men watched as a teenage girl took a pompano off the hook and placed it in a bulging fish bag. She quickly re-baited, casting into the channel.

"Is that Harry's youngest daughter?" Jake asked, admiring the passionate energy. It reminded him of catching pompano as a boy on the bridge, one right after another.

"Yessiree. Damn firecracker. Out-fishes the rest of us most weekends." Garrett paused, shifting the discussion. "Sorry 'bout Nielsen and our land. Sis and me been feeling mighty bad, wishing we never sold."

"All of us have some remorse about the past."

"Yeah. Hey, Sis been talking to the Kerner woman 'bout giving some money to the lab. They been trying to raise two million for fixing up boats and buildings."

Jake recalled the millions the Garretts had received from Nielsen. *This should be easy for them.* "How much are you thinking?"

"Half each."

"So, one million total?"

"Yep."

"Fabulous. Let me know when the donation happens. I'll make sure the *Gazette* writes an article."

"There ain't no need to shout 'bout it. People'll find out when they do. We ain't ones to show off our money."

Old Florida through and through. "Okay. Forget about the *Gazette*. Thanks for doing it."

"Just make sure them state bastards don't build that new bridge. Maybe our old land can be ..." Garrett lunged toward the fishing rod. It was bent well over, straining against the heavy pull on the line. He removed the rod from the knothole and yanked several times, firmly setting the hook. The reel started screaming as the line stripped away rapidly, pulling against the drag.

Too large to be a pompano. Jake patted Garrett on the back. "I need to grab a takeout. Good luck with that big one."

Garrett grinned over his shoulder, holding a firm grip on the bent rod. The taut line continued departing the reel, beelining for the open gulf.

Jake chuckled. *A shark probably ate a hooked pompano and got hooked itself. Or maybe it's a beachcomber kingfish. Big, whatever it is.*

****

The police station was on the east side of City Hall, adjacent to the tavern. Jake opened the front door and entered the cramped operations room.

The weekend duty officer looked up from a nearby desk. "Hey there, Mayor. What brings you in on a Sunday?"

"Good to see you, Homer. This fried shrimp box is for Billy. I'd like to chat with him."

The holding cell was at the back left. Billy reclined on its well-worn bench, facing away, the curly red hair protruding through spaces between the bars. He leaned forward, glancing over his shoulder.

"Sure smells good," said Homer. He looked at his watch.

"Three hours, I'll be chewing some shrump myself."

"Anything up this shift?"

"Naw. Real quiet … being Sunday and all."

"Good. Hey, can you open the cell?" Jake went to the small interrogation room, placing the lunchbox on the table. He came out, noticing Homer grabbing handcuffs from his utility belt.

"No need for cuffs," Jake said.

"It ain't procedure."

"Billy won't cause trouble."

Homer relented but with a warning, facing toward Billy. "I'll be watching from my desk." He unlocked the cell door, swinging it open.

Billy glanced up. The sullenness continued. "Ain't nothin' to chat about."

Jake shook his head in frustration, lips in a tight line.

Billy looked away.

"I brought you lunch from the tavern. Thought you might have a hankering for a jumbo shrimp platter."

"Ain't hungry."

"You and I know that's bullshit. You're always hungry. What are they feeding you in here? Wimpy hot dogs and baked beans? Come on. We need to talk. I put the shrimp in the side room, eighteen tasty ones."

Billy didn't budge.

Jake stared at Billy for a good thirty seconds, finally giving up. "Okay, the hell with it. You can eat it later. I spoke with Harry before leaving the tavern. He says you've agreed to the plea deal."

"Ain't got no choice. Lawyer dude's sayin' a year I don't."

"You'll be in the county jail for two months, followed by a few months of probation. Both timeframes will involve anger counseling."

Billy shook his head, rolling his eyes in disgust.

"Listen, you might want to get a shave and haircut. The

judge still has to agree with the plea deal. She's known for being tough. You should look clean-cut. I can arrange for Roy to come here and do it."

Billy kept his arms crossed, not responding.

Jake sighed. "Sorry it's come to this. Hopefully, you'll stop the feuding with Dirty Dick. You've taken it far enough, okay?" Jake waited again, not getting a response. "Just so you know, the police have put Dirty Dick on formal notice. They've instructed him to stay clear of you and your stuff. They're still investigating if he cut your nets. You'll need to press charges if he did. Far better to let a court handle his punishment than get yourself in bigger trouble."

"The bastard cut 'em. Still a dead man."

How to get past this? Jake shifted tactics. "I'll get your cast nets fixed while you're serving time. The best thing you can do is net mullet when you're released on probation."

"I ain't needin' your help."

No sense arguing, just get the nets repaired. "Okay, whatever. Harry said he'll keep an eye on your place. The police will be keeping your guns in storage. You can't have those during probation."

"Any more bullshit? Or's that it?"

"Harry and I will be coming up to visit you at the county jail. Let us know if you need anything … at least anything allowed. We still care about your ass—something to think about while you're sitting on it for two months."

Billy kept his eyes glued to the floor. His shoulders slumped a bit.

Jake left the cell and pointed toward the interrogation room, speaking to Homer. "Could you put that lunchbox in the cell before you lock it? Thanks."

"Roger that." Homer got up from the desk, grabbing the key to the holding cell.

Jake went outside, turning toward the main entrance of City

Hall. His mind shifted to the movie team's visit the following morning.

****

Satorri's private jet departed Santa Barbara later that afternoon, ascending above the Santa Ynez Mountains. The pilots estimated the arrival into Naples, Florida, at 8:15 p.m., Eastern time.

Nyholm sat on the right of the cabin, facing forward. Jones typed on a laptop in front of her, facing to the rear. Stevansky flanked Jones on the opposite side, marking up satellite images of Marcosta Island with a grease pencil. Krista reclined to Nyholm's left, yawning widely.

Nyholm turned to her cabin window, feeling the tug of gravity against her lower back. Her thoughts were focused on the two alternatives that Jones had shared prior to takeoff: Should the movie begin with Bronson as a young man preparing for war or flip the chronology and start with his memorial service?

Her creative instincts said to start with the memorial, but with a twist at the beginning of the scene, a brief flashback to the heroic combat mission. She envisioned a view from Bronson's cockpit as his fighter plane dove into the ravine toward the Burmese bridge, depicting the dire situation below—the British soldiers pinned alongside a river, a constant hail of bullets preventing them from engaging the much larger Japanese force streaming down the opposite bank, its lead element advancing across the wooden bridge. Dark puffs from exploding antiaircraft fire would appear around the cockpit, along with fiery streaks and smoke trails. The sound of shrapnel piercing the fuselage would mix with the shrieking of the wings. The cockpit view would shift to a close-up of Bronson's raised thumb, positioned above the bomb-release button at the top of the flight control stick, poised to deliver the moment of tremendous carnage.

The scene would fade as Bronson's thumb depressed the

button, transitioning to the elderly British sergeant standing at the memorial podium on a sunny day, the tranquil waters of Passage Channel behind him. The incongruous transition would have an immediate impact on the audience, setting the stage for the rest of the story, the movie ending with the sergeant finishing his impromptu eulogy, turning to salute the emptiness where Bronson and the Florida bridge had once resided.

Fletcher Hastings had attended the memorial on Marcosta Island, capturing the essence of the scene along with a voice recording of the sergeant's eulogy. Nyholm recalled her favorite line: "Galloping like a knight of old in his mighty fighter plane." *We should use it at the start of the opening memorial scene, following the cockpit flashback.* She smiled to herself. *I like it. Much more impactful than the other approach.*

The rest of the scenes would work as Jones had sketched, capturing the day and evening of the wooden bridge fire and explosion in Florida. The day would start with Jake Crawford's return in the dark of early morning, encountering Bronson after being gone for over two decades. The movie team knew that Bronson had become a surrogate father to Crawford, starting soon after Crawford lost his real father, around the age of seven. Hastings had informed Kurt of the special relationship.

Her creative thinking continued, abetted by the cocooning noise of the powerful jet engines. The reunion of the two men offered the opportunity for an intimate, character-driven drama, using the interactions to expose Bronson's troubled psyche and the hidden basis for the turmoil, interlaced with other flashbacks to the war and earlier times on the Florida bridge.

Adrien should love the revised approach. Nyholm knew his preference for nonlinear storylines, the interweaving of present and past to paint the emotional landscape, adding depth and texture to the story and its characters, pulling the audience into the hellishness of war and its lasting effects, physically and emotionally. It would be a challenge to direct but very engaging from an audience perspective.

And Kurt is a master at writing that type of screenplay. The revised approach would require him to learn much more about Crawford's return and what had transpired between the two men on that fateful July day.

The noise of the engines lessened. She felt a moment of lightness as the jet reached the apex of its trajectory, leveling at the altitude reserved for private jets, two miles above commercial airliners. The cabin lights blinked twice. Nyholm unlatched her seat, allowing it to pivot diagonally toward Stevansky. Kurt and Krista did the same. Each seat now faced its diagonal counterpart, arrayed around an empty center point in the aisle. The flight attendant came back, extracting inlaid tables from the lacquered side rails and securing them between the flanking seats.

Stevansky spoke after the attendant had finished. "Smooth climb this time. Almost chipped a tooth on the last one."

Nyholm recalled the turbulence. "That was intense. All those lightning flashes between the mountain peaks."

A motion caught her attention. The flight attendant stood outside the forward galley, holding a pot of coffee and four mugs, his fingers interlaced through the cup handles. Nyholm signaled him back. She waited until he finished serving before engaging with Jones.

"Kurt, I prefer starting with the memorial. But I've come up with an idea for an opening flashback." She glanced left. "It will appeal to your talents, Merv."

Stevansky cocked his head, a teasing expression on his face. "Should I keep my seatbelt on?"

Jones replaced the coffee cup on the side table and focused intently on Nyholm, maintaining a neutral expression.

She gave a verbal sketch of the cockpit flashback and fade-out to the old sergeant, along with the favorite line from his eulogy. Stevansky and Jones remained silent afterward, clearly lost in their respective contemplations. The constant hum of the engines became more noticeable, resonating inside the cabin as the minutes accumulated. Nyholm looked to her immediate left. Krista had fallen asleep, the seat fully reclined, coffee untouched. *Understandable after the late-night preparations.*

Jones reengaged first. "The day of the Florida bridge fire becomes the backbone of the screenplay, driven by character interactions that gain emotional momentum, heading to the town hall meeting. The bridge fire and explosion provide the climactic gut punch. I wouldn't dwell on the memorial initially, only enough to capture the sergeant's description of the galloping knight. It leaves the audience with a big clue, but not enough to spoil the ending, when the old sergeant shows up unannounced at the memorial and agrees to speak." Jones paused momentarily. "Crawford's character is critical to making this work. We need him to extract the relevant pieces of Bronson's troubling war experience and expose the deep-seated turmoil, mostly through dialogue."

Nyholm looked at Stevansky. "Merv? Your thoughts? You'll have a big job capturing all this."

He turned from the window. "I assume we can get Crawford to advise on the interior of the shack. There need to be visual cues for the audience, dramatic and subtle."

"We'll also need him for the verbal and nonverbal nuances," said Jones. "Lines and gestures are always tweaked for these types of close-in character dramas. The nuances make a big difference, yielding interactions that are much more realistic and natural."

Nyholm used their observations to reinforce the island setting. "Yet another reason to film the shack interior scenes on the island. It will make it easier for Crawford to be involved."

Stevansky sat straighter. "I've come around on your suggestion for the shack interior, placing it at the marine lab. It allows the actors to come and go from the luxury yachts, avoiding the paparazzi and groupies."

"Good," acknowledged Nyholm. "Hopefully, the lab site proves worthy. What else about the revised approach? Any other issues jump to mind?"

"Not really," Stevansky said. "The changes remove some of the starting war scenes, reducing the overseas time and the associated budget. The original sketch placed more emphasis on earlier events in the Burma air campaign."

Jones held up a hand. "We wouldn't want to lose what I've learned about those. A pilot from Bronson's squadron provided some key insights. I've been waiting to update you."

"Such as?" Nyholm asked, intrigued.

Jones thumbed through his thick notebook, scanning until he found the relevant notes. "The squadron's air base was carved from a jungle. The pilots had to deal with all kinds of crazy challenges. Here's a good example. During the monsoon season, everything turns muddy. They had to walk on corduroy logs between their tents and flight operations. The insides of the tents were damp but much dryer than the surrounding jungle. Whatever could crawl or slither wanted inside, the worst of which were cobras."

"Aren't they aggressive as hell?" asked Stevansky.

"They'll strike when startled or challenged. The pilots had to search their tents every time they entered, pistols at ready. One unfortunate pilot got bit on the neck when he checked under a cot. Died shortly afterward."

"Whoa!" Stevansky exclaimed, shaking both arms for effect.

Jones kept going. "The old pilot faxed me a copy of their mimeographed survival instructions … about what they would encounter if they bailed out over a Burmese jungle. Blood-sucking leeches were at the top of the list, along with snakes, tigers, and dense clouds of malaria-carrying mosquitos, plus a bunch of other bad shit, including some headhunting tribes. The skies were plenty dangerous. But the jungles? They were terrifying."

Kurt is having fun with the details. Nyholm intervened. "Let's get back to what we can use in the movie. Did Bronson bail out and experience the terrifying jungle?"

"Not that I've found." Jones thumbed a few pages further. "But I did learn new information about his heroic mission. Something awful, assuming it's true."

"More awful than cobras and headhunters?" asked Stevansky. He leaned toward Jones, focused intently.

"The squadron pilot told me a rumor they heard a few months after Bronson had shipped stateside. It came from one of the Chindits that Bronson saved."

Stevansky looked confused. "Chindits?"

"That's what they called the British guys pinned down next to the Burmese bridge. They were the World War II precursor to our modern-day special forces—operating deep behind enemy lines, blowing up Japanese supply lines and attacking high-value targets. They mostly hid in the jungle. True badasses."

"The rumor?" Nyholm asked, trying to keep Jones focused.

"Right. Apparently, the attacking Japanese soldiers herded women, children, and old men from a nearby village onto the bridge ahead of them, using them as human shields, daring the Chindits to shoot them out of the way."

Nyholm glanced at Stevansky. His eyes were glued on Jones.

"The Chindit commander ordered them to hold fire," Jones added.

"But Bronson had other orders," said Stevansky softly, as if musing aloud.

"Maybe he didn't know the civilians were on the bridge," offered Nyholm.

"He likely knew," said Jones. "I reviewed the entire transcript of the British sergeant's eulogy. Bronson's first flyby was to determine the line of attack for the dive bombing that followed. He zoomed past at a low altitude, almost on his side.

The Chindits could see him in the cockpit, looking down at the bridge."

"My God," said Nyholm, suddenly realizing the implications. "It's probably the reason Bronson became a recluse." She looked back and forth at the two men, her creative instincts shifting to high gear. "It would be a dramatic moment to capture. Does he forgo the critical bombing mission and let the Chindits get overrun? Or save them by blowing up the bridge, knowingly killing the villagers? Think of what Bronson would have to endure the rest of his life, all the nightmarish flashbacks of the carnage he caused, including the killing of children, the most innocent of innocent. It aligns with a signature Satorri story, a gut-wrenching, horrible choice of combat and the lifelong mental turmoil it causes."

"Fully agree," Jones said. "Turns out the British sergeant lives in Tampa. I was planning to ask Hastings for an introduction. I'd like to interview the guy, assuming he agrees. He never mentioned the villagers during the eulogy, but that's understandable. It's one of those horrific memories that veterans loathe to share."

"You should definitely try to interview him," Nyholm said. "And I understand your concern about losing the earlier moments of the Burma air campaign. We'll use flashbacks to capture some of them. They definitely add further depth and texture to the screenplay."

"Excellent," Jones said, looking relieved.

"Wait a minute," said Stevansky. He became animated, focusing on Jones. "I know this is your turf, but the Chindit rumor might offer a way to dramatize the suspicious events surrounding the Florida bridge arson, but with an unexpected twist."

Jones remained quiet, staring at Stevansky.

"How so, Merv?" Nyholm asked.

"Portray the fire and explosion as an arson-suicide. Have

Bronson set the flanking fires, and then go back inside the shack and wait for the explosion, finally ending the decades of emotional turmoil once and for all. Show him sitting at a table, smoking his last cigarette, downing a final tumbler of whiskey, the flickering light of the flames getting brighter and brighter until … *boom*."

Jones shook his head. "They failed to prove arson-suicide. I've studied the report by the lead homicide investigator."

"That doesn't matter," countered Stevansky. "Remember what Adrien said, we have creative license. I'm telling you, it would be far more impactful than leaving it to the audience to decide who torched the bridge. And there's little chance of a libel suit, if any." He looked toward Nyholm.

"It's definitely an intriguing twist," Nyholm acknowledged. "We'll need to run it past Adrien. He wanted us to resurrect suspicions about Nielsen, without crossing the line."

"But you know Adrien," said Stevansky. "Of foremost importance is weaving a powerful and gripping story."

Merv's right. "I guess Adrien could find another way to get at Nielsen. He should favor the climactic twist." Nyholm looked at Jones. "Any objection to the arson-suicide?"

Jones rubbed his chin, glancing at the cabin ceiling and musing aloud, making an insightful leap in turn. "It also fits with Crawford's speech at the public council meeting."

"How's that?" Nyholm asked, perplexed.

"Stopping the mental turmoil would be the reason for committing suicide, but why the timing and method? There must be a link with Crawford's public comments that evening—the proposal about returning to ferries and barges rather than replacing the old bridge with a modern one. Maybe Crawford mentioned his proposal to Bronson earlier in the day, unknowingly triggering the arson-suicide."

Nyholm grasped the importance of what Jones had surmised. "Bravo, Kurt, a brilliant insight. We could show Crawford in the shack discussing his proposal with Bronson, advocating the return to waterborne transportation. Unbeknownst to Crawford, Bronson realizes that torching the old bridge would leave the island stranded, requiring the islanders to experience the proposed approach before a replacement bridge could be constructed, buying time for Crawford to show it could work, winning their support."

They all sat for a while without speaking.

Nyholm finally broke the silence. "Great job, both of you. Okay, let's assume the arson-suicide approach is the direction we're headed. We'll organize it for presentation to Adrien after we finish the island visit. You both in favor?"

"I'm in," Stevansky said.

"Me as well," Jones said. He held up an index finger. "One more thing. We should consider adding a romantic subplot involving Bronson."

Stevansky quipped, "With what, a pelican?"

Nyholm couldn't help bursting out laughing.

Jones stared at Stevansky, shaking his head.

Nyholm recovered, asking Jones, "When? Before he left for combat in Burma?"

"No, during his life on the bridge." Jones thumbed through his notes. "Hastings told me that a widowed Cuban woman ran errands for Bronson, starting around 1949, protecting his reclusion. Her husband had died within a year of marriage. She was about nineteen when the relationship started with Bronson—he would have been about ten years older. He paid her to purchase and deliver groceries, including all the booze and cigarettes. The relationship continued throughout the decades, up until Bronson died."

"And was it romantic?" asked Nyholm.

"Hastings didn't say."

Nyholm considered the possibilities. "Is the woman alive? Living on the island? She might object to the romantic portrayal."

"No idea," replied Jones.

"Let's add this to the interview with Crawford," said Nyholm. "He likely knows."

"There's an alternative if she objects," said Jones. "Crawford married an island woman soon after returning."

"A high school sweetheart?" asked Stevansky.

"We need to find out," said Jones.

Nyholm's stomach grumbled. "Another possibility. Let's take a break and eat something. I want to get into the casting discussion. Our schedule aligns with several actors of interest, most notably Draven Barlowe. I mentioned him when we last met at Adrien's villa. I'd like to review the pros and cons of each candidate before we land."

****

Far to the east, another private jet streaked toward Florida, returning Nielsen to Tampa after a Sunday afternoon meeting with Senator Hoxman in Washington, DC.

Nielsen sat in the midsection of the cabin, reviewing a bulleted list. His long-trusted head of personal security occupied the forwardmost seat, directly across from the galley, conversing with the weekend flight attendant; she laughed at something Kevin said. Late afternoon sunlight filled the cabin with an orange glow.

Nielsen returned the list to its folder, his eyes flat. The Blake legislation had passed but with a much narrower margin than expected. Nielsen's state lobbyist wouldn't admit to the real cause, listing a variety of other excuses. It didn't matter, Nielsen already knew. More legislators had called to express concern about the recent *Sentinel* article, afraid of what Hastings would write next. *Chickenshits.* Nielsen had circled names on the list, identifying those who had flipped against the legislation, targeting them for funding opposition in the next election cycle.

The weekend flight attendant came back. “Would you like dinner, Mr. Nielsen? I have your favorite, tender grouper cheeks, baked with Cajun seasoning and lemon juice, along with a small lobster salad, Niçoise-style.”

“Florida lobster?”

“Yes. Lightly grilled.”

“I’ll start with the salad. Could you refresh this?”

“Certainly.”

He handed her the empty tumbler, shifting thoughts to the meeting at Hoxman’s DC residence. It had been a challenging negotiation, still to be finalized. As chair of the Senate Judiciary Committee, Hoxman was well positioned to influence the dismissal of the anticipated Marcosta lawsuit. The federal district judge in Miami was high on the list of potential nominees to the US Supreme Court—his chances would wither without Hoxman’s support.

The attendant brought the refreshed bourbon, following shortly thereafter with the dinner fare.

Kevin came back after she returned to the galley. “Should I make preparations for a rendezvous with Hoxman’s associate?”

Nielsen looked up from eating. “Not yet. I pushed back on the requested amount. We’ll see if the senator blinks.”

“Understood.” Kevin returned forward.

Nielsen finished the dinner, thoughts turning to Hoxman’s suggestion. It would help if a state environmental study contradicted the one performed by the University of Miami, providing cover for the judge’s dismissal of the lawsuit. Nielsen made a mental note to meet with the governor’s chief of staff.

The flight attendant stepped from the galley, delivering fresh coffee to the cockpit, taking the opportunity to flirt with the copilot. The scene reminded Nielsen of Anna Nyholm and what he had initiated with the PI firm. *We’ll see if Nyholm lives up to her reputation.* If she did, the tactic would offer an opportunity to hit Crawford in his soft spot, forcing him to defend his integrity within the island community, right when it mattered most.

Chapter 9

Monday morning arrived much too early, given the three-hour time zone difference. Nyholm yawned broadly, listening through the headphones as Stevansky guided the helicopter pilot, seeking yet another perspective of the island fishing pier.

"Come in low and slow again … this time toward the big mermaid sign on that green building. That's good … hover here."

Stevansky sat in the copilot seat, a map and large sketchpad on his lap. Arrows and notations flanked images of the pier and downtown. He turned to a fresh page, adding a new sketch and set of notations.

Nyholm glanced through the window on the left side, looking down. Twenty feet above the water … at most. She turned toward Jones. His left hand gripped the armrest, eyes shut tight; the right hand formed a fist, a pen in the center, pushing down on an open binder. *Interesting. He's never seemed afraid of flying in helicopters ... but that was over land.*

Stevansky gave new instructions. "Okay, now rise and bank

toward that motel and sandy point on the far right. Stay aligned with the sea wall, just off the channel edge. Go slowly."

The copter rose while banking to the right, leveling about a hundred feet up. Nyholm looked out. *Must be Main Street*. Forty or so people were arrayed on a rambling brick sidewalk alongside the road, looking up and waving; others stood across the street doing the same. She leaned close to the window, staring down at the town hall building, imagining the public meeting when Crawford spoke, the bridge fire occurring soon afterward.

The copter rose higher, bringing more of the island into view. Further south, the roofs of small businesses and houses were intermingled among colorful trees and shrubbery. Nyholm looked back to the left. The raised booms of shrimp boats poked above the tops of palm trees, arrayed like thick antennas along the curve of a harbor, over on the bay side. *The town is more charming than I imagined.*

The copter continued ascending, affording a view down the island's length. The roofs appeared to stop about a mile or two to the south. A water tower and some utility works could be seen at the edge of the large bay, including several windmills. The rest of the island appeared undeveloped, except for a set of buildings in the far distance on the southern tip. She studied the printed map on her lap, turning it to match the island's shape. *It's the marine lab.*

Stevansky gestured to the pilot. The copter made a shallow dive while banking left, leveling about fifty feet above the Gulf of Mexico as it proceeded down the beachfront.

Waves crashed along the white sand, visible at the bottom of Nyholm's window. A few people were walking or wade-fishing, dispersed in front of a sparsely settled stretch of one-story cottages. The copter continued south. Sea grapes and scrub pines dotted the landscape behind the beach. No buildings were evident. A two-lane road ran the island's length.

"Go down the bay side of the island," Stevansky instructed. The copter banked to the left, rising as it turned, heading across the half-mile width of the island and down its bay side.

Nyholm leaned to the middle, looking through the cockpit window. Arrayed ahead was the marine lab, a complex of twenty or more buildings, each with a similar exterior, white clapboard siding with grayish metal roofs. The most prominent building was two stories, in the center of the property, alongside a rectangular-shaped harbor. A thatched hut sat on the bay's edge next to an enclosed pond. *The lab is larger than I expected.*

They came closer. Nyholm focused on three of the buildings, set in sequence along a peninsula between the bay and harbor. Long-handled nets could be seen hanging from pegs next to holding tanks. Scuba tanks and other diving equipment were neatly arranged under an overhanging roof. The last building had a screened porch off the back. A broad stone patio continued to a low sea wall. A set of round wooden tables held collapsible umbrellas. Shallow water was adjacent to the patio. *It might be a good spot for filming the interior shack scenes, positioning it atop an anchored platform.* She made a reminder to discuss the idea with Merv.

"Slide down to that shallow pass and rotate back toward the lab," Stevansky instructed. The copter slid off to the left, ascending to about a hundred feet. Nyholm looked down. The water of the bay gave way to shallow sandbars and undulating rows of oyster beds. She looked at the map. *Clayton's Pass.* The shallow opening separated the south end of Marcosta Island from the northern boundary of the Ten Thousand Islands. A broad mosaic of small mangrove islands dotted the view to the south, as far as the eye could see. *How does anyone navigate that maze?*

The copter rotated to the right, shifting her view toward the Gulf of Mexico. Several large boats were about a half mile offshore, pulling traps from the water, one moving slowly, the others stopped. The copter descended, coming to a low hover above the pass. Stevansky continued sketching, drawing a sharp arrow toward a long rectangle and annotating it. *Merv must love all the filming possibilities.*

Stevansky pointed. "Go over to the point and come up about fifty feet. I want a closer view of the lab harbor."

Boats of all sizes became visible in the harbor, an eclectic mix of research vessels, power catamarans with flat decks, center-console monohulls, small skiffs, and a few sailboats. A gleaming wooden houseboat was docked at the edge of the harbor mouth, along the south seawall, shaped like a Chinese junk. Nyholm assumed some were owned by the staff. *What a romantic life. At the very end of a remote island, surrounded by such beauty. The star actors would do fine in luxury yachts here.*

"Okay, let's land." Stevansky pointed toward the open field at the west end of the harbor.

****

Caitlin stood outside the lab's front office. The helicopter flew over the harbor, hovering above the open field.

Jake and Ida Hoefler waited near the landing area, turning away as the downwash from the blades blew bits of sand and grass through the air. Judith Kerner left the welcoming party and grabbed Dingo, securing his collar to an available dock line.

Caitlin scanned the property. Everyone had paused what they were doing. She could see Dirty Dick standing outside the kitchen door.

The helicopter blades spun to a stop. The left-side passenger door opened. Long legs extended toward the ground, followed by tight-fitting lime-green shorts and an untucked Hawaiian shirt of pastel blue with matching green seashells. Nyholm stood to full height, looking slowly from left to right, her shaggy blonde hair glistening in the morning sunlight. All her movements displayed a sophisticated elegance, the demeanor of a woman accustomed to the limelight alongside famous movie stars. Caitlin had never seen such an appearance. It radiated with feminine dominance. *A dream woman for confident men.*

Jake stepped forward as Nyholm approached, his height several inches above hers. Caitlin stared as Nyholm held out a hand, palm down. Like a Nordic queen greeting a subservient warrior. They came together. Jake held the proffered handshake as he spoke. Nyholm flashed a bright smile. Her free hand came to rest on his shoulder.

Caitlin felt a rare emotion take hold, something she had experienced long ago, back when Jake had left for college. An overactive teenage mind had provoked the jealousy, imagining him in bed with attractive coeds. She looked away, forcing aside the surprising reaction.

A few moments passed before she looked back. Nyholm and Hoefler were exchanging greetings. Two men came around the front of the helicopter, heading toward the assembled group. The gray hair of the older man dangled across his chest in two long braids, yielding the appearance of an oversized Willie Nelson. The other man was younger and shorter, moving forward in a contorted up-and-down motion. Each had sling bags strung across their shoulders.

Caitlin wondered if Krista remained in the helicopter. The pilot left the cockpit, proceeding to unload travel bags from a back compartment. Kerner had rejoined the group. The handshakes and greetings continued.

A modified golf cart pulled up to the copter. Two dockhands helped the pilot load the luggage onto the cart's platform. The duo drove off to the visiting scientist quarters, near the entrance to the property. Caitlin made a checkmark on the clipboard. *First item completed.*

The entourage started toward the front office, Jake and Nyholm in the lead, their longer strides outdistancing the others.

He pointed toward something in the harbor. Nyholm touched his shoulder again, speaking close to his ear, then laughing. Jake grinned broadly. Caitlin forced her eyes to the action list, preparing for the imminent greeting. She grabbed a set of packets from a nearby table.

****

"I've never visited a marine lab before," Nyholm announced as the group approached the front office. "Simply stunning from the air. Such a lovely spot."

"We have information packets for your review and keeping," Hoefler said from behind, her voice elevated. "There's a site map of the facilities and background materials that describe our research and ecotourism programs."

"Hello, Ms. Nyholm. I'm Caitlin Crawford … Jake's *wife*." Caitlin stepped forward and stuck out her right hand.

Nyholm was momentarily startled, noting the extra emphasis on the marital relationship, clearly conveying territoriality. She glanced down, taking the proffered handshake, noticing the well-defined arm muscles. Nyholm released the firm handshake and looked up, only to be startled again, this time by Caitlin's emerald eyes, a perfect complement to the long auburn hair. *A natural beauty. High cheekbones. A radiant smile framed by perfectly formed lips. No obvious make-up. The fabled Guinevere …*.

Caitlin pulled a packet from the set and handed it to Nyholm.

The gesture triggered a realization: *I forgot to acknowledge her introduction*. "Goodness, I'm so sorry. I was admiring your exquisite eyes."

"You're very kind, Ms. Nyholm."

"Please, call me Anna. It's such a pleasure to meet you, Caitlin. We've learned about Jake's amazing past, including what he's accomplished for Marcosta Island. You must be an exceptional woman to have him as a husband."

Nyholm saw a flicker of concern in Caitlin's eyes after the backhanded compliment. *Interesting*. She took the packet and stepped aside, turning to introduce Jones and Stevansky. Jones immediately opened his packet and began reviewing the contents.

"I also have a packet for Krista," said Caitlin. "Is she still in the helicopter?"

As if on cue, the helicopter came to life, the blades starting to spin.

Nyholm's voice rose in concert with the engine noise. "We didn't have room. She'll be dropped off later today. Would you kindly hold it for her?"

"Of course … Anna."

Hoefler stepped forward as the copter lifted away, taking charge. "Let's get started on the tour. There are restrooms along the way. Some refreshments are set up in the dining hall."

Jake left Nyholm's side and stood beside Caitlin, placing a hand on her back. "Enjoy the tour. I need to get back to City Hall. A lab van will bring you all to the north end for lunch and the interview. Sorry for the switch to my office."

"No problem whatsoever," said Nyholm. "We want to see the downtown buildings from ground level. Oh yes, and Merv is eagerly awaiting the lunch specialty at the local tavern. What's was that called, Merv?"

"The Famous Claude Sandwich."

"Well, you're in for a treat," said Jake.

"Why the name Claude, and not Clawed?" Jones asked, spelling the latter.

"Your waiter can explain. It's best to learn about the history at the tavern. There's a good chance you'll witness the local superstition in action."

"I'd love for you to join us for lunch," Nyholm said.

"Thanks for the invite. It will depend on my noon

teleconference."

Nyholm smiled brightly. "Well, we hope to see you there." She removed the aviator sunglasses and shook out her hair, turning to Hoefler. "And now for my very first tour of a marine lab." She repositioned the sunglasses. "Please lead the way."

****

Jake followed Caitlin into the front office. "Everything okay?"

She turned to face him. "Do you find her attractive? So tall and young looking?"

Jake didn't hesitate, quickly stepping forward to hold her. "This isn't like you." He felt Caitlin stiffen.

She averted his eyes.

He let go and stepped back slightly, studying the expression, then reached for her hands, taking them in his. "You are everything to me." He embraced her again, holding her close to his chest, waiting patiently. The stiffness dissipated.

She eased away. "I'm not sure what's gotten into me. I guess it's the uncertainty about my medical situation."

"I meant what I said the other night. You are stuck with me through whatever lies ahead. One thousand percent. No one will ever come between us, and particularly someone like her. I know the type."

Caitlin pointed at his watch. "You'll be late for your next meeting."

"It doesn't matter."

"You should go. I'll call Sandra and let her know you're on the way."

Jake hesitated, watching as Caitlin took a seat and reached for the desk phone. She glanced over, shooing him away with the wave of her hand.

"Okay. Hopefully the afternoon interview doesn't last too long. I'll be home right afterward."

She lifted the handset and started to dial. "I'll be fine. You take whatever time is needed."

****

Jake conversed with Nyholm at his office conference table. Stevansky stood by a back window, staring intently in the direction of the fishing pier. Jones studied the wall painting.

"I'm sorry about Sandra's exuberance," said Jake. "She's a big fan. I should also apologize for the behavior of the commercial fishermen in the tavern. They can be overly raunchy at times. As I warned, we have quite a few characters on the island."

Nyholm placed a hand on his forearm. "No need to apologize. Trust me, they're mild compared to the paparazzi."

Jake removed his arms from the table, leaning back in the chair.

She leaned back as well, an amused expression on her face.

"What do you think of the marine lab?" he asked.

"It has great promise. I'm excited by the location and what I've seen of the island thus far."

"Excellent."

"By the way, you'll need extra security if we film here, well beyond what you've likely imagined."

"Because of the paparazzi?"

"Those guys for sure and the groupies that track movie stars." She pointed in the direction of the tavern. "A paparazzo was already taking pictures during our lunch."

"Where? I didn't see anyone with a camera."

"The middle-aged man at the bar, dressed like a tourist, seersucker Bermuda shorts and a dark polo shirt. The camera lens was under his left armpit, pointed our direction. I noticed him shifting left and right, probably clicking away."

"You've got to be kidding. Already?"

"You'd be amazed. They do stuff like that all the time, trying to catch a photo they can sell to the tabloids, something juicy that enables a sensational headline."

Jake became concerned. *What photos did the guy take?* Nyholm had touched him repeatedly until he conveyed obvious discomfort by shifting positions. Her flirtatious behavior reminded him of the younger socialites he had encountered in Boston, shortly after his ultra-wealth had become public knowledge.

"How about we get started?" Nyholm asked, speaking in the direction of Jones and Stevansky.

Both men returned to the table, extracting notebooks from their sling bags.

Nyholm flashed a quick smile before starting. "Let me provide the context for our interview session. As you will recall, your character serves as the protagonist's helper, enabling the audience to learn about Lieutenant Bronson through your dialogue and interactions.

"The storyline will center on the day of your return, including the evening town hall meeting and your passionate comments about preserving the island's heritage and beauty. Along the way, we'll use flashbacks to capture the World War II events and your life as a young boy fishing with Lieutenant Bronson on the old bridge. We are especially curious what triggered your return and how your interactions in the bridgetender's shack may have impacted the fateful events of that evening. Supporting characters will be used to augment the central storyline. Kurt is well underway on the screenplay."

Jake made a grimace. *Ugh, my character role is much more than I expected.*

"You seem uncomfortable," said Nyholm, studying him closely.

Jake looked away, staring at the painting. *Let it go. Concentrate on the goal.* He refocused on Nyholm. "What about the suspicious circumstances of the bridge fire? How will you represent what happened?"

"Our approach has changed," said Jones. "We …"

"Kurt," Nyholm said sharply, shooting him a stern look.

"Changed in what way?" Jake asked, his eyes shifting back and forth between Jones and Nyholm.

Jones stared at his notepad.

Nyholm sighed. "What I'm about to share must stay strictly confidential—it represents a climactic twist in the movie. We still need Adrien's approval."

Jake heard a bumping sound. He went to the office door and yanked it open. Sandra stumbled into the room sideways. Jake grabbed her by the arm, stopping her fall. "What the hell are you doing?"

She recovered her balance, face red with embarrassment. "Oh … I'm so sorry." She hurried through the doorway and into the outer office area.

Jake closed the door and returned to the table. "Apologies. She's starstruck, but that's no excuse for unprofessional behavior." He sat down. "Where were we?"

"I was about to divulge the confidential shift in our approach. We plan to portray Lieutenant Bronson as the arsonist, committing suicide to escape the mental turmoil from his combat experience." She described the proposed arson action and the scene inside the shack in the moments preceding the fatal explosion.

****

Nyholm observed Jake's reaction, allowing him time to absorb the shift. The center of the conference table held his attention; his eyes unfocused, mouth clenched shut, jaw muscles flexing repeatedly.

He looked up. "It was never proven."

"I know, but the movie is not a documentary. We are using creative latitude."

"You'll be impugning Simon's reputation."

"I understand your concern." Nyholm softened her voice, speaking gently. "I know you care deeply for Lieutenant Bronson. However, we've learned some information that makes arson-suicide the most likely explanation for what happened that evening."

"What information?"

Nyholm glanced at Jones. *Should I let Kurt explain? Best not. He'll provide too much detail.* She refocused on Jake. "Kurt interviewed a surviving pilot from Lieutenant Bronson's squadron. The pilot shared a troubling rumor. If it's true, it could explain why Lieutenant Bronson became a bridgetender and …"

"Took his life that night," Jones interjected. "The timing …"

"Kurt." Nyholm shot him another look.

Jake rose abruptly and walked to the back windows, staring at Passage Channel. An awkwardness settled over the room. Minutes ticked by. Stevansky raised both hands toward Nyholm, palms up, a gesture of "What gives?" She shook her head and raised an index finger, signaling him to hold tight.

Jake returned to the table, continuing to stand, hovering above them. He focused on Jones. "Have you confirmed the rumor?"

Jones glanced Nyholm's direction.

She tilted her head toward Jake, signaling to answer.

Jones responded, "My team has been researching the Chindits, the British group pinned down by the Burmese bridge."

"I know who they are," said Jake.

Nyholm interceded, realizing what he was after. "Kurt is scheduled to speak with Sergeant McGregor on Thursday in Tampa."

"He agreed to meet?"

"Fletcher Hastings arranged it," she replied.

Jake turned away, pacing to and from the painting, eyes aimed at the floor.

Nyholm finally grasped the reason for Jake's behavior. *He already knows about the villagers on the Burmese bridge.*

The pacing stopped. Jake resumed sitting, slumping in the chair. "It negates what you said during your press event."

"Actually, that's not quite correct," said Nyholm. "Arson-suicide fits within the spectrum of suspicious events, but you raise an important point. The Hastings articles left the distinct impression that Nielsen had the bridge torched. It's why our shift to arson-suicide needs to stay strictly confidential, protecting the unexpected twist."

"What's the estimate on timing?" Jake asked her.

"Timing?"

"Of the movie release."

"We'll start filming this summer. A good rule of thumb is about two years from then. Adrien thinks we should release on Veteran's Day, so a bit more than two years."

"So, November of '99?"

"Assuming everything stays on track."

Jake nodded slowly.

Jones reentered the discussion, jumping to a key question. "Did you share your ferry and barge idea with Simon?"

Nyholm watched intently, anticipating the terse response that followed.

"Yes." The painful look in Jake's eyes confirmed what Jones had surmised.

****

Jake reclined in his desk chair, staring up at the rotating Bahama fan, his long legs resting across the desktop, ankles crossed. Nyholm and her colleagues had left a short while ago, returning to the marine lab.

The interview session had proven exhausting. Jones had been incredibly thorough, probing unexpected nooks and crannies. *I can see why he's the best screenwriter in Hollywood—incredibly perceptive.* Most of the questions had centered on Jake's return to the island and his interactions with Simon, all that had transpired on the day of the bridge fire. Nyholm and Stevansky spent the time listening and taking notes, interrupting periodically to augment a question or clarify a response.

Jones revealed an insight toward the end of the interview, something Jake thought no one else would understand. "The arson-suicide, it was more than an escape from the mental turmoil of combat. It was also the loving act of a surrogate father, wanting to protect the reason his 'son' returned home." Jake had observed Nyholm as Jones described the insight. *She's in favor of using it.*

Jake had protested vehemently about portraying Simon and Maria as lovers, emphasizing her Catholic virtues and longstanding dedication to the memory of her deceased husband—the victim of a terrible loading dock accident at Horseshoe Basin. Nyholm relented, shifting to Jake's relationship with Caitlin, describing how the rekindling of their teenage love would help counterbalance the harsher realities of Simon's storyline. *I need to alert Caitlin.*

His thoughts swung to Joneses' impending interview with Sergeant McGregor. Jake had to assume the sergeant would confirm the rumor about the villagers on the bridge. *Why else would he accept the meeting?* Jake had thought about sparing Jones the trip to Tampa, but he had made a solemn promise to McGregor after the memorial service.

Deep inside, Jake understood why they had gravitated to the arson-suicide. Nyholm needed to portray the darkest aspects of war and the lasting consequences. *It's the essence of the Satorri genre.*

Simon's preoccupation with karma came to the forefront, the

continuing effect of his decision to bomb the Burmese bridge—in this case, the effect it would have on movie audiences worldwide. *What would Simon think?* Jake wasn't sure but it didn't matter anyway. *I can't stop the portrayal.*

He noticed the growing darkness outside. *Shit. Caitlin must be wondering.* He glanced at the desk phone, tempted to call, but decided otherwise. The cabin was only a short drive away. He hurried out, locking the front door and heading for his car.

Rain had begun falling. Gulf Drive was all but deserted. He paused for a second, staring at the adjacent police station, remembering that Billy had been transported to the county jail. *The sentencing is on Thursday morning. Remember to set an early alarm.*

He wound himself into the driver's seat, starting the engine. The headlight beams illuminated the white clapboard siding of City Hall. He stared through the streaked windshield, listening to the rain hit the car. A feeling of melancholy came over him. He tried to shake it off. *Get moving.*

The wipers swept back and forth as he drove home, the windshield clear then blurry, again and again. The tires hummed on the wet tarmac. It wasn't long before the cabin mailbox came into view, glistening brightly.

Chapter 10

The Thursday morning drive to Naples took longer than expected. Jake hurried inside the county courtroom. Billy sat at the defense table at the front left wearing a button-down shirt and tie. Likely a singular occurrence in his life. Jake took a seat on the right side, close to the front, hoping Billy would notice his presence.

The big question would be answered shortly. Will the judge accept the prosecutor's recommendation? Jake knew her reputation. She was tough on gun-related crimes, often delivering the maximum sentence. Yes, Billy's crime was a dangerous prank, but not a robbery or the cause of serious bodily harm. Jake crossed his fingers.

The judge studied the sheet of paper the prosecutor presented. She looked over at Billy, leveling a stern gaze. "Mr. Watson, you are charged with reckless endangerment and discharging a firearm on the premises of a public facility. The reckless endangerment charge comes close to being a felony but does not reach that level, in my opinion. As such, both violations will be treated as first-degree misdemeanors. Each carries a maximum penalty of one year in jail. How do you plead?"

"Guilty as hell!" hollered a voice from the rear.

Shit. He's here. Jake turned sharply. Dirty Dick stood in the last row, waving a baseball cap and pointing at the top of his head. A bailiff hurried toward him along the far wall. The judge banged her gavel.

A loud thud echoed across the courtroom. Billy had tipped over his chair, escaping the grasp of his attorney. A second bailiff prevented him from reaching the center aisle, embracing Billy in a bear hug. The judge stood, pounding the gavel harder, yelling for order.

Billy pointed at Dirty Dick. "Get the fuck out of here, you cocksucker!"

The first bailiff removed Dirty Dick from the courtroom. Noisy chatter erupted.

"Order! Quiet!" yelled the judge, her face flushed. "Bailiff, return Mr. Watson to his chair."

Jake had stood, preparing to engage Billy if he had made it into the aisle. *What a shitshow.* He sat, reminding himself to speak with Hoefler about what just happened.

The bailiff marched Billy toward the defense table. They didn't make it.

Billy erupted for the second time, staring at a hard-looking man a few rows from the front. "Hell you doin' here, you son of a bitch?"

The man raised a middle finger, mouthing "fuck you."

It took a moment for Jake to recognize him. It was Eric Jenkins, Caitlin's ex-brother-in-law, probably here to gloat about Billy's predicament. *Wonderful, as if Dirty Dick wasn't bad enough.*

"Mr. Watson, if you have another outburst, you will be cited for contempt of court. Do you understand?"

Billy continued to glare at Jenkins until the bailiff pushed him down in the chair and stood behind, keeping a hand on

Billy's shoulder.

The defense attorney leaned over and said something to Billy.

Billy turned to the judge. "Yeah. I git it."

"And the same goes for everyone else in my courtroom." The judge scanned the audience sternly, daring anyone to step out of line, finally refocusing her attention on Billy. "Please stand, Mr. Watson."

Billy stood, pushing his chair into the bailiff as he got up, causing a noticeable grunt. The defense counsel stood alongside, visibly ruffled from the earlier encounter with Billy, his groomed hair in disarray.

"I've already stated the charges. Mr. Watson, how do you plead?"

The attorney answered, "My client pleads guilty to the charges, Your Honor."

"Is that correct, Mr. Watson? You are pleading guilty to all charges?"

"Guess so."

Once again, the attorney said something to Billy.

"Yeah … Your Honor."

The judge sighed, shaking her head. She turned toward the prosecution. "I've reviewed your recommendation, which falls short. Particularly after the angry outbursts I just witnessed."

Jake grimaced. *Billy's his own worst enemy.*

The judge paused, reviewing the recommendation again and making some notes. Conversations started in the audience. The judge banged her gavel, not looking up. "Quiet."

She refocused on Billy. "Mr. Watson, you clearly have an anger management problem. I'm concerned you will do serious harm to someone if you can't learn to control yourself better."

Billy looked down and muttered something, shaking his head.

"Are you disagreeing with my assessment?"

Billy looked up. “I ain’t meanin’ nothin’.”

She looked at her notes. “Very well then. I am doubling the recommended two-month incarceration. You are hereby sentenced to four months in the county jail. During that time, you will receive anger counseling three times a week. If you miss any of the counseling sessions, your jail sentence will be extended accordingly. A six-month probationary period will commence upon release from prison. You will continue the mandatory anger counseling during the probationary period, scaled back to once a week. If you miss a weekly session, your probation will be revoked, and the remaining time spent in jail.”

She paused, continuing to study her notes. “Your probation carries four restrictions: First, you are confined to your home from sunset until one hour before sunrise. Second, you are not allowed on the premises of any establishment that is licensed to sell or serve alcoholic beverages. Third, you must stay at least one hundred feet away from Mr. Richard Cybert, the man you endangered in the shooting incident. Fourth, and not the least, your guns will remain in the safekeeping of the Marcosta Island Police Department. And let me be perfectly clear, if you are found in possession of a firearm during probation, you will be arrested and returned to jail for one year for violating my order.”

The judge continued, “Lastly, and in lieu of a monetary fine, you are sentenced to eighty hours of community service on behalf of the City of Marcosta Island. The hours must be completed during the six-month probation period. The specific services will be determined by the city’s mayor.”

Jake acknowledged with a quick nod when the judge glanced in his direction.

“Mr. Watson, do you have any questions regarding the sentence I have imposed?”

Billy shook his head.

“Please answer my question, Mr. Watson.”

“Nope.”

She banged the gavel. "The sentence is effective immediately. Bailiff, please escort Mr. Watson from the courtroom and remand him to the county jail authorities."

Jake waited for Billy to leave before standing up. *It could have been worse.* He counted the months to Billy's release, thinking about the hours of public service. *I'll have him net a supply of fresh mullet for the summer seafood festival. Maybe we can do it together.*

Someone approached from Jake's left. "Well, looky here. If it ain't the big shot mayor hisself."

Jake turned to face Eric Jenkins. The two men squared up. Jenkins was shorter but built like a human pit bull, displaying an upper torso of bulging muscles under a tight-fitting camouflage T-shirt. His face was pockmarked from severe acne.

Jake felt a surge of masculine energy, struggling to contain his anger.

Jenkins escalated the provocation. "How's my brother's ex-bitch?"

Jake clenched his fists, shortening the distance between them. Jenkins matched the gesture. Both men were now inches apart, glaring hard.

The judge banged her gavel and pointed it at them. "Whatever is going on must stop immediately."

A bailiff hurried over.

Jenkins ignored the judge, putting a finger on Jake's chest. "You and Billy ain't worth shit."

The bailiff forced himself between them, pushing Jenkins away. The judge banged her gavel again, pointing toward Jenkins. "Remove that man from my courtroom. Mayor Crawford, please approach."

Jake complied, going through the swinging fence at the center of the bar and approaching the judge's bench. "I'm sorry, Your Honor."

"I saw him come at you. What was that about?"

Jake limited the answer. “It’s someone who has a challenging history with Billy Watson. They’ve fought in the past.”

“Recent past?”

“I don’t believe so. Years ago.”

“And that man still harbors a grudge?”

“Apparently so, Your Honor.”

“Why’d he come at you?”

“He knows I’m Billy’s close friend. I’m also the spouse of his brother’s ex-wife, Caitlin McKenzie.”

The judge reacted with surprise. “That was Mark Jenkins’s brother?”

“Yes, Eric Jenkins. You know of Mark?”

“Too well, I’m afraid. Do I need to issue a restraining order on Eric? He clearly accosted you.”

“It’s unnecessary. He lives in Copeland now.”

The judge remained silent for a moment. “You should reconsider if he threatens again or causes trouble for Mrs. Crawford.”

“Understood, Your Honor.”

****

The governor’s chief of staff exited the private meeting in Nielsen’s private jet, heading toward the flight operations base at Tallahassee Regional Airport. Nielsen watched as she entered the building. “Why such reluctance?” His question was aimed at Diaz, sitting across the aisle.

“She’s wrestling with the potential blowback on the governor.”

Nielsen turned to Diaz. “Which I don’t understand—the blowback would be minimal.”

“It’s a very short timeframe,” warned Diaz. “The data and findings will be strongly challenged by Fred Thompson and his expert witnesses."

"It won't matter," said Nielsen. "Dangle another campaign donation to get the study done faster."

"You just did $500,000."

"Up it to a million, but only if the study report is completed by the end of May."

Diaz made a notation on his legal pad. "I'll call her tomorrow."

"No, meet with her in person. In fact, use this jet to get back here first thing in the morning. It underscores the importance I place on this—the medium is the message."

"You're headed to Orlando tomorrow morning."

"I'll use the helo." Nielsen pushed a button on the side console.

The weekday flight attendant came out of the galley, brushing something off her uniform.

"Tell the pilots to get moving."

"Yes, Mr. Nielsen. Do you want lunch now?"

"No. More coffee."

Diaz leafed to another page of his legal pad. "There's an update from the Marcosta source. The movie team met with Crawford for almost five hours on Monday, talking in his office."

"And?"

"It sounds like the storyline will center on the day and night of the bridge fire. They plan to portray Crawford as a central character."

"And you find that surprising? Crawford spent most of that day with the old bridgetender. He mentioned it during the town meeting the night of the fire."

"I thought you'd like to know."

"Did his chatty assistant learn anything of value? Like how they plan to portray the suspicious events?"

"No. Apparently, she had nothing else to report."

The engines spooled up. The jet began taxiing toward the south end of the airport. Nielsen watched as they passed a long row of private jets. *A busy day for lining pockets.*

He refocused on Diaz. “And the PI firm? Did their guy get pictures of Crawford with Nyholm?”

“That’s what they said. I haven’t received the photos yet.” Diaz held up an index finger. He thumbed to a page, placing his finger on a specific item. “I forgot, Nyholm spotted the PI guy taking their pictures.”

“What the hell? Is this amateur hour?”

“It won’t matter.”

“Why’s that?”

“She assumed he was a paparazzo.”

Nielsen chuckled. “A perfect cover. We’ll see if he caught something useful.”

****

The car ferry departed the island transport dock, heading to the mainland side. Caitlin stood by the starboard railing alongside Jake. Their cabin came into view at the far end of Eletz Point. Munson Bay stretched beyond, the waters bluish-green in the afternoon sun.

Visiting Boston in February sounded surreal. A camping trip with Jake was the farthest north she had traveled, back when they visited the Smoky Mountains in their late teens—*but that was in the summer.* The anticipation of harsh winter weather added to the anxiety she felt. Jake had reassured her, insisting that she keep the medical appointments. *He only wants the best of care for me. What did he say? No errors or omissions are allowed.*

A warm breeze swirled above the channel waters. The high tomorrow in Boston would be ten degrees Fahrenheit, below zero overnight. She could barely tolerate sixty-degree weather. It caused her to shiver thinking of such inhumane temperatures. Jake's arm came around her shoulders, pulling her close.

The ferry approached the mainland transport dock. Jake let go and opened the passenger door, closing it after she was seated. They drove down the ramp and onto the tarmac, heading along the winding road toward the Tamiami Trail.

"How're you doing?" he asked.

She gave a quick smile, masking the anxiety. "I'm fine. By the way, I overheard Ida talking about the courtroom incident with Dirty Dick."

Jake shook his head, frustration apparent. "He knew Billy would explode. It's a dangerous game he's playing—Ida needs to rein him in."

"Are you worried Billy will seek revenge, even after the anger counseling?"

"I'm beyond worried." Jake rounded a curve, dodging a land crab scurrying across the road. "It didn't help that Eric Jenkins showed up too." He refrained from telling her all of what had transpired.

"Eric's awful. Mean-spirited to the core. In some ways worse than Mark."

"I wonder how he knew about the court timing."

"I'm sure he stays in touch with some of the island fishermen," said Caitlin. "Word travels fast with all the tavern talk. Mark probably knows about Billy as well."

They rode in silence, eventually turning onto the Tamiami Trail. A road sign announced the remaining distance to Miami. Ninety-five miles.

Caitlin noticed the new mobile phone, retrieving it from the cupholder. "Have you used this yet?"

"Only during a test at the store. There's still no signal on the island. I'll turn it on when we get to Miami.

"Who has the number?"

"Miriam, Sandra, Ed Dickerson, and Chief Wilkinson. I'll

share it with several others once we get to Boston, including Bill Atkins in Chicago."

"Why Ed?"

"You may have forgotten; he's deputy mayor. I asked him to handle minor matters during my absence."

Caitlin replaced the phone, looking out the passenger window at the flocks of birds standing in the wetlands, many driven south by the winter weather.

They drove a while before Jake reengaged, surprising her. "I found a cruising yacht. A Bertram 38 with twin diesels. She'll fit nicely at the cabin dock."

Caitlin smiled to herself, recognizing his attempt to discuss a pleasant future. "Where'd you find her?"

"Snead Island Boatworks in Palmetto, near the mouth of the Manatee River."

"New or used?"

"Used. She's in solid mechanical shape—mostly needs cosmetic work."

"What's her name?"

"It's been sanded off. We'd change it anyway."

"To what? *Reel Tight Genes II*?"

Jake shook his head. "That name stays with the Boston days. I have a new one in mind, regarding something long ago, back when you and I were kids. I hope you like it."

"Try me."

"Can I give you a hint first?"

"Sure."

"Remember the billowing clouds on the gulf horizon? How the formations offered endless opportunities to imagine animals and other things? We would point them out: rabbits, dragons, cars, pumpkins, flags, teapots … making a game of it."

Caitlin recognized where the discussion was leading. "And you wanted a big yacht with a flying bridge … so we could reach those clouds and touch them."

She reached forward, tapping the dash with both hands, creating the sound of a drumroll. “And the name is?”

“*Cloud Catcher*.”

“Aw … I love it, Jake.”

“I thought you would. As soon as I wrap up being mayor, we’ll go chase the clouds.”

“It sounds wonderfully romantic.” She paused, studying him. “So, you’re not seeking reelection?”

His eyes stayed focused on the road ahead. “The island is at a tipping point—Nielsen gets his way or we put a stop to him, once and for all. Either of those outcomes removes the need for me to be mayor. I’ll never preside over the transformation of the island into a playground for wealthy snowbirds. And if we can stop him, it’s time for someone else to take over, hopefully continuing what I’ve started.”

“And you think the outcome will be determined before November?”

“Most likely. But that doesn’t matter. I still won’t seek reelection.”

“Why not?”

“I want to focus on you and me. We need to make up for lost time, more than two decades’ worth.”

Caitlin became quiet. *Is he worrying about the Boston results? That I might not have much time left?* She stared ahead. A car approached, heading in the opposite direction. It made her think of the return trip from Boston, wondering if their homecoming would be a happy one.

PART II

Chapter 11

Five months had passed since the initial visit to the Albright Medical Center in Boston. Jake stood at the south end of Horseshoe Basin, watching as Billy prepared for another day of netting mullet.

The temperature gauge on the wall of Hawkers Fish Company registered eighty-five degrees Fahrenheit, on its way to the mid-nineties, typical for mid-July. High tide hid the barnacles on pilings. The commercial boats pulled tightly against dock lines, their decks wet with morning dew. The strong aroma of Cuban coffee accented the stifling humidity. Sweat glistened on faces and forearms.

"Thanks for heading out again," said Jake. "Festival attendance will be much larger this year."

Billy finished arranging his cast nets and reached for the ignition switch on the steering console. "Eight hours left. Ain't no more after today."

"Good for you. I'll notify the judge's office."

The outboard motor fired up. Billy revved the engine. A cloud of gray smoke spewed from the exhaust, lingering in the calm air. He untied the dock lines and backed the skiff away, spinning the bow toward Munson Bay.

Jake hollered above the engine noise. "Let's go netting soon. Like old times."

Billy responded by jamming the throttle forward. The skiff jumped to a level plane, skimming across the shallow flat in the middle of the basin, a route that could only be taken at the top of the tide.

Jake watched as Billy veered southeast, wishing the resentment would end. *At least he's quit fuming about Dirty Dick.*

The deep-throated resonance of diesel engines replaced the sound of Billy's motor. The shrimper fleet rounded Eletz Point, returning from a night of trawling in the gulf. The laden boats slowed as they approached the docks, hulls riding low in the water. The Saturday seafood festival held claim to the shrimp in their holds.

Jake glanced at his watch. The teleconference with Fred Thompson was scheduled for 10:30 a.m., three hours away. His thoughts shifted to the movie production, wondering if the daily filming activities were already underway at the marine lab. Several days had passed since he last checked on the progress. *Best to head there next.*

****

Caitlin was still at the cabin, preparing for another half day of work. She spread a dab of steroid cream along the scar lines on her left breast, wiping away the excess. The painful sensations were more pronounced this morning, a reason to pause and take a deep breath. They had a medical name: *post-mastectomy pain syndrome*. Her oncologist said the damaged nerve tissue might need excision to remove the discomfort. The thought of more surgery caused her to grimace.

She faced the bathroom mirror, straightening to full height, her lower back slightly arched, turning from side to side. The skill of the elderly surgeon was remarkable; the reddish-pink scar lines were the only notable difference between left and right. Fortunately, the diagnostic findings had supported a partial mastectomy, enabling preservation of the areola and nipple.

She replaced the support bra and leaned toward the mirror, studying the closely cropped hair. The patchiness had all but disappeared. *Time to let it grow.*

Dark circles showed below bloodshot eyes. The application of eyedrops reduced the redness. Makeup offset the haunting look.

Medications rounded out the morning routine. Four pills, followed by self-injection of Jake's drug. Her cancer had proven responsive to it, unsurprising given the drug's broad success. *Nonetheless, if it wasn't for his decades of absence ....* She squeezed an area of skin on the abdomen, injecting the pinkish solution using a preloaded cartridge.

A baseball cap completed the day's ensemble, matching her khaki shorts. The empty cartridge was deposited in a biohazard container. She tidied the bathroom before heading to the kitchen.

A small orange light glowed on the coffeemaker. The aroma was finally appealing, a welcome change after months of morning nausea. Extra cream helped reduce the coffee's acidity. The first sip proved successful.

A copy of the *Gazette* lay on the kitchen table, resting alongside Jake's empty cup. The cover photo caught her attention. Jake and actor Karl Svenson flanked Anna Nyholm, both men of comparable height. Nyholm seemed delighted by the moment, her mouth wide with laughter, an arm around the waist of the grinning Svenson. Jake stood apart from the duo, arms dangling down, showing a polite smile.

Caitlin set the paper aside. The multiple surgeries and months of radiation and chemotherapy had left her drained, physically and emotionally, sapping her self-confidence and libido. Nyholm stood in defining contrast, a younger woman of unblemished beauty and vibrant sensuality.

Jake continually reassured her that his interactions with Nyholm were all business. Caitlin hated making him worry, wishing she could snap her fingers and return to her former, confident self, knowing she could trust Jake completely. He had wanted to resign immediately when the breast cancer was confirmed. *But I insisted otherwise, placing him in that photo.*

She turned away, grabbing the coffee cup and exiting through the back porch and across the tree-covered yard, heading for the bench at the end of the cabin dock. Shafts of morning sunlight illuminated the colorful assortment of tropical underbrush, mostly bougainvillea, hibiscus, and firebush. A royal poinciana tree dominated the overhanging canopy, its reddish crown on full display. Dew dripped from the leaves and dangling Spanish moss.

Ahead, *Cloud Catcher* rose up and down in a gentle, undulating motion. The restored yacht was secured on the bay side of the cabin dock; its bow pointed toward the mainland. Jake had placed heavy mooring anchors to the starboard side, enabling him to pull the yacht away from the dock, keeping the port rail from rubbing against the pilings.

Caitlin walked along the dock. Yellowish streaks on *Cloud Catcher*'s stern caused her to pause. *Jake needs to clean those; I can't do it.* The sunset cruise the previous evening had proven too much, the gulf swells more than she could handle, becoming seasick soon after leaving the calmer water of Passage Channel.

What remained of the coffee she tossed in the outgoing tide, its taste no longer appealing. A deep inhale ensued, followed by a long sigh. She retraced her steps, forgoing time on the bench, heading back to the cabin and departing for work.

****

Jake's drive from the basin to the marine lab had been troubling. Survey stakes had been erected at varying intervals along the three miles of Nielsen's property, a stark reminder of the impending threat. He crossed his fingers, hoping the federal judge would rule in favor of the preliminary injunction. The decision was expected soon.

A uniformed guard stepped from a check station at the lab gate. Jake held out a security pass as he approached.

"Ain't no need for that, Mayor. Just making sure it's you." The guard pointed behind Jake's car. "Can't trust them assholes."

The rearview mirror showed a line of cars and vans parked along both shoulders of Gulf Drive. Paparazzi stood outside their vehicles talking, cameras within reach.

Jake refocused on the guard. "Any more trouble?"

"Yeah. One of the stupid shits waded into the mangroves, trying to get to the actor yachts. Skeeters nailed his ass … bad. Started screaming bloody murder. Actor's bodyguards caught him, letting the skeeters have at him 'til police arrived. Ain't gonna try that no more. No-sir-ee."

Jake chuckled, hooking a thumb rearward. "They'll be broiling soon enough. It's headed into the mid-nineties today—heat index will be near a hundred. Where should I park?"

"Usual spot."

"Got it, thanks." Jake studied the nearby palm trees. The fronds were motionless. *Bay water should be calm, a good morning for filming.*

He drove through the gate, tires crunching on the oyster shell driveway. A helicopter was ahead to the right, sitting motionless in the field next to the harbor. A production team worked close by, organizing videography equipment. The sight caused Jake to recall the previous day. Aerial filming had lasted for most of it, targeting the drawbridge and shack replicas at the far end of the fishing pier. The back-and-forth noise became more and more annoying as the day wore on.

Three luxury yachts could be seen ahead, two of them tied stern-to-stern along the south side of the lab harbor. The smallest of the three sat beyond the others, near the harbor entrance to the bay—Nyholm's personal quarters.

Draven Barlowe and Kurt Svenson were visible on the afterdeck of the first yacht, a steward serving them breakfast. The stern of the sibling yacht was empty. Jake wondered if Eileen McRaith was still on location. The Irish actress was an excellent match for Caitlin's character.

Development of the romantic subplot had triggered questions from Kurt Jones right when Caitlin was least able to tolerate the interactions. She had managed through it, relying on extra doses of anti-nausea medicine. Jones had come away enamored, saying she's one tough woman. High praise considering the congenital hip disability that he had endured since birth.

The rest of the production staff and secondary actors occupied the dormitories and small cabins on the opposite side of the property. Spaces in other buildings had been coopted for wardrobe, makeup, equipment storage, and props of various shapes and sizes.

A long hydraulic arm extended above the harbor fuel dock. It had replaced the lifting crane on the back of *HML Explorer-2*, one of the lab's primary vessels. The top of the hydraulic arm hosted a remote-controlled video camera. A support team was busy on the vessel's wide afterdeck. One person spoke into a handheld transceiver that sported a footlong whip antenna.

Jake continued scanning the surroundings, driving slowly toward the front office parking spot, noting that Caitlin had yet to arrive. People and equipment were in motion in every direction. A security patrol boat headed out of the harbor and into the bay.

He parked and exited the car, attempting to reach the dining hall. The bustling activity kept disrupting his progress, becoming more challenging the closer he came to the destination. He diverted to the chickee to observe the action.

Dirty Dick could be seen in the hut as Jake approached, his silhouette backlit by the bay waters. The paunchy cook sat on one of the benches that ringed the perimeter, hunched forward, elbows on knees, spindly legs tucked underneath. One hand grasped an open beer can; the other held a lit cigarette. Dingo lay close by, tethered by a leash to one of the chickee poles, a concession to numerous complaints. Dingo jumped up, yapping loudly. “Shut up.” Dirty Dick cuffed the top of Dingo’s head, causing the dog to whimper and lie down.

Dirty Dick glanced up as Jake entered the hut. “Well, if it isn’t the leader extraordinaire of Hollywood Island. To what do I owe the honor of his eminence?”

Jake ignored him, turning toward the dining hall. Nyholm could be seen in the shade of the back porch, perched atop a raised director’s chair, Jones seated alongside. She was pointing toward one of the video monitors arrayed in front. Stevansky stood behind her. Others hovered nearby.

The adjacent scene was impressive. A full-size replica of Simon’s shack had been constructed next to the dining hall, sitting atop temporary pilings anchored into the shallow bay bottom. A wide gangplank connected the shack platform to the seawall, providing easy access for the actors, camera crews, and stacked rows of multimedia cabling. Large video cameras stood on tripods, aimed into the shack interior through its open windows.

Jake kept half an eye on Dingo. The dog’s libidinous reputation had become the subject of humorous anecdotes at Harry’s Tavern, elevating the terrier to exalted status among the commercial fishermen. He turned to Dirty Dick. “Do you live at the lab?”

The cigarette pointed in the direction of the harbor; the

response punctuated by exhaled smoke. “On one of the sailboats.”

“You’re a sailor?” Jake asked, incredulous.

“Hell no. I only sleep in it, which isn’t so easy now, not with all the thumping and humping on *SS Loveboat*.”

Jake assumed he was referring to the yacht that housed Svenson and Barlowe. “Thumping and humping?”

“Whatever they call music nowadays, the thumping part. Humping is humping.”

Jake shrugged. *Not too surprising for movie stars, I guess.* He hoped they didn’t wreck interiors like rock stars.

Dirty Dick pointed the cigarette toward the dining hall. “Most nights I sleep on a cot in the kitchen storeroom. Hell of a lot quieter in there.”

Jake studied the bay. Private boats could be seen in the distance, anchored along a large semicircle of warning buoys. Occupants stood with telephoto lenses and binoculars pointed toward the dining hall. Two security boats patrolled inside the perimeter.

Dingo jumped up barking, causing more head-cuffing.

Caitlin approached, speaking first to Jake. “I wondered where you went. Melissa said you were here. Hello, Dick.”

He raised the beer in acknowledgment.

Jake turned to him. “Thanks for staying clear of Billy. He seems to have moved past the feud.”

“Don’t be fooled. He hasn’t changed.”

“Hopefully you’re wrong. Meanwhile, keep your distance. Don’t rile him up again.”

“Yes, your eminence.”

Jake took Caitlin by the hand, moving out of earshot from the hut. “How are you feeling this morning? Your color looks better.”

“Early sunlight helps … plus some makeup.”

“Any nausea?”

"I managed to drink a little coffee. Extra cream helped."

"That's progress. How's the stamina so far?"

"Okay. I need to stick with the half-days, if that's what you're asking. The afternoon naps are a must."

"I'm glad Ida hired you two assistants. Not sure how you'd keep all this straight."

"They're a godsend." Caitlin glanced in the direction of the dining hall, releasing Jake's hand. "Are you headed back to City Hall?"

"It's a slow start this morning. My first meeting isn't until ten thirty."

"So, you'll be talking to Anna?" Caitlin's voice sounded flat.

"Briefly. It's been a few days since I checked in. Come over there with me." He attempted to take her hand again, but she moved apart.

"I wouldn't want to spoil the fun." She turned, heading toward the front office.

Jake caught up, touching her shoulder.

She stopped, avoiding his look. "I don't know why I said that."

"Don't be hard on yourself. It's the side effects of the medications. They're known to cause mood swings."

"I know, I know … but I hate acting that way, adding to your concerns. You don't deserve it."

"I tell you what, there's no need to check on the filming. They seem to be doing fine. How about we take a walk on the beach?"

"In the rising heat? I'd be puking in no time."

"Well … at least let me walk you back to the front office."

"I'll be fine. Go check on the action."

Jake studied her. She stuck her face toward him, chin jutting out, eyes insisting he'd better do it.

****

The studio guard gestured toward the back of the dining hall, allowing Jake to pass. Nyholm waved him over, shooing Krista from the seat to her left. Jones sat to Nyholm's right, Stevansky behind. All wore headphones.

"Come join us," Nyholm encouraged. "We're reviewing some cuts from yesterday. You can listen in." She handed him Krista's headphones.

Jake took the proffered seat, securing the headset.

"Replay the last one," Nyholm instructed. She and Jones held three-ring binders on their laps, opened to a page of the movie script.

A nearby technician restarted the current segment of interest. Jake stared at the monitor. The camera angle showed the inside of the shack, focused on Barlowe and Svenson. The men were seated opposite each other at a small kitchen table. Barlowe smoked a cigarette. *Remarkable how they can age him.*

A glass tumbler rested on the table alongside a bottle of Ancient Age. A pile of lychee peelings occupied the center. Jake assumed the tumbler was filled with iced tea. But then again, maybe not.

The dialogue came through clearly.

Svenson (Jake): "The medal. Is it pinned to the uniform in your footlocker?"

Barlowe (Simon): "No … it's on the bottom of the channel." He pointed toward the rear of the shack.

Svenson: "What? Why? You should be extremely proud. Such courage under fire."

Barlowe: "I realize it's confusing. The Distinguished Flying Cross is most often awarded for courage while killing. And killing always shifts karma in the wrong direction."

Svenson: "But you were fighting an occupying enemy."

"Stop," said Nyholm abruptly. "Kurt, let's switch to … 'a

brutal enemy.' It aligns with herding the villagers onto the bridge."

A commotion broke out to the left. A small entourage had come around the corner, Karl Svenson in the middle, towering well above the others.

He announced his presence in a booming voice, "Morning, everybody."

Nyholm removed the headset. "Karl, you are a sweetheart for coming over this early. I need to show you a few segments we want to rework. Is Draven close behind?"

"He'll be here in a bit. Another bad headache."

"Not surprising. What time did you guys get to sleep?"

Svenson ignored her question. "I told him it's better to start early. Hotter than hell inside that thing." He pointed at the shack replica. "Damn sauna on steroids. The Bahama fan is worthless. Only stirs the heat."

"I understand, but active sweating makes the scene more realistic, especially with the related gestures."

Svenson grimaced, turning his attention to Jake. "Hey, is it okay to swim off the back of our yacht? Or do their relatives come in the harbor?" He pointed toward the shark pond, shifting his palm vertical, gesturing like a fin cutting through the water.

"It's fine," Jake replied, having removed the headphones. "You might encounter a couple of manatees, but they're gentle creatures. Getting chewed on by a boat propeller is your biggest risk."

Nyholm tapped Jake's shoulder. "Do you mind letting Karl sit there?"

Jake stood and handed the headset to Svenson, relieved to escape quickly. "Looks like everything is in full swing. Give a holler if something requires my attention."

****

The 10:30 a.m. call with Fred Thompson had started thirty minutes late. Jake remained standing, leaning against the wall of his office, listening to the attorney's voice on the speakerphone. Ida Hoefler and Judith Kerner sat at the corner conference table, along with Miriam Wilson. Sandra sat apart, taking notes.

"Hold a second," said Thompson. A voice could be heard in the background. He returned to the teleconference. "We just learned that Judge Trestor will issue the ruling tomorrow."

"What's our odds?" asked Wilson.

"At best a toss-up. The state study contradicts the academic findings."

Kerner leaned toward the speakerphone, spitting out words of frustration. "The state study is total bullshit. They only sampled two months of limited data. The university research lasted more than a year and captured a much more robust dataset for modeling the predictions."

"I emphasized that to the judge."

"So, why the toss-up?" Kerner asked.

"The matter involves more than science. There are complications of late."

"I assume you're referring to our wonderful US senator?" Hoefler asked sarcastically.

"Afraid so," acknowledged Thompson. "Unsurprisingly, Hoxman just announced a committee hearing on federal court interference in state-level matters."

Jake surmised the maneuver underway. "The state study is nothing but optics, offering Trestor a convenient excuse to deny our request."

Thompson concurred, adding a related insight. "Trestor's on the shortlist for the next US Supreme Court nomination. He can't get there without Hoxman's endorsement."

"Why does it always come to this!" Kerner exclaimed.

"Money and politics … and the deceptive use of sham science."

"Calm down, Judith," Hoefler admonished. "We can't be naive, especially when it involves Florida real estate and billions of dollars."

Jake grimaced, thinking of the recent visit to the island by the state's civil engineers. They had arrived unannounced to survey the pier and its connection to Gulf Drive. *They clearly expect a favorable ruling.*

Hoefler queried Thompson, "What about an urgent appeal? Assuming Trestor rules against us, which sounds likely."

"The federal appellate docket is overflowing. I highly doubt they would consider this an urgent matter."

Silence ensued. Jake stared at the fishing pier. The memorial showcase had been temporarily repositioned to the back lawn of City Hall. The movie helicopter hovered on the bay side of the pier about fifty feet above the water, a cameraman harnessed to a side platform, filming in the direction of the replicated drawbridge and shack.

Jake had monitored the surveying activities of the state engineers. From what he could determine, they intend to bring the new bridge on the same path as the old one, requiring the removal of the pier. *If that happens sooner than later, it will halt the filming.* He made a mental note to speak with Nyholm. *We need Satorri's direct involvement.*

****

Jake followed Hoefler and Kerner out of his office. They departed for the lab, despondent. He headed to the tavern for lunch.

The patrons quieted as he entered, an odd occurrence. He scanned the room. Many averted their eyes. No one waved or acknowledged his presence. *Strange. Wonder what's up?*

Jake caught the attention of the hostess, pointing toward the bar. She gave a thumbs-up. He took the first available stool.

Harry entered from the rear deck, coming down the back of the bar. He grabbed a manila envelope lying alongside the cash register, placing it in front of Jake, keeping a hand on it. "This shit was on a table. Best open it at your office—I'll get your lunch over." He glanced above Jake's head, looking toward the dining area. "It ain't good, man. Everybody seen 'em."

"Seen what?"

"Photos of you with the Nyholm woman … and some other fancy chicks. Like I said, it ain't good. People are pretty upset. Thinking you might be cheating on Caitlin. And with her hurting so much and all. It just ain't right."

Jake turned around. Many of the tavern patrons stared back, a near-universal look of disdain on their faces. He swung back to Harry. "This is utter bullshit. I'd never do anything to hurt Caitlin." He ignored Harry's suggestion and opened the packet. Greasy fingerprints covered the photos. Most of the images showed him with Nyholm, captured in suggestive moments. The others were of women from his time in Boston, years ago. A surge of anger boiled up. *Who planted these?*

Jake jumped off the stool, turning to face the room, holding the photos aloft as he spoke. "It's not what you think. Someone's trying to make me look bad."

Someone shouted, "What about her sitting on your desk?"

Others murmured in support of the challenge.

"Those are Karl Svenson's legs in the photo, not mine."

Dismissive guffaws sounded from the tables. Many looked away in apparent disgust, heads shaking.

Jake felt a sudden panic, realizing the island would be consumed with the juicy gossip. The last thing he wanted was for Caitlin to experience more distress. *I need to explain the photos before she hears from someone else.*

He exited, hurrying to his car in front of City Hall. Caitlin had turned onto Eletz Point Lane minutes before, heading home after the half day of work.

****

The cabin interior felt hot and humid. Caitlin removed the ball cap, going from room to room, pulling the chains on the Bahama fans to the highest speed. An attic fan sucked outside air through open windows and out the roof vents. They eschewed air conditioning, preferring the fans and shade of overhanging trees to moderate the inside temperature.

She went to the bedroom and undressed, allowing the fan-driven air to sweep across her skin. A faded cotton muumuu hung from a wooden peg on the wall. She slipped it on and glanced at the queen bed. It was unmade, the top sheet thrown back from each side toward the middle. The symmetry caused her to pause, thinking of how long it had been since the bed coverings lay in chaotic disarray … *far too long*.

Jake had been more than understanding, knowledgeable of chemotherapy and its after-effects, telling her it was the reason for her loss of libido and not to worry, that it would come back in due time.

Caitlin paused, attempting to recapture the missing desire, imagining him coming home early, removing the muumuu, and taking her to bed. Usually, the thought would have brought arousal. Instead, it made her feel tired and drained, wanting only to nap. *How long can Jake wait before …*

She pushed the thought aside and went into the kitchen for a glass of ice water. Jake's car pulled into view, visible through the kitchen window, surprising her. He got out quickly and walked toward the side door, a large manila envelope in hand.

****

The stack of photos occupied a low table in front of their couch. The topmost commanded Caitlin's attention. She leaned forward, staring at an image of Jake wearing a tuxedo, his head lowered to one side. A duo of beautiful women flanked him, his arm around one of them. The other had a delicate hand on his shoulder, her lips close to his ear, almost touching, whispering or delivering a kiss. Both wore provocative, deeply V-cut evening gowns. A caption proclaimed, "Boston's Most Eligible Bachelor." The copyright belonged to a high-society publication.

She glanced over. Jake sat in his reading chair watching intently, a slight grimace evident. She took a deep breath and slowly exhaled, returning to the stack and exposing the next photo, another from the same publication. Jake stood on an outside balcony with a different young woman, both her arms around his waist. Behind them were rows of large sailing yachts. His hair was slicked back, beard neatly trimmed. He wore a chic black T-shirt and dress blue jeans. The woman wore a revealing, one-piece bathing suit. Her breeze-swept, honey-blonde hair presented the look of a model at a photo shoot. Jake beamed with delight.

Caitlin recalled their previous discussions about his Boston past. She knew he had been transported overnight into the world of ultra-wealth, eventually becoming disgusted, not only with what he encountered but also with himself. *These women are flings from the past. The only thing that matters is that he walked away and came home to me.*

She flipped to the next photo. Her hand went up, covering her mouth. The telephoto image was taken from outside City Hall at dusk, exposing a portion of Jake's lighted office, visible through a side window. The view showed Nyholm sitting on his desk wearing a lightweight shift, her legs uncrossed. Jake's legs were visible in the bottom left of the image, the rest of him obscured. Nyholm's outstretched arms disappeared behind the window frame, clearly reaching for him.

Roiling emotions welled up, a volatile mix of jealousy and anger. Caitlin's breathing became rapid and shallow.

"Those are Karl Svenson's legs," Jake explained. "I'm hidden to the right, seated at my conference table. They were play-acting, Svenson as a mobster mayor and Nyholm his moll. They can confirm what I'm saying."

Caitlin began to calm down. "Why were they at your office so late?"

"Nyholm wanted Svenson to see the inside of town hall, in preparation for filming the public meeting. They stopped by my office afterward. He asked me to verbalize my comments from that night using the movie script. They brought a bottle of wine and finished it quickly, which led to the impromptu mobster scene."

Caitlin had continued to view the remaining photos, another eight images or so. She bit at her lower lip, working to maintain composure. Each showed Nyholm seated alongside Jake at a tavern table, leaning close and touching him, giving the appearance of something more than a business relationship.

"The other photos were taken when Nyholm first visited the island," Jake said. "Back in February. There was a paparazzo at the bar with a camera. I've tried to stay clear of her flirtations ever since."

Jake left the reading chair and came alongside Caitlin on the couch, attempting to place an arm around her.

She fended off the attempt, shifting apart and turning, studying him closely. His eyes showed concern and worry. He started to speak, but she held up a hand, silencing him. "Why would someone leave these in the middle of the tavern?"

"Clearly to discredit me. The photos make me look like a heedless prick, considering what you've been through. Whoever did this must have understood the impact it would have within our small-town community. I'm sorry it's happened. The last thing I want is to cause you added stress."

"Do you think Nielsen would do this?"

"He has the most to gain. Finding those Boston photos took

some research. He likely had someone dig into my past."

"Do you think he knows about my medical situation? How this might impact me?"

"Almost everyone on the island knows what you've been through. It may have reached him."

"But how did he get the paparazzo photos?"

Jake hesitated before responding. "I don't have a good explanation. Unless it wasn't a paparazzo after all."

They sat in silence.

Having to deal with the island rumor mill became an overwhelming thought. Caitlin felt exhausted. "I need to take a nap," she announced, standing.

Jake stood as well, attempting another embrace.

She fended again, heading toward the bedroom. "I need some space."

****

A luxury yacht lay anchored near Egmont Key on the western edge of Tampa Bay. Late afternoon sunlight shimmered across the water. A powerboat approached the stern, coming alongside the fantail.

Kevin's voice followed three quick taps on the stateroom door. "Your guest has arrived."

Nielsen reclined on the stateroom bed, catching his breath. "Out in a moment." He attempted to rise.

The weekend flight attendant put a hand around his neck, trying to pull him down.

He gently released her grasp. "This shouldn't take long." He grabbed an index card from the nightstand and stood, donning a silk bathrobe before heading topside.

A gray-haired man with narrow shoulders sat at a varnished table on the raised afterdeck, facing astern. The boat that brought him drifted behind the fantail; its bowline tied to a stern cleat. A young man stood behind the center console.

Kevin maintained a discreet distance, leaning against the aft bulkhead, keeping an eye on the visitors.

Nielsen took a seat opposite Hoxman's longtime associate and bagman. A satellite phone waited on the table. "You're a half hour early."

The man pointed toward the east, keeping his eyes on Nielsen.

Nielsen turned. A line of dark thunderstorms was approaching the large bay; lightning flashed across the upper reaches; thunder rumbled in the distance.

"Got it," said Nielsen, turning back. "Let's get this over with." He reached for the phone, expecting the man to provide an account number for the offshore transfer.

"There's a matter we must discuss first."

Nielsen pulled his hand back, eyes narrowing.

"The senator has learned you're trying to purchase the marine lab property on Marcosta Island. He assumes it will be used for some kind of yacht club, tied to your development plan."

"And why is that of interest?"

"The US Fish and Wildlife Agency has jurisdiction over the daily traffic limit of harbored boats with direct access to the south half of Munson Bay, which is part of the Ten Thousand Islands National Wildlife Refuge. The current limit is well below what you would require."

"Ah, so let me guess. The senator could influence the raising of that limit."

The man made a small smile, more of a smirk. "Senator Hoxman sits on the Senate appropriations subcommittee that funds the agency. I wish he was interested in your yacht club, but he's not."

"Get on with it. How much?"

"Twice what you offered for the Trestor ruling."

Nielsen laughed. “You’ve got to be kidding.”

“Not in the least.”

Nielsen grabbed the phone, removing the index card from his pocket, the number for a Mauritius banker written across it. “Let’s complete the current transaction. As we agreed, fifty percent now, the remainder to be transferred once Judge Trestor dismisses the lawsuit.” He gestured for the man to pass over the destination account number, waggling an index finger.

“What about the boat traffic?”

“I’ll think about it. In the meantime, there’s something your boss should understand.”

“Such as?”

“Many of my wealthy friends are looking forward to joining the Marcosta Island Yacht Club. Most of them have been sizable donors to the senator’s campaigns. Perhaps they should know of his lack of interest in their future enjoyment.”

Chapter 12

Jake turned onto Gulf Drive from the cabin road, coffee and donuts the current focus. A yawn spread across his face, the result of a fitful night's sleep. He had risen early and decided to skip breakfast at the cabin, leaving before Caitlin awakened, giving her more time and space.

He parked in front of City Hall and went over to Spud Nut. Voices muted as he entered. He took a seat at the counter. Freshly prepared donuts floated on the surfaces of the deep-fat fryers, bubbling at their edges.

Ms. Appleton appeared behind the counter, tearing off a sheet of wax paper and placing it in front of him, her voice flat. "How many?"

No pleasantries? He eyed her cautiously. "How about three?"

She spun around and hooked a trio of donuts from the deep fat fryers, allowing excess oil to drip away before depositing them on the wax paper and heading to another customer.

No one came over to talk. Normally, two or three patrons would already be engaged in discussion about island issues. Jake scanned the tables. Heads turned away; eyes dropped. *The gossip network is alive and well. Descriptions of the photos must have spread like wildfire.*

He grabbed the nearest carafe and poured a cup of coffee. Next came the shakers filled with powdered sugar and cinnamon crystals. A heavy dusting coated the fresh donuts.

He ate in silence, experiencing unfamiliar self-pity. *This is what I get? Guilty before innocent? After everything I've done for the island?*

Most of the islanders knew about Caitlin's abusive first marriage and the challenges of her breast cancer. She was a native daughter who had never left, especially for a Yankee city like Boston. *Yep, I'm guilty before innocent.*

Ms. Appleton came back. "More?" Her terseness betrayed the prejudice.

Jake brushed away crumbs from his beard. "I'm done."

A counter ticket slapped in front of him. He put a five-dollar bill on it and exited, crossing to City Hall.

Sandra pulled into a parking spot alongside his, her car nicely polished.

Jake joined her on the walk to the main doors. "So, where in Ohio does he live?"

"Who?" she asked.

"Who? How about your sweet uncle?"

"Oh yeah … Columbus … close to Ohio State University." She pulled the main door open, heading briskly for the office suite.

Jake followed his customary route over the gator tail, wondering about the true source of the car money. He decided to call the county sheriff's office, knowing of their involvement in the regional drug task force. *Maybe she's on the DEA's radar from illicit activities up in Tampa, coming here to lay low.* If so, it wasn't smart to buy a new car using cash.

The day had barely begun, and Jake already felt drained. He

sat, elbows on the desktop, hands on head, staring down. Dents and pockmarks mottled the wood surface. *How many times have the other mayors sat like this, feeling maligned despite their best efforts?* He glanced at the bridge painting and dropped his hands. *Snap out of the funk.*

****

Nyholm's day started later but also on a bad note. She yanked off the headphones and traversed the gangplank, squinting in the bright sunshine, careful not to trip on the thick stack of multimedia wiring. She navigated around the camera operators, stopping just inside the shack doorway. Svenson and Barlowe were seated at the small kitchen table. A tumbler of iced tea sat in the center, faking whiskey, along with an ashcan filled with cigarette butts. Barlowe held a lit cigarette. Both men sweated profusely.

"Are you hungover again?" Nyholm asked, focused on Barlowe. "You keep wincing."

"No!" he exclaimed, clearly wincing when doing so. "This is my normal expression when sitting in a fucking sauna with bloodsucking mosquitos."

Nyholm sighed in frustration—*becoming a spoiled brat.* "Let's take an hour break and try again. You guys should hydrate. And use more bug repellent." She exited the gangplank. Staffers hurried across to the shack, water bottles and bug spray in hand.

Krista caught her attention, coming close and whispering. "We need to talk in private."

Nyholm looked around. People were scurrying about, securing equipment for the hour break. Svenson and Barlowe came across the gangplank, doting assistants in tow.

Nyholm pointed. "Let's head to the chickee. I need to get away from this."

They walked past the shark pond. Nyholm glanced at a larger one swimming past. A cylindrical orange tag protruded from the base of its dorsal fin. She couldn't help thinking that many in Hollywood should be tagged like that—always circling, waiting to strike at the first sign of weakness.

They sat on a bench under the shade of the thatched roof.

Nyholm noticed a muscular, red-headed guy about fifty yards away, wading the shallows near an anchored skiff. He rotated, heaving a spinning circular net across the water's surface. She turned to Krista. "What's up?"

"Unkind rumors about you are circulating the island."

"Unkind? In what way?"

"A packet of photos was discovered on a table at Harry's Tavern. Apparently, the images show you in suggestive moments with Mayor Crawford." Krista looked at her with apparent suspicion.

"Suggestive? I haven't done anything inappropriate with him."

"It's how the photos are being described. I haven't seen them."

Nyholm refocused on the red-headed guy, watching as he emptied a net full of fish into the back of the boat. *Working hard out there*. She considered the scene. *The netting activity might be an interesting cutaway, adding to the local color of the island.*

"Well, whatever," said Nyholm. "If anything, it was only brief touching. You know my expressive style. The photos they captured can't be much. Crawford has kept a noticeable distance ever since we first visited the island."

Krista continued the look of concern.

"Why's this bothering you so much?" challenged Nyholm.

"Locals are saying your behavior is heartless, a slap in the face to Caitlin … because of everything she's been dealing with, the mastectomy and chemotherapy, the loss of her hair."

Nyholm stared at Krista, temporarily speechless.

Krista looked away.

"My God, Krista, I had no intention of causing Caitlin distress." Nyholm got angry. "Was it a paparazzo that took those photos? And left the packet in the tavern? We need to find out who did it. I'll skewer the bastard."

"It doesn't sound like paparazzi. The packet also contained photos of Mayor Crawford with other women, during his days in Boston. He's the main target of the backlash. The locals are really upset at him. The culture here is old-fashioned, nothing like Hollywood."

Nyholm watched as the red-headed guy boarded the skiff and departed, heading across the bay toward the other side. She reflected on the motive for the packet at the tavern. Someone had clearly done it to impugn Crawford's reputation, maybe realizing it would be amplified by Caitlin's medical status. *And my expressive behavior helped make it possible.* She chastised herself, deciding to deal with it head-on. "Is Caitlin at the lab today?"

"I saw her about an hour ago … when I picked up your mail."

****

Caitlin stifled a yawn, hands over her mouth. The awkward phone calls from friends had left her drained. *I need to get out of here and take a nap.* Knowledge of the photos had also circulated the lab, first made evident by Hoefler stopping by to express her concern and support. Others had come through soon afterward, doing the same. Caitlin had defended Jake repeatedly, exhausting herself in the process.

She contacted Melissa and arranged to have the front office covered earlier than usual. She started collecting personal effects, taking a moment to look at the picture of Tommy. A kissed fingertip touched the glass cover.

The office door opened. Caitlin spoke over her shoulder, zipping the purse shut. “That was fast.”

No response was forthcoming. Caitlin turned, expecting Melissa.

Anna Nyholm stared down at her. “I’m sorry if I startled you. Do you have a few minutes?”

Caitlin looked away, fiddling with the zipper and strap. “Melissa should be here any moment. I’m heading home.”

“I don’t need her help. It’s about you.”

Melissa came through the doorway. She stopped, looking back and forth at Caitlin and Nyholm. “Oh … I didn’t … I should come back.”

“No,” said Caitlin. “You stay. I’m leaving.” Caitlin grabbed the purse, pushing past Nyholm and Melissa, heading out the front door toward her car.

Nyholm followed. “Caitlin, wait. I just heard about the photos. I meant no harm. It’s only my expressive style. I’m truly sorry it’s caused a problem.”

Caitlin turned and faced her. “Did Jake ask you to talk with me? If he did, it’s totally unnecessary.”

“He did not. Krista told me about the photos and the awful gossip that is circulating.”

Caitlin stared intently at Nyholm. “I’ve known and loved Jake since I was a little girl and trust him completely. We have a lasting bond that will never be broken, not by you or anyone else. What makes me upset is someone trying to discredit him in front of our hometown community. He doesn’t deserve it.”

Nyholm reacted with a surprised look.

Caitlin opened the driver’s door, throwing her purse onto the passenger seat.

“Caitlin, wait.” Nyholm came closer. “What you just said about Jake … the long, trusting bond you have. It’s truly special.” Nyholm’s voice grew softer. “It’s something I …” she stumbled, unable to finish, looking away.

It was Caitlin's turn to be surprised, never expecting Nyholm to exhibit vulnerability.

Nyholm turned back, her eyes expressing an inner pain. "My apologies. This moment is not about me."

Caitlin studied her, instincts guiding the response. "I'm sorry about what happened between you and John Clanders."

Nyholm's lips came tight, the pained expression deepening. She nodded slightly.

"Maybe we should go somewhere to talk, away from the lab." Caitlin's tone had softened, shifting to kindness. "I know a remote spot along the beachfront, about a mile from here."

"You were headed home."

"It can wait. This is more important."

Nyholm looked toward the lab's entrance. A gated barrier prevented observation of the movie activities. "I doubt we'll get past the paparazzi without them noticing me."

"They ignore my car. You can curl up on the back seat. I'll cover you with a blanket I keep in the trunk."

Nyholm surveyed the surrounding area, identifying a nearby staffer and gesturing him over, speaking as he approached. "Jimbo, head down to the set and let Merv know that we're done filming the interior scenes for the day. He can keep going on the aerial filming. Tell Draven I said to catch up on sleep."

The staffer acknowledged, hustling toward the dining hall.

Caitlin smiled, opening the rear passenger door. "I'll grab the blanket."

****

Jake reflected on the attitude of the Spud Nut patrons earlier that morning. He wondered if the gossip had made it to the marine lab, worrying about what Caitlin would encounter.

Sandra came into his office. "Here's the affidavit attesting to Billy's completion of community service." She handed it over.

Jake scribbled his signature to the right of the red sticker, yawning widely.

"Can I get you a refill?"

"I've had enough coffee, thanks."

"Okay. I'm concerned about the seafood festival. My voicemail is full of requests for info—from all over the state. People have heard the movie stars may be attending."

"How the hell did it get out? It was highly confidential."

"I don't know. It wasn't me."

The direct line rang on his desk phone. "It's my call with Fred Thompson. We'll finish the discussion about the festival later." He waved her out and punched the button.

"Jake here."

"Mayor Crawford, this is Mr. Thompson's office. Please hold while I connect you."

Thompson came on the line. "Hello, Jake. Unfortunately, it's been a difficult day for us."

Jake braced himself for what came next.

"I won't sugarcoat it. Judge Trestor granted the State's motion to dismiss the lawsuit … with prejudice. As expected, he cited the conflicting research studies along with the need to avoid federal interference in a state matter."

Jake shook his head, grimacing, feeling trapped with no way out.

"As I said before, an emergency appeal would almost surely be denied. The regular appeals process will take a minimum of two years, given their docket."

"Does this mean the State can overrule our referendum at any time?"

"I'm afraid that's correct," said Thompson.

"It's over then. State engineers have already been surveying the island entryway for the new bridge."

"I'm sorry the lawsuit didn't work out. Senator Hoxman wields too much clout, both nationally and around the state."

Jake went silent. Seconds ticked by. He stared at the pier through the window. Barlowe's body double and a small boy fished near the shack. The movie helicopter hovered at a distance, a harnessed cameraman standing on a sideboard, filming the action. *Hopefully, Satorri can delay the State action.*

Thompson interrupted the thought. "I'll await your decision on whether to file an emergency appeal. If we do, anticipate a quick denial."

"Forget the appeal. There's no hope with Hoxman against us."

****

A mango tree graced the front yard of the cabin. Caitlin balanced on the top of a short stepladder, stretching upward with her right hand. She pulled hard. The stem broke free, almost causing her to lose balance. She descended the ladder. The fresh picking joined three siblings in a wicker basket.

The sound of crunching shells announced Jake's arrival from work. He parked and walked over, glancing at the colorful harvest. "Ripened to perfection. Need some help?"

"You can grab the ladder." She lifted the basket and walked toward the cabin.

Jake fell in step alongside, ladder in hand. "How was it at the lab today?"

"You mean regarding the photos? It was uncomfortable. Everyone knows about them."

"Same for downtown. I almost got tarred and feathered in Spud Nut." He diverted to the toolshed to store the ladder.

Caitlin continued to the kitchen. She rinsed the mangos and placed them on a wooden cutting board.

He walked in, retrieving a beer from the fridge.

"What happened to you in Spud Nut is unfair," said Caitlin. "People need to realize it was all Anna, not you."

Jake looked relieved. “As long as you believe me. That’s all that matters.”

“I would believe you regardless, but Anna sought me out, confirming what you told me, including what happened in your office … her playacting with Karl Svenson.”

“I didn’t ask her to say anything.”

“I know.”

He took a swig of beer and set it on the counter. “Well, that’s good to hear. Someone yelled ‘cheater’ when I left City Hall to drive home. It came from the direction of the tavern parking lot.”

“What? Why such hostility? The photos aren’t that bad.”

“Except in the context of your medical challenges … and what you experienced in your first marriage.” His eyes mirrored the tone of frustration.

Caitlin went to him, wrapping her arms around his waist and holding him tightly, the side of her face against his chest. “They’re so terribly wrong about you.”

She held him a few moments longer, then released him and stood back. “Anna and I are going to put a halt to the stupid gossip.”

“What are you talking about?”

“You’ll see. We have a plan.” Caitlin smiled. “And I learned something today. What you and I have is even more special than I thought. I mean, I’ve always known it, but Anna reminded me how fortunate I am.”

“This is a twist I could not have imagined.”

“We spent most of the afternoon talking, sitting on a dune near the beachfront. I feel for her. All the pressure—having to live up to the Hollywood stereotype of being beautiful and exciting. Deep inside she’s a regular person, wanting a loving partner who will stick by her side through thick and thin, growing old together.”

“Well, how about that? So, what’s the plan you’ve cooked up?”

"Nothing less than being seen in public together, getting along fabulously."

"And where would that be? The tavern? It would cause chaos with the paparazzi. Harry would go berserk."

"Have you forgotten what's happening on Saturday?"

Jake tapped his forehead. "Ah, the festival."

"No better place or moment. Most of the island will be there."

"Along with a thousand others." He drained the first beer and went to the refrigerator, retrieving a second one.

Caitlin studied him. "What does that mean?"

"He took a long swig, wiping his beard with the back of a hand. "The secret got out about the actors attending. We are besieged with requests for festival information … from all over the state."

"Who divulged it?"

"I'm not sure. Sandra denies doing it." He drained the rest of the beer. "Chief Wilkinson and I met late today. He's not happy. We'll be adding more security, but I still wouldn't agree to his full request. We're already well over budget."

"The ferries can only transport a limited number of visitors," said Caitlin. "Hopefully that will reduce their numbers."

"We've learned that many are planning to arrive in private boats, from as far away as Tampa and the Florida Keys."

Caitlin shook her head in dismay. "You certainly don't need another challenge."

Jake grabbed a third beer and sat at the kitchen table. "There's much worse news. The federal judge dismissed our lawsuit with prejudice. The State is unleashed, free to overrule our referendum whenever they want."

She placed a hand on his shoulder before taking the opposite seat. "You've tried so hard to stop it."

He gave a tired look. "They're not wasting time. The State's project manager called me late this afternoon. We're set to meet in the morning."

"So, there's no hope?"

"At best a potential delaying action. The construction activity would interfere with the remainder of filming on the north end. Satorri has agreed to intervene personally. He'll be contacting the governor to request a delay."

"But the delay wouldn't last long," said Caitlin. "Anna told me they only have a month of filming left, at the most."

Jake stood, grabbing the beer. "I need to check a couple of things on *Cloud Catcher*. I might take her into the bay tonight and drift under the stars for a while." He studied her. "You up for joining me? The bay water should be calm."

Caitlin didn't hesitate. "I'd love to. I'll throw a quick dinner together and take my evening meds."

****

Caitlin released the slack line from the bow cleat and threw it on the cabin dock. *Cloud Catcher* drifted away, caught in the flow of an incoming tide. She watched as Jake reversed one throttle while pushing the other forward. The bow swung from west to east, the twin propellors working in opposition. He brought the throttles together, motoring *Cloud Catcher* into the darkness of Munson Bay, barely above idle speed. Flanking red and green running lights cast their hues to port and starboard, coloring the left and right gunnels. A white stern light illuminated the afterdeck. The bay waters remained calm. A three-quarters moon rose slowly above the mangroves on the far shoreline. Lights from other vessels were nowhere to be seen. *We have the bay to ourselves.*

Caitlin navigated the port gunnel to the afterdeck, going up the steps and joining Jake at the captain's console, coming inside his outstretched arm. She put both of hers around his waist, enjoying the peacefulness of the moment. The synchronized engines resonated with a deep humming sound. She hugged him tightly, imagining their overdue honeymoon trip, the two of them cruising the Bahamas.

After a while, Jake pulled the throttles back and shut off the engines. *Cloud Catcher* drifted quietly in the middle of the bay. He took her hand, leading them to the bow. They reclined on the foredeck, their backs against the slope of the cabin top. The moon rose higher.

"We should do this more often," she said.

"I was thinking the same thing."

She turned her head, looking toward Eletz Point. Several dim lights designated their cabin dock. "It feels like we are far away. Now I understand why you had that fancy fishing yacht up in Boston, needing to escape."

"It kept me sane amidst the challenges. But I could still see the broad light pollution above Boston on clear nights, even when fishing on Georges Bank."

"How far at sea was that?"

"About seventy miles."

"And all we have is the small nighttime glow from Naples." She felt him tense.

His words explained the reaction. "Marcosta will be glowing in a few years, thanks to Nielsen. We shouldn't stay to witness it."

What does that mean? She raised on her forearms. "Where would we go? This is our home."

Jake remained silent. Only the sound of tiny waves could be heard, lapping gently against the hull.

She eased back as the minutes passed, awaiting his answer, finally forthcoming.

"I want to find an island that can never be threatened by overpopulation."

"Where? In the Bahamas?"

"More specifically, the southern Bahamas."

"Have you been there before?"

"No, but I've studied maps and read a few articles in yachting publications. We should check out Crooked Island on our honeymoon. It looks the most promising."

"After the November election?"

"Or sooner."

Caitlin sat up fully, wishing she could see his eyes clearly. "Are you thinking of resigning?"

Again a long pause before Jake responded. "It was naive to think I could stop Nielsen. The loss of old Florida is inevitable. There's an endless supply of snowbirds wanting to live down here. I won't preside over the demise of our culture and the trampling of this native beauty."

"It's not like you to give up."

"It's not? I gave up my research career."

"But that was different."

"Maybe in specifics, but the underlying motivation is the same."

"The disillusionment with misguided wealth?"

"Yes."

"Who would you support as mayor?"

"The way things stand, no one will want my support. But since you ask, it would be Delores. She's most aligned with my thinking … except, of course, for the filming on the island. Becoming the interim mayor could help her win in November."

"How soon would you resign?"

"We'll see. It depends on how things play out in the days and weeks ahead."

Chapter 13

Seagulls worked the early morning tide in Passage Channel, swooping to snatch baitfish schooling just below the surface. Jake watched the timeless dynamic, standing on the seawall behind City Hall. He recalled seeing similar schools the previous night in Munson Bay, rippling patches on the moonlit water.

The State project manager stood alongside, discussing plans for the bridge entrance onto Gulf Drive. "We'll keep the transport dock in operation until the new bridge is completed. But that forces us to take down the fishing pier to connect with the roadway embankment."

"Why not place the entrance on the east side of the transport dock?"

The project manager confirmed what Jake had anticipated. "It would require us to assert eminent domain on several private residences, which would cause a significant delay … unless the homeowners agreed without a legal fight."

One of the cottages belonged to Ray Garrett. *He'd battle the State to the last of his money*. Jake came to grips with the State's plan; the transport dock had to stay in operation until the bridge was completed. "What is the estimated timing for removal of the pier?"

The project manager pointed. "The current runs strong in that channel. We can't work until the tide slackens enough, which limits us to a couple of hours or so, twice a day during daylight hours. It will take a good two months to tear it down and remove all the submerged pilings. It's why we're starting the pier demolition from the outset."

Jake recalled when the State had removed the leftover pilings from the old bridge fire. It had taken them several months for the same reason. He glanced toward City Hall, checking his watch. "Hank Tucker and Miriam Wilson are probably waiting on us. Hank heads our municipal works department. He'll be your primary contact. Miriam is our city attorney."

The project manager walked to Simon's memorial and studied the photos. "So, this is the fighter pilot bridgetender?" It was more a statement than a question.

"Yes," Jake replied flatly. "You'll be removing what remains of the bridge he loved. Keep that in mind as you demolish it."

"I'm just following orders."

"As did Simon … it haunted him for the rest of his life. Karma."

"What the hell are you talking about?"

"Never mind. Anything else you need to tell me?"

"Nothing I can think of."

"Okay then. Come inside. I'll introduce you to Hank and Miriam."

****

Jake finished the impromptu meeting, exiting the police station. Nearby activity grabbed his attention. Volunteers were hard at work erecting canopied booths in the town hall parking lot. He walked over to check on the progress, reflecting on the tense discussion with Chief Wilkinson. Last-minute plans were being finalized for festival security. The county sheriff agreed that off-duty deputies could moonlight for extra pay. Chief Wilkinson would also be deputizing some of the residents to patrol the island's perimeter in their private boats. They wouldn't carry firearms, only police-band radios. If they saw a problem, they were to notify the dispatcher of the location and situation, keeping an eye on the alleged perpetrators but not intervening.

The projected number of visitors kept growing. *Hopefully, the festival stays civil.* Jake had considered banning the sale of alcoholic beverages but decided against it. *I'm already in the doghouse; no sense adding to the backlash.*

Ray Garrett came from the direction of the Hawkers Fish Company booth, an angry look on his face.

Jake shifted his route, pretending not to notice.

"Now you hold up, dammit," hollered Garrett.

Jake stopped and faced him.

"What's them state assholes doing round my cottage, pointing at this and that? They better not be thinking what I think they're thinking."

"They won't be touching your property."

"You sure 'bout that?"

"I spoke with the project manager this morning. They're bringing the new bridge on the same route as the pier."

Garrett looked stunned, his face screwing up, turning redder by the second. "What? The hell you say. They're knocking it down?"

"That's the plan."

"You're shitting me. How soon?"

"They'll start shortly after the State overrules our referendum, which is expected any day. I'm trying to delay the pier demolition, but that remains to be seen."

Garrett snorted in disgust. "They ain't gonna allow no fishing on the new bridge. 'Fraid we'll whack some fancy car with our sinker weights. Never shoulda sold the land." He shook his head, muttering as he walked away, shoulders sagging.

Jake headed to City Hall, ignoring the scowls along the way. Afternoon thunderstorms bore down on the island from the east, causing the festival volunteers to quicken their efforts. He wondered if Satorri had been able to reach the governor.

****

Nielsen's helicopter sat in an open field next to the practice range at his private golf course, thirty miles southeast of Tampa. Kevin reclined in an electric cart nearby, keeping an eye on the surrounding area as Nielsen hit practice shots. His aviator sunglasses reflected the afternoon sunlight.

A close replica of the famous St. Andrews clubhouse started at the end of the practice range and rambled across the back of the number-one tee box and eighteenth green. The rest of the golf course spanned the distance to the horizon, a Scottish "links" design, replete with undulating fairways, impenetrable rough, deeply cut sand bunkers, and enormous greens. Nielsen was the only member of the private club, owning 100 percent of the shares. Anyone who played there was an invited guest, part of an ultra-exclusive list that included favored politicians, celebrities, and business executives, along with a small group of touring professionals.

An older woman came out of the clubhouse, waving at Kevin.

He drove over in the cart.

"Mr. Satorri will be calling in fifteen minutes."

****

The dark elegance harkened to the 1800s in Scotland. Nielsen stood at the window of the second-floor study, awaiting the incoming call from Satorri. He watched with envy as a tour professional hit a low approach to the long eighteenth green. The ball landed well before the front apron and released forward, rolling over a low rise and coming to rest two feet from the cup.

The intercom came alive. “It’s Mr. Satorri, sir.”

“Put him through.”

Nielsen allowed five chimes to pass before lifting the handset. “Ah, the famous Adrien Satorri. Such an honor. I’m a big fan.”

“*Not* a reverse sentiment,” said Satorri.

Nielsen’s eyes narrowed. “Well now, that’s a bit harsh, don’t you think.”

“Actually, I was being nice. You’re the last person I care to speak with. Unfortunately, it’s become a necessity.”

“And why is that?”

“Your governor wouldn’t take my calls. I decided to bypass him and reach the guy who pulls his strings.”

“So, here we are,” said Nielsen, tacitly acknowledging the characterization. “Shall we get down to business? I assume you’re calling about the bridgetender movie.”

“My production team is three weeks from finishing the filming on Marcosta Island. I need you to stop the State from interfering until then.”

“That’s it?” Nielsen asked, genuinely surprised. “Three weeks?”

“Yes.”

“Works for me. Incidentally, I’m glad you got the script right. I always suspected the bridgetender committed suicide.”

“How the hell …” Satorri stopped the reaction. “Forget it, I’m sure you have informants everywhere. We made a creative choice, not a statement of belief. Otherwise, you’d be the obvious villain.”

“In which case I’d own a lovely villa north of Santa Barbara. It sounds like prime development land.”

“You are an exquisite bastard.”

"Very unoriginal for a such creative genius. I've heard the expression many times."

"I'm certain you have … and much worse."

Nielsen watched as the pro holed the short putt, standing on one foot while looking skyward, his caddie laughing. "Speaking of your creative talents, I'm curious: What if I hadn't agreed to the three-week delay? What was your next line of attack?"

"Let's see, how many press interviews can I do in a day? Six … eight … ten? In case you've forgotten, the bridgetender was a decorated war hero—somebody who protected your freedom to acquire billions of dollars. I'd make sure everyone in the world knew that you denied my request, choosing to dishonor his courage and sacrifice … simply to gain a few weeks of additional profits."

Nielsen took a moment to suppress the concern and form a worthy retort. "And you think that would matter? I'd point out how you've used the heroics of combat veterans to amass your wealth, hiding behind a veneer of patriotism. You could have used that wealth to support the veteran community. Instead, you built a luxurious villa and surrounded it with vineyards and four thousand acres of exquisite coastal land, all of it for your private enjoyment."

Satorri hung up.

Nielsen tapped the handset in a palm, reconsidering Satorri's request. He shrugged, punching the intercom button.

"Yes, Mr. Nielsen."

"Get me the governor's chief of staff. Call her mobile number."

****

The fishing action held Jake's attention, watching from his office window. A group of boys were on the pier, snitching shiners with bare hooks, immediately casting the snagged baitfish into the water below. Schooling Spanish mackerel struck swiftly, bending rods and stripping lines. The boys hollered with excitement. Two movie cameramen filmed the action, one from the helicopter and the other from the drawbridge replica. Jake had suggested the scene, recalling those special moments as a young boy.

Sandra entered. "I just received a call from Mr. Tucker."

"And?" Jake asked, turning from the window.

"He just received an update from the State project manager. The start of the new bridge construction has been delayed for three weeks."

"Okay. Thanks again for working late."

"No problem. I think all is set for tomorrow's festival—at least what's on my task list."

"Did Hank order the extra bank of portable toilets?"

"He said they'll arrive first thing in the morning."

"Good."

Sandra studied him. "You doing all right? Almost everyone's upset at you about those photos."

"They aren't what they seem."

"I heard the Boston women were beautiful … and that one was a swimsuit model. Was she in *Sports Illustrated?*"

Jake stared at her. "Those photos are none of your business, or anyone else's for that matter. They were taken well before Caitlin and I got back together."

"I just think it's kinda cool. I didn't realize you could be that way."

"I'm not, dammit. Listen, my life is not a *National Enquirer* story."

"Okay, okay. Sorry I said it." She turned and exited his office quickly.

He listened as she gathered her stuff and headed out. *I should terminate her employment once things calm down ... or maybe let the next mayor decide.* Jake went to the painting, thinking about an unpleasant discussion earlier that day. *The movie-*

making already had Delores upset … and now the damn photos.

Chapter 14

The seafood festival was underway in earnest. The crowd was larger than the uppermost estimate, at least three times higher than the previous summer. Jake surveyed the increasingly chaotic scene, standing apart from the main crowd.

Most of the festivalgoers were from elsewhere. An armada of private boats lay anchored on the bay side of the island. Enterprising commercial fishermen were making fast money, using their skiffs to taxi visitors to offloading points at Horseshoe Basin. Some of the visitors used small dinghies or kayaks to come ashore. Adventuresome others swam the distance, holding shirts and footwear overhead.

The star actors and Anna Nyholm could be seen in a canopied booth outfitted with interlocking metal barriers to protect them from the encircling groupies and paparazzi. They had tried to visit other booths but had to retreat. Studio bodyguards and local enforcement worked the booth perimeter, inside and out. A lab van was parked close by, prepared to remove the celebrities on short notice.

Karl Svenson and Eileen McRaith stayed busy signing

autographs, accepting and returning caps, shirts, and other items thrust at them across the barriers. Draven Barlowe sat at an interior table, finishing a platter of fried seafood; five empty beer bottles rested alongside. Anna and Caitlin stood nearby, gesturing and laughing. Jake watched Anna give Caitlin a brief hug, followed by simultaneous grins. Camera strobes flashed repeatedly.

Curly red hair caught his attention, brightly lit by the light of the impending sunset. Billy was navigating the crowd, heading toward the town hall. Jake wasted no time traversing an intersecting route. “I’m glad you came. Just remember, if Dirty Dick shows up, keep clear of him—at least a hundred feet away. I haven’t seen him.”

Billy grimaced, screwing up his face. The frustrated look shifted quickly to anger. “What the fuck? What’s that asshole doin’ here?” Billy was glaring in the direction of the movie booth.

Jake followed his line of sight. Eric Jenkins was moving through the crowd with two other men, neither of whom Jake recognized. Billy started in their direction.

Jake grabbed his arm. “Let it go. You can’t violate probation.”

Billy shrugged off Jake’s grasp. “You gonna stop him? He ain’t there for the movie folk. Fucker’s gonna throw shit at Caitlin.”

“That’s my worry now, not yours. I’ll deal with him.” Jake pointed toward the western sky. “It’ll be sundown soon. Don’t violate your curfew—and stay away from the booths serving alcohol.” He turned toward Caitlin and Nyholm. Jenkins and his buddies pushed closer.

****

“Hey, hey, slutty babe!” Eric Jenkins leaned across the barrier, only six feet away.

Caitlin recognized his voice, turning her head sharply.

A studio guard shifted position, pushing Jenkins backward. A local man shoved Jenkins from the side. He fought back, his two buddies joining the fray. A bystander fell against the barrier, hitting her shoulder. More people joined the fight. Whistles blew. Several deputies waded into the expanding melee, pushing the combatants apart.

Caitlin watched Jenkins slip away in the midst of the chaos, trailed by his buddies. She shook her head in frustration, lips tight.

"Who was that awful man? The one that yelled at you?" asked Anna.

"Nobody worth discussing."

The head of security for Satorri Productions came over, directing his comment at Nyholm. "That's it. We need to pull the plug." He jerked his thumb toward the van.

Anna turned to Caitlin, giving her a quick embrace and kiss on the cheek. "Sorry to scoot. I enjoyed the festivities. Quite a memorable scene." She hurried away, joining the actors. A phalanx of security guards shepherded them into the van. Paparazzi held cameras high in the air, strobes flashing. The swirling groupies moved away as the van departed, heading to other booths.

Jake entered the movie booth, separating two of the barriers. He put an arm around Caitlin. "You okay?"

"This is a madhouse. Did you see Eric Jenkins? And the men with him?"

"I watched them. They left the festival and headed down Heron Avenue. Did you recognize the two men?"

"I've never seen them before. Definitely not from the island."

Chief Wilkinson came through the parted barriers, trailed by Perkins. "It's gotten totally out of hand. Food and drinks have run out. The portable toilets are overflowing."

Perkins was visibly upset, pointing a finger in Jake's face. "I warned you." She spun around and stormed off.

The chief piled on, "And I warned about more security. It's going to be hell making all these people leave. The sooner we start, the better."

Jake scanned around. "Okay, I'll end the festival. Have someone get to the Naples passenger ferry. Instruct the captain to stay docked until the maximum load is aboard."

The chief departed, shaking his head.

Jake turned to Caitlin. "Find some friends to walk you home. Be sure to lock up, including the windows."

Caitlin watched as he hurried off, frustrated at the way Perkins and Chief Wilkinson treated him. She scanned the crowd for familiar faces.

****

Jake headed around the back of the town hall. Country R&B played loudly through outside and inside speakers. He entered the last exit door and went on the stage, motioning to the disc jockey.

The DJ took off his headphones as Jake approached.

"I need to make an announcement," Jake shouted, slicing a palm in front of his neck. "Stop the music."

The DJ acknowledged, turning a large knob and handing Jake a handheld microphone.

Jake took a deep breath. "I need everyone's attention. Attention please." He kept repeating the last phrase until the chatter had mostly quieted. "Thank you. I'm Mayor Crawford. You've been a fantastic crowd. Biggest we've ever had. Guess what, folks? You've cleaned us out of everything. The Gulf of Mexico is officially empty!"

Jake paused before continuing, hearing some laughter. "The

Naples ferry is at the transport dock, waiting to take a full load. For those who parked on the mainland side of the channel, there are flattop boats running back and forth from the island transport dock, located on the other side of the tavern. If you came in your own watercraft, please return to your vessel. Thank you so much for coming. Be safe going home. The 1997 Marcosta Seafood Festival is over!"

Hoots and catcalls swelled up from the crowd. Jake held up a hand. "Please stay orderly. All visitors should leave at the earliest opportunity. Please maintain orderly behavior. Thank you."

Some started to exit the hall. Jake glanced out the side windows. Part of the crowd headed toward the tavern. Others walked to the opposite side of Gulf Drive, in front of other downtown buildings. Most remained in place. One guy appeared at a town hall window, peering in and shooting Jake the middle finger.

What a shitshow. Jake left the stage, going out the opposite exit door from where he entered, navigating toward the front of City Hall. Chief Wilkinson came into view on the brick sidewalk, returning from Heron Avenue.

A couple of drunk visitors cussed at Jake as he walked by. He intercepted the chief. "All the officers and extra deputies need to stay downtown until the visitors are gone."

"No shit," replied the chief. "We just stopped a fight next to IGA. Two windows got smashed."

Fighting and vandalism had never happened at previous festivals. Jake shook his head in frustration, scanning the crowd's behavior. Most had drifted across Gulf Drive, milling outside the various buildings in the downtown area. Some of the locals had stayed behind to help with the cleanup. Others took protective positions in front of buildings, interspersed between police officers and sheriff deputies. Another fight broke out in front of Spud Nut, quickly spreading as locals rushed to help the officers and deputies. A small group of nonlocals came around the corner of Osprey Avenue, purposely starting another fight, causing Jake to wonder if gang members from Miami or Tampa had arrived within the deluge of outsiders, hellbent on causing trouble.

Chapter 15

A loud siren woke Jake from a brief sleep. He raised his head, glancing at the wall clock in his office. 12:50 a.m. *Dammit, more trouble?* He had tried multiple times to leave for the cabin, only to have another incident demand his attention, finally giving up and catnapping at his desk.

The siren kept wailing. He hurried out of City Hall, looking toward the volunteer fire station. The pumper and tanker pulled forward from their bays. Several pickup trucks raced into the station parking lot. Volunteers jumped out, joining the drivers in the cabs. The fire engines took off on Gulf Drive, red lights flashing, heading south around the curve by the Catholic church. A police cruiser shot past, coming from the east, most likely from Horseshoe Basin. Another pickup truck turned onto Gulf Drive from Osprey Avenue, trailing the cruiser.

Jake ran to his car, speeding off to catch the procession, tires squealing in protest as he rounded the curve. The flashing red and blue lights were already beyond Egret Avenue. *Shit. It's the marine lab.* He pressed the accelerator to the floor. *What more could go wrong?*

The aftermath of the festival had become a near riot, badly scarring the downtown area. Most of the windows along Gulf Drive were smashed. Numerous fights had broken out between locals and visitors. Harry had to clear the tavern, waving a shotgun to herd everyone outside, standing out front and firing overhead warning shots to ward off vandals.

Jake had endured a stream of invectives from all sides. Someone sucker-punched him in the back.

The arrival of additional county sheriff's deputies finally quelled the unruliness, but serious physical and psychological damage had been done to the island. The lack of a bridge made the situation much worse, delaying the arrival of needed reinforcements.

An orange glow filled the sky above the marine lab, visible a half mile away. *Did the vandals hit there too? Hopefully, everyone is safe.* The speedometer of the old Honda Accord reached ninety miles per hour, causing the steering wheel to shake.

****

Tall flames shot above the opposite side of the marine lab dining hall. A ship's bell clanged repeatedly. People were running, some with extinguishers in hand. Sirens wailed in the distance, coming closer.

Anna Nyholm stood on the hatchway steps of her yacht, her face illuminated by the fire.

A man called out from below, "What the hell is happening?"

She retreated down the steps, turning. Karl Svenson stood naked in the stateroom doorway.

"Our shack's on fire," she replied, her voice tense. She pushed past him, throwing off her bathrobe and grabbing some clothes. The sirens grew louder. She dressed quickly.

Svenson went to the hatchway and looked out. "Holy shit!"

“Holy shit is right.” She slapped him on the butt. “Up or down. I need to get over there.”

Svenson went to the foredeck.

She exited the gangplank, hollering back, “Find Merv. Maybe he can film something useful. Hurry up.”

****

Judith Kerner stood alongside Ida Hoefler, part of a growing crowd that had gathered near the shark pond. They watched as the raging inferno consumed the shack replica. Hoefler remained tight-lipped, eyebrows twitching in the fiery glow. Kerner recalled the fire and explosion that had destroyed the old wooden bridge and killed Simon. The burning replica was eerily reminiscent. *Thank God the dining hall is not on fire.*

Fire trucks arrived, the volunteer firemen moving in rapid coordination to contain the flames, their training evident.

Flashing blue lights soon joined the red ones. Chief Wilkinson pulled up in his cruiser, exiting quickly and hurrying toward the fire team. A red pickup truck arrived a short time later —the volunteer fire chief joined the action, taking charge. Flames diminished under the spray of the firehoses.

Kerner noticed a security guard talking to the chiefs, pointing toward the bay.

Nyholm came alongside. “What happened?”

“We’re not sure,” Kerner said. She gestured toward the chiefs. “The guard seems to know something.”

****

An old Honda Accord pulled in next to the police cruiser. Jake jumped out, hurrying toward the chiefs. He came close, in time to hear the security guard’s fateful words.

“… bushy red hair. Took off in one of those odd fishing skiffs. Outboard motor forward, near the bow.”

Jake's heart sank. *Billy, what have you done?* He noticed the bay water was higher than normal. A full moon cast its glow across the surface.

"You're certain he had red hair?" Wilkinson asked.

"Yes, sir. No mistaking it. Bright red in the light of the fire."

"And the skiff took off north? Up the edge of the bay?"

"That's right."

Wilkinson reached for a handheld radio on his belt. "Michael?"

Pearson's voice crackled in response. "Hey, Chief. I'm halfway to the lab."

"Turn around and head to Billy Watson's cottage. Arrest him for suspected arson. Be careful when you arrive. We have his guns, but he could still be armed."

"Roger that, Chief."

Wilkinson aimed the radio antenna toward the burning shack, querying Jake. "Any idea why Billy would do this?"

"I never heard him say something negative about the filming." Jake pointed skyward, his tone flat. "It's a full moon."

Wilkinson glanced upward, uttering a shared sentiment. "Damnedest thing."

Stevansky appeared to their left dressed only in boxer shorts, filming the fire scene with a portable movie camera. Svenson trailed him wearing a woman's bathrobe. They moved toward the firemen on the hoses.

"What the …?" exclaimed Wilkinson, waving them away. "Get the hell back, dammit!"

A fireman shouted, "Hey! Over here!" He stood on the seawall holding a large flashlight. The beam pointed at something glistening, bobbing among the smoldering ruins.

Jake followed Wilkinson and the fire chief. The beam illuminated a melted cocoon of monofilament netting. Two sets of charred fingers protruded through a section of the netting, contorted fingernails evident at the tips.

The radio came alive. "Chief, it's Pearson. Just arrived at Billy's. No lights on at the cottage."

Wilkinson responded, "Get Glenn as a backup. A burned body's been discovered wrapped in cast nets. It's probably the cook."

"You're shitting me. Hell, I shoulda checked on Billy tonight."

Wilkinson stared with frustration at Jake. "We were too damn busy. Confirm the skiff's at the dock. Let me know if it's missing."

"Roger. I'll get Glenn."

"People need to look for the cook," Wilkinson said, still focused on Jake. "Tell them not to disturb anything that looks suspicious." He pointed the antenna toward the charred fingers and netting. "But I bet that's him."

Jake shook off the shock, his voice subdued. "I'll get the search going." He went to the chickee, acknowledging Anna with a quick grimace before focusing on Hoefler and Kerner. "We need to find Dirty Dick. Can you get the staff searching for him?"

Hoefler's eyes went wide. "They think Richard caused the fire?"

"A burned body has been discovered in the debris. It might be him." Jake avoided mention of the melted nets and likely perpetrator.

"Oh, no!" Hoefler exclaimed, a horrified look on her face, tears forming.

"I'll get the staff looking for him," said Kerner, touching Hoefler on the shoulder.

"If anyone finds him, let Chief Wilkinson know," instructed Jake. "Tell the searchers not to disturb anything that looks suspicious. And be sure to check the kitchen storeroom."

Jake returned to the seawall. Wilkinson was on the radio, issuing instructions to the dispatcher. "Contact the sheriff's department. I need a homicide team at the Hixon Marine Lab. A body has been discovered. Burned and wrapped in melted monofilament netting … floating in shallow water next to the lab's dining hall."

"Sounds terrible," said the dispatcher.

"Confirm back with their ETA."

"Roger that, Chief."

Wilkinson turned to the fire chief. "Tell your men to avoid further disturbance of the area. I'll get some crime scene tape from my trunk." He stepped away from the seawall.

Jake followed him. They stopped after a short distance, standing face to face.

"I thought Billy was over it," said Jake. "I haven't heard him mention Dirty Dick for over a month."

The radio crackled to life. "Chief, it's Pearson. The skiff's at the dock. Just waiting for Glenn to arrive."

"Roger. Take note of Billy's condition. Anything that suggests he's been out tonight."

"Got something already. Only the bow was tied off. Billy left the skiff floating partway in the basin. The engine's still warm. There's an empty five-gallon gas can on board. No nets in the stern."

"Roger that," Wilkinson acknowledged. "Leave everything as you found it."

"Glenn just pulled up. We'll look for Billy."

The chief reminded him to be careful.

Jake hung his head, the enormity of the arson-murder grabbing hold.

Wilkinson became visibly angry. He started to say something but stopped, storming off in the direction of his cruiser. Judith Kerner intercepted him on the way.

****

Jake drove away from the lab, heading for the police station. The dashboard clock showed 3:45 a.m.

Pearson had confirmed the arrest. Billy came to the door wearing boxer undershorts, professing innocence and claiming to have been home all night. He appeared to have just awakened. Pearson was en route to the station when he had radioed the update. Loud cursing could be heard in the background.

Dingo had been discovered lying unconscious under an overturned cot in the kitchen storeroom, a nasty gash on his head. Ned Callahan had offered a grim assessment, noting the terrier's dilated pupils and erratic heartbeat. Dirty Dick was nowhere to be found.

Jake continued north on Gulf Drive, despondent. A space of open terrain exposed a view of the gulf beyond the dunes. A bright swath of moonlight cut across the expanse of water.

Throughout his scientific career, Jake had heard anecdotes about full moons and how those nights correlated with an increased number of births and acts of violence; almost every emergency department had its stories. *Billy clearly has a problem during full moons. But premeditated murder? Causing a life-threatening injury to a dog?* Jake couldn't fathom how his longtime friend would have gone that far. Remorse joined the despondency. *What if I had spent more time with him? Would I have seen the telltale clues of a mental disorder?*

Two sets of flashing blue lights approached. A car and van sped by. *The homicide investigation team.*

The drive north continued, Jake's emotions swirling. A twisted irony became apparent, the symmetry of another fiery death inside Simon's shack, albeit a replica. Jake's scientific objectivity wrestled against a growing belief in a negative karmic force. *Everything seems caught in a downward spiral, orbiting a dark center.*

He slowed at the Catholic church, navigating the curve. The gap between the Coquina Motel and the town hall enabled a view of the mainland shoreline, visible in the moonlight. A television news van could be seen under the lights of the mainland transport dock, a satellite dish on its roof. *They must have been monitoring the police channel.* Stories about the deadly arson would likely hit the morning news, combined with images and local interviews about the post-festival vandalism. The intersection with a Satorri movie would drag the news into the global spotlight, forever tarnishing the island's tranquil image. Jake shook his head. *Could the downward spiral get any worse?*

City Hall approached on the left. Jake couldn't bear to look at the vandalized buildings. Pearson stood outside the police station, speaking on his radio. Jake slowed, pulling into his reserved parking spot.

****

Jake followed Pearson into the police station. A group of agitated vandals stood in the cramped holding cell, awaiting transfer to the sheriff's department for processing. A deputy stood nearby, hollering at them to quiet down.

"Where's Billy?" Jake asked in a raised voice.

Pearson pointed toward the interrogation room.

Jake went to an inset window. Pearson followed. Billy sat at the table in his boxers, chin slumped against his chest, wrists shackled to the bolted rings anchored in the tabletop.

"Why not let him get dressed before coming here?"

"Chief said not to disturb anything at the cottage."

"Did you read him his rights?"

"Yeah. When we stuck him in the cruiser."

"Did he say anything?"

"Yelled about being innocent and cussing a blue streak."

Pearson pointed. “Finally shut up when we stuck him in there.”

Headlight beams shone through the front windows.

“Should be the chief,” Pearson noted, yawning widely.

Wilkinson entered. He bypassed Jake and Pearson without a word, glancing briefly at Billy.

Jake followed to the chief’s desk.

Wilkinson sat and removed his glasses, pulling out a handkerchief to clean the lenses. Bloodshot eyes looked up. “Billy’s always been a pain in the ass. But damn, never thought he’d kill somebody—least not like that. Christ, wrapping the guy in cast nets and burning him to death? Like some kinda Miami drug hit? Can’t believe it. I’ve known him since he was just a little fella.”

“I can’t believe it either,” said Jake. “If he did it, he must have some kind of psychiatric disorder. Maybe something organic, like a brain tumor.”

Wilkinson stared at Jake. “You already working some kind of insanity angle, being his close buddy and all?”

“It’s a real possibility. Billy’s not been himself for the past six months, maybe longer. I’ve seen what brain tumors can do to people. Some develop psychotic pathologies, like paranoia and increased aggression. There’s a wide spectrum of neurological disorders that can cause aberrant behaviors.”

The chief shook his head. “That’s a bunch of mumbo jumbo to me. All I know is what I saw and heard. Far as I can tell, he went down there, whacked the dog and probably the cook, then wrapped the cook in the cast nets, stuck him in that shack, poured a bunch of gas, and set it on fire. That takes real planning. It’s revenge, pure and simple; payback for the cut nets. That’s probably why he used them.”

“I know it looks damning. But it also makes no sense how it happened. If Billy did it, why make it obvious that he’s the killer? Good grief, using cast nets? Leaving the scene in his mullet skiff, visible in the light of the fire? He might as well sit on the seawall and wait to be arrested."

Wilkinson pursed his lips. "I hear ya. But maybe he wasn't thinking too smart. Like they say: dig two graves before seeking revenge." The chief yawned widely. "I need some shut-eye. A few hours from now, all hell is breaking loose. People seeing and hearing all the shit that's gone down."

"Who's leading the homicide investigation?"

"Detective Harper. You can tell him your thoughts about Billy being crazy. I need to focus on the vandalism."

Jake grimaced. Detective Harper had directed the investigation of Simon's death, leading to a tense encounter between the two of them in the very interrogation room where Billy now sat. "Harper and I don't get along too well."

Wilkinson replaced his glasses and shrugged. "Your problem, not mine."

"Have they confirmed it's the cook?" Jake asked, recalling the certainty of Wilkinson's comments.

"Yeah. Not all his face got burned off. The bay water saved part of it."

"Who identified him?"

"Ida Hoefler. She's pretty tore up."

Jake glanced toward the inset window. "Has Harry been told?"

"Ask Pearson. I just got here."

****

Caitlin awakened to the sound of the shower running. She rose on her forearms, glancing around, struggling to surface from a deep sleep. The nightstand clock showed 6:13 a.m. Jake's side of the bed was unused.

The previous evening came rushing into focus. She had left the festival right after it ended, heading home with a few neighbors, finishing the final distance alone. She had kept a close eye when passing the turnoff to Horseshoe Basin, concerned about Eric Jenkins and his buddies.

Why didn't Jake make it to bed? She jumped up, grabbing a lightweight bathrobe. The shower stopped as she exited the bedroom.

The bathroom door opened. Jake walked out, a towel around his waist, hair and beard still wet. His eyes expressed concern and lack of sleep.

"Were you up all night?" she asked. "Did things get worse?"

"Far more than you can imagine." He removed the towel and finished drying, continuing into the bedroom, Caitlin trailing behind.

"Are you going to tell me?"

He got dressed while describing the vandalism and the death of Dirty Dick, including Billy's arrest. The discussion carried them out of the bedroom and into the kitchen. He started fixing a pot of coffee.

Caitlin slumped in a chair. "Billy? A murderer? It can't be."

Jake finished loading the coffeepot, coming over and sitting opposite. "If Billy is the murderer, which appears likely, something must be wrong mentally. Look at the way the murder was committed. It's almost like he wanted to get caught, as if he couldn't help himself. I wish I had spent more time with him the past year. Maybe I could have prevented what happened."

"Don't be so hard on yourself. You thought Billy had let go of the revenge." She glanced at the fresh pot of coffee. "You're not getting some sleep? How will you manage?"

"I used to pull all-nighters during my research days, sometimes several in a row."

"And you were much younger."

He stood and fixed a cup, leaning against the counter as he drank the coffee. "I'm sorry that I didn't get home until this morning."

"I understand now. What can I do to help you?"

He finished the cup, placing it in the sink. "I realize it's Sunday, but maybe you should go down to the lab. Ida identified Dirty Dick's body. I'm sure she's distraught … and Anna has to be reeling from the loss of the shack replica."

"Poor Ida. She had strong affection for Dirty Dick."

"Were they a thing at one time?"

"Lovers? Unlikely. I've heard she's of a different orientation."

Jake checked his watch. "I need to scoot. They were notifying Harry about Billy when I left. I want to find out the latest."

"You can't leave without eating some breakfast, at least a bowl of cereal."

"I'll be okay." He gave her a quick kiss and hurried out.

Caitlin watched as his car drove away, disappearing past the hibiscus bushes and stand of bamboo. She fixed a cup of coffee and walked onto the back porch, looking toward the bay. *Cloud Catcher* rose and fell alongside the dock, riding the swells from a passing commercial boat.

The sight of the undulating yacht caused a realization, a recognition of what might lie ahead. She scanned the surroundings. *He loves this cabin and location. But is it enough to keep him here?*

****

Yellow tape blocked access to the back of the dining hall. Caitlin stood by the chickee hut along with others from the lab. They watched the grim process of removing Dirty Dick's body from the crime scene. The coroner's van departed with the remains.

A helicopter spooled at the opposite end of the property, the rotating blades gaining speed. Caitlin watched Anna hug Draven Barlowe. He climbed aboard. The copter lifted away, heading west over the beachfront before banking north. Nyholm walked toward the front office. Caitlin exited the group, waving to catch her attention. The two came together. Anna had a strained look.

"Is Karl leaving too," Caitlin asked, "and Eileen?"

"Maybe. We might try to film the town hall scene before they go." She pointed at the robotic camera on the boom above *HML Explorer 2*. "We were supposed to shoot close-in segments on the pier, but Draven demanded to leave."

Caitlin grimaced, shaking her head in dismay. "It's just as well, I drove through downtown this morning. Most of the buildings were vandalized, including the town hall. All the windows were smashed." She paused, looking down. "Local residents are blaming Jake for what's happened, believing he misled them about the benefits of having the filming here."

Nyholm grimaced as well. "It was a big mistake for the star actors to be at the festival. What surprises me is how the rumor got out so broadly. It was supposed to remain a secret until they showed up. Krista only informed Jake."

"Directly or through his assistant?"

"I'm not sure."

"Jake wouldn't have divulged it."

Anna circled back. "The town hall windows don't matter. Our set designers can replace them. But your comment about the locals … are you saying they won't participate as extras?"

"It would be difficult now. I've received calls from friends this morning. Islanders are irate about the festival vandalism. The anger will worsen when they learn about the murder."

"I recall the red-haired guy throwing a net, just the other day. Over there along the bay." Anna pointed north of the chickee hut.

"That was Billy. Jake and I have known him since we were little. We can't believe he would go this far, plotting to kill someone."

Anna looked toward the dining hall. "It's a serious setback for us. Three of our main camera systems were destroyed, along with a bunch of other equipment. Adrien wants me to pull the plug, so to speak."

Krista hurried toward them, raising her voice. "You need to call Adrien right away—something about an investor meeting this afternoon." She left after delivering the message, heading toward the dining hall.

Anna emitted a long sigh.

"I'm sorry about what's happened," said Caitlin.

"It's not your fault."

"I know, but I still feel bad."

"We'll get past it. The bulk of the island filming has been completed. The remainder can be accomplished using studio sets and CGI."

The two women stood quietly for a few moments.

"It must be hard for you, watching the backlash at Jake," said Anna.

"I hate it. He doesn't deserve the wrath, not after everything he's done for the island, working to protect our way of life."

Anna nodded, glancing toward the front office. "Can I use your phone to call Adrien?"

****

Nielsen strolled the widow's walk atop his Bahamian vacation house, enjoying a weekend change of scenery. A modest settlement occupied the opposite side of Staniel Key, a smaller island in the Exumas chain. Several large yachts were tied along a marina dock. At the island's center, the carcass of a dismembered DC3 cargo plane rested in a weedy field next to a modest airstrip, a reminder of the cocaine shipments that had frequented the island during the late seventies and early eighties. The metal carcass still served as a source of materials for locals. Nielsen's smaller jet was parked nearby.

He reached the eastern side of the widow's walk, looking downward at the clear water. A young woman swam laps near the shoreline, her shadow flowing in parallel across the sandy bottom. Kevin walked in sync along the water's edge, monitoring for sharks.

A loud beeping brought Nielsen to a nearby lounge table. He brought the satellite phone to his ear. "Yes."

"Diaz here. Ugly news out of Marcosta."

"What's that?"

"Looks like Billy Watson murdered the cook last night."

Nielsen stared toward the eastern horizon, eyes squinting against the brightness of the morning sun. "Where and how?"

"Down at the marine lab. He allegedly set fire to the replica of the bridgetender's shack. Firefighters discovered the cook's body floating in the charred debris, wrapped in cast nets. The monofilament line was melted into his remains."

"Ghastly. Was the movie set destroyed?"

"Apparently. The location is now a crime scene. I think the murder will spook the movie folks. The news is garnering national attention, given the Satorri connection."

"Has Watson been apprehended?"

"He's in an island holding cell, awaiting transfer to the county jail in Naples. First appearance before a judge is tomorrow."

"Any other news from Marcosta?"

"The summer seafood festival became a riot of sorts, causing damage to downtown buildings, mostly broken windows. There was a large invasion of movie groupies and other revelers. Many arrived by private boats."

"Unfortunate. Hopefully, no one was hurt."

"I didn't hear mention of injuries. The islanders are royally pissed. Much of the anger is directed at Crawford."

Splashing caught Nielsen's attention. Kevin had hurried into the water, grabbing the woman by the arm. A dark shape could be seen about twenty yards away, cutting a path to their location. The duo quickly exited the water as the shark came close. It circled in several tight loops before heading back to deeper water. The woman covered her mouth with both hands. *Good job, Kevin.*

Nielsen turned away from the scene, finishing the discussion with Diaz. “I wouldn’t want to be in Crawford’s shoes right now. Keep me updated.”

Chapter 16

Angry islanders congregated at the front of City Hall on Monday, the number growing as the morning wore on. Chief Wilkinson had positioned an officer to keep them from entering the building. Jake could hear the hollering from his office. The blinds on his office windows were closed, a rare occurrence.

Sandra hurried in, appearing distressed, eyes glistening.

Miriam Wilson got up from the conference table, putting an arm around her. "Goodness, honey, what happened?"

"Someone knocked Mayor Crawford's box lunch to the ground. They're shouting awful things." Sandra sniffled, placing Jake's favorite candy bar on the table. "I got this from the vending machine."

Jake glanced at Wilson, tipping his head toward the door.

"Here now, you come with me," Wilson said, directing Sandra out of the office.

Jake stared at the candy bar, imagining what Sandra had encountered, his frustration rising another notch.

Wilson came back, retaking her seat.

"Let's continue," said Jake. "You were about to explain the conflict of interest."

"Billy's alleged actions violate multiple city ordinances. You can't fund his legal fees. It would be in direct conflict with your duties and responsibilities as mayor."

"You look irritated."

"I know you and Billy are longtime friends, but I can't understand why you are defending his actions. What he did is horrible."

"The murder *is* horrible, but Billy remains innocent until proven guilty, including innocence by reason of insanity. He needs a thorough psychiatric examination plus a top defense attorney who has handled that type of pleading." Jake slid from the chair and stood. "Which is why I need to help him financially. He can't afford a lawyer, much less one of the best." He paced to the painting and back. "And there won't be a conflict of interest. I'm ready to resign, but not until I can vote on the interim mayor. I need you to make that happen."

Wilson stared at him, a look of disbelief on her face.

Jake waited, allowing her to consider his request.

"Are you certain?" Wilson asked.

"Completely. Do you understand what I'm requesting?"

"I think so. The council must elect one of its members to finish your term … but you don't want to resign until you can vote on your replacement."

"You understand it perfectly."

"It's irregular, but I can see a route."

"Which is?"

"I could write up a council action based on your *anticipated* resignation; something like, 'Should the current mayor resign within the next seven days, council hereby elects …."

"And I can vote on that council action?"

"I don't see why not."

"Good. One more question: does it need to be done in a

public forum?"

"What do you think?"

"Okay, but it will be a noisy meeting." Jake shifted to an official tone. "Please draft the proposed action and issue a public notice of the council meeting. Whatever is the shortest time allowed."

"The customary forty-eight hours. I need to provide the purpose."

"Describe it as you suggested. It's for the selection of an interim mayor to finish my term, should I choose to resign in the next seven days. Circulate the proposed action among the council members as soon as possible."

"And you're absolutely sure you want to do this?"

"Yes. The community needs healing, which will be delayed if I stay in office. Resigning also frees me to help Billy and spend much more time with Caitlin."

"What about fighting the State and Nielsen?"

"That's why I want to vote on my replacement."

Wilson nodded slowly. "So, you want Delores to be mayor."

Jake maintained a neutral expression.

"Or maybe Ed. Both are against the new bridge and Nielsen's plans." She expressed a corollary thought, more of a self-reminder. "There will need to be a special election to fill the vacant council seat, to occur within sixty days."

Jake glanced at the wall clock. "Ed set a meeting with me for three thirty this afternoon. Any idea what it's about?"

"I can only think of a thousand things."

"No kidding."

She stood. "I'll draft the proposed action and get the public notice issued." She departed the office, pulling the door closed.

Jake already felt the burden lifting. He shifted his thoughts to Billy. *I need to find the top defense attorney and push for a comprehensive psychiatric assessment.*

****

The three thirty meeting enabled Jake to disclose his intentions, disrupting Dickerson's whining about the vandalism and uproar among the Spud Nut regulars.

Dickerson reacted skeptically. "Really?"

"Yes. Delores is best suited for the job. We share a strong belief in protecting the island's heritage and natural environment."

"As do I," said Dickerson. "I did a solid job as deputy mayor while you were on those Boston trips with Caitlin … unless you've changed your opinion."

It was Jake's turn to express skepticism. "And you would fight the State and Nielsen as fiercely as Delores?"

"Most definitely."

Jake shrugged. "Frankly, I'm fine with either of you, but she's my preference."

"Delores can be hot-headed. It doesn't sit well with the other council members. Plus, the island has never had a woman mayor."

"That shouldn't matter one iota. Hanna Sawyer is mayor of Key West and doing an outstanding job."

"Yes, but that's Key West. Our cultures are entirely different. Marcosta is far more conservative."

"Have you forgotten Margaret Thatcher?"

"Delores is a flaming liberal, not a Margaret Thatcher."

"Well, make that your issue, not her gender." Jake pointed at the painting. "There's no question about her deep love for the island."

Dickerson softened a bit, speaking while looking at the painting. "She does have the longest legacy among the council members."

"Which is why she keeps getting reelected, despite the liberal orientation. Look, Delores is as tenacious as a pit bull, which is precisely what the island needs right now. Nielsen has pulled a fast one. She'll battle him tooth and nail, in many ways better than you or me. And besides, you can always run for mayor in November."

Dickerson stayed quiet for a while, lips pursed, finally yielding to Jake's request. "All right, I'll support her as interim mayor. I'm just sorry this is happening in the first place. I know you believed the movie would help us."

"It's my karma," said Jake. He yawned, eyes watering.

"What?"

"My fate. Delores was right about not filming the movie here."

Sandra stuck her head through the doorway. "Sorry to interrupt. Fred Thompson is on line one, returning your call."

"I'll be right with him."

Jake refocused on Dickerson. "Thanks for supporting Delores. The public meeting announcement will be posted on the outside bulletin board late this afternoon and in the *Gazette* tomorrow morning. Miriam will be sharing the proposed action with council members shortly."

Jake stood, shaking hands. He returned to the desk, punching the blinking button as Dickerson exited. "Fred?"

"Hey, Jake. Sorry I couldn't take your call earlier."

"I assume you've heard our bad news … about what happened at the festival and marine lab."

"Yes. Terrible … just terrible."

"It is. The prime murder suspect is Billy Watson, a lifelong friend. His first appearance is tomorrow, late morning. I need a referral to a top defense attorney in Miami, someone experienced with capital murder cases and pleading insanity. I'll fund personally whatever it takes to provide Billy the best representation."

Thompson didn't hesitate. "Esther Graham is who you want. Her office is on Biscayne Boulevard, a block from mine."

"What's her track record?"

"In which regard? Win-lose? Or reduced sentences?"

"Both," Jake replied. "I think Billy is suffering from a mental disorder."

"Esther is known for defending tough murder cases, including the pleading of not guilty by reason of insanity. She's got a superb record, not perfect, but far more successes than not."

"Okay then. What's the next step?"

"I'll contact her. Given the timing, you can expect a quick follow-up." Thompson paused momentarily. "But I have a concern regarding your funding of Watson's defense."

"You mean the conflict of interest, given I'm mayor?"

"So, you're aware."

"Miriam took me to the legal woodshed. It won't be an issue. I'll no longer be mayor in a few days."

"I see."

"The wheels are already in motion."

"And who will take your place?"

"Most likely Delores Perkins."

"Well … I'm sorry you've decided to resign."

"It's the right decision. Thanks for contacting Ms. Graham. Hopefully, she's available and willing to take the case."

"I'll ask her to call you today, if possible. Take care of yourself. And good luck with whatever is next."

Jake hung up, yawning again. He glanced at the wall clock, wondering how much longer he could remain upright and functioning.

Chapter 17

A foggy dawn enveloped the cabin, the surrounding bushes and trees appearing as ghostlike apparitions. Caitlin heard Jake stirring. She jumped off the couch and headed into the bedroom, wrapping her bathrobe tightly. She found him sitting up. "I thought you were dead when I got home. Do you remember me pulling your pants off?"

Jake glanced down at his work shirt. He fell back, resting his head on the pillow. "No. I only remember coming home for a nap. What time is it?"

"Approaching 6:30 a.m." She came over to the bed and sat next to him, holding one of his hands. "I heard it was rough at City Hall yesterday."

"Yeah. Has the *Gazette* arrived in the driveway?"

"I haven't checked. Are you expecting more news about Billy?"

"Yes, and other news." Jake swung his legs over the side of the bed, rubbing fingers briskly through his hair. "Billy got transferred to the county jail yesterday afternoon. His first appearance is later this morning."

“Are you going to attend?”

“No. It’s a brief session. Harry will be there, along with a defense attorney that I retained, assuming Billy agreed to her representation.”

“What’s the other news?” asked Caitlin.

“Notice of a public meeting tomorrow evening, regarding my impending resignation.” Jake explained the conflict of interest.

“Just as well,” said Caitlin. “I can’t stand how you’re being treated.”

“It goes with the territory.” Jake stood and removed the wrinkled shirt. “By the way, how’s Ida doing?”

“She’s holed up in her apartment at the lab.”

“I should visit her. What’s the status of the injured dog?”

“Dingo’s at a vet hospital in Naples. Alive but still unconscious. It doesn’t look good. He’ll probably be put down.”

“Billy would never hurt a dog.”

Caitlin held up an index finger, reminded of something. “Judith wants to discuss Billy’s full moon behavior. It has something to do with her graduate advisor.”

“I’ll find her after I visit Ida.”

Caitlin took him by the hand. “Come on, there’s a fresh pot of coffee waiting. I’ll toast some bread to get you started. You must be starving.”

Jake pulled away. “I need to use the bathroom.”

“I bet. Hopefully, you have some time before heading out. There’s something I want to discuss.”

****

Cloud Catcher rocked gently from side to side, the starboard mooring lines pulled tight by the outgoing tide. Caitlin stood with Jake on the dock, both dressed for work. Their breakfast discussion continued.

"I insist," said Caitlin. "Take the scouting trip. Find the best spots for our honeymoon cruise. Get away for a month. Hopefully, people will regain their senses by the time you return."

"I'm not leaving you behind."

"I called the oncology nurse. She said I shouldn't attempt a cruise for at least three months. I have plenty of friends who will keep an eye on me." Caitlin observed his expression as he studied *Cloud Catcher*, worry lines evident across his brow.

He turned to face her. "I need to ensure Billy's defense is handled properly."

"Didn't you just hire a top lawyer? And don't murder trials take a long time to get started? I doubt a one-month absence will matter. You can call from marinas to check on what's happening."

"I suppose."

She touched his arm. "Don't use Billy as an excuse not to go. If something serious comes up, you can always dock somewhere and fly back."

Jake returned to studying *Cloud Catcher*.

She imagined the things churning in his mind. *Come on, Jake, just let it all go. Take the long-needed break.* She placed both arms around his waist, looking up. "I know what you're like on the ocean, so much at peace. You've always been that way. It's the healthiest thing you could do right now."

"I'll get a satellite phone to stay in touch."

"Perfect. We can talk each evening. It will allow me to enjoy the cruise as you go along, hearing about the beautiful scenes—above and below the water. It will make me even more excited about our honeymoon."

His eyes stared into hers, searching.

She tilted her head slightly and placed a hand behind his neck, pulling him down for a long kiss before letting go.

He chuckled, the worry lines relaxing. "You should have

been in sales." He glanced at his watch. "Okay then. I've got a bunch of things to prepare before leaving, particularly with where I'll be headed." He started toward the cabin.

She grabbed him by the hand, slowing his progress and falling in step alongside. "There's something else I want to discuss. It's about Sandra. I wonder if she's connected to what's been happening. Did she know about the actors coming to the seafood festival?"

"Yes, but she claims it wasn't her that leaked it."

"How did it get out so broadly? Who else did you tell?

"Chief Wilkinson … and Miriam."

They continued across the back yard. Jake stopped before reaching the cabin, turning to face her. "I suppose it could have been Sandra. But I doubt she purposely caused the problem. You know she's starstruck. Maybe she told one of her friends from Tampa, too excited to keep it secret.

"Sandra came from Tampa?"

"I thought you knew that."

"You probably told me, but I forgot."

"She used to work for a law firm up there."

"And that doesn't worry you? If she told a friend at the firm, it could have reached Nielsen's ears."

Jake grimaced. "I guess that's possible too."

Caitlin let it go, having made her point, returning to the earlier discussion as they approached the porch steps. "You said something about where you'd go in the Bahamas. It sounded remote."

"It is."

"Are you going to tell me?"

"Part of me wants to keep it a surprise."

"What if something bad happens? Imagine the situation in reverse. Would you like being in the dark about my location?"

He paused, studying her, then shrugged. "Nothing bad is going to happen—but I take your point. I'm going to the Bight of the Acklins. It's an enormous bay, covering almost a thousand square miles of shallow flats and tidal cuts; Crooked Island frames its northern boundary. I'll get you a nautical map of the area before I embark."

"Wonderful. That way I can track your anchorages."

Jake glanced at his watch. "I'll check on Ida before dealing with City Hall." He gave Caitlin a quick kiss and headed up the porch steps.

She reminded him, "Remember to talk with Judith."

****

Morning sunlight glowed from behind the tall office windows, casting a shadow of Nielsen through the elegant glass desk. He looked up from the *Tampa Sentinel*. "This is the kind of news coverage I like to see." He held up the front page to Diaz, seated in front. The headline article continued the paper's sensational coverage of a grisly murder at Satorri's movie location.

Diaz reacted with an expression of concern. "The cook's murder?"

"Of course not. The side article about the movie pulling out." Nielsen tapped the lower-right of the page. "The State can get started on the bridge construction."

"Oh … yeah, great to see."

"And the murder is beyond terrible," Nielsen acknowledged reassuringly. "Watson should get the death penalty."

"Definitely," said Diaz, studying his notepad. "Speaking of which, I have an update about his legal defense, plus some important news about Crawford—you'll be pleased."

Nielsen replaced the paper on the desk. "What's the Crawford news?"

"He's resigning."

Nielsen pushed the paper aside, resting his hands on the desk, one palm atop the other. "Say again?"

"Crawford's resigning … on Thursday. The Marcosta City Council is meeting tomorrow evening to vote on his replacement."

"Is he being forced out?"

"Probably. Most of the island is pissed at him."

"Who's his likely replacement?"

"I would guess the Dickerson fellow. Delores Perkins is a possibility, but I doubt she would receive a majority vote … much too liberal."

"I remember her. Dead set against us. Dickerson isn't a whole lot better. Too bad it's not that corny ex-mayor. He's a blustering buffoon but harmless."

"There's the other thing I wanted to share. Esther Graham will be defending Watson. She's a prominent criminal defense attorney from Miami."

"Didn't she save that Palm Beach financier from the death penalty—the guy that drowned his elderly wife in a Jacuzzi? What was his name? Something Dutch. Van der Vorson?"

"Something like that. Maybe 'der Verdon.' Graham's expensive."

"Crawford likely hired her."

"My assumption as well. Watson's first appearance is later this morning," said Diaz.

"He'll need every bit of Graham's talents. Sounds like a conviction is all but assured. Gruesome way to kill somebody, particularly if the cook was wrapped alive in those nets—a recipe for the death penalty, in a manner of speaking. Anything more?"

"That's it for now."

"Keep me updated about Crawford's next moves. His resignation may be a smokescreen masking some kind of maneuver. I don't want to be blindsided." Nielsen reached for his mobile phone, waiting for Diaz to exit before hitting a speed dial number.

The governor's chief of staff answered immediately. "Hello, Derek."

"Did you see the news about Marcosta Island? The murder and the rioting at the festival?"

"I did. Looks awful."

"And the other news? About Satorri stopping the filming?"

"That as well."

"You can remove the construction delay."

"I figured."

"The current mayor of the island is resigning in two days. I need the bridge underway before his replacement can cause any trouble."

"I'll ask the governor to weigh in directly."

****

Jake found Judith Kerner behind the wet lab, reaching into a large holding tank with a hand net. They exchanged quick greetings.

"Have you seen Ida this morning?" Jake asked.

"No. She's probably in her apartment."

"Have you spoken with her recently?"

"Last night. She seemed better."

"Caitlin mentioned you have something to discuss about Billy's full moon behavior."

Kerner stepped away from the tank, replacing the net and grabbing a towel, drying her hands and arms. "I thought you might want to hear my advisor's theory."

Jake peered into the tank. Juvenile snook swam lazily—about twenty or thirty in total, each about ten inches long. All had pink bumps around the base of their fins. "What's with those lesions?"

"It's caused by an invasive insect from Brazil, during its larval stage." She pointed at a labeled bottle on a nearby table.

"We're testing a treatment."

"Is it working?"

"We dosed the tank yesterday. I should know within a few weeks."

Jake grabbed a nearby stool and took a seat.

Kerner provided context for her advisor's theory, leaning against the tank. "As you likely know, the term 'lunacy' is derived from a historical belief that lunar cycles can cause human madness, particularly on full moon nights.

"My advisor postulated a theory based on evolution. She's a comparative physiologist, specializing in the intertidal regions of marine ecosystems. Human predecessors evolved from the ocean, as evidenced by our close homology with the genes of certain marine species."

Jake leaned forward, intrigued by the genetic connection. "Go on."

"A full moon causes the highest of ocean tides, flooding the uppermost tidal pools, every thirty days. The females of some marine species use that opportunity to lay eggs in those pools. And the males fight each other for positioning to fertilize them. Once the highest tide recedes, those uppermost pools remain isolated until the next full moon, protecting the fertilized eggs and hatchlings from ocean predators. When the full moon tide returns, the maturing offspring escape into the ocean with a running start, increasing their chance of survival."

Jake grasped the evolutionary connection to humans. "The uppermost tidal pools function like a womb, providing a protective environment. And the thirty-day lunar cycle correlates with the average monthly ovulation cycle for women."

"That's correct. My advisor theorized that the human ovulation cycle is matched by a complementary hormonal cycle in males, perhaps with an outsized effect in a subset of the male population. It could explain why some men are more prone to violence on full moon nights."

Jake believed that many human behaviors could be explained by the influences of distant biological evolution, particularly those related to hormones. He reflected on Billy's situation. Lunar-driven aggressiveness may have been a male advantage eons ago in those uppermost tide pools, but it was definitely a disadvantage in human society.

Kerner continued, "Unfortunately, scientific studies have failed to prove a significant correlation between male violence and full moons."

"Are you aware of any full moon studies involving a subset of men with diagnosed psychiatric disorders?"

"I don't think those studies have been conducted."

"The theory is intriguing," acknowledged Jake. "Unfortunately, the lack of scientific proof prevents it from being used at Billy's trial. The prosecution would denounce your advisor's theory as pure speculation, hearsay."

"I assumed that would be a problem." Kerner gave Jake a kind look. "I thought you'd still like to hear her theory, given your close relationship with Billy. It might make it easier to reconcile his behavior."

"I appreciate it. The full moon connection has been baffling."

Kerner shifted topics. "There's something else I wanted to discuss. I read the *Gazette* announcement about your impending resignation. Are you considering a return to scientific research?"

"I haven't thought that far ahead. I'm taking it a step at a time."

"Well, keep us in mind. Marine organisms can get cancerous lesions. Maybe those tumor pathologies could shed light on new drug candidates for humans. We would be thrilled if you joined our team."

****

Caitlin exited the front office, having spotted Jake coming from the direction of Hoefler's apartment. She waited until he was within earshot. "Sandra just called. Detective Harper is willing to meet with you tomorrow morning."

"Good."

"I thought you and Detective Harper don't get along."

"We don't—I want to seed some thoughts. The county jail is co-located with the sheriff's department. We can prepare a box of goodies for Billy. I'll drop it off before seeing Harper."

"Should I include a card, expressing our love and concern?"

"It can't hurt."

"By the way, Sandra said it's a much smaller group outside City Hall this morning."

"I was expecting more of the same or worse."

"I certainly hope not. I called some friends this morning and gave them an earful."

A familiar voice shouted their names. They turned to see Nyholm approaching from the dining hall.

Caitlin waved in response. Jake lifted a hand in brief acknowledgment.

"Have they allowed your team to retrieve anything?" Caitlin asked as Nyholm walked up.

"The forensic team needs one more day. I'm learning what's involved in a true crime scene investigation. It's rather tedious and boring."

"Was the damaged equipment insured?" Jake asked.

"Yes, but the biggest cost is the time disruption, which isn't insurable—at least not for a reasonable price."

"Regrettable what happened," said Jake.

"Adrien demanded we stop all filming and pack up. I'll be heading to Los Angeles tomorrow morning; a cleanup crew will remain behind." Nyholm shifted topics. "I heard you're resigning. Is it because of what happened at the festival?"

"That's part of it."

"I should never have allowed the star actors to attend."

Jake shrugged. "Hindsight offers clarity, but it can also be deceptive."

Nyholm looked perplexed. "How's that?"

"The clarity makes us believe we could have done better, belying the unknowns that faced us at the time, including the potential for bad luck, which is inherently unpredictable."

"If that's the case, then why resign? You couldn't have foreseen what happened. The festival could have been a smashing success." Nyholm caught herself. "Sorry, poor word choice."

Jake shrugged again. "The deception of hindsight is rarely appreciated, and especially in the realm of politics."

Caitlin didn't want Jake to reconsider his resignation, returning to the movie discussion. "Do you plan to finish the island filming elsewhere?"

"Definitely," replied Nyholm. "We have enough footage to do the remaining island segments with blue screens and CGI. Then off to Thailand for filming the Burma segments."

"Can you still make Satorri's timing?" asked Jake. "Veterans Day '99?"

"I believe so. Speaking of which, both of you will receive invitations to the movie premiere. It typically occurs a week or two prior to the broad release."

"Will it premiere in Hollywood?" Caitlin asked excitedly.

"Possibly. Adrien prefers New York City, but he may offer me the choice as director."

"We look forward to attending, wherever it's held," said Jake. "I'm late for a meeting. Safe travels home."

Nyholm extended a handshake. "Our financial manager will be in touch to square accounts."

Caitlin observed their interaction, noting the businesslike

formality, a stark contrast to when Nyholm had first arrived on the island.

Anna watched him depart, then turned to Caitlin. “Is there anything I can do to help the situation? Jake seems demoralized, which is certainly understandable.”

“Thanks for offering. He just needs to resign and get away for a while. Hopefully, people will come to their senses by then.”

“And what about you? After everything you’ve been through.”

“I should be fine. The doctors seem pleased with my progress.”

“I’d like to stay in touch. Assuming that’s okay.”

Caitlin smiled. “I’d be delighted.”

“You have a standing invitation to visit me in Hollywood. I can show you around as my honored guest.”

“I’m doubly delighted. And you should come back to visit us. We can sit on my favorite dune and discuss what matters most in life.”

“I can think of nothing better.” Anna placed both hands on Caitlin’s shoulders, a kind look in her eyes. “You have taught me an invaluable lesson … in words and actions. Thank you.”

Caitlin leaned forward, giving her a hug.

“Shall we get back to our work?” said Anna.

They turned and walked up the driveway, parting at the front office.

Chapter 18

Jake leaned against the railing of the car ferry, bound for the county jail and the late-morning meeting with Detective Harper. Other stops would include a Naples flea market and a nearby dive shop. The round trip should take most of the day, allowing him time to consider the evening council meeting and his departing comments.

Pulsating reverberations could be heard above the noise of the ferry. A civilian helicopter zoomed past, heading north in the morning sunlight. He wondered what Nyholm was thinking as she departed, especially after experiencing the arson-murder. *Probably glad to put the island behind her.*

The ferry approached the mainland transport dock. Jake returned to his car and started the engine, idling in place until the ramp lowered. The goody box rested on the back seat—contents included an assortment of favorite candy bars and two mangos. Jake still wasn't allowed to talk with Billy, which was one of the topics he wanted to discuss with Harper.

The more important topic involved Billy's mental status. Esther Graham had called the previous afternoon, shortly after the first appearance. The circuit judge had cited the gruesome details of the murder before denying bail. Graham sought permission to seek an assessment of Billy's psychiatric status. The arraignment would be scheduled after the judge's decision on the request.

Jake's thoughts shifted to the flea market. A recommended gun dealer had a booth there, offering the defensive weapon of choice for cruising the Caribbean on a private yacht. The short barrel, pump-action shotgun was well-suited for fending off ill-intentioned boarders; its galvanized finish minimized corrosion from the saltwater spray and tropical humidity.

Spearfishing gear prompted the need for the dive shop visit —to purchase a set of Hawaiian slings and multiple spear shafts. The simplistic weapon was far less dangerous than modern pneumatic spearguns. Self-impalement was the last thing Jake needed while cruising alone in a remote location.

He had discussed the dive shop errand with Caitlin but not the flea market, reluctant to worry her. *And besides, the shotgun is only a precaution.*

****

Jake left the county jail, traversing the outside corridor to the adjoining sheriff's department. He entered the main door and approached the front counter, stepping aside to allow a handcuffed man and deputy to pass. The pungent odor of marijuana explained the man's bloodshot eyes.

"Jake Crawford. I'm here for a meeting with Detective Harper."

The attendant dialed an internal number, making contact. "He'll be right out."

A side door opened a short while later. Harper motioned Jake over. A roomful of desks and swirling activity were visible behind him.

They shook hands, forgoing pleasantries.

"Follow me." Harper navigated the bullpen toward a meeting room on the opposite side. Along the way, he grabbed a half-full coffee mug from a messy desk. "Can I get you some coffee?"

"I'll pass."

They entered the room. "Have a seat." Harper closed the door, sitting opposite Jake at the table.

"This feels familiar." Jake recalled the tense interview with Harper after the '94 bridge fire.

Harper wasted no time in acknowledgment. "I've heard you're funding Watson's defense."

"Is that a problem?"

The detective ignored the question. "Rumor has it you're pushing for an insanity defense."

"It's why I'm here. I've known Billy since I was a little kid. If he did the crime, he must have a psychiatric disorder, possibly something organic, like a tumor or serious neurotransmitter imbalance. You should keep that in mind during your investigation."

Harper gave him a skeptical look. "Does your scientific background also include expertise in psychiatry?"

"I've seen bizarre mental disorders many times in my scientific career, mostly stemming from brain tumors. Look, Billy's behavior doesn't add up. Why make the crime so obvious, using cast nets and leaving an empty five-gallon gas can in the skiff? It's irrational at a minimum and, most likely, insane."

"Or just plain stupid," countered Harper. "I recall your theory back in '94, about the car backing off the burning bridge with its headlights on. I'll tell you again what I said back then: You give way too much credit to criminals. Most are dimwits, not masterminds. You're accustomed to being around highly educated people, not the lowlifes I deal with."

This is going downhill fast. Jake shifted the discussion. "Why prevent me from visiting with Billy? His brother has seen him. I'm Billy's closest friend. You can't deny me visitation rights."

"We can under special circumstances. The state prosecutor agrees with me. We don't want you coaching Watson."

"To do what?"

"Act insane."

Jake laughed derisively. "You've got to be kidding."

"You just claimed to know a lot about mental disorders. Plus, you'd be a strong influence."

"And you think just-plain-stupid Billy would be able to remember the telltale signs and act convincingly? Give me a break."

Harper shrugged dismissively. "You can protest all you want. There's no way you're visiting him until after the psychiatric evaluation is completed, assuming the judge even agrees to that request. And trust me, I know the judge well. He'll agree with the prosecutor if you try to escalate the matter."

Jake decided to back down, reflecting on the potential need for a second psychiatric assessment, preferably from an expert he knew at Columbia University. *Billy needs a full neurological workup, including a comprehensive brain scan.* He would bring it up with Esther Graham.

Harper disrupted Jake's reflection. "Did you have something else to discuss? Or is that it?" He glanced at his watch.

Jake stood. "Nope. That's it. I'll let you get back to the human beings you call lowlifes."

****

The town hall was packed. All but one of the council members were seated behind the table on the front stage, the center chair empty. Jake entered at the last minute, coming through the main doors and heading down the center aisle, discussions muting as he passed.

The hall had quieted by the time he ascended the stage. He stood behind the empty chair, scanning the audience. Many of the attendees exhibited disapproving expressions, some showing outright scorn.

The clock on the back wall hit 7:00 p.m. Jake looked at Pastor Burnside and nodded.

The pastor delivered a longer-than-normal prayer, emphasizing the need for community healing. The hall stood for the Pledge of Allegiance.

Jake took his seat along with the others, pulling the table microphone close. "Thank you, Pastor Burnside. Your words set the foundation for tonight's meeting."

Jake held up the agenda. "This was on your chairs. As evident, a single matter requires the council's attention."

"Why ain't we the ones to vote?" shouted someone.

Jake gestured toward Miriam Wilson.

She leaned to her microphone. "Our city charter states that a majority of the council shall appoint an interim mayor, in the event the current mayor's unable or unwilling to serve the remaining term."

Murmuring rose from the audience. Another voice hollered out, "Then why the hell are we sitting here? There ain't no public comments."

Jake gestured again to Wilson.

"The council discussion and vote must be done with public transparency—it's required by Florida's Government-in-the-Sunshine statute. There's no additional requirement for seeking public comments."

Somebody yelled, "Sun done already set." Sporadic laughter could be heard. About twenty people left their seats, exiting the hall. Discussions broke out.

Jake leaned back, observing the behavior in the room. Most of the attendees seemed frustrated. The hall grew more agitated. He glanced left and right at the other council members. Each stared at him expectantly. Glenda Vickers turned her palms upward in a gesture of "What gives?"

****

Caitlin wondered why Jake was allowing the audience to get so worked up. Fingers tapped her shoulder from behind.

Harry Watson leaned to her ear, whispering loudly, "Why ain't he doing something?"

She shook her head, putting her hands in the air.

Jake finally banged the gavel. The room quieted. He leaned to the microphone. "Last February I encouraged all of you to support the filming of the movie on our island. The unfortunate events of the past two weeks have proven me wrong."

"Damn right," someone hollered.

Others shouted similar remarks. Caitlin's anger grew, upset by all the negative comments. Her face felt flushed.

Jake continued, causing the heckling to diminish. "I believed the filming would help delay the construction of the new bridge, buying time to thwart Nielsen's latest maneuver. It hasn't turned out as I had hoped. In the process, I have subjected the island to great disruption."

The heckling returned.

He continued to speak, raising his voice above the noise. "I also failed on a personal level, not spending enough time with those closest to me … in their time of need."

Jake placed both hands on the table, staring downward. The hall fell quiet again. He looked up. "It's been a privilege to be your mayor. Hopefully, you can forgive me over time."

It was Caitlin's turn to look downward. *This is so wrong.*

Jake concluded his remarks. "As Pastor Burnside emphasized, of foremost importance is community healing. The first step in that process is my resignation, which will take effect tomorrow."

Some people clapped. Others took exception, shushing them.

Caitlin wanted to cover her ears. She looked at Jake, startled to see him staring at her with a calm expression. He made a slight up-and-down motion with his right hand, signaling to stay calm as well. She took a deep breath, grimacing.

Jake shifted his attention to the left. "Delores, you warned me, all of us, about bringing the movie filming into our midst. Had I listened, the disruption to our island would not have occurred. I did you a disservice and apologize accordingly."

Perkins remained expressionless, staring back at Jake, then leaned to her microphone. "Apology accepted. Can we please move forward with the matter at hand?"

Caitlin sighed. *Good for her.*

****

Jake looked away from Perkins, refocusing his attention to the right. "Vern? You've been the island mayor four times. Which council member should be the interim mayor … and why?"

The trademark Panama hat sat next to Tompkins's microphone, a bright-yellow feather stuck in the band. He didn't hesitate, leaning forward. "Well now, seeing as the State's gonna build us a spanking new bridge, I do believe Glenda should be our next mayor. Yes indeedy. She's done a mighty fine job heading up the Chamber. Dang, there'll be lots of business and money coming at us."

Intermingled applause came from the audience. Vickers scanned the hall, a broad smile on her face. Catcalls came from the commercial fisherman at the back right.

Jake looked to his left. "Your turn, Ed."

Dickerson rubbed his chin, glancing in the direction of Vickers and Tompkins. He pulled his microphone closer. "I hear you there, Vern. But we must keep a balance. Hell, if we let him, Nielsen will pack the island with wealthy snowbirds, driving most of us away. We need a mayor who'll fight back, keeping him in check."

More of the audience responded with applause. Some of Vickers's supporters reciprocated, catcalling in response.

The gavel banged. "Let's be civil," admonished Jake.

"You be civil," someone shouted.

Another hollered at the person, "Shut your trap."

"I ain't shutting nothing."

Pastor Burnside stood, turning to face the audience. The verbal sparring stopped.

"Please continue, Ed," encouraged Jake.

"Like I was saying, we need someone to keep Nielsen in check. I can think of no one better than Delores."

Discussions broke out, along with limited applause. No one hollered, in large part because of Pastor Burnside. He remained standing, sweeping a stern gaze back and forth across the audience.

Jake glanced at Caitlin. Her expression was downbeat. He banged the gavel to quiet the room again. "It appears we have two candidates for consideration, assuming they want the job." He turned to Vickers. "Glenda? Are you interested?"

She cleared her throat, right hand touching Tompkins on the arm. "Thank you for the kind comments, Vern. I also appreciate the show of support in the room." She turned to her left. "Ed, the handwriting is on the wall. We can't keep our heads in the sand, fighting progress forever. Some would like to believe we are capable of self-rule and sustaining our needs, fully independent, like being our own country. Like it or not, we are part of Florida and must accept what that means. I'm well qualified to work with the State and Derek Nielsen … to ensure we modernize the island properly." She leaned back.

The pro-business supporters applauded again. No one catcalled. Pastor Burnside returned to sitting.

Jake turned left. "Delores. How about you?"

She struck a defiant tone. "I've lived on this beautiful island from the time I was born, seventy-one years ago—well before most of you and long enough to witness other attempts to modernize the island. If it hadn't been for our founding settler, Cyrus Garrett, it would have happened long before now. He fiercely protected the bulk of the island land, the land that Nielsen now owns. I wish his grandchildren had done the same.

"The threat facing Marcosta Island is far worse than anything I have witnessed along the Florida Gulf Coast. Our sibling islands to the north didn't get overrun in one fell swoop—it took decades. That's not what Nielsen is planning. He intends to grow our population almost forty-fold within the next three to five years, from six hundred to over twenty thousand. The island I've long known and loved won't exist when he's done. Everything will have changed.

"If I become mayor, I will fight Nielsen day and night, forcing him to grow our population in a responsible manner, ensuring that those of us with simpler means are not forced out by tax hikes and zoning restrictions that only the wealthy can afford. You have my solemn promise."

Many more in the audience applauded in support.

Jake looked left and right. "My thanks for the member comments. I have nothing to add. Miriam, could you call the vote of council?"

Chapter 19

Diaz caught up with Nielsen at the far side of Tampa International Airport. The two men continued across the tarmac toward a small corporate jet. Dark clouds blocked the morning sun.

"Crawford officially resigned this morning," said Diaz, slightly out of breath. "Delores Perkins is the interim mayor."

"Is Perkins keeping the chatty assistant?"

"Our source believes so."

Nielsen looked confused.

Diaz clarified, "The assistant comes over for after-dinner drinks on the source's back porch. Free liquor helps with the visit frequency and chattiness."

"So, who is …?" Nielsen stopped himself. "Never mind. Any update on Crawford? Have we heard what he's doing next?"

"Nothing to report as of yet."

The copilot came down the boarding stairs as they approached. Nielsen pointed toward the eastern skyline. "Is that squall line a problem?"

"We should be fine. There's a gap between the thunderheads.

It's flyable if we leave soon."

Nielsen turned to Diaz. "Have the PI firm keep an eye on Crawford."

"It will be difficult to avoid detection on the island."

"They did it before."

"The paparazzi made for easy cover. They're gone now."

"Figure it out. The PI firm should have some ideas. Just don't lose track of him. As I said before, I don't want to be blindsided by something he's cooked up."

Nielsen headed up the short stairway. The jet's engines started spooling.

Diaz raised his voice. "Do you still want updates about the movie?"

The engines spooled louder. Nielsen turned in the doorway and hollered down, "No. It's irrelevant now. Focus on the new bridge project. I want it started yesterday."

****

Wrinkled fingers caressed the top of the mayor's desk, feeling the mix of smoothness and pockmarks. Mayor Perkins reflected on the myriad of matters that had happened at the desk over the years, thinking of the stories it could tell. She looked at her painting on the wall, recalling when she had presented it to Mayor Pettigrew. *I was only twenty-three. Never in my wildest imagination could I have envisioned sitting here.*

Perkins studied the day's agenda: *two meetings and five phone calls*. Next to the agenda sat an opened envelope—the contents were from Jake, a bulleted outline of key issues and initiatives, along with next steps and the key people involved. He also included a personal note expressing his best wishes.

The weight of being mayor settled over her, along with some unexpected anxiety. She glanced again at the painting, reminding herself of what was at stake. *Settle down. You can do this.*

Sandra entered the office. "Fletcher Hastings, line 1, regarding your interview with the *Sentinel*."

"Thank you. Please close the door on your way out." Perkins slowly inhaled and exhaled. *Ready or not.*

****

Nyholm pushed aside what remained of lunch, sitting back and observing the Pacific Ocean, visible at the distant edge of the sloping hills. Brisk steps could be heard crossing the deck, heading in her direction.

"That was Charles Hastings," explained Satorri. "The investor group has finally calmed down. Also, Crawford resigned this morning."

"Unfortunate," said Anna. "The news about Jake."

Satorri poured a fresh glass of chardonnay from his vineyard. "Why so? We've been delayed at least a month. He should have done a better job of providing security."

"He couldn't have foreseen what happened. And besides, I've taken steps to recover most of the lost time. We should be done with the studio filming by late next week … then off to Thailand."

Satorri set the wine glass on the table, studying her for a moment. "Okay, let's forget what happened on the island. Stay focused on the success of the movie."

"Not to worry, I've been reviewing what we've filmed to date. It's superb. The actors have performed at the top of their game, despite Barlowe becoming a pain in the ass. If Thailand goes as planned, we should receive numerous award nominations and realize a box office hit."

Voices could be heard. Jones and Stevansky came up the side steps in conversation. Anna glanced at her watch. *Plenty early this time.*

The group assembled around a coffee table, taking seats.

Jones wasted no time getting started. “My Asia researcher delivered her report. The eyewitness accounts from Japanese veterans aligns with what we’ve learned from the squadron pilot and Sergeant McGregor.”

Nyholm provided a reminder for Satorri. “This is about the herding of women and children on the Burmese bridge.”

“And old men,” Jones added.

“They confirmed the first flyby?” Nyholm asked him.

“Yes. Bronson didn’t use his weapons on the first pass, clearly assessing the situation. He had to see the villagers.”

“How many civilians were on the bridge?” queried Satorri.

Jones restudied his notes. “The bridge was wider than we first thought. About eighty villagers got blown up, along with a company of Japanese soldiers. So, almost three hundred were killed by the dive bombing. That doesn’t count all the deaths from the repeated strafing runs.”

The group sat quietly. Anna finally spoke. “Anything else from the researcher?”

“The Japanese veterans she interviewed showed a great deal of remorse. Several broke down and cried.”

“Remorse about the villagers … or their lost comrades?” Stevansky asked.

“She didn’t say. All we know is Bronson caused a great deal of carnage. One of the veterans said the river was choked with dismembered bodies, the water flowing red.”

Stevansky looked at Satorri. “How far should I go with this? Graphically speaking?”

Satorri didn’t hesitate. “The full extent, especially from Bronson’s perspective. It’s why he became a recluse and eventually committed suicide. The audience needs to internalize the turmoil right from the start. The graphic imagery should haunt them throughout the storyline, always present in their minds.”

“The special effects will be expensive,” Stevansky noted.

"And it's definitely an R," added Jones. "Along with a warning label about graphic violence."

"My customary rating," said Satorri.

"Anything further of relevance?" Anna asked Jones.

"There're things I need to share with Merv. How the Japanese pinned down the Brits and approached the bridge, herding the villagers, shooting the ones that jumped in the river, other details and nuances."

Stevansky gave a related update. "We found a functional P51-A in Australia. It's being flown to the remote Thai airfield by the owner. He has a knowledgeable mechanic that will join him on location, traveling separately with a load of tools and spare parts."

"Excellent," said Satorri.

Nyholm added, "The advance team is already recruiting locals to represent the Japanese soldiers and Burmese villagers. We'll use mobile housing for the extras from Australia, India, and Singapore, representing the Chindits. Filming starts in six weeks. Everything has been accelerated, all teams working around the clock."

****

Preparations for a very different trip were underway on Marcosta Island. Jake sat at the varnished table inside *Cloud Catcher*'s main cabin. A satellite phone technician leaned against the galley counter, sweating from the late afternoon heat. A passing commercial boat caused the yacht to pitch and yaw alongside the cabin dock.

"Say that again?" Jake asked, stopping his beer from sliding.

"You'd have to stay connected to the satellite network to receive calls—which would be prohibitively expensive." The technician wiped his face with a rag.

"So, how does someone reach me?"

"I recommend establishing a daily call-in timeframe, say fifteen minutes in duration. Connect to the satellite service during that time to see if anyone makes contact. Share the phone number and timeframe with whoever matters."

"Not ideal, but I get it." Jake thought of another question. "What about dense cloud cover? Will I lose the connection?"

"You should be fine, given the transmitter wattage and size of the antenna dish. There might be short disruptions during an intense thunderstorm—the electrical interference from lightning. Strong solar flares can also be a problem, but they're infrequent."

"Got it."

"Other questions?"

"That's it for now."

The technician collected his tools. "When are you shoving off?"

"In about a week."

"Have a good voyage. Here's my card. Call if you need anything." The technician exited, his footsteps echoing in the cabin as he crossed the afterdeck.

Jake considered the daily call timeframe, deciding to use 7:30 to 7:45 a.m., Eastern time. *That should work for Caitlin, Delores, and Esther Graham. And Bill Atkins arrives at work by 6:30 a.m., Central time.*

Jake left *Cloud Catcher* and headed to the cabin. The technician's van could be seen departing between the hibiscus bushes. Jake entered through the side door to the kitchen and reached for the wall phone, dialing a Chicago number.

"Atkins."

"Bill, it's Jake."

"Doctor Crawford. Are you heading to sea soon?"

"That's why I'm calling." Jake provided the satellite phone number and call timeframe, explaining why he couldn't be reached at other times.

"What's your crossing route and first port of call?" asked Atkins.

"The first overnight anchorage is below Everglades National Park, near Sandy Key. I'll stop briefly in Islamorada to top off the fuel tanks and then head for the southeast corner of Cay Sal Bank, not far from Isabela de Sagua, Cuba. The last leg will take me to Clarence Town, Long Island. I'll clear Customs and refuel at a marina there, before continuing to the Bight of the Acklins. Clarence Town is the first port where I could receive documents to review and sign, assuming the marina has a fax machine. I'll let you know the other ports as I go along."

"Long Island? Funny to hear that name in the Bahamas."

"It's definitely not the Hamptons."

"How long will it take to cross the open ocean?"

"Two days, assuming the weather and seas cooperate, about 380 nautical miles in total … a relatively short leg to Cay Sal Bank, followed by a longer leg to Clarence Town. I'll get you the name of the marina there."

"Will Caitlin make the trip?"

"She needs more recovery time. I'm scouting locations for our overdue honeymoon cruise."

"Well, it sounds wonderful." Atkins shifted his tone, sounding slightly downbeat. "Although it's unfortunate under the circumstances … everything that's happened recently."

"Speaking of which, have you finalized Billy's defense account and drawing rights with Esther Graham?"

"The account is funded as you instructed. JPMorgan is still awaiting her firm's signature on the paperwork. I'll pester her assistant again today."

The bank's name reminded Jake of another matter. "Any update on the Cortisolix payout?"

"I spoke with the sell-side banker late yesterday. The upfront payment should hit your bank account in about a month. The parties settled on seventy percent, with the remainder to be paid on the fifth-year anniversary of the acquisition. You'll receive a total of twenty-three million and change, so about sixteen mil upfront."

"I'll be on the voyage when the first payment hits."

"Same diversification strategy as last time?" asked Atkins.

"No. Put all of it in three-month T-bills. I'll provide more guidance when I return. I have some new donations in mind."

"Easy-peasy. Incidentally, if you have any biotech investing tips, please let me know."

"I'm not a biotech investor, at least not in the typical sense. Cortisolix couldn't afford my consulting fee in its early days. I accepted their common stock instead. I never expected the shares to attain such a high valuation."

The sound of crunching oyster shells came through the open kitchen window.

"Hey Bill, Caitlin just got home from work. I'll reconnect before I depart on the voyage."

****

Caitlin found Jake in the kitchen as she entered. She placed her handbag on the counter and gave him a tight embrace, looking up. "How'd it go this morning?"

"Your breast pain must have lessened considerably." He gave her a quick kiss before answering. "It was uneventful. Delores seemed nervous, but she'll do fine."

"Was there a celebration?"

"Yes."

"For you?"

"No, Delores, but that's okay."

She stepped back. "It's not okay."

"The value of my tenure is questionable. How's it going at the lab?"

"The dining hall is back in operation with a temporary cook;

turns out one of the dockhands has some culinary talent. The movie team removed whatever equipment could be salvaged, which wasn't much. Water from the fire hoses caused a lot of damage."

"What about Ida?"

"She's upset about your resignation. You may want to visit her again. I think she's worried about your funding support."

"I'll consider stopping by. I still have a lot to accomplish before leaving."

"How long before you're ready?"

"Six to seven days."

"Not seeing you for a month will feel like an eternity. I miss you already."

"It'll go by faster than you think. The satellite phone got installed today. Remember, I'll be calling every evening around sunset."

She grasped Jake's hands, looking up with concern. "One of the marine lab captains reminded me … you're heading into the worst of hurricane season."

"Have you changed your mind about me going?"

"No, you should go, just promise me you'll come back in one piece."

Jake squeezed her hands before letting go. "I'll be fine. Hey, I spoke with Bill Atkins right before you came home. He's squared away on current legal and financial matters."

She studied him. "That doesn't sound reassuring. Why tell me you'll be fine and then say something like that?"

"I was referring to Billy's defense funding. Plus, I needed to deal with the Cortisolix payout."

"Is it what you expected?"

"Well beyond." He shared the amounts and timing of the two payments.

"You certainly have the Midas touch."

"I continue to be lucky."

"Is that why you give away most of the money? You think it's undeserved?"

"I used to think I deserved it, believing I was especially hardworking and willing to take significant career risks. But so are many others who never attain a similar level of financial success. I eventually understood the outsized impact of luck. It has far more to do with exceptional financial upside than most wealthy people are willing to admit. Doing so would greatly diminish their puffed-up belief in personal capabilities." Jake went to the refrigerator and grabbed another beer.

Caitlin grinned, looking mischievous. "Isn't there another reason for giving away the money? Something to do with real-tight jeans?"

Jake made a pained expression. "I prefer honest, sincere relationships. Excessive wealth attracts the opposite." He shifted topics, explaining the need for the morning call timeframe in case she needed to reach him. "Otherwise, expect my evening contact."

She smiled. "I'll be sitting right here, waiting with bated breath for the phone to ring. You can regale me with your adventures of the day. I'll fix a Corona and lime and pretend I was there, right alongside you."

PART III

Chapter 20

A week had passed since Jake resigned. His remaining preparations had gone smoothly, enabling him to depart on schedule.

Cloud Catcher motored into the middle of Passage Channel, heading toward the Gulf of Mexico. He turned and waved to Caitlin. She stood on the dock bench, a hand raised high.

He returned to the job of captaining. Ahead lay a disturbing image. Two barges were tied off on opposite sides of the memorial fishing pier. One held a crane. The other contained a pile of dismembered wood planks. Demolition workers were busy with chainsaws and crowbars, preparing the next load for the crane to lift.

A feeling of sadness welled up. Jake closed his eyes, pretending the old wooden bridge still spanned the channel. He envisioned the radio exchange that would be occurring with Simon.

"Marcosta Bridge, *Cloud Catcher*. Over."

"Go ahead, *Cloud Catcher*."

"Inbound, bay side. Quarter mile out. Approaching at seven

knots. Request drawbridge open. Over."

"Roger, proceed to drawbridge."

Recalling the sound of Simon's voice enhanced the vision. Jake could picture the worn Zippo lighter, the gnarled fingers lighting a smoke, followed by Simon leaving the bridgetender's shack and heading into the control shelter, preparing to lift the drawbridge. The feeling of sadness deepened as *Cloud Catcher* passed through the imaginary opening, leaving both Caitlin and Simon behind as he headed toward the gulf.

Jake opened his eyes. The partially demolished pier went by, followed by the remainder of the downtown waterfront. No one came out to wave as he passed. He wondered how long it would take for the community to forgive him for what happened. *Maybe never*.

Sand Point marked the beginning of a submerged sandbar that ran well into the gulf. Large waves crashed against its length, signaling the impending encounter with rough seas. The weather report called for twenty-knot winds from the southwest, gusting to thirty. Stronger than he liked but manageable. *Good thing Caitlin is not aboard.*

He rounded the end of the bar. The harmonic vibrations of the twin diesel engines mixed with the pounding of gulf waves against the hull, each impact vibrating the deck under his feet. Jake eyed the instruments as he turned the helm and eased the throttles forward, attaining the desired southerly heading and cruising speed. The direction allowed the bow to quarter the wind-driven swells, lessening the vertical drops. *She's handling well.*

****

Caitlin sped south on Gulf Drive, driving parallel to the beachfront. She had stopped near the Coquina Motel to watch *Cloud Catcher* enter the gulf and turn to the south, pulsing spray bursting off the hull in a rhythmic pattern. Just seeing the yacht's motion made her slightly nauseated. *Jake has an iron stomach. He should be fine.*

Feelings of happiness and apprehension battled within her as she drove. She had observed the positive change in Jake's demeanor, the apparent excitement about the cruise; that was the happy part. The other part, the apprehension, stemmed from the distant past. They had not been long apart since Jake had returned to the island. The fear of losing him again was deeply embedded, resurfacing quickly.

Her special pathway to the beach approached on the right. She pulled onto the sandy shoulder, quickly exiting the car and hurrying to the high dune, clambering to the top and standing by the scrub pine.

Cloud Catcher had moved offshore, about a mile out. She felt the urge to wave but didn't, recognizing the futility. She held a branch tightly in the stiff breeze, the wind whistling loudly through the pine needles. *Cloud Catcher* grew smaller and smaller—the diminishing size amplified her loneliness.

The yacht became a tiny speck, finally disappearing from sight. All that remained was the empty expanse of white-capped waves and a line of billowing clouds that spread across the horizon. The clouds swirled, changing shape. For a moment, she imagined a billowy hand, waving a final goodbye. She raised hers in return. *Godspeed, my love. Catch the clouds for us.*

****

A lone pelican came into view on the port side of *Cloud Catcher*. It traveled beyond the bow, flying just off the surface, flapping and gliding in a repetitive pattern, rising and falling in concert with the undulating waves, avoiding the stronger wind above.

A starboard pull on the helm adjusted the heading to south by southwest, bypassing the shallower water near the western shoreline of the Everglades National Park. Jake passed the mouth of the Shark River, heading for the overnight anchorage in Sandy Key Basin, at the edge of Florida Bay, directly south of Cape Sable. He and Billy had fished the basin for tarpon as teenagers, betting on who would land the largest. Billy still held the record at 178 pounds, estimated by measuring the fish's length and girth.

The thought of those trips triggered a humorous recollection of the infamous mosquito attack on the south end of the park, near the Flamingo Campground, the two of them running pell-mell for a cinder block cabin they had rented for the night. They had anchored their skiff at dusk, holding their clothes overhead as they waded to the shore, butt naked. A large swarm of mosquitos had descended immediately upon reaching land, biting incessantly. Hundreds of the whining devils were carried inside before the cabin door could be shut. Wet towels had become the defensive weapon of choice, resulting in hundreds of the enemy smashed against the white walls and ceiling, along with the contents of their feasting, tiny splatters of blood everywhere. The chaotic fury had lasted for a good thirty minutes, both men cussing and laughing throughout. It took weeks to recover from the itchy bites, some in the worst of locations.

The recollection became bittersweet, the innocence of the youthful adventure offset by current reality. Jake still couldn't believe that a right-minded Billy would commit premeditated murder. Esther Graham promised to make contact once she received the results of the psychiatric assessments.

The sun sank lower in the west. Jake glanced at his watch, making a quick calculation. *I'll call Caitlin once I'm anchored ... about an hour from now.*

A tide table rested on the captain's console. *Cloud Catcher* required almost five feet of draft. Jake estimated the depth of the destination. The deeper part of the basin looked sufficient, plus the bottom was composed of sand and turtle grass, nothing rocky. *But it could be a tight fit at dead low tide.* Worst case she would rest on the soft bottom for a brief while, floating free when the tide returned.

He adjusted the heading, shifting to the southeast, aiming for the deepest entry into the basin. The new course brought the waves directly against the starboard hull. The piloting became trickier, the bow wanting to surf the waves. He reduced speed. The yacht yawed in an awkward motion, sinking and raising while rolling to port and starboard. A slight feeling of seasickness set in, causing him to yawn. He kept his eyes on the horizon, helping to minimize the vertigo. A small plane flew toward him, passing to port before turning east. The vertigo got worse, bringing more yawning and excess saliva. He drank some water from a nearby bottle, forcing his thoughts to the southern Bahamas, trying to forestall the full onset of seasickness.

There was still much to learn and consider during the exploratory cruise. This much he knew—the next place to live had to be an island that would never have a bridge to it or a deep harbor for cruise ships. Someplace with a sparse population and robust marine environment. *Crooked Island still looks the most promising.* He was eager to explore the underwater diversity of the nearby waters, most notably the Bight of the Acklins.

Cape Sable appeared to the southeast, its sandy shoreline a warm color in the late sunlight. He rechecked the heading. *Shouldn't be long before the waves lessen.*

****

Nielsen reclined in a chair outside his villa on Anna Maria Island, hundreds of miles to the north of Jake's anchorage at Sandy Key Basin. The broad portico extended from the rear of the villa's main residence to the edge of Tampa Bay. Nielsen shifted the chair to afford a better view of the impending sunset, careful not to spill the bourbon on his favorite Brioni jacket. A mobile phone rested on the side table.

A young woman approached wearing an elegant evening gown. "Our guests are arriving."

"Keep them entertained for a bit. I'm expecting a call. It won't take long."

She touched him softly on the neck. "You look especially handsome tonight."

He took her hand. "Hopefully a worthy counterpart. Is that the new necklace from Bulgari's?"

"Yes. It's utterly exquisite."

Nielsen looked past her to the expansive great room, visible through a wide set of windows. A large architectural rendering stood on an easel near the grand piano, a bold title at the top: *The Landings of Marcosta Island.* The guests of honor entered the room through a main archway, elegantly attired. "The governor's chief of staff and her husband just walked in. I'm sure you can keep their attention until I'm finished. It won't take long."

He watched as she retraced steps and entered the portico doors, returning his view to the setting sun. A soft chime announced the incoming call. Nielsen set the tumbler on the table, speaking as the phone touched his ear. "Is Crawford heading as expected?"

"The spotter plane tracked him down the western edge of the Everglades. He's anchored about five miles southwest of the Flamingo campground."

"Good," said Nielsen. "Sounds like your intel is correct. Let me know when he starts across the Gulf Stream. No need to track him afterward. We'll assume he's heading to the Bight of the Acklins."

Nielsen hung up, exchanging the phone for the tumbler, standing and downing the remaining bourbon. He raised the empty glass in salute as the top of the sun disappeared below the horizon. *Bon voyage, Crawford, and good riddance.*

Chapter 21

The fourth morning of Jake's voyage found *Cloud Catcher* anchored inside of Long Cay, on the northwestern edge of the Bight of the Acklins. A strong incoming tide pulled against the anchor line, pointing the bow to the west. The orientation positioned the afterdeck with an expansive view of the large bight. On a map, it resembled a watery Africa, bounded to the north, east, and south by two large islands, Crooked and Acklins. Long Cay defined the northwest portion, a smaller island that had once been home to a thriving population of Lucayans, before European explorers decimated them with disease and extraction into slavery.

The fecundity of surrounding waters provided a good reason for the Lucayans' choice of location. The waters of the shallow bight provided a constant supply of mutton snapper, hogfish, lobster, and conch. Yellowfin tuna, wahoo, and other blue-water species could be found in quantity to the immediate west of the cay, where the shallow water dropped precipitously to a depth of over two thousand feet only four hundred yards offshore, the blue-water fish easily accessible by dugout canoe on calmer days.

Jake glanced at the nautical clock—7:45 a.m. No one had called during the set timeframe. He disconnected from the satellite network, departing the cabin for the openness of the afterdeck. A warm breeze blew from the southeast. No other boats were in sight.

He walked to the edge of the stern. An inflatable dinghy drifted behind the yacht, attached by a thirty-foot line. Its small outboard motor enabled him to explore nearby cuts and channels that coursed through the shallow flats and shoals. He looked forward to a full day of free diving and spearfishing in the clear water, drifting with the tide and wind, observing the teeming array of exotic marine life. Protective diving gloves would help with capturing lobster and conch. Inshore fish could be speared using a Hawaiian sling; the large, blue-water fish required a stout rod and deep-sea reel loaded with heavy line.

The sound of a small plane caused him to raise a hand to his forehead, shielding the sun and scanning to the northeast. He watched with curiosity as it changed course, banking to the southwest and heading toward him. *High-winged with struts. Probably a Cessna.* Jake squinted into the sunrise as the plane flew by at about a thousand feet of altitude.

The plane continued southwest for about a mile before banking and heading back. Jake ascended the ladder to the flying bridge, grabbing a pair of binoculars.

Sunlight illuminated the plane as it passed beyond the bow at about the same altitude. *No markings other than a tail number.* The plane flew on, continuing to the north, finally disappearing in the brightening sky.

Jake grew concerned by the potential surveillance. He was aware of the occasional piracy of private yachts in remote areas of the Bahamas, accompanied by the disappearance of the occupants, likely murdered and thrown overboard in the open ocean. The violent crimes were most often drug related, the pirated yachts taken to the Florida coastline near Miami and subsequently set afire or sunk after the offshore transfer of illicit cargo, usually many kilos of cocaine.

I need to shift my anchorage before nightfall—best to move further south. He went below and retrieved the loaded shotgun, placing it on the galley table along with an open box of buckshot.

****

Caitlin stared out the window of the lab's front office. The harbor seemed much larger without the luxury yachts. A movement caught her attention toward the harbor mouth. Steve Moore was departing in his guide skiff with an angler aboard, turning toward the southeast of Munson Bay.

She returned to her desk. A picture of Jake now stood alongside the one of Tommy, both men smiling broadly. The one of Jake had been taken after their marriage on Sand Point, dunes in the background. She smiled in return. *The loves of my life.*

Judith Kerner entered through the rear office door, heading toward the copier. "So, did you hear from Jake last evening?"

"I certainly did," said Caitlin brightly.

"Has he made it to the Bight of the Acklins?"

"Yes, it sounds beautiful."

Copies started ejecting into the receiving tray. Kerner came over. "He made great time."

"The seas had calmed by the time he departed Cay Sal."

The copier stopped. Kerner went over and started another run, returning. "Well, I hope the trip proves restful for him, after everything that's happened recently."

"Me too. He seems in much better spirits."

"I don't know if he mentioned it. We wish he would return to science and join us."

Caitlin reacted with surprise. "Here at the marine lab?"

"That's our hope."

"But he's not a marine scientist."

"Some of the most important medical research has been performed on marine organisms."

"Including cancer research?"

"Many marine organisms get cancerous tumors: porpoises, whales, turtles, fishes, sharks, rays, even sponges and corals."

Caitlin considered Kerner's comments, negating the wishful thinking. *No way Jake would drive back and forth through Nielsen's resort to work here.*

Kerner retrieved the copy sets. "Let Jake know we're thinking of him." She exited through the rear.

Caitlin reflected on Jake's idea of moving to the southern Bahamas. The thought of leaving Marcosta Island seemed daunting. *This is all I have known.*

She understood why he might want to leave. He had returned to the island with the desire to live a simpler life, in harmony with its natural beauty, recapturing what he had known and loved growing up. It wouldn't exist after Nielsen's plans were realized.

And Jake isn't alone. Many native Floridians had left after their hometowns had been overrun with snowbirds, reestablishing in the hills and mountains of western North Carolina or northern Georgia, locations their ancestors and families had long used to escape the summer heat and humidity —*like my parents*. But the Bahamas? She couldn't recall anyone from southwest Florida moving there.

The offsetting factor was the financial resources they had available. Before departing, Jake had discussed the idea of earning a pilot's license and buying a twin-engine seaplane. Explaining how it would enable flights back and forth to Miami for medical visits and spending time with friends on Marcosta and elsewhere. *But I still dislike flying on big planes*. Flying in a small one sounded much worse.

Her thoughts shifted to the present moment, wondering if he

was already out free diving and spearfishing. She had heard the excitement in his voice the previous evening, listening to him describe the endless opportunities for exploring the vast bight.

The thought of him diving alone in such a remote location remained a lingering concern. She reminded herself that he had been an accomplished free diver since childhood, spearing fish in the gulf, often going alone. He would return with large grouper and snapper, along with periodic stories of "sporty" shark encounters. Over time, his nickname, "Guts," had come to mean more than barely surviving a childhood disaster with fish guts and rampaging sharks at Horseshoe Basin. Eventually, the moniker's legacy grew to encompass a teenager who chose to spearfish in places others wouldn't dare. In an odd way, the thought reassured her. *He'll be fine.*

Caitlin sighed, focusing on the pile of work in her inbox, occasionally glancing at the wall clock, counting the hours until she could go home. Corona beer and limes awaited Jake's evening call.

****

Steve Moore poled his flats skiff along the edge of the mangroves on the southeast shoreline of Munson Bay, standing on a platform above the outboard engine. The higher elevation made it easier to spot fish in the shallow water ahead. His client stood ready on the bow, a saltwater fly rod in hand.

Moore spotted a large snook, calling out its position, "Just beyond that mangrove root at one o'clock, the one jutting out the farthest. See the long shape above the lighter turtle grass?" The snook remained stationary, just inside the shadow of the overhanging branches, a poised assassin lying in wait.

"Yeah, I think so," answered the angler, sounding unsure.

"Point your rod."

The angler obliged, aiming the rod tip.

Moore corrected him. "No, the other light spot, further left … about five feet."

"I see him now," the angler whispered loudly.

Moore poled the skiff out and around to the left, working to get a better angle for the impending fly cast. "Lower your profile. He might see you as we move into sunlight."

The angler stooped, casting the line softly across the surface, dropping the fly into position ahead of the fish, the tiny splash barely perceptible. The big snook took notice, approaching slowly.

"Perfect," whispered Moore. "Strip the line."

The angler retrieved the fly line using short pulls. The action caused the feathered fly to dart forward, pause, and then dart again in an enticing baitfish motion.

"He's coming at it. Long strip."

The angler complied. The explosive attack and hookup embodied a classic fishing photo; the upper body of the snook extended partway out of the water, its head shaking violently, the spray glistening in the early sunlight.

"Keep the pressure on," Moore instructed.

The fish veered close to the mangroves. The angler tried but failed to move the fish toward the open bay. It turned suddenly, streaking into the mouth of a small creek, heading up the center, the line peeling off the fly reel.

"Shit!" Moore exclaimed. He strained hard against the pushpole, propelling the skiff toward the creek mouth. "We're hosed."

The creek narrowed at its back end, at most six feet wide. A forest of red mangroves framed both sides. The angler did his best to slow the fish, adding more drag against the line. Overhanging branches forced Moore to come down from the poling platform. Both men crouched low. The fish hurtled up the creek, the taut line disappearing underneath a tangle of lower branches. Large webs of banana spiders spread across the limbs in varying directions.

"Tighten the drag to full," Moore instructed. "Either he stops or the line breaks."

The line stayed taut for a moment, then snapped.

The angler retrieved the remaining line. "Smart bastard. Knew right where to go."

"What the hell is that?" Moore said, pointing toward the swampy maze of curved roots at right, spread across the base of the shadowy mangrove forest.

The angler looked over. "Not sure what you're seeing."

"That red clump of seaweed, about twenty feet in, hanging across the highest root. I've never seen that color in the mangroves before." Moore pushed to the edge of the creek. "Keep hold of a root."

Moore stepped onto the curved roots, avoiding the swamp muck, grabbing overhead limbs for support as he navigated to the seaweed, stooping to look closely. *What the hell?* Moore broke off a small branch, using it to lift a portion of the clump, exposing an interwoven skull cap of white mesh and a tag marked XL. "I'll be damned. It's a curly red wig."

****

Sharon turned away from the dispatcher console, taking off the headset. "Chief, I need you here. It's Tim Olsen with the Florida Marine Patrol."

The chief walked over, putting on the headset. "What's up, Tim?"

"We got us a big discovery in the southeast corner of Munson. Steve Moore came across a curly red wig hanging in the mangrove roots … up a small creek. It's in there a ways, well beyond the high tide mark."

"Why's that a big deal?"

"Doesn't that Watson fella have curly red hair?"

"Christ almighty!" Wilkinson exclaimed.

"Just what I said."

Wilkinson rapidly considered the implications. "You guys got crime scene tape on board?"

"Nope. Not something we cart around."

"I need to get Detective Harper and his team out there. Can you stay till they arrive? Make sure no one messes with anything."

"How long's that gonna be?"

"I can't be sure. Probably a few hours."

"Okay, I guess. We'll hang tight."

"Thanks. Was anybody with Moore when he discovered the wig?"

"He's got a client aboard. They hooked a big-ass snook that hauled up the creek. That's when Steve spotted the wig."

"Ask them to stay put. Harper will want to speak with them."

"You got it, Chief."

"Good. Sharon will get back to you with Harper's ETA."

She gave a thumbs-up.

Wilkinson handed her the headset and headed for his desk phone.

Pearson came over. "What's going on?"

"I'll put the call on speaker. You can listen in." He dialed a direct number at the county sheriff's office.

A voice answered gruffly. "Harper."

"Detective. Chief Wilkinson. You're not gonna believe this."

****

Crime scene tape encircled the trunks of nearby mangrove trees, the red wig at the center. Detective Harper swatted at the mosquitos swarming around his face and ears. The constant, high-pitched whine could drive a person crazy.

The dense canopy of leaves and branches cast a deep shadow

over the immediate area despite the afternoon sunlight. The flash of a camera strobe penetrated Harper's closed eyelids. "How much longer?"

"Almost done." The photographer shot another perspective of the red wig. "Okay, that's it."

Harper opened his eyes, scanning around. Others on the team were using flashlights to help search for clues. Hands kept slapping at ears and noses. *Thank God for bug spray. We'd be bloodless corpses by now.*

He pulled on a pair of latex gloves, squatting by the wig. "Jerry, shine the flashlight here."

A skinny man in his late twenties came alongside.

The beam illuminated the wig details. Harper retrieved a pair of stainless-steel tongs from his shirt pocket. He probed the wig, slowly untangling it from atop the roots. The polyester strands stuck firmly, making the extraction tedious. "It's been here a while." The wig finally came free. "Who's got an evidence bag?"

"Me," answered a woman's voice. She headed slowly toward him, balancing on the curvy roots.

Harper held the wig, turning it in different directions, spreading the artificial hair with his gloved fingers.

Jerry kept the light focused, standing slightly behind, casting the beam over Harper's left shoulder.

"It didn't float to this spot," Harper concluded. "Somebody threw it back here."

"How can you tell?"

"It's too clean inside. Floating into the mangroves would have impregnated it with sand particles and pieces of detritus. Only the surface hairs have debris on them, probably wind-blown. The other clue is where it landed, hanging well above the high tide mark."

"Here you go," said the woman.

Harper sealed the wig in the evidence bag. "Mark the date, time, and GPS coordinates."

She navigated away, heading for the evidence locker on the sheriff's boat.

"Shine the light where the wig was attached." Harper studied the surrounding roots and mucky ground. *Nothing else*. He stood, grasping an overhead branch and stretching his back. "Anyone discover something of interest?"

"I can't find anything."

"Me either."

"Nope."

"Okay. Leave the tape up. Get back to the boat before we need blood transfusions."

Harper led the way out, the rest of the team following slowly, navigating atop the curving roots. The sheriff's boat lay anchored at the mouth of the creek, too wide to go up it.

Harper glanced at Steve Moore and his angler. They sat in Moore's flats skiff, anchored about twenty yards away. A breeze blew down the bay from the northeast. The skiff's exposed position helped keep the mosquitos away.

Harper had requested them to hang tight in case he had more questions. The investigation team finished boarding the sheriff's boat. Harper instructed the captain to motor to the skiff.

"Thanks for sticking here so long," Harper said as the boats came together. "I know it's been a long day for you guys."

"What do you think?" asked Moore.

"Interesting discovery," Harper replied. "Have you been further up that creek?"

"Not for six months or so. It's a bitch to work through the overhanging branches and spider webs."

"Where does it lead?"

"To a small inner bay. It's maybe a hundred yards in diameter, about four or five feet deep. Snook congregate there during January and February, along with a ton of deer flies. It's not a spot for the faint-hearted."

"What surrounds the inner bay? More mangrove swamps?"

"Mostly. There's an area on the east side covered with white mangroves and some thatch palms, probably firmer ground. I've never gone ashore there."

Harper glanced at the creek mouth. He turned to the deputy captaining the boat. "Brad, radio HQ and ask them to send your replacement for the night … along with a gallon of bug spray. We'll work the exchange at the mainland transport dock. I want this creek under surveillance, in case someone of interest has spotted us here." Harper turned to Moore. "What's the best way to get up that creek and into the inner bay? Your skiff?"

"No. It's too big. I have a modified canoe … flat stern with a small outboard and tiller steering."

"How many does it hold?"

"Barely two people."

"You up for taking me in the morning? I'd like to explore that firmer ground you mentioned."

Moore glanced at his client. "You okay with giving up a day of fishing?"

The angler signaled a thumbs-up.

Moore focused on Harper. "Wear a lightweight, long-sleeve shirt and pants, plus knee-high snake boots or leggings. I'll bring my rifle in case of frisky gators."

Harper grimaced. "Not a Disney cruise. You up for going early?"

"I'll meet you an hour after sunrise, here at the creek mouth."

"Thanks." Harper addressed the entire group. "Keep the wig discovery quiet until I say otherwise. Lips sealed."

****

Fish Cay lay a hundred yards to starboard, a tiny island at the western edge of the Bight of the Acklins, eight miles southeast of Jake's previous anchorage. The waning light of sunset cast a golden glow across the island's scrub brush and sandy shoreline. A flock of noisy terns flew by, hurrying to an overnight destination.

Cloud Catcher rode anchor in a deep cut. Winds were light from the southeast, the tide incoming. Jake made a mental note to reposition the anchor when the tide turned.

He took the ladder to the top of the flying bridge, grabbing the binoculars and scanning all directions. *Good. No vessels in sight.* He focused on Fish Cay. A shallow lagoon defined the northwest corner, a protected spot to come ashore with the dinghy. The beach along its western shoreline looked like a nice place to take a walk. *Maybe after the call with Caitlin.* Thunder grumbled; a squall line approached from the southwest. *Then again, maybe not.*

He clambered down the ladder and entered the cabin. The shotgun remained on the table. He rechecked the safety switch. It had been a long time since he had discharged a shotgun, back when he and Billy were teenagers hunting turkeys in central Florida. *Remember, your left eye is dominant.*

He turned his attention to the transmitter, connecting to the satellite network and dialing Caitlin. The phone rang once on the other end.

"Jake?"

"Hi, love."

"Your voice is much clearer tonight."

"So is yours. How are you feeling? Doing okay?"

"I'm fine, other than missing you terribly. The cabin feels so empty … as does the dock."

"You're definitely coming with me next time."

"I can't wait. Are you anchored in the same spot?"

"I moved eight miles south, alongside a little island called Fish Cay."

"I'm marking it on the chart. Tell me about your day. Is it as beautiful as you hoped? Did you spear some dinner?"

"Beyond expectations. The cuts are teeming with mutton snapper and grouper. I speared a smaller mutton. Hard to imagine a tastier fish."

"Better than hogfish?"

"Hmmm … that's a toss-up."

"What about sharks? Hopefully, nothing sporty happened."

"I saw a few."

"Did they leave you alone?"

"For the most part."

"What exactly does that mean?"

"One got a little nosy. But I dealt with him."

Caitlin remembered something. "I got a call from Harry late this afternoon. Billy's initial psychiatric evaluation is tomorrow."

"Good."

"And I received a nice letter from Anna. They're headed to Thailand soon to film the Burma scenes. She made it sound like everything was back on track."

"She wrote you?"

"We agreed to stay in touch. She asked how you're doing."

The satellite connection started crackling. A loud thunderclap reverberated throughout the cabin.

"What was that?" Caitlin asked, her voice garbled.

Rain pelted the starboard windows.

"A squall line is passing. Lightning is interfering with the connection."

"You're … breaking …"

A bright flash illuminated Fish Cay, followed almost immediately by another thunderclap, much louder than the first.

Jake spoke slowly, hoping his words would make it through. "Best if I get off this thing. I'll call tomorrow evening at the scheduled time. Love you."

****

The wind gusted from the southwest. Jake maneuvered in the nighttime darkness toward the shallow lagoon at the northeast corner of Fish Cay, finally reaching calm water. He tilted the small outboard motor, enabling the propellor to thrash just below the surface, pushing the inflatable dinghy across the shallows toward the edge of the cay, the sandy shoreline vaguely outlined by starlight on the moonless night.

A push of the tiller button stopped the engine. He stepped over the side, wearing swim trunks and a T-shirt, standing barefoot in a foot or so of water. He waded the final distance to shore, pulling the dinghy onto the sandy slope.

A yellow dry bag contained a four-cell battery flashlight. Illumination of the dinghy interior exposed a grappling anchor and coil of line. The line unraveled as he walked up a slight incline. A large piece of driftwood lay above the high tide mark; it became the anchoring point, preventing the dinghy from floating away as the tide rose. He set the dry bag next to the driftwood and turned off the flashlight, temporarily closing his eyes.

He had tried to fall asleep but had given up, his mind whirling about the troubling fates of Billy and Marcosta Island. A nighttime walk on the beach became attractive, a way to seek some peace.

More and more stars filled the sky as the night vision returned. Jake went around the north point to the western beachfront, his bare feet leaving a trail in the soft sand. He stopped, making a quick check of *Cloud Catcher*. Her anchor light cut a narrow swath across the dark water. Frothy wave tops glittered in the path.

The sandy beach extended for over a half mile in length. He continued slowly down the shore, navigating the flotsam, mostly pieces of driftwood, their presence made evident in the faint light from the Milky Way galaxy. Wind and crashing waves dominated the soundscape.

After a while, he arrived at the southern tip, reclining against a small dune. The damp sand was pitted from the passing rain. The squall-driven winds slowly diminished as time went by. He closed his eyes. Waves hit the beach and receded, over and over, a soothing melody. It calmed the troubled thoughts, caressing him to sleep.

Chapter 22

Jake awoke suddenly. *What the hell?* A familiar sound reverberated from the north, twin diesels revving louder. *Shit! She's been boarded.* He turned on the flashlight, directing the beam in front, running along the beach. After a distance, he stopped, gathering his wits. *Turn off the beam. You're a dead man if they see you.* The lack of light slowed his pace; the driftwood and flotsam making it difficult to move quickly.

He stopped. Another sound had joined the diesel engines, the synchronized roar of outboard motors. A spotlight came around the north end of Fish Cay, traveling at a fast speed, its bright beam sweeping the beachfront.

The speeding boat turned south, paralleling the shoreline. Jake wasted no time scrambling into the scrub bushes that covered the interior of the little island, finding a shallow depression. The boat closed the distance rapidly, the powerful beam probing the beach and scrub brush. He lay motionless, the right side of his face pressed against the limestone muck. The beam passed overhead, illuminating the limbs and leaves, a foot above his position.

He got to his knees, peering above the scraggly bush tops. Backlight from the search beam outlined a center console boat, about twenty-five feet long, with two large outboard motors on its stern. The silhouettes of three men were visible, one directing the handheld spotlight, another driving, the last holding what looked like an assault rifle. The boat continued to the south end of the cay and spun sharply, reversing its route. The beam continued to search, aimed further into the interior. Jake went prone again, pressing deeper. The beam passed inches overhead, the slivers of light just missing his presence.

Jake let a minute pass, slowly lifting his head as the motor sound diminished, clearing limestone muck from over his right eye. The boat continued up the cay, finally going around the island's north end, repeating the process up and down the opposite side. Again, Jake lay flat each time the beam passed.

The sound of the outboards finally subsided at the north end. Jake stood, trying to gather his wits. A few more minutes passed. POP. POP. POP. *Gunfire*. Flames followed, shooting skyward in the vicinity of the dinghy. The twin outboard engines roared back to life.

Cloud Catcher started out to deep water, the anchor light moving to the northwest. The other boat trailed behind, riding in the wake. The anchor light suddenly went dark. Only the engine sounds remained, eventually no longer audible.

Bastards. Jake kicked himself. *The anchor light is how they found her. What the hell was I thinking? I didn't need it out here.* He worked through the scrub brush and onto the beach, bleeding from minor cuts on his arms and legs, the result of sharp limestone outcroppings buried in the muck. The fiery glow had diminished in the direction of the dinghy. He returned his gaze to the western darkness. *Probably drug pirates, planning to load her with cocaine and head to a rendezvous point off Florida. She has enough fuel to get there. And then what? Scuttle her?*

It dawned on him that the fast search boat might return soon, the pirates wanting to finish the job, either tonight or at daybreak. He listened intently for the sound of the outboards. *Nothing.* He left the flashlight on the beach and entered the waves, working to remove the caked muck, listening periodically. Eventually, he retrieved the flashlight and headed for the north end, slowly navigating the flotsam-strewn beach in the dark.

****

The pirates had doused the dinghy with gas from its fuel can and set it ablaze. Jake pushed apart the charred remains, searching with the flashlight. Metal objects were the only survivors, including a spear shaft. The outboard engine lay on its side, several bullet holes in the cowling. Multiple footprints surrounded the scene of destruction, along with the bullet casings.

He spotted the burned end of the anchor line and traced it to the driftwood. The dry bag remained untouched. He emptied the contents onto the sand. Only one item stood out as helpful: a set of goggles, like the ones worn by competitive swimmers.

No food or fresh water. Jake considered the situation, recognizing survival opportunities: raw seafood could be captured using the goggles and spear to harvest crabs and lobster; passing rain squalls could supply a small amount of fresh water, modifying the dry bag to serve as a collector.

The thought of returning pirates brought another auditory scan and a realization. *Still nothing ... but I can't stay here.* He considered the options for escaping, each of which involved swimming. A small cay lay to the north, about three miles away; he had passed it motoring to the current location. The route meant crossing several deep channels through which the tide passed strongly, in and out of the bight, twice daily. The chance of getting swept out to sea or into the bight was too great. Plus, the pirates would likely return from that direction.

Being swept out to sea was by far the worst outcome, particularly floating at night with tiger and mako sharks in abundance. He considered the risk of being swept the other direction, into the vast bight. It would require almost a twenty-mile swim to reach the islands of Crooked or Acklins, drifting whenever possible with the incoming tide. *But I'd need to pull aside on shallow flats when the tide flowed out, losing precious time.* His clinical training calculated the risk of severe dehydration. *Much too high.*

The remaining option involved swimming during slack tide to another small cay that lay to the south, about the same distance as the one to the north. If he recalled correctly, there was only one channel to cross.

He had encountered large bull sharks in the channels near Long Cay. He had to assume they would occupy the channel to the south. The spear shaft could be used for fending nosy ones. *But I'll have to swim sidestroke using only one arm, the other holding the spear.* Regardless, the southern route seemed the least risky. When he made it to the next cay, he would prioritize collecting rainwater while awaiting rescue. *Caitlin will likely contact authorities if I don't call this evening ... certainly after two missed calls.*

He went to the edge of the nearby cut, shining the flashlight beam into the water, watching as clumps of reddish-brown Sargassum weed passed in the current. The tide continued to fall from the bight, heading west. He judged the speed of the tide and depth of nearby shallows. The tide would likely slack in about three hours before flowing back into the bight, roughly an hour after sunrise. He grabbed the goggles and spear shaft along with the dry bag, setting off for the southern tip of Fish Cay.

****

Harper stayed low in the stern, watching intently for dropping banana spiders.

Moore kneeled up front, using his left hand to grab overhanging branches, pulling the canoe through the last stretch of the narrow mangrove creek. His right hand held the headless shaft of a golf club, ready to clear the next spider web that occupied the route.

Mosquitos and deer flies swarmed. The men sweated profusely.

Moore pointed the shaft at a branch ahead. "See the broken limb … and yellowish-green leaves? The break must have happened in the past two months." He swung the shaft back and forth sharply.

Harper flinched, quickly flicking away a spider that landed on his pant leg. *Big bastards*. "How much longer to the inner bay?"

"About eighty feet. Around the next bend."

A loud splash erupted just ahead, followed by a series of bumps and a slight lift of the canoe

"What the hell was that?" Harper exclaimed.

"A nice size gator."

Harper touched the revolver in his shoulder holster. "You come through here to go fishing? And get paid for it?"

"No pain, no gain. The little bay gets loaded with snook and small tarpon in January and February. The flyfishing is insane at times."

Harper looked past Moore. The mangrove leaves had thinned in front, the inner bay becoming visible.

Moore pulled them through the final twenty feet and into open water.

Harper scanned the surroundings. *Moore's right. Maybe a hundred yards in diameter ... at the most.*

A large mullet jumped in front of the bow, making a noticeable splash. Ibises burst from the mangrove branches to the right, emitting guttural grunts, wings whistling in harmony. A squawking blue heron joined the auditory mix—it stood on the east shoreline, next to a cabbage palm and within the area of interest. A couple of gators could be seen to the far left, near the northern edge of the little bay, their heads visible in the lee, exposed on the surface. Wind ripples ran toward the canoe. One of the gators started moving in their direction, disappearing below the surface.

Moore submerged a hand in the water. "Really warm right now. That's why the gators are active this early."

Harper touched the revolver again.

"I'll motor us to the east side," said Moore. "We need to switch ends. Shimmy to the middle, staying low—just don't lean to the side." Moore worked his way to the stern, crossing overtop of Harper, keeping his hands and boots on the narrow gunnels, his weight evenly distributed. "Okay. Take the bow seat, keep to the center."

Harper glanced at the remaining gator on the surface, wondering if the other one had reached the canoe. *And the center it will be. No way I'm falling in.* He carefully seated up front, continuing to scan the surrounding water.

Moore pulled the starter cord and engaged the forward gear, idling slowly to the eastern shore. He revved the engine at the last moment, thrusting the canoe's bow partway onto the low embankment, alongside the cabbage palm. The blue heron had already departed, squawking in protest.

"Hold up, Detective," Moore advised. He reached for the rifle case, retrieving the carbine. He loaded several large cartridges and chambered a round. "Check the immediate surroundings before you step off. Don't want you bit by a rattler or water moccasin."

Harper grabbed a two-way radio from a dry bag and clipped

it to his belt. A GPS navigator went into a pants pocket. "Okay if I get my gun out?"

"Wait until you get on land, just in case you fall. I don't want a bullet in me."

Harper made a visual scan before climbing out of the canoe. The ground was firmer than he expected. He stepped aside, retrieving the revolver and scanning again.

Moore came up the middle of the canoe and onto the terrain, pulling the canoe further up the embankment.

Both men stood still for a moment, studying the immediate area, neither seeing anything unusual.

Harper swept his hand back and forth, gesturing. "Probably best to look along this shoreline before going deeper into the brush."

"All right. I'll head that way," Moore said, pointing south. "You head north. Pay attention to sunny spots. A gator or snake might be warming there."

Harper stared at Moore's rifle. "Uh, I think we should stick together … it's best to have a corroborating witness if something is found."

Moore smiled. "Okay. Makes sense. Wasn't thinking like a detective. Which direction first?"

****

Harper took the two-way radio off his belt and keyed the mic. "Dispatch? Harper, here."

"Go ahead, Detective."

"I need a CSI team to the glades, near southeast Munson Bay. They should come by swamp buggy from the Tamiami Trail. Tell everyone to dress for snakes and bugs."

"Roger. What's your coordinates?"

Harper retrieved the handheld GPS navigator. "Let me know when you're ready."

"Fire away."

Harper provided the numbers. The dispatcher read them back.

"Correct," confirmed Harper.

"Back soon with the team's ETA."

"Thanks. Standing by.

"Roger. Out."

Both men stared at the kayak, hidden in a dense thicket of Brazilian pepper, about fifty feet from the edge of the small bay. Its camouflage pattern closely matched the leaves and limbs. A brown, double-ended paddle stuck through some lower branches at a downward angle.

"Keen eye, Detective," Moore said. "I walked right past it. Never saw the damn thing."

"Been at this a while." Harper went partway around the thicket, studying an opening between two cabbage palms, heading further east. He pointed. "The likely route for whoever left this."

"Agreed."

"Take it slow," Harper instructed as they headed for the opening. "Scan for gum, cigarette butts, boot prints, anything manmade or unusual looking."

"Roger that." Moore retook point, the rifle pointing down and to the left.

They worked through the vegetation, taking the route of least effort, assuming the kayaker would have done the same. The route led them to a small prairie of muhly grass, about a hundred feet long and half as wide. Several game trails crisscrossed the grass.

"What's that?" Harper pointed toward a nearby cabbage palm. A glint of sunlight reflected from the middle of the trunk. The reflective object was hidden within an arrangement of dead palm fronds.

They went over. Two glass portals were visible through

cutouts in the fronds, embedded in a green plastic case. Harper shined a small flashlight into the portals, shifting his head to see the interior from different angles. “Damn thing has a camera and some kind of optical sensor.” Harper stepped around the side, parting the fronds and checking the back of the box. “US Fish and Wildlife tag on the back.”

“A wildlife camera trap,” Moore surmised. “I’ll bet the second lens is a motion detector. They must be counting animals that run these trails.”

Harper couldn’t believe the potential good luck. He grabbed the two-way radio off his belt, holding it to his mouth, keying the mic.

“Dispatch? Harper.”

“Go ahead, Detective.”

“Have Jerry contact the local US Fish and Wildlife Office. I need the name and number of whoever placed a remote wildlife camera near the GPS coordinates I provided.”

“Roger, Detective. Anything else?”

“That’s it.”

“The CSI team still owes me their ETA. Looks like y’all are in an area called Hell’s Butt.”

Harper chuckled. “Gotta love the old-timers who named these places.”

“Ain’t that the truth.”

“Okay. Standing by.”

****

The incoming tide strengthened much sooner than Jake had estimated, pulling him further into the bight. He kicked hard but still lost ground—the one-armed sidestroking prevented him from attaining sufficient thrust to overcome the current. He had considered switching to the backstroke, but it would have required letting go of the spear shaft and dry bag, a bad decision if he failed to reach the cay. The dry bag would provide some needed flotation.

The attempted crossing had been unnerving. Multiple times he had used the spear to fend off nosy bull sharks. *Damn thugs.* The last one stuck around, nosing in repeatedly, only veering when the spear tip struck its face. It finally gave up, but the encounters had cost precious time.

The incoming tide steadily accelerated. His right arm stroked in concert with the scissor kick of his legs. The left hand held the spear at ready. His legs were cramping, worsening as the minutes passed, finally causing intense pain, forcing him to stop swimming and float with the incoming tide. *At least I'm heading into the bight and not out to sea.* The destination cay slipped away to the west.

The depth shallowed as he drifted further into the bight. *About seven feet now.* He lifted his head from the water and glanced toward the sun's position. *Almost directly overhead—maybe slightly to the west.* He estimated the time of day between noon and 1 p.m. The tide would turn in about four or five hours, the current flowing toward deeper water. *I'll need to find a shallow sandbar to anchor myself.* The thought of spending the night in the bight seemed daunting.

Several hours passed. The lengthy submergence in salt water caused him to urinate frequently, aggravating the already serious dehydration. His thirst became unbearable. *Try to relax and conserve energy.* He floated with little motion, using the dry bag for added buoyancy. Every so often, he observed the bottom contours, hoping to find a shallow spot that offered a place to kneel or sit until low tide exposed it to the air, offering the opportunity to sleep without choking on water.

****

Harper and Moore stood to the side of the small prairie clearing.

A swamp buggy with huge tires was parked nearby, covered with mud and debris from the difficult trek to the current location. Its owner sat high up in the open driver's seat. The retrieved kayak was strapped lengthwise to the buggy's roll bar, tilted upward, its stern secured to an enormous spare tire on the back. Several members of the homicide team stood nearby, swatting at the incessant mosquitoes.

"It's getting late, and the bugs are going nuts. You still okay with taking your canoe back through the creek?" asked Harper.

"I'll be fine. The winds are calm enough to cross the bay."

Harper studied an aerial photograph that had been brought by the team, pointing at a specific area. "What do you think of this clearing near the Tamiami Trail? I'm thinking it might have been a spot for the kayaker to have left a swamp buggy or get picked up by one."

Moore scanned the map, then pointed at a faint line. "That's probably a well-used game trail that leads from this spot to the clearing. The kayaker may have known about it."

Harper nodded and hollered for one of the team members.

The man came over. "Whatcha need, boss?"

Harper traced the route with his finger. "We'll be searching along this game trail and into that clearing as we head out of here." He handed the aerial photo to the team member. "Show the buggy driver and the others. We're leaving shortly."

"You got it." The man headed away.

"So, what do you think?" asked Moore. "Sure looks like someone framed Billy Watson, throwing the wig in the roots and hiding the kayak."

"That's a leap at this point. For all we know, it's someone who likes to fish the little bay, hiding the kayak rather than transporting the thing back and forth. The team said the buggy driver had a really hard time getting out here. He thinks the federal wildlife guys use an airboat to check on that camera system."

"I've never seen anyone else fish the inner bay, or even heard someone talk about it," countered Moore.

"That may be, but you aren't there every day of the year. And don't fishermen like to keep their best spots secret?" Harper glanced over. The team had assembled, ready to search the game trail. He turned back to Moore. "We'll see if the wildlife camera captured something of relevance, but don't hold your breath. Thanks again for the help. Remember, lips sealed about this."

****

Jake rested his head on the floating dry bag, arms holding it snug. His knees rubbed against a shell-strewn bottom in about three feet of water.

Lightning flashed to the west. Each illumination showed evidence of billowing thunderheads, briefly outlined against the nighttime darkness. *Keep coming, keep coming.* Rain from the incoming squall might help offset the increasingly severe dehydration. He hoped it would be a deluge. *Open the dry bag and your mouth. Catch what you can.*

Something swirled, brushing against his left thigh. Its skin felt like sandpaper. The swirls and brushing had happened multiple times. *Probably a small lemon shark.* He rocked slightly in the wind-driven chop, his knees slipping a few inches across the broken shells; some had sharp edges. His knees and toes stung from numerous cuts.

His left arm remained looped through the dry bag tether; his right hand grasped the spear shaft, fingers cramping spasmodically; toes were dug into the bottom, helping to hold him against the outgoing current. The tide continued to retreat, sending tons of water out of the bight. The depth had dropped a foot or more in the past hour. *How shallow will this spot get?* He hoped the bar would be exposed at low tide, allowing him to lie down and sleep. Thunder rumbled in the distance.

A sad thought came to mind. Simon's Bhagavad Gita book and its two enclosed photos were aboard *Cloud Catcher*, probably lost forever. Jake had read the underlined passages multiple times over the past two years, gaining a greater appreciation for what they represented, particularly considering what had happened at the Burmese bridge. The book and photos were irreplaceable.

Thoughts of those passages brought the current situation into perspective—not just karma but also dharma. *And here I am, kneeling in obeisance to the cosmic order of all things, awash in the primordial sea.*

The lightning flashed closer. He counted the seconds to determine the distance, another lesson he had learned from Simon. *One thousand one, one thousand two* .... Twenty-one seconds passed before the resulting thunder arrived. *Three miles away.*

The wind rose with the advancing squall line. Jake's head bobbed up and down in a rhythmic motion, the waves rising in concert with the wind. The rocking caused his knees and toes to slip a short distance. The sandpaper skin immediately brushed his leg, followed by a strong swirl. *Definitely a small shark.* He wondered if the cuts were bleeding much. The thought made him laugh, imagining Caitlin worried about him diving with large sharks. *Maybe this little guy will be my denouement. Ha, ha.*

The rhythmic rocking eventually lulled him to sleep. His head shifted, sliding off the bag. Salt water filled his mouth and nostrils. He sputtered. *Can't sleep yet, dammit.* He repositioned his head on the bag, trying to rest, thinking of Caitlin. *Here I am, love, a speck so slight, bobbing in a vast bight, enjoying my plight, at night. Ha, clever rhyme.*

A wave slapped his face, restoring sense to his thoughts. He wondered if Caitlin had called the Bahamian authorities. But then what? He felt a sinking feeling. Would they believe her? An American woman calling in a panic after a single missed call from her cruising husband? Satellite phones can have transmission difficulties. *They'll likely wait for more time to pass.*

A bright flash ruined his night vision, followed almost immediately by a loud clap of thunder. His eyes shut reflexively. *Shit! That was close, maybe a quarter of a mile. What is the electrocution range in salt water? A hundred yards? More? Less?* Another lightning bolt hit, followed quickly by another. *Is this how soldiers feel in an artillery barrage? A sitting duck with nowhere to hide?* He clutched the bag tightly. The water seemed shallower, the bottom closer, the current slowing.

Chapter 23

Caitlin's imagination had run the gamut after Jake failed to call, resulting in a night of fitful sleep. She told herself to calm down, recalling the garbled ending to their last phone conversation. *The lightning must have caused a problem with the satellite transmitter. I bet that's it.*

She placed the box of preloaded drug cartridges back in the fridge and glanced at the kitchen clock—6:47 a.m. Less than an hour before the morning call timeframe. The wait would be interminable.

She went to the bathroom and ran warm water against the cartridge while rotating it, warming the contents before placing it in the injector. The baseball cap hung on a hook next to the sink. Her hand reached toward it but stopped, pulling back. She studied herself in the mirror. The auburn hair had grown out an inch or so, the straightness replaced by curls. The oncology nurse said it was the result of the chemotherapy, a side effect that could last up to a year.

She tousled the curls with her fingers. *This is different.* She wondered if they would stretch into waves as her hair grew longer.

The cap remained on the hook. *The time has come to go without it.* She administered the injection and exited the bathroom, thoughts returning to Jake, wondering if the speared mutton snapper had contained roe sacs, imagining him frying and eating them for breakfast.

The kitchen clock approached 7:00 a.m. She decided to call him from the lab rather than wait at the cabin. *Hopefully the satellite transmitter is working.* She grabbed her purse and headed out the door.

****

A delirious vision held Jake in its grasp. An auburn-haired mermaid left the wall of a shimmering tavern, dropping her beer mug and stone crab, swimming upward in an undulating, rhythmic motion. The hair turned a deeper color as she came closer, arms outstretched. *Caitlin.* Her emerald eyes glowed brightly, glittering with passion and delight. He reached out, bringing his mouth to hers. *My love. I love you. ...* His fingers became entangled in slimy hair. Sharp tips scratched against his face. He recoiled. The vision evaporated, chased away by the scratching and a choking cough. Wracking chills shook his body. Both legs cramped, the pain intense. He tried to scream, but no sound came out, gasping for air. A surge of adrenaline shot from the center of his torso. He flung the slimy seaweed aside.

The cramping lessened, enabling other senses to take hold, the feel of the sand and broken shells against his skin, watery ripples hitting his feet. He attempted to raise his head, failing, the effort exhausting. His face remained against the sandy wetness; one eye closed. The other stared across the partially exposed sandbar. A nearby horse conch loomed large, its wet shell glistening in the early sunlight. Intermittent clumps of Sargassum weed dotted the sand, each the color of auburn hair.

A short stretch of white sand stood out, further down the bar. What was left of his logic recognized the need to get there before the tide rose higher. He attempted to move. Another round of chills coursed through his body, joined again by the painful cramping. A hoarse scream followed. The cramps held tight. Red-hot pokers stuck inside his muscles. He gasped for air, panting hard. A wave of nausea hit, adding retching to the mix of torturous spasms. It seemed an eternity before the pain and retching subsided. He closed his eyes, utterly exhausted. The rippling water rose higher, reaching his ankles.

****

Nielsen stopped the treadmill and walked to the wall-mounted television, keeping his eyes glued to the CNN morning news. An aerial video showed a partially burned yacht, its bow under water, the stern rising and falling in the waves. The camera zoomed to the stern, exposing the vessel's name and home port. He turned up the volume, listening intently.

"… *Cloud Catcher,* was discovered by a cargo ship early this morning in the Gulf Stream, halfway between Fort Lauderdale and Bimini. The US Coast Guard has searched the vessel and surrounding waters. No survivors have been located. Law enforcement sources have told CNN that the abandoned yacht is likely the victim of a drug-related piracy. Captured vessels have been used in the past to smuggle illicit drugs from the Bahamas, Cuba, and other Caribbean locations, typically rendezvousing with large speedboats in the Gulf Stream near Miami, then set afire and scuttled. We expect to learn the name of the yacht's owner within the next hour. Turning now to other breaking news …"

Nielsen turned off the TV. An attendant stood nearby, holding a towel and a small glass of freshly squeezed orange juice. He ignored the offering, exiting the second floor of the exercise facility and continuing across a covered walkway to the main section of his villa. He turned right and walked through an archway, entering the spacious master bath. The overhead rain shower had been turned on ahead of his arrival, a cool mist forming in the air. He headed through another archway to the bedroom, removing the mobile phone from its nightstand charger and checking the screen. *No voicemails.* He continued to the balcony. Early sunlight glinted off the Sunshine Skyway Bridge in the distance. Two sportfishing boats raced toward the Anna Maria City Pier, heading for the open gulf.

Nielsen tossed the mobile phone in his hand. *Tracking Crawford's departure will look bad if traced to me.* He debated calling the head of the PI firm and reinforcing the importance of keeping the tracking confidential. Instincts suggested otherwise, winning the debate. *Don't draw attention to the concern.*

He replaced the phone on the charger, retracing his steps to the master bath, luxuriating in the refreshing shower when a thought hit. *I'll get my aviation fleet involved in the search.* He stepped from the shower and toweled off, heading to the wall intercom and pressing a button.

"Yes, Mr. Nielsen."

"Contact our head of flight operations. Tell him to call my mobile phone, as soon as possible."

****

A flat-bottom, twenty-seven-foot sailboat slid across the shallow flats of the Bight of the Acklins, its centerboard fully retracted. The sails were set wing-on-wing, filled with a following northeast breeze, the foresail to port and the mizzen to starboard. Ben Grotebek stood in the cockpit, bare-chested, an inch over six feet, manning the upraised tiller—the tough-minded Vietnam veteran had stayed in great shape, lean and muscular, belying his forty-nine years. He kept a close eye on the bottom contours, easy to see in the clear water and morning light.

The wooden sailboat was made of his hands, built alongside his small cottage on Big Pine Key, in the Lower Florida Keys. *Ibis* was almost identical to *Egret*, her long-ago ancestor and famous sharpie that had plied the waters of Miami and Key Biscayne in the late 1800s. The modified New England design enabled running the shallow waters of Florida and the Bahamas while being able to cross the Gulf Stream in reasonable weather.

Ben hollered at Kara Newsome, his adventurous companion on the bow, twenty years his junior. "Careful up there. You don't want to be keelhauled in these shallows."

"The bight is huge!" she exclaimed in return.

****

Kara clutched the foremast tightly. Unlike Ben, she preferred to wear a T-shirt while underway, having been chafed across her breasts more than once by shifting rigging. After two months of sailing, the Bahamas had streaked her dark-brown hair with blonde tinges.

She looked back at Ben appreciatively. A man of strength and courage, the physical scars of an awful war to prove it. The other women in her Outward Bound class had been far less admiring, finding his style of survival instruction overly masculine and chauvinistic, rooted in a bygone era. Kara saw him differently: a self-made man who had dutifully volunteered for combat when many evaded it. *The other women can have their preppy "outdoorsmen." I prefer a man who's endured true hardship.*

She returned to the job at hand, monitoring the waters farther ahead. Moments passed before something caught her attention. A driftwood log with a yellow float lying alongside.

She yelled to Ben, "Exposed sandbar ahead. Directly on our heading. About two hundred yards."

"Should I fall to port or starboard?"

"There's deeper water to starboard, just off the bar."

"Hold tight. I'm lowering the centerboard a notch and jibing the mizzen sail."

Kara hugged the foremast close, keeping her eye on the yellow float and log. The bow turned about ten degrees to starboard. *Ibis* lurched, heeling to port as the mizzen sail swung across the aft section, refilling immediately with the wind.

Ben hollered, "How's the heading?"

Kara looked toward the bar and then back at the stern. Ben sat in the cockpit, having ducked the swinging boom. She shouted into the following wind, "More to starboard. About five degrees." The adjusted heading would allow *Ibis* to pass the bar without grounding the centerboard.

The bow pointed further to the west, causing the foresail to block her view of the approaching sandbar. She came forward a step, peering around the foremast. The driftwood log was partially submerged in the rising tide. It had a blue material caught around its midsection. *Probably a piece of tarp.*

A sudden movement caught her attention. She focused intently. Something moved again at the bottom of the log. *What is ...?* "*Ben! Oh my God! Ben!*"

She let go of the foremast and lowered her hands to the deck, scrambling over the cabin top and into the cockpit, pointing frantically. "A man is lying on the sandbar. His legs just moved!" They both lowered down, looking under the bottom of the mizzen sail.

Ben didn't hesitate. "Stay down!" He pushed the tiller hard to port, forcing *Ibis* to pivot right, swinging her bow directly into the wind, the two sails luffing. "Furl the foresail."

Kara scrambled back to the bow. She uncleated the halyard line and dropped the foresail and its boom to the deck. Both were soon furled around the foremast, tied securely in place with the halyard.

Ben had kept the mizzen sail from grabbing the wind, bringing it tight to center and shifting the tiller back and forth as *Ibis* drifted backward, using the rudder to steer in reverse, keeping the bow to the wind, allowing the mizzen to act like a wind vane. "Hold the foremast," he hollered, pushing the tiller away while shifting to the port side of the cockpit. The bow fell off the wind to starboard, heading toward the cut that bordered the bar.

"Get the anchor ready," Ben shouted.

"The Danforth?"

Ben glanced at the sandy bottom before confirming her choice.

Kara retrieved the chosen anchor from the forward hatch, along with its connected chain and line.

Ben navigated to a spot upwind of the man, once again holding the bow directly into the wind, allowing *Ibis* to slide backward. "Let out forty feet of scope."

Kara slid the anchor into the water, the tips of its flanges facing to the rear. The anchor quickly settled on the sandy bottom at a depth of about four feet. She threw the estimated forty feet of line into the water, securing it to the bow cleat.

Ben continued steering backward, pushing and pulling on the tiller, allowing *Ibis* to back down without the mizzen filling.

Kara clutched the foremast. The sharpie jolted as the flanges of the anchor buried deeply in the sand, the anchor line coming taut. She looked over. *Ibis* sat parallel to the prone man, about twenty feet off the edge of the sandbar. His legs moved sharply again, clearly cramping.

"Get the smaller water jug," Ben instructed. "Only give small sips. I'll drop the mizzen and bring the emergency kit."

Kara located the jug in the cabin and returned topside, jumping in and swimming sidestroke to the bar's edge.

The tall man lay face down, his legs partially submerged in the rising tide, head turned to the left. His hair and beard were encrusted with sand and seaweed. The blue swim trunks were ripped open, exposing most of his left buttock. A deep, ragged wound oozed blood; sand and detritus were stuck in the exposed tissue.

She came forward and kneeled by his upper torso, feeling for the carotid artery. *Pulse is rapid and weak.* She brought her face close to his. “Hey. Can you hear me?” The man stirred slightly, making a croaking sound. His lips were badly parched.

She slid her knees back, reaching under his left armpit and midsection, trying to roll him over. *Way too heavy.* A large splash hit the water behind her. She glanced over. Ben held the emergency medical kit in the air, side-stroking.

More croaking.

She opened the jug of water, pouring a small amount into its cap, repeatedly wetting her fingertips and gently rubbing them inside the man’s lips. He started to suck against her fingers.

Ben came up. “We need to get him higher on the bar.”

****

“What’s wrong?” Caitlin asked, immediately concerned. Ida Hoefler and Judith Kerner had entered the front office wearing downcast expressions.

Hoefler came over, touching her shoulder. “Let’s go to the chickee. Melissa will be here shortly to cover.”

“Why? What’s going on?”

“It’s best if we talk there,” Judith added gently.

Jake had been unreachable during the morning timeframe. Caitlin glanced at his picture. She looked up, tears forming. “Tell me.”

Hoefler reached for a tissue and handed it to Caitlin, placing a hand on her shoulder while explaining what they had seen and heard on the news. “… but there’s always hope. Jake is very resourceful. He could have survived.”

Caitlin broke down, sobbing inconsolably.

****

A woman's voice swirled at the fuzzy edge of Jake's consciousness. *Caitlin?* A sensation of lightness joined the sound of words and tones. He felt his body moving across the sand. *But how?*

Fingers flicked his face. The taste of fresh water came back. He sucked at the wet fingers, wanting more. The flicking returned, followed by water entering his mouth. *Lovely*. A hard slap this time, the fingers bigger, rougher—a deeper voice. *Simon*?

Encrusted eyelids made the awakening more difficult. Jake squinted in the sunlight. The blurred image of a woman's face appeared, then faded.

"His eyes just fluttered."

Not Caitlin. Large hands brought his head and shoulders forward, resting Jake against something cushioned. A bottle touched his lips. More fresh water flowed into his mouth. *Glorious*. The attempt to swallow failed, causing sputtering and coughing. The shivering returned. Sharp pains coursed through his legs and torso.

The deeper voice again. "Severe dehydration … mix these broth cubes."

A different fluid soon entered Jake's mouth, salty and meaty tasting. He gagged immediately. Retching in spasms. His eyes opened slightly. The blurred image of the woman reappeared. She leaned toward him on her knees. Jake blinked, his vision still blurry. A man stood behind her. *Who is …?* Jake tried to raise, falling back.

The man spoke. "Easy now, buddy."

****

Kara brought the bottle back to the man's lips, placing a hand behind his head and feeding the broth more slowly.

He gagged less, swallowing most of the salty fluid, then shivered, muscles cramping painfully. "Arghhh!"

"We need to get him out of the sun," said Ben.

The man raised a hand, reaching for the bottle.

Kara pushed the hand down, bringing the bottle to his lips, providing more volume this time. "How do we get him aboard? He's really tall … and heavy."

"I'll bring *Ibis* closer to the sandbar. We'll rinse him off and slide him over the gunnel and into the cockpit. Keep giving him the broth. There're two more cubes in the kit." Ben reentered the water.

The man swallowed most of what she provided, followed by a single word, barely audible, his voice weak and hoarse. "Name."

Kara leaned close. "My name?"

He gave a slight nod.

She smiled. "Kara. What's yours?"

"Jake." Spasms rippled throughout his body, causing a shaking seizure that wouldn't stop.

She grasped his head, pressing her body against his until the seizure subsided. She went back to kneeling, bringing more broth to his lips. "Let's take it slower, Jake. Focus on keeping this down."

****

Caitlin pulled into the tavern parking lot, wanting to monitor the news.

The sign on the outside wall read "Closed." She checked her watch—11:15 a.m. The tavern would open in fifteen minutes.

Harry Watson came out the door, turning left. A chalkboard easel commanded his attention. He erased the first digit and changed the price of steamed crab claws, now $7.95 a pound.

Caitlin hurried from the car, intercepting him. She didn't have to say anything.

"Really sorry about Jake." He held the door open.

The wait staff had gathered at the bar, watching the television on the back counter. Caitlin approached them.

One of the older waitresses saw her coming, breaking from the group to provide a hug, starting to cry. "Baby, I'm so sorry."

Caitlin closed her eyes, hugging back, fighting the resurgence of tears.

Others in the group moved apart, allowing Caitlin to sit on a stool closest to the television. The CNN anchor was announcing an unrelated news item.

Harry returned with a box of tissues and a glass of iced sweet tea.

Caitlin took a tissue and dabbed at her eyes, trying to compose herself.

A young waitress put her arm around Caitlin's shoulder, attempting to strike a hopeful tone, expressing her belief in God's goodness. "The Lord will protect Jake. I know he will."

An advertisement replaced the news, the triteness of the upbeat jingle clashing with the heavy mix of fear and despair that roiled inside Caitlin. She placed her hands over her ears, staring at the bar top. A few tears dripped on the worn mahogany.

The advertisement faded, replaced by the next news segment. Caitlin stared with horror at the background image of *Cloud Catcher*, half submerged and buffeted by waves. Most of her superstructure and upper deck were missing, the remnants charred from flames. A United States Coast Guard vessel maintained a position close by. Divers could be seen affixing inflatable bags to keep what remained of the yacht afloat.

"We go now to Sherri Jennick in Tallahassee with more

breaking news about the burned yacht discovered floating in the Gulf Stream off of Fort Lauderdale."

"Thanks, Lynne. The yacht's owner is Jacob Crawford, the former mayor of Marcosta Island in southwest Florida. The island has been the subject of recent news regarding an arson-murder on the set of a new movie by Adrien Satorri."

The anchor cut in. "Sherri, you heard Retired Admiral Tom Davis, former head of the DEA, describe the burning and sinking as likely foul play by drug smugglers. Have you heard if Mr. Crawford was cruising on the yacht and who else might have been with him?"

"We've learned he was on a solo voyage to the Bahamas. That's all we know at this time."

"Well, we sincerely hope Mr. Crawford is found alive and unharmed," said the anchor. "That was Sherri Jennick reporting from Tallahassee. Stay with us through the commercial break. New information has just been released regarding the Ukrainian airliner that disappeared over Cyprus."

Harry turned down the volume and focused on Caitlin. "You want something stronger than iced tea? Southern Comfort? I remember you drinking it long ago. Might help some."

Caitlin nodded, biting her lower lip. *This can't be happening. Not to my Jake. I should never have encouraged him to go.* She felt numb.

Several locals arrived for an early lunch, noticing Caitlin and the assembled waitstaff, heading over to check on what was happening. Harry came back with the Southern Comfort, intercepting their questions.

****

Ibis remained anchored alongside the sandbar. Kara stood in the cockpit, arguing with Ben. Jake dozed fitfully in the forward berth, his head toward the bow.

"You're being paranoid," she said. "He seems nice."

Ben shook his head in disagreement. "We know nothing about him. Only a first name."

"You need to put that away; you're scaring me." She pointed at the shotgun resting on top of the cabin, just beyond the open hatchway. "This is the peaceful Bahamas."

Ben raised his voice, sounding irritated. "You're being naïve. The Bahamas has drug gangs. They've been known to murder people." He pointed toward the cabin. "What the hell happened to him? Something peaceful? It's likely the result of foul play, a drug deal gone bad."

Kara shook her head in frustration, pulling off her damp T-shirt and throwing it on the cabin top next to the gun. She stepped backward through the hatchway, her look defiant. "Fine. Keep the gun out." She grabbed a dry T-shirt from a nearby cubbyhole, donning it before heading to Jake.

Ben hollered after her, his voice carrying through the open hatchway. "We're sailing to a different location for the night. I'm pulling anchor."

Kara came to the edge of the bed, sitting in an open spot on the corner, her feet resting on the cabin floor. Jake lay on his stomach, diagonally across the bed, his torn swim trunks removed. His feet dangled off the opposite corner, twitching frequently. Gasps followed periodic bouts of cramping and shivering. She wanted to cover him with a blanket, but Ben had instructed otherwise, not wanting further loss of electrolytes from sweating.

She went to her knees on the bed, closely studying the cuts and abrasions that covered the length of Jake's body, head to toe. *The ragged wound on the left buttock is gnarly.*

A brief snort brought her face parallel to his. His blue eyes opened, darting in apparent confusion. She leaned in closer, giving his hand a squeeze. "Jake, you're on a bed in a sailboat." She grabbed an extra pillow, propping his head higher, squeezing his hand again.

This time, he squeezed back. “Water.”

“You bet.” She left the bed for the small galley.

Heavy footsteps went across the cabin top above them.

She filled a third of a cup with watery broth and returned to Jake’s side. “Can you lift yourself up?”

Jake managed to inch further up on the pillows, grimacing in the process. He turned to his right side and reached for the cup with his left hand, propping his right arm to raise his head and shoulders.

More footsteps could be heard overhead, followed by the anchor line dropping on the foredeck.

She positioned the cup in the open palm, helping guide it to his mouth.

Jake closed his eyes after swallowing, returning to the prone position. He continued to lie on his stomach, shivering in waves.

The anchor chain rattled onto the deck, followed by a loud thunk as the anchor was dropped into a hatch on the other side of the bulkhead. Footsteps hurried across the cabin roof toward the stern.

“Ben just pulled anchor,” Kara explained. “He’s taking us to a better anchorage for the night.”

A jet plane could be heard in the distance, the sound rising and falling.

Jake raised his head, his voice wavering. “Not … west.”

Kara cocked her head, studying Jake’s expression of concern. “Don’t sail west?”

He nodded, lowering his head.

“Why?”

“Men … tried to kill me.”

“Where?”

“Fish Cay.”

“I’ll tell Ben.”

Kara went to the hatchway.

Ben took his eyes off the horizon. "A private jet is going back and forth … no official markings on the fuselage."

"Did you signal it?"

"Hell no. I don't trust whoever is searching."

"What are you talking about?"

"The jet might belong to a drug cartel, some drug kingpin." He pointed past her toward the cabin. "I don't want us mixed up in whatever is going on with him."

Kara wanted to argue but stopped, remembering Jake's warning. "Don't go west. Jake said some men tried to kill him that direction. Near Fish Cay."

Ben shot her a look that said *I told you so*. He studied the eastern side of the bight, pushing the tiller more to port. The other hand reached for a line that controlled the centerboard, lowering it further. "Okay. We're heading for the northwest corner of the Acklins. I'll be tacking into the wind. It'll take a while to get there."

****

Officer Pearson had delivered a message and phone number, finding Caitlin at the bar.

She opened a creaky door on the tavern's second floor. The narrow room resembled more of an oversized closet than an office. Milk crates occupied the left side, stacked on their sides for easy access, filled with wrinkled T-shirts, shorts, and other clothing. Camouflage hunting apparel hung on wall hooks to the right. A desk filled the end, cluttered with paperwork and tacky objects, mostly bawdy mermaid figurines. The wall above held a black velvet painting and a calendar from an airboat manufacturer; the August photo fit with the figurines. Noise from the bar and restaurant permeated the floorboards. She grabbed the phone handset and dialed the Miami number, sitting at the desk.

A woman's voice answered, "FBI, how may I direct your call?"

Caitlin glanced nervously at Pearson's handwriting. "Agent Nolen, please."

"May I ask who's calling?"

"Caitlin Crawford."

"One moment." Music played briefly, followed by a series of clicks.

"Thanks for returning my call, Ms. Crawford."

"Please tell me my husband is alive." She held her breath.

"I'm sorry, I wish I could."

She exhaled slowly, the moment of hope dissipating, replaced with a sense of dread.

"I was hoping you could provide me with some information," said Nolen.

Caitlin remained silent, struggling to compose herself.

"Ms. Crawford?"

"What information?"

"Did your husband communicate with you during his voyage?"

"Yes. He had a satellite phone."

"When did you last speak with him?"

"Two evenings ago." She thought of Jake's crackling voice at the end of that call. *Will that be the last time I hear it?* It already felt like an eternity.

"Did he mention his location when he called? We know he cleared customs at Clarence Town on Long Island. The entry form states the next port of call as Georgetown, Exumas."

"He was on the west side of the Bight of the Acklins, near a little island. Fish … Fish Cay, I think."

The sound of pen to paper came through the handset.

"Okay, thank you. Do you know of anyone who may have wanted to harm your husband?"

"The news said it was a drug gang."

"Yes. However, at this stage we have to consider other potential suspects."

Caitlin didn't hesitate. "He's been a thorn in the side of Derek Nielsen, the Tampa real estate developer."

"We've learned of their adversarial relationship. Anyone else?"

"No, unless it's someone from his days in Boston. Many of our island residents are upset at him, but none would do something like this. Can you tell me anything about the search? How long it will continue?"

Nolen paused before answering. "I'm not able to say."

"Who can?"

"Afraid I'm your point of contact. The FBI is now leading the investigation, working in concert with the DEA."

Caitlin's heart sank. "Do you mean Jake is assumed to be …?" She couldn't bring herself to say the word.

"There's always the possibility your husband survived, but we must be realistic, given the pattern and circumstances. The information about his last known location might extend the search timeframe, but I'll have to check. That area may have already been surveyed."

Caitlin stared at the coffee-stained blotter below, a hand against her forehead, elbows resting on the desktop. She fought against the impact of the agent's words, the ultimate despair trying to take hold. *I can't give up hope. Not yet.*

****

Ibis lay anchored in the lee of Acklins Island, positioned on the eastern side of the bight. The centerboard was fully retracted, allowing the flat-bottom sharpie to float in a mere foot of water, affording added security. Large outboard engines would run aground well before reaching the shallow anchorage. The muddy bottom made wading virtually impossible—the limestone muck would sink a grown man to his waist.

Jake reclined on the forward berth, leaning partly to his right side to keep pressure off the left buttock. He slowly flexed his legs and arms. It felt like everything hurt, inside and out. *At least I'm alive.*

The butt wound had been cleaned and doused with an iodine tincture. Ben tried to close the ragged tissue with sutures but had given up. The buttock was crisscrossed with strips of medical tape. An underlying wad of gauze absorbed the bloody oozings. The iodine antiseptic also coated the numerous smaller cuts and scrapes, coloring them amber.

Ben sat on the hatchway step, wiping down a shotgun of a comparable design and finish to the one Jake had purchased. Kara stirred a pot of stew on the single-burner galley stove. The remnants of a spectacular sunset lit the underside of cumulus clouds, visible through the open hatch.

"Need to piss yet?" inquired Ben.

Jake pushed against the waistband of the loaner gym shorts, testing the fullness of his bladder. "Nope."

"Drink a larger quantity."

Jake grabbed the nearby jug of fresh water, downing a third.

"We need to get you to a medical clinic," said Ben. "There's bound to be one on Crooked. It's only a matter of time before some of those wounds get infected, especially the one on your butt."

"There's no need to put me ashore," said Jake, worrying about the likelihood of local gang members. "I can get a seaplane sent down from Miami. Do you have a satellite phone on board? I'll cover the cost."

Kara chuckled. "The only communications we have are a weather radio and semaphore flags."

Jake reacted with surprise. "You're kidding?"

"I'm not. Ben's a throwback. Loves the old ways of the sea."

Jake pointed at a lantern near the hatchway. "Let me guess

… it burns whale oil."

"Don't throw me that far back." Ben returned the shotgun to the cabin top. He stared at Jake intently. "Seaplane, huh? Just snap your fingers and down it comes. You must have some fancy connections in Miami."

Jake noted the suspicious tone. *Probably thinks I'm mixed up in drug smuggling. It would fit the circumstances.*

The wind had rotated to the southeast. Ben stood in the open hatchway, announcing a need to reset the direction of the anchor. He left, crossing the cabin's roof toward the bow.

Kara ladled some of the stew, bringing Jake a half-filled bowl. "I hope you like conch and potatoes. Ben pounded the meat yesterday. It shouldn't be too hard on your gut."

Jake's appetite had returned with a vengeance. "Thanks." He stirred the bowl to cool its contents. "How long have you and Ben been together?"

"About six months. We met at Outward Bound, up in Maine."

"Hurricane Island?"

She seemed surprised. "You've been there?"

"No. I saw a presentation during a fundraising event in Boston."

"You donated to the program?"

"Not a large amount."

"You don't sound like someone from Boston."

Ben came back, resuming his perch in the hatchway.

Jake responded to Kara, "I'm from Marcosta Island, off the coast of southwest Florida."

She turned to Ben. "Jake's been a donor to the Hurricane Island program."

"Nice of you," said Ben, looking slightly surprised. "I remember Marcosta Island on the map. Outward Bound has a program that operates out of the Lower Florida Keys in the winter, using pulling boats with rudimentary sails. We come across Florida Bay to the west side of the Everglades and isolate students along the shoreline—solo survival training."

Jake finished the bowl.

"More?" Kara asked, looking pleased.

"It's delicious. I'll have more in a bit." Jake pushed himself off the bed, wincing from the bite wound and numerous cuts. "Now I need to piss."

****

Detective Harper muted the department TV, returning to a desk in the middle of the bullpen, his mind racing. *Crawford's friend may have been framed for murder, and now Crawford himself has likely perished in an attack on his yacht.* Harper tapped a ballpoint pen against the freshened cup of coffee, wondering if there was a connection. The other hand scratched at mosquito bites on his neck. He glanced at the large wall clock—7:34 p.m.

Jerry walked over, waving a yellow Post-it note in the air, clearly pleased with himself. "I got the home phone number of the US Fish and Wildlife researcher. He lives in Immokalee."

"Good job. Speaking of home, why don't you head out and get some rest? It's been a long two-day stretch."

"What, and leave you with all the fun?"

Harper smiled. *The kid's a keeper*.

"Are you contacting the wildlife guy tonight?" asked Jerry.

"Thinking about it. Curious what they're doing with that camera system."

"Me too."

"Reheat a cup of joe and meet me in the conference room. We'll call him on the speakerphone."

Jerry held up a hand. "Before you get up, I've got the other thing you wanted." He placed a printout on Harper's desk. A map of the Everglades was covered with crisscrossing trails. "There's the network of swamp buggy routes. The red dot is the clearing near the Tamiami Trail."

"Damn. Looks like a plate of spaghetti. A buggy could have reached the clearing from lots of locations."

"Here's what I don't get," said Jerry. "Why walk to the clearing for pickup? It's a tough slog, but a swamp buggy could have made it to the hidden kayak."

"Assuming the kayaker is our perp. He might not have wanted fresh buggy tracks leading to that little bay, planning to retrieve the kayak after enough time had passed. Plus, it was nighttime. The buggy driver would have needed to use headlights or a spotlight to navigate the route, potentially arousing suspicion. Frog hunters operate at night in the swamps."

Jerry looked confused. "So how did the perp get the kayak to that hiding spot in the first place? There were no drag marks or indication of buggy traffic. The kayak's too heavy to carry all the way from the clearing."

"It could have arrived by a boat during the festival, which suggests accomplices. There were kayaks in the bay that evening, coming ashore along with dinghies from anchored boats. The perp could have hidden the kayak close to Horseshoe Basin, retrieving it after bringing Watson's skiff back from the arson-murder, then headed for the narrow creek on the other side of the bay. It's only a four-mile crossing."

"It would have to be someone with intimate knowledge of the creek and inner bay," Jerry noted. "Someone from the island, maybe?"

"Or the mainland. Possibly Everglades City or one of the residential enclaves that are connected to these buggy trails." Harper checked the wall clock. "Let's go call the wildlife researcher. If we're lucky, he'll save us a lot of time and effort."

****

The threesome sat in the cockpit of *Ibis*, their faces illuminated by the light of the lantern. Lightning flashed in the western sky. The squall line ran from north to south, out near Fish Cay.

Jake wore one of Ben's T-shirts. It was a tight fit, rubbing against some of the cuts and scrapes. He inclined to the right, keeping pressure off the painful butt wound. Ben and Kara sat on the other side. The questioning continued.

"Then what happened?" Ben asked.

"They took *Cloud Catcher* westward, out to deep water."

"Why didn't you stay on Fish Cay? Why try the risky swim?"

"I thought the pirates might return."

"Are you mixed up in drugs?" Ben finally asked, exposing his suspicion outright.

Jake gave a short laugh. "I was, but not how you're thinking. I invented biopharmaceuticals."

"Your Boston connection," Kara concluded.

Jake nodded. *Perceptive.*

Ben shifted to another angle. "Why'd you go back to Marcosta?"

"There were multiple reasons."

"And then what, you run for mayor after inventing drugs?" asked Ben skeptically.

"I never intended to be the island's mayor. There was a groundswell of support after I led an effort that blocked a billionaire resort developer."

"A billionaire?" asked Kara. "Is he vindictive?"

"He uses shady tactics, but I highly doubt he would stoop this low, and particularly now. He's managed to circumvent the blockage."

"You don't seem like a politician," said Ben.

"Gimme a break. I never wanted to be one. As I said, I'm a

scientist."

"Ben," Kara said sternly. She folded her arms, leaning back, clearly frustrated by his continued suspicion. No one spoke for several minutes, the tension palpable. Jake shifted his seating to ease the butt pain, leaning further right.

Ben reengaged, apparently noting Jake's discomfort. "We'll get you ashore, near the road that runs the length of Crooked Island. You can find a medical clinic from there. But I don't want us seen with you by locals."

"Ben Grotebek, stop it!" Kara exclaimed.

Jake looked down. *I'm causing serious tension between the two of them—and after they saved my life.* He thought about the pirates and their attempt to find him on Fish Cay. They could definitely be locals. *Ben's right. I might be putting them at risk.*

Ben stood. "It's getting late."

"I'll stay out here," said Jake. "It's the only thing that makes sense, given the limited space below."

Ben arched his back, twisting from side to side. "Okay, but nothing funny." He grabbed the lantern and held out a hand to Kara. "Let's get below."

She didn't respond, arms still folded.

"You're right," Jake said abruptly. "Just take me near shore in the morning. Somewhere that keeps you from being seen. I'll remove the bandages and change back to my swim trunks, then slip over the side and wade or swim the final distance. The salt water should remove the iodine stains. It'll look as though I made it across the bight on my own."

"That's absolutely ridiculous," said Kara.

Ben wasted no time agreeing with Jake. "Great plan. We'll pull anchor once there's enough light to navigate the shallows." He headed below, making obvious the retrieval of the shotgun from the cabin top, laying it along the edge of the bed.

"You should go with Ben," Jake said quietly.

Her jaw muscles were clenched tightly, visible from the glow of the lantern.

Jake tried again. “Listen, Ben has the right instincts. The pirates are likely part of a Bahamian drug gang. There could very well be locals involved. He just wants you to be safe.”

Ben came back to the hatchway, handing a blanket to Jake. “Kara?”

She let out a sigh, then stood and went below. Ben grabbed the lantern and closed the cabin door, lowering the hatch.

A short while later, Jake could hear the muffled sounds of an argument. He moved closer to the stern, adjusting position to ease the buttock pain. The argument died out, allowing the night sky to envelop the moment. Jake pulled the blanket around him as a gentle breeze caressed his face. Wavelets lapped at the hull in a metronomic rhythm. Exhaustion completed the task, bringing welcome sleep.

****

Caitlin stood, holding the bar to steady herself, wondering what Harry needed to say. He came around, helping her navigate to the far edge of the back deck. The dark waters of Passage Channel flowed toward the gulf, the tide going out.

He continued to hold her arm, a sorrowful look in his eyes. “That FBI dude called again. I hope I done it right. Said you was too tired to talk and all. There’s more news coming … in about a half hour. He was wanting you to know first. They ain’t searching for Jake no more.”

Caitlin closed her eyes, her lips quivering. The thought of jumping into the channel flashed through her mind.

Harry shared the details, the reason for stopping the search. “They done found Jake’s dinghy on some small island … all burned up, bullet holes in the motor. Dammit, looks like the worst done happened.”

Caitlin’s knees buckled, the depth of the loss overwhelming.

My Jake is gone forever, dying violently in the middle of nowhere. A howl of despair echoed across the channel waters.

Harry caught her, going to his knees to buffer the collapse, holding her tight. Caitlin sobbed uncontrollably, eventually starting to retch. He eased her gently to the edge of the dock, allowing her to vomit into the water below.

A waitress came close. “How can I help?”

“Get a wet washcloth—and a wad of paper towels.”

The sobbing and retching continued.

The waitress returned. “You need something else?”

“Naw, thanks.” Harry used the washcloth and towels, gently wiping and drying Caitlin’s mouth and face.

She unwound from his grasp, sitting with her back against a piling, inhaling fitfully. She took the washcloth and finished the job.

“I’ll drive you home,” offered Harry. “One of the staff’ll follow and get me back.”

The thought of the empty cabin was too much to bear. “I don’t want to go home.” She took several deep breaths before gesturing toward the bar area. “The news. I want to hear it.”

Harry helped her up, leading her inside. The stool remained empty. The group parted to let her through. She sat, staring numbly at the partially filled tumbler. The steady supply of Southern Comfort had helped dull the emotions, taking her to the edge of drunkenness. She downed the remainder. The sweetness of the Southern Comfort removed the taste of the retching. Childhood friends closed ranks. Someone placed an arm around her. Others made sure she knew they were there, expressing their support.

Chapter 24

L*oud snoring?* Caitlin reached across the bed, fingers grasping at the emptiness. *Who's here?* She threw the covers aside, swinging her legs and sitting up, still dressed in the previous day's clothes. *Ugh.* She rubbed fingers through her hair, head down. The curls felt sticky. A recollection surfaced amid the pounding headache.

Harry slept in Jake's reading chair, his bald scalp visible as she left the bedroom. He snorted and jerked, resuming the snoring.

A full bladder encouraged a timely pace to the bathroom, walking lightly. She finished and stood in front of the sink. An open bottle of ibuprofen sat on the side. She swallowed two tablets, then another, drinking multiple cups of faucet water—the alcoholic dehydration demanding its morning tribute.

The mirror exposed her haunting, disheveled appearance. Dark circles and streaks of dried tears gave evidence of the fitful sleep, the nightmarish violence unrelenting … replaying over and over. *Jake murdered at the hands of a drug gang.* A loss too great to comprehend; a void that could never be filled. She made no effort to address the mirror's reflection; her appearance befitted a grieving widow.

The phone rang. She flushed the toilet, hurrying from the bathroom.

Harry lurched in the chair, coming awake.

"Hello?" said Caitlin, squinting. Sunlight filled the kitchen window.

"This is Kathy with the Sylvester Cancer Center in Miami. Am I speaking with Caitlin Crawford?"

"What's this about?"

"I'm calling with a reminder of your Wednesday appointment. I also have some pre-visit questions and instructions."

"I … I won't be coming."

"Dr. Baird believes the scheduled tests are very important."

"My husband has been murdered."

"My goodness, I …"

Caitlin hung up.

The toilet flushed again. Heavy footsteps approached, creaking across the cabin floorboards. She turned to face Harry. He clearly hadn't slept well either.

"You didn't need to stay," said Caitlin.

"Maggie said you shouldn't oughta be alone." He scratched at the bottom of his beer belly, exposed below a wrinkled T-shirt. "She told me to stick here."

Caitlin touched his shoulder, her voice subdued. "Thanks."

"Maggie wants to come over. Supposed to call her when you's up.

"I'd rather be alone."

"You sure? You don't look too good."

"I'm sure."

"Okay, then. Guess I'll be heading on. Really sorry about Jake." Harry hugged her and left through the side door, driving away.

She drank another glass of water, leaning against the sink counter, a resurgence of sorrow overtaking the emotional numbness. The phone rang again.

"Hello."

The caller's voice was somber. "Caitlin, it's Bill Atkins in Chicago. I heard the terrible news. I wanted to say how very sorry I am."

"Thank you," she said softly.

"Now's not the time, but I will have some important matters to discuss. Please call me when you're ready."

"What kind of matters?"

Atkins hesitated before answering, "Most important is obtaining death certificates. We will need to get the process …"

"I'll call back." She hung up, squeezing her eyes shut, trying and failing to suppress the horrible image of Jake's death. *Such a good man. It can't have happened to him—no, No, NO!* A scream filled the cabin, a shriek of pure agony. She fell to the floor sobbing, curling into a fetal position, suffocating under the weight of an enormous loss. The sobbing continued, slowly diminishing as minutes passed.

The phone rang again. She rose to her knees, stretching to reach the handset, barely composing herself to answer. "Hello?" The line crackled. For a moment, her heart jumped.

"Caitlin? Is that you?"

"Anna?"

"We just learned the devastating news over here. Oh, Caitlin, I'm so very sorry."

Caitlin tried to reply but failed. She sat with her back against the wall. The sobbing returned.

The line continued to crackle. A voice could be heard in the background, someone hollering.

Caitlin struggled to contain the sobs, managing to utter "thank you" before the sobbing regained momentum.

Nyholm spoke again, her voice filled with emotion. "I can't

imagine the depth of your heartbreak. Is there anything you need? Anything I can do?"

Caitlin sniffled. "No. I'll …" She couldn't continue, starting to sob again.

The line crackled. "I'll be back in touch soon. Please, please, know I'm thinking of you." The crackling stopped.

Caitlin stayed sitting, elbows on knees, fingers spread through the curls. The phone handset lay beside her, beeping. Swallowing the entire bottle of pain pills became an obsessive thought, wanting to escape the agony of her broken heart, longing to join Jake. She grabbed the kitchen counter and stood, starting for the bathroom.

The crunch of footsteps could be heard outside, followed by a loud knock on the kitchen door.

Caitlin stopped, hanging her head, unable to move.

A raised voice joined another round of knocking. "Caitlin, it's Donna. Barbara and Francis are with me. Honey, you shouldn't be home alone."

****

Jake remained below, lying on the forward berth, observing Ben and Kara through the open hatchway. Discarded bandages were gathered in a bucket close by.

Ben stood on the port side stern of *Ibis*, a hand on the raised tiller. The centerboard remained fully retracted, allowing the flat-bottom sharpie to slide over the shallow flats at a fast clip, the sails again set wing-on-wing, this time filled with a southerly breeze. He pushed the tiller slightly to starboard, navigating toward the channel that split the islands of Crooked and Acklins. Kara sat in the forward section of the cockpit, finishing a bowl of rolled oats and evaporated milk.

Moments later, she came through the hatchway, placing the bowl on the galley counter. "Ben says about twenty minutes.

Ready to remove the bandaging from the butt wound?" She reached for a towel.

Jake rolled to his right side, preparing to grit his teeth.

She kneeled next to him, positioning the towel before spreading the torn swim trunks. A large wad of tape, yellow-red gauze, and closure strips joined the other bandaging in the bucket. "You can roll back. Try to keep your butt on the towel. The wound's still seeping blood." She washed her hands in the sink.

"Thanks for the care." Jake reached for the nearby jug of water. Ben had encouraged him to hydrate in anticipation of the trek ahead.

"I'm sorry that Ben is making you do this."

"It's fine. I wasn't thinking clearly. The last thing you need is bad guys coming aboard."

"But something might happen to you. If the bad guys *are* on Crooked Island, you'll be walking right into their hands."

"It's a chance I have to take. The butt wound needs prompt attention."

She shook her head. "I still don't like it."

"Look, I should be dead on that sandbar, getting chewed on by crabs. I'm forever indebted to both of you." Jake slid down the bed, sitting at the edge, holding the towel against the wound. He pointed at a notepad on the galley counter. "I wrote down a name and phone number. Bill Atkins is my attorney in Chicago. If you or Ben are ever in need, call him."

Ben hollered from the cockpit. "Hey! Last-minute instructions."

Kara clambered out of the cabin, allowing Jake to enter the hatchway.

"You can come out," said Ben. "There's no one around."

Jake repositioned to the cockpit.

Ben pointed toward the bow. Dead ahead was a small, low-lying island framed by deeper cuts on either side. "Those cuts converge on the opposite side of the island, forming a larger channel that separates Crooked from Acklins. I found a good entry spot on the map—there's a sandy cove that's used by a ferry that runs between the two islands. The landing connects to a road that goes all the way to Pitts Town on the north end of Crooked. Brown's Settlement is about a three-mile walk to the north. If they don't have a medical clinic, try to catch a ride to one that does."

Jake turned so Ben could hear him. "Are you dropping me at the landing?"

"No. The outgoing tide will be running strong in the larger channel, heading east into the open ocean. I can't get caught in the flow; otherwise, we won't make it back to the bight until nightfall. I need you to go overboard on this side of the small island—angle with the current toward Crooked and come ashore near the cove." Ben switched hands on the tiller. "Get ready. I need to come about soon."

Jake continued to stay low, working toward Ben, preparing to exit off the stern.

Ben stuck out a free hand.

Jake took it, the handshake firm. "I'm forever indebted. I left a name and phone number on the notepad in the cabin. Kara will explain."

Kara came alongside, bypassing Jake's outstretched hand, choosing to hug him instead. She backed away. "Stay safe, and good luck."

"Okay, coming about." Ben and Kara sat down in the cockpit, anticipating the swinging boom. Ben lowered the centerboard and pushed the tiller, coming off the wind.

Jake made a shallow dive from the stern as the boom swung around. The tidal flow pulled him toward the small island, the salt water immediately causing his wounds to sting. He looked back. *Ibis* moved away to the west, heeling to starboard, her twin sails filled with the southerly breeze, Ben and Kara seated in the cockpit. *My guardian angels.*

He turned toward the south shore of Crooked Island and started swimming, reflecting on the unlikely rescue, a few hours from the top of the tide and certain death. *Maybe the downward spiral is finally reversing.* He stroked harder in the fast-moving current, eventually reaching shallow water.

****

Detective Harper was surprised at the small size of the US Fish and Wildlife building, imagining a more extensive operation. The administrative assistant escorted him down a short corridor, trailed by Jerry. They stopped in front of a closed metal door; a residential refrigerator stood to the right.

The admin pressed a button on the wall intercom. "The detectives are here."

"Just a minute," came the response. The man's voice sounded high-pitched.

The assistant headed back up the corridor.

"Appreciate the help," said Harper, calling after her.

The door opened, exposing a lanky, middle-aged man wearing thick glasses and a lab coat stained by photographic chemicals. He stuck out a hand. "Reggie Washington."

"Detective Harper. Thanks for seeing us on short notice." He hooked a thumb. "This is Jerry."

The men finished shaking hands.

"As you can see, we have limited funding," said Washington.

The cramped photo lab underscored his comment. Harper surveyed the layout. A stainless-steel sink ran down the right side of the narrow, rectangular room. Above the sink were shelves stacked with metal cylinders and bottles of chemicals. A raised wooden table supported a film enlarger at the other end of the room—underneath were shelves of photo paper. The left side of the room had two rows of braided fishing line strung lengthwise between the back and front wall, pulled tight and connected by eye screws, about seven feet above the floor. Several lengths of black-and-white negatives hung drying in loose curls, attached by plastic clips at the top. A stool sat in front of the sink.

"Okay if I look at one of those filmstrips?" Harper asked.

"No problem. Hold it by the edges."

Harper raised a selected strip to an overhead light. The inverse images showed the small plain that he and Moore had discovered. All were taken during the night, the sky a light gray, capturing images of nearby animals. *The optical sensor must recognize night from day.*

"How often do you see Florida panthers?" Harper asked, acknowledging the purpose of the research.

"Rarely. They're coming back from near extinction, but very slowly."

"How many of those camera traps have you deployed?"

"Five."

"All near Hell's Butt?"

"No, they're miles apart. Covering known chokepoints."

"Chokepoints?" Jerry asked.

"Much of the 'glades is swampy, loaded with gators. We look for narrow stretches of firm ground between flanking swamps. Panthers go across those land bridges and interconnected clearings, along with everything else that wants to avoid becoming gator food."

Harper thought back to the narrow game trail they had surveyed on the way to the clearing near the Tamiami Trail. *Yep, swampy ground directly to either side.* He got to the critical question. "How often do you capture images of people in Hell's Butt?"

"Never seen anyone, but we've only reviewed through March of this year."

"It's already August," Harper noted, surprised by the long delay.

"We have enough funding to capture nightly images, but not enough to keep up with developing and reviewing them."

"Where do you store the undeveloped film?"

"In the refrigerator outside the door."

"And you have the rolls cataloged by dates?"

"Of course. We retrieve them weekly."

"I'm interested in a specific week … from July."

"It will be a while before we get to it."

Harper stared at the researcher. "As I mentioned on the phone, you may have evidence that relates directly to a murder investigation. This is a time-sensitive matter."

"Uh, okay. How soon do you need it?"

"In fact, let me be clearer, I need to walk out of here with whichever roll of film covers the evening in question. Our crime lab folks will develop it to maintain an evidentiary chain of custody. Depending on what's found, we may have to hold selected images in confidence for a while."

"What if the film captured a panther?"

"You'll be notified in a timely manner."

"I need the approval of my supervisor in Miami."

"Let's make the phone call."

****

Jake kneeled again in shallow water. The butt wound was painful to touch, stinging the most. He probed the hard swelling that had formed around the wound's perimeter. *It's definitely getting worse.*

He rose from the shallows and waded toward the cove, the depth reaching his chest as he entered a narrow cut that enabled the ferry to reach the shore. A staked sign denoted the landing zone. Shallow ruts populated the sandy edge. He exited the water and looked to the south. The small ferry was visible across the channel, its bow ashore at the north end of Acklins Island. No people were evident.

He went up a path to the connecting roadway. Its surface consisted of dirty, hard-packed sand, making it easier to walk. Striding on land felt invigorating after being on the water for a week. He jogged for a short distance, succumbing quickly to the pain in his left buttock. He continued to walk northward, favoring the left side with a limp.

The eastern shore came close to the road after a mile or so. He decided to take a break, slipping through a short stretch of scrubby brush and onto a long, white beach. The clear water exposed a group of coral heads only fifty feet or so offshore. He stood and looked toward the horizon, imagining the sails of the *Santa María*, *Pinta*, and *Niña* approaching. *The native Lucayans must have been terrified seeing those ships. Rightfully so.*

Jake heard the sound of a car coming from the north. He hurried back to the road. A beat-up Toyota Previa minivan came around the curve ahead, slowing as the driver caught sight of him. The van stopped short, about thirty feet away.

A gray-haired Caucasian woman stuck her head out the driver's window. "Who the bloody hell are you? Tarzan?"

Jake started walking toward her, trying to place the accent. *British? Australian?*

She hollered again. "Stay where you are, dammit." She leaned toward the passenger seat, reaching for something.

Jake stopped immediately.

She leaned her head out again. "What's your name?"

"Jake Crawford. I need medical help."

The driver's door swung open. The side panel displayed a painted name: SHARK LADY. The woman stepped out, one hand behind her back. She was barefoot, wearing a drab, purple-and-yellow muumuu, its floral pattern badly faded. "You the bloke who got pirated?"

Jake hesitated before answering. "Yes."

She stared at him. "You look like bloody hell. Better than

being cactus, I suppose."

"Cactus?"

"Dead. Croaked."

Jake glanced at the painted panel. *Why not?* He turned around, spreading apart the torn swim trunks and exposing the ugly bite wound, speaking over his shoulder. "A shark took a chunk."

She cackled. "A rippin' ankle biter got your bum."

"Still hurts a bunch. It's likely infected."

"Come on now. Let's get you to the clinic." She waved him over. Whatever she was hiding went back in the van.

Jake approached, remaining wary.

She slid open the rear passenger door and positioned an old towel on the single captain's seat. "Put that wounded bum in here."

Jake got in, sitting at an angle to relieve the pressure. The other side of the van held an assortment of well-used fishing tackle, mostly heavy rods and reels, the lines sporting large hooks attached to wire leaders.

She glanced at him in the rearview mirror. "Ten US dollars a klick. It's ten klicks to the clinic."

"Ten dollars a klick? That's more than New York City cabs. Highway robbery."

"Your rate's about to double."

"Do I look like I'm carrying money?"

"What else do you have?"

"A pair of torn swim trunks."

"What size?"

Jake finally realized she was messing with him. "I can have some money wired to your bank account."

"I only take cash."

"Okay then, do you have a bank or Western Union on the island? Somewhere to receive a wire transfer?"

"Where do you think you are? Nassau?" She grinned

broadly, the rearview mirror exposing the absence of multiple teeth. "We'll work it out. Let's get you to the clinic first. The sharks won't miss me today." She maneuvered the van, turning around and heading north.

He looked left and right around his seat—the seatbelt was missing. "Where's the clinic located?"

"Colonel Hill settlement."

Jake recalled Kara's concern. "How'd you know I was the guy who got pirated?"

"Your picture's all over the bloomin' telly. Took me a minute. You look much older."

Caitlin must be frantic. "Does the clinic have a phone? I need to make a collect call."

"If it's working. Batelco's no bloody good … hit-and-miss at best." She reached between the seats, pulling out a two-way radio. "Let's see if our walloper's in range. Constable Fergie lives in Moss Town, other side of Colonel Hill. Never know, he might be near the clinic."

Walloper? She's an Aussie.

****

Jake winced for the umpteenth time. The Bahamian nurse continued her work, abrading and cleansing his butt wound with a rough sponge and soapy water. She had injected a local anesthetic, but not enough. The sponge went deeper and harder. More pain broke through, causing him to flinch repeatedly.

"Nasty bite you have here … badly infected. You'll be staying on the antibiotic for a while."

"What about stitches?"

"It's too wide to bring together with the sutures. I'll pack and tape it. The scar will not look so good, but you'll have a good story to tell your grandchildren. Most important is ridding the infection." She walked to a nearby counter, retrieving a bottle of rinse water and a dark-colored antiseptic.

Someone knocked on the exam room door.

"Yes," said the nurse.

"Constable Ferguson," came the reply.

"You okay if a copper sees your bum?"

"Sure."

"Come in, Constable."

The wiry Bahamian officer entered, exchanging brief pleasantries with the nurse. He walked over and stooped down, turning his head to look Jake squarely in the face, holding a cutout newspaper picture for comparison. He stood, addressing the nurse. "How much longer?"

"Twenty minutes, perhaps. He has many small cuts and scrapes and a deep bite wound that became infected—a moderate sunburn but not too bad, mostly his face and shoulders."

The constable walked out, closing the door.

Jake grew uneasy. *No greeting or introduction?* He thought again of drug gangs. *Could this guy be on the take?*

"Is he normally like that?" Jake queried.

"Like what?"

"I expected an introduction or at least some questions."

"He'll be back. Most likely he's outside on the radio, confirming it's you."

"Confirming to whom?"

"Police headquarters in Nassau I would suppose. Sharky said you have been in the news."

"That's her nickname?" Jake felt stupid as soon as he asked the question, wincing as the antiseptic was applied.

"Oh yeah. Sharky loves catching and eating them; black tips being her favorite."

"I profess a different theory. I don't eat them, so they don't eat me."

The nurse chuckled. "Well, a small one skipped your lecture." She finished bandaging the bite wound, applying some lotion to his upper shoulders. "I'm done back here. Let's get you turned over." She covered his midsection with a towel as he rotated.

The constable stuck his head through the doorway. "Nurse Pinder, a moment."

"Stay like you are," she instructed, removing the surgical gloves and exiting the room, closing the door.

Jake couldn't discern the muffled exchange.

Nurse Pinder reentered. "Looks like you are getting some special treatment."

"How so?"

"The constable will explain." She reused the gloves and continued to apply antiseptic and bandages to his front-side cuts and scrapes, focusing mostly on the knees and feet. Lotion was spread on parts of his face, avoiding the small wounds.

"Thanks for patching me up."

"It's what I'm paid to do."

"I have to give you an IOU like I did Sharky. I have no money with me."

"Sort it out with Constable Fergie. I need to find you something to wear. Your swimming togs have seen their last." She picked up the torn trunks from the floor and threw them into a trashcan, along with the gloves. The bottom row of a shelving unit held surgical tops and pants. She grabbed a set from the far right. "My last set of extra-large. Too small for you, but they must do."

"Is it okay if I try the clinic phone again? Maybe it's working now."

"Constable Fergie said no calls allowed. He told the same to Sharky. We must keep quiet about you."

Jake stared at the door, growing concerned again.

****

Harper was back at his desk in the department bullpen when the phone rang. He glanced at the incoming extension. *Crime lab.* He reached for the handset, crossing fingers on the other hand.

"You need to see this," said the technician.

Harper hung up, addressing Jerry as he hurried past the adjacent cubicle. "Lab tech has something. She sounds excited."

Jerry jumped up, trailing a few steps behind.

They exited the bullpen and walked briskly down a corridor to the opposite end, entering the lab.

The red light above the darkroom door was turned off. Harper went over, entering a brightly lit room. The technician stood to the left, staring at three black-and-white photos lying side-by-side on a drying rack, still wet from processing.

Harper studied the eight-by-ten-inch prints. The first showed a faint gray beam originating from the right side of the image, along with a large hand holding a flashlight. The beam aimed downward, illuminating the nearby game trail. The second image held the prize, capturing the man's face as he looked in the direction of the hidden camera. The third image showed the man moving away, following the trail toward the other side of the clearing, his full silhouette captured by the faint backlight from the flashlight beam.

Harper focused on the second photo. *Late thirties? Maybe early forties. Caucasian, with dark hair, deep-set eyes, and high cheekbones.* He studied the third photo. *Approximately six feet tall, weighing around two hundred pounds, with broad shoulders and a muscular upper build.* The man's left hand held the flashlight. The right grasped another object. *A gun?* The graininess of the silhouette made it difficult to tell.

"That's a red beam from the flashlight," observed the tech. "The wildlife camera uses a special low-light film. A regular flashlight beam would have blown out the image."

"How do you know it's red?" asked Jerry.

She explained, pointing out the distinction. "The derived shade of gray from red is darker. The muhly grass is mostly green. You can see the difference between the grass and the beam exiting the end of the flashlight."

Harper added the reason. "A red beam preserves night vision." He studied the facial image in the second photo. "Can you enhance the resolution?"

"I can send the negatives to the state crime lab. They perform the computer-enhanced rendering."

"How long will that take?"

"Two to three days."

"What if we fly up there and stand around stomping our feet?"

The technician hesitated, coming to an estimate. "They could probably do a single image in a few hours."

"And I could access the digital file, right? Downloading it using a modem?"

"That's right. It would probably take an hour or two to transfer, given the file size."

Harper glanced at the photos, deciding on next steps. "Make a duplicate of the film for safekeeping. Jerry and I need the phone number and street address of the state lab, plus these prints when they're dry."

He shifted to Jerry. "Get the original filmstrip after she's finished making a copy. Book the first available flight to Tallahassee. I'll call ahead and pave the way."

****

The small café was located next to the Pitts Town airstrip at the northern edge of Crooked Island. Jake ate at the bar, relishing a hogfish filet grilled in lime juice and butter. Kalik beer and a platter of conch fritters rounded out the dinner fare. He glanced over. Constable Ferguson sat alongside, his back against the bar, observing two groups of sport fishermen at nearby tables. Several had amused expressions. A middle-aged waitress stood at the end of the short bar, holding the microphone from an air-traffic radio, engaged in a bawdy discussion with a commercial airline pilot who flew miles overhead en route from Buenos Aires to Miami.

Jake glanced at the phone to the left of the radio, wishing he could contact Caitlin. Constable Ferguson still wouldn't allow it. Jake only knew one thing about what was transpiring: an incoming FBI plane would be removing him from the island. Otherwise, the constable remained tight-lipped about the process underway.

One of the anglers signaled the waitress. She left the radio, grabbed two beers from the back bar cooler, and headed to his table.

Another angler hollered over, "Hey, Doc, where's the operating room?"

Jake chuckled. *I must look funny as hell. Undersized surgical smocks. Hair and beard in need of washing.* He remained barefoot; no shoes or sandals were large enough.

Three clicks emitted from the air-traffic radio. The runway lights came to life, followed by an incoming transmission: "Pitts Town. Piper 21662. Inbound 9. Long final."

The waitress hurried to the radio handset, looking at a small weather monitor and then out the nearest window. She keyed the mic: "21662. Pitts Town. Runway clear. Winds southeast at ten, gusting fifteen."

"21662. Thanks."

An angler went to the screened windows, looking toward the west. Jake lowered his head to see out. The landing lights of a plane were visible about a mile away.

Constable Ferguson tapped Jake on the shoulder, pointing toward the runway turnout. "Hot transfer."

Whatever that means. Jake gave a thumbs-up and engulfed the remaining hogfish and beer. A small plane zoomed in for a landing, touching down close to the water's edge, a twin-engine Piper Aztec. Jake remembered flying in one from Boston to a summer research conference in upper Vermont. *Bumpy as hell.*

The constable tapped Jake's arm and crooked a finger.

"What about the tab?" asked Jake.

"I'll be handling it."

They exited, heading toward the small apron at the edge of the runway. The constable scanned the surrounding area. The plane taxied up the runway at a quick pace.

The plane came onto the apron and rotated, facing the runway. No markings were apparent other than the tail number. The propellers continued spinning at a modest RPM, the pilot holding position with the brakes.

Jake glanced at the café. The anglers stood along the screened windows watching. He smiled. *They must be completely baffled.*

The copilot door opened after two tries, buffeted by the thrust from the propellors. A middle-aged man struggled to climb out. He descended along the inner edge of the wing, hair blowing wildly, his short-sleeve shirt and khaki trousers flapping at the edges—a badge and holstered handgun were attached to the belt. His left hand clutched a small packet.

Constable Ferguson took Jake by the arm, walking toward the plane as the FBI agent stepped to the ground. The men came together.

The agent shouted above the engine noise, "Dr. Crawford, Special Agent Nolen. Nice outfit." They shook hands.

Agent Nolen handed the constable a regular-sized envelope, its thickness telling. "Thanks for the help. Use this to cover the local expenses."

Jake turned to Constable Ferguson and shook his hand. "My thanks as well."

"Come on," Nolen hollered, turning toward the plane. "Let's get you out of here."

Chapter 25

Caitlin had spent the rest of the previous day and overnight at Donna's house. Word had traveled rapidly, close friends gathering in caring support. They knew of Caitlin's history with Jake, the deep love that started long ago. Her heartbreaking loss became a cause of repeated tears and embraces, the remembering of special moments with Jake, all of them growing up together.

She had slept fitfully again, despite the tranquilizer prescribed by Doc Harris, the imagined horrors of Jake's death unrelenting. Morning finally arrived, along with a need to escape another regathering of friends—the thought of another day of well-intentioned sentiments and memories seemed exhausting. She fought against their insistence on staying, convincing Donna to drive her home.

The final attempt at dissuasion found Donna standing in the cabin driveway next to her open car door. "Are you sure, honey? We're all so worried about you being home alone. Now, you call me if it gets overwhelming."

"I'll be okay. Thanks for caring so much." Caitlin entered the kitchen through the side door. The table and countertop remained a mess from the previous morning: cups partially filled with coffee, an open jar of jelly and a dirty spoon resting on the cutting board, and pieces of toast on paper towels. A half stick of butter had melted in a saucer near the stove.

She headed to the main room. The sight of the couch caused her to pause, thinking of the many moments lying there with Jake. She closed her swollen eyes, wanting beyond all else to put her head on his chest and hear the pounding of his heart, buried safely within his loving embrace.

The kitchen phone rang, ripping apart the wishful moment. She hesitated at first, the thought of another expression of sorrow unappealing. Only a dial tone could be heard when she finally lifted the handset, now wondering who called.

She replaced the handset and glanced at the refrigerator, reminded of the morning injection of Jake's drug. She extracted a fresh cartridge and headed for the bathroom, warming the contents in a fisted hand. The phone rang again. She hurried back to the kitchen, bringing the handset to her ear.

A woman's voice could be heard on the other end, the line crackling. "Hello? Mrs. Crawford?"

"Who's calling?"

"The US Embassy in Nassau. Is this Mrs. Crawford?"

Caitlin braced herself. *They've found Jake's body.*

"Is this regarding my husband?"

"Please hold."

Several clicks could be heard. The next voice caused her to gasp.

"Caitlin … it's Jake."

She dropped the cartridge and sank to the floor, a hand against her chest, leaning against the wall. She burst into sobs, overwhelmed, unable to speak.

"I've been trying to reach you since last night."

She struggled to stop the sobbing, inhaling and exhaling several times.

"Caitlin? You there?"

"I … we all … I thought you were …" She failed to finish.

"I'm sorry you thought the worst. They wouldn't let me call from Crooked Island."

She managed to suppress the sobbing, regaining enough of a voice, immediately conveying what she felt so deeply. "I love you, Jake Crawford … with every ounce of my being. I … I never thought I could tell you again."

"It was only you I thought of during the worst of it."

"Are you hurt?"

"Just cuts and scrapes … one nasty wound on my butt. But I'll be fine."

"What happened? Did they try to kill you?"

"It's a long story."

"Are you coming home today? Where can I pick you up? Miami? Naples? I will never let you out of my sight again … *ever*."

He hesitated. "Unfortunately, it may take a bit longer before I'm allowed to leave."

"Why?"

"The Bahamian government wants partial reparation for their search costs. They're claiming I made a misleading statement on the Customs entry form, regarding my next port of call, costing them extra time and resources. I can't leave until the State Department settles the matter."

Caitlin got up from the floor. "How much do they want?"

"One hundred and fifty thousand dollars. The State Department is pushing back, something to do with treaty obligations. I offered to make the payment, but the US ambassador rejected it on principle."

Caitlin looked at the kitchen clock, making a quick decision. "I'm coming to Nassau. Don't you try to stop me."

"You can't come."

"Why not?"

Jake hesitated again before answering, "There's another reason I'm at the embassy."

"Are you still in danger? I got a call from an FBI agent."

"Agent Nolen?"

"That's him."

"He's just outside the room."

"What's going on, Jake?"

"The State Department demanded that I harbor inside the embassy rather than a Bahamian facility. The drug gang that pirated *Cloud Catcher* has deep pockets and operates with some impunity. I'd give anything to be with you, but we'll have to wait until I get home."

"What are you saying? That they still might try to kill you?"

"I guess there's intel suggesting the gang believes I can identify the pirates." A voice could be heard in the background, followed by Jake saying, "Okay. I'll be right out." He explained, "Looks like the reparation spat got resolved. The embassy wants to prep me for a live news event, occurring in a half hour. It's part of the resolution."

"Jake, please, *please* stay safe. I can't bear the thought of losing you again."

"I'll be okay. The FBI guys are pros. I have to run. Always know I love you."

The line went dead.

****

Harry came out of the tavern office and down the creaky stairs. "Hold your fucking horses." The rapid pounding continued. He unlocked the front door.

Caitlin's eyes were filled with joy. "Jake's alive!" She flew past him, heading for the stool across from the TV. "Hurry, the news event starts soon. Jake will be there."

"I'll be damned!" Harry hustled around the back of the bar,

turning on the TV and switching the station to CNN. "How'd you find out?"

"He called me a little while ago … from the US Embassy in Nassau."

"Hallelujah Almighty. I'll get some coffee started." Harry returned to the back counter.

A commercial filled the screen, advertising a new online service called AOL Instant Messenger. The commercial ended, followed by a summary of headline news.

Caitlin stared intently at the screen, gripping her hands together nervously atop the bar. She suddenly pointed at the TV. "It's starting. Can you turn up the sound?"

Harry grabbed the remote, raising the volume. A podium with a State Department emblem filled the center of the screen. US and Bahamian flags hung on flanking poles in the background. The TV camera zoomed out. A small group of reporters milled about in front of a few rows of chairs. A large caption filled the bottom of the screen: "Breaking News • US Embassy, Bahamas."

The CNN anchor narrated the scene. "We're standing by for an early news conference at the US Embassy in Nassau, Bahamas. What we know at this point is …"

Shouts erupted from the reporters, silencing the narration. Jake's tall figure entered the room limping, trailing a man and woman, each of whom wore dark business attire; Jake's white T-shirt and khaki shorts offered a sharp contrast. Bandages covered his extremities, neck and forehead. Sunburnt, peeling skin showed on one side of his face. The unkempt hair and beard rounded out the appearance of a man who had been lost at sea.

Caitlin covered her mouth with both hands.

Harry stated the obvious. "He's been through hell and back."

A small entourage of lesser officials trailed Jake, a mix of Americans and Bahamians. They assumed positions behind the central threesome.

The woman went to the podium, raising both hands, silencing the assembled reporters. “Thank you. Please be seated.”

Jake stared without expression.

She continued, “Good morning. I am US Ambassador Mary Chenowith. To my immediate left is the Honorable Prime Minister of the Bahamas, Malcolm Pinders.” She leaned toward the microphone, looking behind and upward to her right. “And with much relief, may I introduce Dr. Jacob Crawford.”

Jake nodded in acknowledgment, presenting a tight-lipped smile. Several reporters shouted questions; others clapped.

Ambassador Chenowith raised her hand. The room quieted. “As you know, the combined coast guards of the Bahamas and the United States searched extensively for Dr. Crawford, the victim of piracy-at-sea. It is believed that the perpetrators used his stolen yacht to deliver illicit drugs near Miami. The search for Dr. Crawford was terminated after all hope had been lost for his survival.

“As we have come to learn, Dr. Crawford eluded his attackers by hiding on a tiny island. He subsequently managed to swim and drift for two days across the Bight of the Acklins, a distance of nearly twenty miles, finally coming ashore on the southern end of Crooked Island. He received prompt treatment at a local medical clinic.”

She paused, looking to her left. “The United States would like to express its utmost gratitude to the Bahamian government for their diligent efforts to locate and protect a US citizen.” She turned and shook hands with the prime minister, exchanging positions.

“Thank you, Ambassador Chenowith.” He stood erect, staring into the TV camera. “We are most pleased that Dr. Crawford is with us this morning, after experiencing such a harrowing event. The Bahamian government is firmly committed to ensuring the safety of all who visit our beautiful islands. Our police are actively coordinating with agencies of the United States to find the perpetrators of this heinous crime. May I assure you, we shall not rest until they are captured and prosecuted to the fullest extent of our laws." He exchanged places with the ambassador.

She leaned toward the microphone. "Dr. Crawford would also like to express his gratitude, after which we will address your questions."

****

The ambassador concluded the question-and-answer session. Nielsen turned away from the TV on the wall of his headquarters office.

A three-dimensional model had been set up next to the glass desk. He bypassed the display and went to the tall windows. The calm waters of Tampa Bay lay before him. Patches of small baitfish rippled on the nearby surface. Seagulls swooped and dipped, feasting from above.

Crawford's pretty beat up, but it could have been much worse. Nielsen felt the concern lifting, believing the ambassador's account of the piracy would quiet any suspicions. He returned to the 3-D model of the planned marina and yacht club for Marcosta Island. The expansive layout encompassed a curving harbor in the shape of a wide U, like a horseshoe.

****

Detective Harper stared at the computer screen, watching the progress bar impatiently. The download of the digitized image had taken over an hour, thanks to the slow speed of the dial-up modem. "Okay, it's opening now." He spoke to Jerry at the state lab in Tallahassee.

The black-and-white image filled most of the screen, showing a much-improved image of the man's face.

"I don't recognize him either," said Harper. "I'll check around the office before heading to the state prosecutor. It's up to him to decide on next steps. We can't share this outside the department until cleared to do so, given the risk of publicity." He started a printout of the image.

"What about sharing the photo confidentially with Jake Crawford, before seeing the prosecutor?" Jerry asked. "I assume you've heard the good news."

"He's lucky to be alive. Why Crawford?"

"Just thinking he might know who'd want to frame Watson. You said Crawford and Watson were close friends from way back."

Harper kicked himself. *Getting slow in older age.* "Good thought. I'll try to get the photo to him. It's worth a quick check."

****

A red crossbar blocked the entrance to the embassy side street. Jake looked down from a second-floor window, observing two marine guards, wondering if they normally stood at that location.

He returned to the conference table, retaking a seat. Only crumbs remained on the lunch plate. Two bottles of beer rested nearby, one empty, the other half full. The walls held photos of Ambassador Chenowith performing her formal duties, captured as she visited various Bahamian locations and ceremonies. The sounds of voices, phones, and printers could be heard through the open doorway.

Agent Nolen walked in. "Sorry for the delay. Did you get enough to eat?"

"I did, thanks."

"Something needs your attention. Come with me, please."

They went across the hallway and into a busy operations room. Nolen led Jake to one of the cubicles. A young man sat in front of a large computer monitor.

Jake stared over the young man's shoulder. A black-and-white photo filled the screen. *What the hell?*

"Do you know that man?" asked Nolen.

"Yeah, unfortunately. It's Eric Jenkins, the brother of my wife's ex-husband. What's this about?"

Nolen turned to the young man. "The photo is confidential. No sharing unless I instruct otherwise."

They returned to the conference room. Nolen retrieved a note from his shirt pocket. "I believe you know Detective Harper." Nolen used the table speakerphone, glancing at the note as he dialed.

"Harper." Voices and ringing phones could be heard in the background.

"Detective, Special Agent Nolen. Crawford is with me. He has a positive ID. I'll leave you to talk." Nolen exited the room, closing the door.

"Who's the guy?" asked Harper, forgoing pleasantries.

"Eric Jenkins," Jake replied, explaining the sibling relationship with Caitlin's ex.

"Does he live on Marcosta?"

"Not any longer. Caitlin said he moved to Copeland to hunt gators."

"Does gator hunting involve swamp buggies?"

"Those and airboats, sometimes pickup trucks and ATVs."

"Does he have a beef against Billy Watson?"

"Definitely … for decades. Do you mind telling me what this is about?"

"I can't at this time, but it would help if you could characterize their adversarial relationship."

Jake described the fights on the elementary school playground.

"Have Jenkins and Watson had any recent encounters?"

Jake recounted the courtroom incident.

"Why the continued bad blood?"

"It's related to Caitlin. Eric's brother was forced to leave Marcosta or face charges of spousal abuse."

"Sorry to hear about the abuse. But how does that involve Watson?"

Jake explained Billy's chivalrous protection of Caitlin, including Eric's broken jaw. "It occurred while I was away from the island, working up in Boston."

"Got it," said Harper. "Anything else you can think of?"

Another incident leapt to mind. "Eric was at the recent seafood festival on Marcosta, the same night of the arson-murder, along with two of his buddies. He hollered something ugly at Caitlin. A scuffle broke out with some of the locals who heard him."

"Did anyone see Jenkins and his buddies leave the island that night?"

"No idea. I saw them head down Heron Avenue after the scuffle. You'll recall there was extensive vandalism of downtown buildings. Maybe he and his buddies stuck around and participated. Others might have seen them."

"I'll have Chief Wilkinson check the police reports and ask around. Does Heron Avenue offer a route to the south end of Horseshoe Basin?"

"It's not the shortest, but you can get there easily."

"Anything else?"

"Not that I recall."

"Okay, appreciate the help. Keep this strictly confidential. It's in your buddy's interest to do so." He disconnected.

Jake sat back. The last comment suggested a connection with the arson-murder. He wondered how.

****

The front office had been busy since Caitlin's mid-morning

arrival at work. The news about Jake brought a steady stream of visits and calls from well-wishers.

Her phone rang. She answered brightly, "Hixon Marine Lab, how may I help?"

"Let's see, how about some fresh mango ice cream when I get home."

Caitlin grinned at Jake's picture. "Am I dreaming? Is it really you?"

"One and the same, I'm afraid."

"I've been wondering when you'd call back. What took so long?"

"They've kept me busy. Hey, I'm cleared to leave. The embassy provided a new passport. I should be home late tonight."

Her spirits soared. "Where are you arriving? Miami?"

"No need to pick me up. I may not be at the cabin until after midnight."

"Why so late?"

"I'll explain when I get there. Make sure the key is under the wooden pelican."

"Are you kidding? Do you think I'm going to bed? No way I could fall asleep."

"By the way, I need to see Doc Harris first thing tomorrow, assuming the clinic is still open on Saturdays. Could you try to arrange an appointment? Otherwise, we'll need to drive to Naples."

"First thing? Why?"

"A small shark bit me on the butt. The wound needs attention."

"Can't you get it treated over there?"

"I did. I'm already on an antibiotic. Doc just needs to excise the infected tissue and repack the wound with iodine impregnated gauze. One more day shouldn't matter."

"Promise me you'll be safe coming home."

"Agent Nolen just walked in. See you soon, love. Can't wait."

****

Jake replaced the handset, focusing on Nolen. "Still on track?"

"Does your island car ferry run all night?"

"It stops at 11:30 p.m."

"That moves up our timeline a bit."

The speakerphone buzzed. Nolen lifted the handset. "Agent Nolen. Yeah, he's right here. Who? Okay, let me check." He muffled the handset against his stomach. "The embassy operator has a guy on hold claiming to return your call. Last name is Atkins."

"I need to take it."

"Remember, limit the details until we get you stateside."

"Not to worry."

Nolen spoke to the operator. "Put him through." Nolen handed over the handset and left the room, closing the door.

"Bill?"

"One moment," said the operator. "Go ahead."

"Jake?"

"Hey, Bill. Thanks for calling back."

"You must have one hell of a scary story to tell. How are you doing?"

"Okay. Mostly cuts and scrapes from seashells and sporty marine life. The biggest problem is a sore butt, from being bitten."

"By what?"

"A small shark."

"Yikes. I can't even watch those things at the Shedd Aquarium. Do you need some cash wired down? I could work with the embassy to arrange it."

"No need, but I do have a couple of instructions." The

painful butt wound kept throbbing. Jake came off the seat, placing a knee on the chair for support. The conference room felt warm, causing him to sweat.

"Fire away," said Atkins.

"You might receive a call in the future from a guy named Ben Grotebek, or his friend, Kara Newsome, asking for help. Find out what's needed and contact me. Try to get a callback number."

"Duly noted. What's the other thing?"

"You'll get a call from the Bahamian prime minister's office in a week or so. They'll provide some information, including wire transfer instructions. I'll be donating funds to help their remote medical clinics, mostly for the purchase of needed supplies."

"How much?"

"I'll let you know. Have JPMorgan convert 500K of the T-bills to cash in preparation."

"The donation won't help with US taxes."

"It doesn't matter."

"Okay. Hey, I've already filed an insurance claim on *Cloud Catcher*. The adjuster declared her a total loss."

Jake grimaced. "I lost something invaluable when they took her: a treasured book and two old photos."

"Those might be okay. Not everything got destroyed."

"What are you saying? Did they salvage her?"

"What remains of the yacht and its contents is impounded at a boatyard on the Miami River, under the custody of the DEA. She's considered evidence until released."

"How will I know if the book and photos survived?"

"I'll follow up with them. They should have a list of the salvaged items. What else do you have for me?"

"That's it for now. I should be at home the next time we talk."

****

Harper sat in front of a large desk, observing the upside-down writing.

The state prosecutor finished a final notation and leaned back in his chair, leveling a stern gaze. “You should have informed me sooner.”

Harper ignored the admonition. “I need an arrest warrant issued for Eric Jenkins.”

The prosecutor removed his glasses, retrieving an optical cloth from a side drawer. He spoke while cleaning the lenses. “I’m not there yet. The evidence is compelling, but there are some loose ends.”

“Like the missing red wig from the dummy stunt?” asked Harper. He had interpreted the notation.

“I noticed it wasn’t discovered during a search of Watson’s cottage after the murder … and that he’s refused to answer questions about it.”

“He’s refused to answer *all* my questions. Is the dummy wig still relevant? Given the strength of the other evidence? Jenkins had a combative history with Watson, including the recent courtroom incident.”

“Which points to another loose end: Why would Jenkins frame Watson for capital murder? Why not kill him outright?”

“Jenkins would be a top suspect. He probably realized that.”

“But is he clever enough to plot an elaborate frame-up?”

“He may have had help.”

“Who? His buddies at the festival? The ones in the scuffle?”

“Maybe. There are two others to consider, but I would need to investigate further.”

“Care to elaborate? Like whom?”

“Mark Jenkins for one, Eric’s brother. He had a big axe to grind.”

“With Watson?”

"No, with Caitlin Crawford, his ex-wife. The report mentions why he had to leave Marcosta. The Jenkins brothers get three birds with one stone by framing Watson. Think of the emotional turmoil a death sentence would cause, not only for Watson but also the Crawfords."

"Seems like a stretch. Who's the other person of interest?"

Harper shifted in his seat, anticipating the reaction that would follow. "Derek Nielsen."

"The Florida real estate magnate?" The prosecutor looked incredulous.

"Through a possible murder-for-hire. At the time of the arson-murder, Jake Crawford was the mayor of Marcosta Island, leading efforts to block a multibillion-dollar resort that Nielsen wants built. They've been adversaries for several years. Maybe Nielsen wanted to cause great personal turmoil for Crawford, knocking him off balance."

The prosecutor waved his hand in a gesture of dismissal. "I'd tread *very* lightly on that ground. Nielsen's a big donor to the governor and many state legislators." He tapped the report, returning to his original concern. "The wig in the mangroves could have been the one from the dummy, planted by a friend, making it look like Watson was framed. What about the fishing guide? Is he a friend of Watson's?"

"We've checked. They're not considered friends by the island residents we interviewed. And besides, as I reported, the guide had an angler aboard when the wig was discovered—a retired judge from Montana. They both gave sworn statements that the snook took them up that creek. Otherwise, they had no reason to go up there."

"Maybe snook always go up that creek when hooked nearby. The guide would know their behavior."

Harper shook his head. "Also a stretch. The key question is what was Eric Jenkins doing in Hell's Butt the night of the crime? In close proximity to where the wig and kayak were found."

"How do you know it's the same night? The image wasn't timestamped."

"The wildlife researcher retrieves the film on a set weekly schedule. He could tell the specific day by counting the lighting cycles, dusk-to-dawn. That's also in my report."

"I must have missed it. Regardless, I wish the dummy wig had been found. It would remove the opportunity for the defense to sow doubt, assuming Eric Jenkins is indicted." He looked at his watch. "We'll take this a step at a time. Bring him in for questioning when you're ready. I want to observe the interrogation before seeking the arrest warrant."

"What about Billy Watson?" Harper asked.

"I'm considering dropping the murder charge. If I do, he'll remain a person of interest, restricted to the county pending further investigation."

"Because of the missing dummy wig?" asked Harper, verifying the reason.

"Yeah, it's nagging me."

Chapter 26

What should have been a night of joyous reunion had been displaced by an escalating threat, this time from the exponential growth of microscopic enemies. Jake had arrived at the cabin shortly before midnight, feverish. He now lay sweating under a blanket, curled in a fetal position on his right side, shaking from racking chills.

Caitlin shared aloud the latest thermometer reading, a jump of one degree in the past hour. "104.2. We're not waiting for your appointment; I'm calling Doc Harris." She clambered off the bed, wrapping her bathrobe.

"Wait … tell him …" Intense shivering racked his entire body, teeth chattering. He closed his eyes, arms crossed, hands clenched into fists.

Caitlin hurried to the kitchen.

****

Doc Harris finished drawing blood, followed by an intravenous injection. "We need to get him to the hospital, urgently." He left the bedroom to use the kitchen phone, closing the door.

Caitlin could overhear bits of his conversation with the Naples hospital, her concern ratcheting sharply. "… ICU … acute septicemia … temperature 105 … medevac transport …." The click of the phone receiver was followed by the sound of three keypad tones, the last two the same. She opened the bedroom door to hear more clearly.

"This is Doctor Harris. I'm at 17 Eletz Point Lane, Marcosta Island. I have a critically ill patient in need of emergency transport to the town hall parking lot. Name is Jake Crawford, forty-four years of age. I've already requested medevac transport—the helicopter should arrive in about twenty minutes." He hung up and returned to the bedroom.

Caitlin gave him an imploring look, eyes teary, a hand across her mouth.

He picked up the spent syringe on the nightstand, covering the needle and placing it in the side pouch of his bag alongside three vacutainer tubes of blood. "I gave Jake a heavy dose of a broad-spectrum antibiotic." He grabbed another pharmaceutical bottle and a new syringe, speaking as he administered an injection in the upper arm. "Hopefully this limits his fever."

"A helicopter? Is it that bad? He was already on an antibiotic."

"Whatever antibiotic he received didn't work. His blood pressure is dropping. There's a significant risk he's going into septic shock, a critical condition. We're in a race against the bacteria that invaded his bloodstream. Every hour counts."

"I want to go with him," Caitlin insisted.

Doc Harris glanced over. "Dress quickly. The island ambulance will be here shortly." He left the room with the doctor's bag in hand.

Caitlin squeezed Jake's hand. It was wet and clammy. He didn't squeeze back. A siren could be heard in the distance.

****

A medevac helicopter came across the channel from the mainland, its reverberations mixing with the wailing of the island ambulance. It flared above the rear lawn of the town hall, settling quickly. The ambulance sped past on Gulf Drive; Doc Harris's car followed close behind. Someone sat beside him in the passenger seat.

Mayor Perkins had just arrived at City Hall for some Saturday catch-up work, stopping on the brick sidewalk to observe the emergency in process. *Probably a badly injured commercial fisherman.* She closed her eyes, saying a quick prayer.

Michael Pearson rode up on his patrol bike; his radio broadcasted the dispatcher's reply.

"It's Jake Crawford. He's being airlifted to Naples."

"He's back?" asked Pearson. "What's wrong with him?"

"He's really sick. That's all we know."

"Oh my." Perkins hurried toward the town hall parking lot. The helicopter departed, heading north across the channel.

Doc Harris saw her approach, coming over. "It's Jake Crawford."

"I heard."

Perkins looked around. "Where's Caitlin?"

"She's with him."

"How bad is it?"

"He's severely ill from an infected wound. Everyone needs to start praying."

Perkins looked in the direction of Spud Nut. "I'll spread the word."

****

Caitlin stared through the ICU window. A critical care physician and two nurses worked diligently in Jake's room, gowned head to toe, wearing special face masks and eyewear. Jake lay unconscious, heavily sedated, a ventilator tube down his throat due to fluid infiltration in his lungs.

Her emotional roller coaster had gone to the bottom, then to the top, and now toward the bottom again, the whipsawing unbearable. Caitlin recalled the joy of Jake's arrival home, holding him tightly, not wanting to let go, the initial happiness thrown aside by a sharpening concern.

Her eyes teared again, seeing him lying motionless in the ICU bed, subjected to an array of monitors, tubes, wires, and hanging fluid packets, realizing all she could do was stand there helplessly, praying that modern medicine would somehow turn the tide.

Fingers tapped her shoulder. She turned, wiping at her eyes.

A middle-aged woman had come alongside, the richness of her ebony skin accentuated by a white lab coat. "You're Mr. Crawford's spouse, correct?"

"Yes."

"I'm Dr. Olsen, the infectious disease specialist. I'm sorry about your husband. I need to ask a few questions."

Caitlin nodded, sniffling.

"Did your husband mention how he got the wound on his left buttock?"

Caitlin cleared her throat. "He believes it was caused by a small shark."

"But he didn't know for sure?"

"He said it happened at night. All he remembers is the tugging and thrashing. He was delirious when it happened … suffering from severe dehydration."

"Do you know the location of the attack? Was it in the Gulf of Mexico?"

"He was in the southern Bahamas—in a huge bay."

"Oh, so not around here. How long ago was the attack?"

"I would guess four or five days, maybe six. Why is the location important?"

"It could help determine what is causing the infection. Do you know if his wound became exposed to a mangrove swamp or muddy area of some kind?"

"I have no idea."

The critical care doctor came out of Jake's room, looking first at Caitlin. "We've stabilized his blood pressure, but it's touch and go." He focused on Dr. Olsen. "Culture and sensitivity?"

"Not yet. Histology shows a predominance of gram-negative rods in the wound tissue. I should have the initial C-S results within the next two hours. The blood cultures might yield something by tomorrow morning."

The critical care doctor turned to Caitlin. "I wish I had better news. Unfortunately, his lactate levels are extremely high. Other blood chemistries indicate multi-organ involvement. We are doing everything we can at this point."

"Will he survive this?" Caitlin braced herself for the answer.

"I wish I could be more optimistic."

Caitlin tried to hold his look, finally lowering her eyes and fighting back tears. "So, not likely?"

"Septic shock is a very tough battle. The hours ahead will be the most challenging."

A familiar voice could be heard in the direction of the nurses' station. Caitlin glanced over. Pastor Burnside was headed toward her.

He briefly acknowledged the two doctors and embraced her. "I'm so sorry, Caitlin. The entire island is praying mightily for Jake. Many have gathered at our churches. I'm here on behalf of all of them and our Lord above."

The doctors moved away in discussion.

"Am I allowed to go in?" the pastor asked after them.

"Please follow those instructions," said Dr. Olsen. She

pointed at a typed list on the room door. “The gowns, gloves, masks, and goggles are in the cabinet drawers at right.”

One of the two nurses left the room, catching up with the doctors.

The pastor turned to Caitlin. “Let’s pray with Jake.” He took her by the hand to the cabinet. They followed the protective instructions and entered.

The remaining nurse exited the room, allowing the private moment.

Pastor Burnside went to the opposite side of the bed, gently taking Jake’s left hand and gesturing for Caitlin to hold the right.

Jake’s hand felt lifeless, causing her a moment of panic. She glanced at the monitor over the bed. The heartbeats were behaving erratically. The pastor extended his free hand across the bed. She took it, closing her eyes, the prayer circle now formed.

“Merciful Father, show your compassion and healing in this difficult moment ….”

Chapter 27

Almost a month had passed since the unfortunate news about Jake Crawford. Detective Harper worried that his visit was premature. Caitlin sounded subdued when they spoke on the phone, but that could only be expected.

He exited the Marcosta car ferry, taking the first left onto Eletz Point Lane. The golden light of sunrise warmed the colorful hues of the trees and bushes that lined the road. Shadows crisscrossed the tarmac, presenting a mosaic of leafy patterns. He entered the last driveway as instructed, admiring the secluded location. *Old Florida at its finest.* A wooden cabin appeared as his car passed between two large hibiscus bushes. Munson Bay glittered beyond.

Caitlin stood at the far end of the dock. She raised a hand, heading toward the cabin. Jake sat motionless on the bench, facing the bay.

Harper met her at the entrance to the dock. "How's he doing this morning?"

"Okay. Less frustrated than yesterday."

They walked toward Jake, moving slowly in discussion.

"Strokes are tough," said Harper. "You said he has speaking challenges?"

"He slurs some letter combinations. Mostly consonants followed by the letter L, like *Florida* or *quickly*. But you'll be able to understand him."

"How's his comprehension?"

"Fine … as far as they can tell."

"And the other challenges?"

"The wheelchair lasted three days." She pointed ahead. "It's resting on the bottom of the channel, off the end of the dock."

Harper couldn't help but grin.

Caitlin continued, "He struggles with a cane. I'm only allowed to help on stairs."

"Is the right or left side affected?"

"Right. You'll notice his mouth droops that direction."

"Right-handed?"

She nodded. "He tried writing with the left, but it's messy. The neurologist says the stroke could have been much worse. Thank God the ICU doctor and nurses were in the room when it struck—the fast response lessened the damage."

"Is it permanent?"

"The main symptoms should diminish over the next six to twelve months, but there's no guarantee." She stopped, glancing toward Jake. "Do you need to talk with him alone?"

"No, you should stay, especially under the circumstances."

She placed a hand on Harper's shoulder. "Before I forget, thank you for getting Billy released. He came over yesterday to deliver some early-season mullet roe. It was heartwarming to watch the two of them on the bench. He kept an arm around Jake the entire time, gesturing with the other. The lithium medication is clearly working—Billy's his old self again."

Harper made a quick grimace, imagining the mental turmoil Watson had endured— moderately bipolar and in jail for over a month. *But there's a silver lining—the undeserved murder charge also triggered the psychiatric assessments.*

He responded to Caitlin's expression of appreciation. "Steve Moore deserves the bulk of the credit, along with the big snook that ran up that creek. It's a good reminder to keep an open mind in my line of work—expect the unexpected."

She placed a hand on Harper's back. "Jake's waiting."

****

Jake and Caitlin sat side-by-side on the dock bench. Harper stood facing them, leaning against an outer piling.

"No coffee cup?" Jake asked, pacing his words.

"Not this time." Harper scanned the surroundings. "Quite the spot you have here. When was the cabin built?"

"Early 1900s," said Jake, the first word slurring. *Dammit. Slow down and enunciate.*

"Modern houses lack the charm of these old Florida cabins," noted Harper. "You don't see many in Naples anymore."

Jake stayed silent. A tingling sensation swept the right side of his face. *Weird as hell.* He shifted attention to the barges in Munson Bay, anchored a few hundred yards away, awaiting slack tide. Two had large cranes. Others held stacks of dismembered wooden planks and pilings. One barge sat empty, having arrived the evening before. He swung his gaze. Another row of barges had dropped their anchor pylons on the mainland side, the decks stacked with prefabricated concrete sections. The two sets of barges symbolized the transformation underway. *Out with the old and in with the new.*

"I'm sorry about your stroke," said Harper. "You've been through the wringer the past two months."

Jake flicked his left hand in dismissal, pacing the response. "Lucky to be alive."

Caitlin issued a quick reminder. "Jake has a ten o'clock

appointment at the island clinic."

Harper glanced at his watch. "I need an hour, at most. Appreciate the time." He paused momentarily. "As I mentioned on the phone, I have some questions related to the arson-murder investigation, which is ongoing. What I discuss needs to stay confidential."

A sucking *pop* erupted below the dock, along with a large splash.

Harper jumped away from the piling. "What the hell was that?"

Caitlin chuckled. "The pet snook Jake has been feeding. It probably attacked a floating crab."

Harper peered over the edge.

"Why is Billy still a person of interest?" asked Jake. "He's clearly innocent."

Harper resumed his former position. "That's one of the reasons I'm here. It's my understanding that you were in Watson's cottage, shortly after he violated house arrest."

"His brother Harry let me in. We didn't want Billy using the dummy again."

"What happened to the dummy's wig?"

"I have it." Jake hooked a thumb over his left shoulder toward the cabin. "It's in my tool shed. Along with the rest of the dummy."

Harper reacted with surprise. "Why didn't you throw the dummy away?"

"Harry wanted me to store it."

"For what reason?"

"Something about a Halloween surprise at the tavern."

"Why didn't he store it there?"

"He didn't want anyone to discover it."

Harper visibly relaxed, sounding relieved. "This is good news. I'll need you and Harry to give sworn statements attesting to the dummy retrieval and why you kept it. But I'll need to take the wig as evidence."

"Evidence for what?"

"The state prosecutor has been bothered by the missing dummy wig, wondering whether it could have been the one discovered in the mangroves."

"It's still stuck to the crab float. You'll see how." Jake reached for his cane. "The shed's on the other side of the cabin."

Harper held up a hand. "Hang here a bit longer. I need to discuss Derek Nielsen."

Jake removed his hand from the cane. He and Caitlin exchanged glances.

Harper reemphasized the need for utmost confidentiality, focusing his attention on Jake. "Do you believe Nielsen had anything to do with the arson-murder? I've become aware of his offer for the marine lab property. He would benefit by disrupting the movie filming and causing negative press for the lab. It also caused a big problem for your mayorship."

"It wouldn't surprise me," Caitlin interjected. "Nielsen's also the most likely person behind the planted photo packet."

"What photo packet?"

Caitlin explained what had transpired, including the broadly leaked rumor about the actors attending the summer festival. "Someone wanted to discredit Jake and succeeded. It had to be Nielsen."

Harper extracted a small notepad from his shirt pocket and entered some information. He looked at Jake. "What do you think?"

"Nielsen's shady as hell, but I don't believe he'd purposely cause a murder."

Harper reacted with surprise. "That doesn't jibe with your belief about the '94 bridge fire. You tried to convince me that Nielsen was behind the death of Lieutenant Bronson."

Jake stared down at the dock planking. *The time has come to set the record straight.* He met Harper's look. "Nielsen didn't do it. Simon burned the bridge, committing suicide."

"As I've always suspected. Is that something you knew when I interrogated you?"

"I didn't know it at the time."

"How could you know it afterward?"

"It's a long story."

Harper checked his watch. "Can you give me the highlights?"

Jake obliged, providing a summary of what had transpired, including what he had learned from Sergeant McGregor and the discovery of the photos in Simon's book.

Caitlin shifted closer to Jake as the summary unfolded, taking his hand.

Harper looked skyward when Jake finished. "I can only imagine the horrible burden he carried all those decades." He looked down, refocusing on Jake. "Do you still have the book and photos? They would help with closing out the '94 case, along with a written statement about what you learned from Lieutenant Bronson and the British sergeant."

"The book and photos were in my pirated yacht. I doubt they survived the incident. Whatever was salvaged is under DEA control in Miami."

"I'll contact them." Harper studied Jake. "Nielsen had to put up with unwarranted suspicion for more than two years. Something you allowed to happen."

"I know."

No one spoke for a while.

Harper finally broke the silence. "But I can understand why you kept it quiet, wanting to honor the promises you made. I would probably have done the same under the circumstances."

Jake was looking in the direction of where the old bridge once stood. He acknowledged with a grimace and nod.

"So, back to Nielsen," said Harper. "I'm only exploring a possible connection with the cook's murder. Nielsen may never be charged with wrongdoing. It's why you need to keep this discussion confidential."

"But only in regard to the murder," clarified Caitlin. "Our community needs to know about his likely involvement in the photo packet and festival rumor. Jake incurred so much anger and resentment."

"I'd be very careful what you say, unless you have ironclad proof," advised Harper. "He'll sue you for slander."

Caitlin stayed quiet.

Jake struggled to stand, relying on the cane for support. "Let's get the wig."

****

Jake and Caitlin sat at the kitchen table. Harper had left with the dummy parts sealed in large evidence bags. The wig was firmly stuck to the crab float with hardened wads of chewed bubble gum. Harper mentioned analyzing the gum for Billy's DNA—in case the prosecutor had any lingering doubts.

Jake reached for the freshly poured cup of coffee, using his left hand, taking a sip from that side of his mouth. The coffee dribbled down his beard, coming out the right. He emitted a sigh. *Drooling like a baby.*

Caitlin leaned across the kitchen table, aiming a napkin.

He pulled his head back.

She put the napkin aside. "I know you're embarrassed, but don't be." She pointed to her curly hair. "I recall you saying similar words."

"You got me there." He gave a crooked grin.

She reached over, taking his right hand in both of hers. "I understand now."

"Understand what?"

"Our first dinner together, after you returned from Boston, the night of Simon's memorial service—you seemed troubled.

Why didn't you tell me what happened with Sergeant McGregor and the discovery of the photos in Simon's book?"

"For the same reason I withheld it from Detective Harper … because of the promises I made to Simon and Sergeant McGregor. I came close to telling you several times. Maybe I should have divulged it. But it doesn't matter now. The Satorri movie will expose Simon's awful choice."

"How did they find out?"

"Kurt Jones learned about it during an interview with one of the pilots in Simon's squadron."

They sat in silence for a while.

"Do you feel like eating now?" Caitlin asked, standing. "You'll need energy for the physical therapy session."

Jake raised his left thumb.

She headed to the stove. The smell of sizzling mullet roe soon filled the air.

Jake smiled to himself, realizing what she was doing. *Trying to hasten my recovery.* His mother used to serve grilled mullet roe sacs on the morning of school exams, calling it "brain food," something Caitlin had learned.

She came back to the table, retaking her seat. "I didn't hear what you and Detective Harper discussed in the tool shed."

"He believes the dummy wig will exonerate Billy, once and for all." Jake spied smoke swirling across the ceiling, raising his left hand and pointing.

"Oh my, I set it too high." She raced over, switching off the burner and opening the kitchen door. A dish towel flew up and down, fanning the smoke. "I hope you don't mind extra-crispy roe."

"I like it that way."

Caitlin positioned the roe sacs on a plate, along with a half stick of butter and a puddle of maple syrup, placing the arrangement in front of Jake. "Eat up, kind sir. Your exercises await."

****

Caitlin spent the remainder of the morning with Jake at the clinic, watching him labor through the exercises. He retired for a nap after lunch, exhausted.

The daily mail remained on the kitchen table alongside the lunch dishes. Caitlin flipped through the small stack. A postcard surfaced. An arrow had been drawn to a bamboo hut along with a handwritten label: “Asian Chickee!” She flipped to the back. The Thailand filming was going well and would be wrapping up soon. Caitlin smiled. Nyholm’s high school sweetheart was flying in from Sweden for a weeklong stay. *Good for her.*

The kitchen phone rang. Caitlin answered quickly, not wanting Jake awakened. “Hello.”

“Caitlin, it’s Mayor Perkins. How’s Jake today?”

“Exhausted from physical therapy. He’s taking a nap.”

“Will you both be attending the celebration for Billy tomorrow evening?”

“Jake wouldn’t miss it.”

“I’m glad he’s coming. Many want to see him.”

“That’s good to hear.”

“Is there a chance you all could stop by my office before the celebration? I’d like to speak with Jake before he gets overtaken by others.”

“How much time do you need? His stamina’s not great.”

“Thirty minutes should do it. Is 5:00 p.m. okay?”

“That should work. I can wait outside while you talk.”

“No, no, I want you to join the meeting. I will see you then.”

Chapter 28

The stuffed gator remained in its menacing position, yellow eyes glistening, jaws open wide. Jake attempted to step over the long tail, following his customary path across the City Hall foyer.

Caitlin caught his arm as he teetered to the right, leaning against his side to prevent a fall. "Not your best idea." They went over the tail together.

A young man emerged from behind the admin desk as they entered the mayor's suite. He stood erect, extending his right hand toward Jake. "Hello, Mr. Crawford."

Caitlin intercepted the gesture. "Hi, I'm Caitlin Crawford."

"Pleasure to meet you, ma'am. I'm Jimmy Taylor, assistant to Mayor Perkins." His voice carried a tone of self-importance.

"You're Sandra's replacement?" asked Jake.

"Temporarily. She took a few days off to show her uncle around. He's down from Ohio."

"I know your grandfather," said Caitlin. "My parents also live in Sylva. How's he liking North Carolina?"

"The winters, not so much. Loves springtime, though, seeing

the mountain laurel and flame azaleas in bloom."

"Tell him Caitlin McKenzie sends her best."

"Sure thing. I'll let Mayor Perkins know you're here." The wall painting became visible beyond the opened door.

Jimmy reappeared, gesturing for them to go in. "Mayor Perkins is at the conference table."

She stood as they entered. "Thank you both for coming."

Jake went to the painting, completing his entrance ritual. He took a deep breath and slowly exhaled, working his way to the table.

Perkins offered them seats, speaking first to Caitlin. "How's Tommy doing?"

"Good, thanks. He's returning from Bosnia later this month."

"That's wonderful news. I'm sure you'll be relieved."

Jake tilted his head at the painting. "I hope all mayors keep it on the wall."

Perkins glanced at her artwork. "I think you love that scene as much as I do."

"Did you meet Sandra's uncle?" he asked.

"She brought him by. Seems like a very nice man. He treats her like a daughter." Perkins rested her hands on the table. "I thought you should hear an update about the ongoing battle with the State."

Jake gestured toward the channel. "You mean the *losing* battle?"

"I'm afraid that's true. And it's getting worse by the day, which is why I wanted to speak with you."

"Let me guess, Nielsen is trying to buy all the properties along Horseshoe Basin."

Perkins reacted with surprise. "How did you know?"

Jake took his time in explanation, pacing the words. "Billy told me he was approached by a Miami real estate company, making a sizable offer for his cottage. I assumed Nielsen was behind it. The basin is the other option for a marina and yacht club."

Perkins nodded. "Fred Thompson did some digging. A subsidiary of Nielsen Enterprises owns the Miami company."

Jake envisioned a live performance of the Miami International Boat Show going back and forth in front of the cabin dock. He looked out the back windows, watching pelicans floating in the channel. "Has the Miami company also made offers for downtown properties?"

"I haven't heard of any."

"Only a matter of time."

"Which brings me to the main topic," said Perkins. "The special election for your vacant council seat. Ed Dickerson and I will be blocked, three to two, if the seat goes to a pro-Nielsen candidate. Would you consider running? Many on the island feel bad about how you were treated, considering what has happened."

Jake shook his head. "I'm finished with politics."

"He couldn't do it anyway," said Caitlin. "At least not for a year. He needs time to heal."

Perkins shifted her focus to Caitlin. "Then what about you? Would you consider running? I believe you'd win handily."

Caitlin reacted with surprise, glancing in Jake's direction.

He kept a neutral expression, curious how she would respond.

"I … I don't know what to say."

"Well, please think about it. Among other things, I want to create a special Heritage Committee … an offshoot of our Zoning Board. It will designate historical buildings for lasting protection, like your cabin. I can't do it without a majority of the council in agreement."

Caitlin made a show of checking her watch. "I need to manage Jake's time. We should head to the tavern."

They stood. Jake worked toward the doorway, then stopped. He pointed the cane at the wall painting. "Would you paint our cabin from the perspective of the bay, with Caitlin and me sitting on the dock bench? I would pay whatever you normally expect."

Perkins smiled. "I would be honored."

****

Caitlin's car sat empty at the far end of the Coquina Motel parking lot. Jake's desire for peace and quiet had prompted an early exit from Billy's celebration. The walk to Sand Point had been arduous, his cane sinking in the sugar-white sand.

They reclined against the outermost dune, a starry panorama above. An offshore breeze carried distant music and laughter from the tavern. Periodically, a double cheer could be heard: "Hail to Claude, Hail to Billy." Jake smiled. Billy would always be one of their own, regardless of his difficult history—a born and bred island man who wore the white rubber boots of the commercial fishermen.

Caitlin rested her head on his chest.

She must be exhausted, as well, handling the nonstop interactions. Jake reflected on the swirl of well-wishers, reducing their sentiments to a single word: *redemption.*

The outpouring had been aided by a rumor that swept the island throughout the day, spilling with momentum into the tavern celebration. Supposedly, the "authorities" had discovered that Derek Nielsen was behind the festival disruption and planting of the photo packet, devious ploys to discredit Jake's leadership.

Jake mused aloud, his tone slightly suspicious. "Hmmm, I wonder how the Nielsen rumor got started?"

Caitlin lifted her head. "I'm glad it did." She shifted, resting her back against the dune and looking skyward. "By the way, I forgot to mention that Donna and I spoke early this morning, catching up on some things. She's doing well."

Jake smiled, recognizing the admission. Donna was at the

center of the island gossip network.

Caitlin pointed, her raised arm silhouetted against the haze of the Milky Way. "Wow. That one had the longest tail I've ever seen."

Jake missed the falling star.

She lowered her arm, finding his hand and holding it.

"I'm curious," said Jake.

"About what?"

"Your thoughts about the council seat. Would you consider running?"

"Have you changed your mind about moving to the Bahamas?"

"Crooked Island and the surrounding waters are exquisite, but I'm concerned about our safety after what happened. And besides, Marcosta Island is our home and always will be." He had come to realize she didn't want to leave, despite what Nielsen would do to the island.

"Are you sure? The cabin is only a block from Horseshoe Basin. If Nielsen puts a yacht club there …"

"We can keep the cabin but not stay in it. I like the idea of making the property a historical site."

"But where would we live?"

"At the marine lab."

She rose, leaning against his side, her face toward his. "You're kidding. Where? In the scientist quarters?"

Jake chuckled. "No, on a boat in the harbor, along the far seawall; where Nyholm's yacht was positioned, directly behind Steve Moore's houseboat."

"You've been thinking about this. Did you already discuss the idea with Ida?"

"I believe she'll agree."

"Tell me more then. Will you be taking up science again? Doing what Judith suggested?"

"I think so."

"And what about the type of boat? I'm not sure I could have lived on *Cloud Catcher* year-round."

"The boat must work for everyday living, but I'll also need to get away periodically. We'll find something that enables short cruises along the western Everglades, going up the rivers and into the back bays. Maybe a nice wooden houseboat—custom built to your liking by a talented ship's carpenter."

She relaxed, resting her head on his chest again, snuggling close.

They grew quiet. Over time, a line of thunderstorms became active on the gulf horizon, lightning illuminating their upper reaches. Jake observed the primal display, recalling a similar squall line that had marched toward him in the Bight of the Acklins. The long night on the sandbar had taught the ultimate perspective, alone but not alone, thinking only of Caitlin and their enduring love as he descended into delirium.

Lightning flashed. Thunder rumbled across the gulf.

"Are you asleep?" she whispered.

The sweet sound of her voice meant everything.

—

www.ingramcontent.com/pod-product-compliance
Lightning Source LLC
LaVergne TN
LVHW010635110826
845149LV00014B/2846